Books by Bestselling Author Jerilyn Dufresne

Praise for Jerilyn Dufresne and the *Sam Darling Mysteries*

Dufresne has created a charming, nosy, and slightly irreverent character in Samantha Darling, the heroine in **Who Killed My Boss?**, *a fast-paced cozy that takes place in the small town of Quincy, Illinois.*
Beth Amos, author of the Mattie Winston Mystery series (as Annelise Ryan)

The plot kept me guessing until nearly the end and I am looking forward to reading further adventures! Fun and entertaining read...highly recommended...well done!
Anne Kelleher, author of the Tilton Chartwell Mysteries

Don't miss Sam Darling's latest adventure in Jerilyn Dufresne's lively and delightful series of mysteries. A great read for plane and train trips or for a week at the beach.
Mary McHugh, author of the Happy Hoofer cozy mystery series

What readers are saying…

Sam Darling is the kind of gal you wish you could know in real life.

Very exciting plot and hard to put down.

The combination of humor and mystery was perfect.

I love Sam Darling, her family, her friends, and I adored her dog!

This book was very well written and I loved all the humor sprinkled throughout the story.

The writing is light-hearted and the whole book is a total fun read!

TRIPLE TROUBLE

Who Killed My Boss?
Any Meat in That Soup?
Can You Picture This?

Bonus story: Sam's Prom Night Fiasco

Jerilyn Dufresne

TRIPLE TROUBLE
A Sam Darling mystery series box set

© 2016 Jerilyn Dufresne

Edition: June 2016

Published by eFitzgerald Publishing, LLC

Cover design by Keri Knutson (www.alchemybookcovers.com)
Formatting by Jason Anderson of Polgarus Studio
(www.polgarusstudio.com)

eFitzgerald Publishing, LLC strives to create a professional product and a smooth reading experience for readers of indie ebooks. Please report typographical or other errors to
eFitzgeraldPublishing@gmail.com.

Want to find out about new books by Jerilyn before anyone else does? Sign up here. http://eepurl.com/z30jv

To my very own Gus.

Contents

About
WHO KILLED MY BOSS?
(Sam Darling Mystery #1)

Moments after hiring Samantha Darling as a therapist, Dr. Burns is murdered. Stunned by his sudden death and desperate to keep the job she just got, Sam vows to find the killer.

She has two things going for her. The first is that her brother Rob is a cop, and she figures the crime-solving thing has to be genetic. The second is that Sam is a little bit psychic—so finding the culprit should be a snap for her. If only she could tell the difference between her psychic vibes and indigestion….

With the help of her landlord and her dog, Sam sets out to solve the murder. Along the way, she spends time with the hot new guy in town and tries *not* to spend time with the old high school boyfriend who stood her up on prom night.

Using her vibes, her wit, and her charm, Sam solves the mystery, but not before going in the absolute wrong direction more than once.

WHO KILLED MY BOSS?

To the eight other J's, the brothers and sisters who inspired the five Darling siblings, although the Darlings aren't nearly as sarcastic and fun as you are.

ONE

I beamed as Leonard Schnitzer plucked an enameled pen from the ceramic elephant on his desk, gave it a flourish, and began to sign the personnel authorization form. I would soon be an official employee.

A scream brought us both to our feet. Schnitzer jumped up ready to investigate. I wasn't as excited as he was. Hell, this was a psychiatric clinic. People yelled in psychiatric clinics.

Before he could escape, I acted on a hunch and hollered, "Sign this first. Sign the paper." I grabbed the contract and held it under his nose, fearing that if he didn't sign it before he left the room, he never would. "Sign it," I commanded. I wanted that job. "Sign it *now*."

Shocked, he signed.

I held on to the paper for dear life and followed Schnitzer's skinny behind right out of the room.

We joined a stampede that led to the office of my brand new boss, Dr. Burns. A woman stood near the doorway with her back to me, papers spilled at her feet. My gaze followed hers through a maze of curious onlookers. She stared at Dr. Burns. He stared back serenely, but he wasn't seeing anything. The scene looked almost peaceful except for the blood that defaced his beautiful Persian rug.

Using offensive skills that the St. Louis Rams would envy, I pushed the group forward so I could be closer to the action. As I entered the room I clutched two strangers on either side of me when a dizzy spell unexpectedly hit. I shook it off and took a few more steps into Burns' office.

I was pretty sure Dr. Burns was dead, but then I'm a social worker and not a medical expert. Someone with a white coat and stethoscope around his neck checked Burns' pulse and stopped another man from beginning CPR, as he slowly shook his head from side to side and quietly pronounced Burns dead. White Coat must have been a doctor. But the blood on the floor told the tale, even to an amateur like me. This guy had lost a lot of the red stuff. I'd never seen this much blood in one place except at a Red Cross blood drive. He was a goner.

There goes my job.

I knew it wasn't very charitable to be concerned about my job with Dr. Burns dead on the floor, but self-preservation is a powerful motivator. I'd started my job less than fifteen minutes ago, after spending months searching for, and finally landing, a position in the private sector. Suddenly I recalled the significant piece of paper glued to my sweaty hand. A smile twitched and it was difficult to suppress it, but hallelujah—I had the contract, signed by both Burns and Schnitzer, the personnel officer. My job was secure. At least for now.

A sudden chill reminded me how serious the situation was. My shaking body convinced me I really did feel the intensity of the situation. Everyone else was shaking too—making me think we were a company full of empathy. Then I noticed that an office window was open and a freezing wind blew into Burns' death chamber. So much for empathy. No one moved to close the window.

Now that I didn't have to worry about receiving a paycheck, my concern about my erstwhile boss's death surfaced. I wondered how he died. Was it a horrible accident? Did a patient kill him? Or did he kill himself?

I surprised myself by my lack of fear, but wrote it off to being in shock. I'd probably pay for it later.

After a few moments, reason overcame my curiosity and I said, "Don't touch anything." I looked around and zeroed in on someone who didn't look panic-stricken. "Will you call the police?"

She looked down from her better-than-six-foot height, with her eyebrows raised nearly to the ceiling. "And just who might you be?"

I bit back the retort I'd been ready to shoot at her. After all she towered over me by at least a foot. "Sorry. I'm

Samantha Darling and I work here. I'm a new therapist. Someone's got to call 911. Will you please call the police?" I spoke in my nicest social worker voice. Seemingly satisfied, she turned to leave.

Every person in the room seemed to flash a cell phone at me sarcastically as the guy in the white coat said, "We already called 911. Didn't you hear the yelling?"

I hadn't heard anything. But that didn't surprise me. I often tuned in to my inner voice and tuned out reality.

I turned to the rest of the curious bystanders. "Okay. Now that we know the cops and paramedics are on their way, will the rest of you please leave? We don't want to mess up the crime scene. I'll stay here and wait for the police to arrive."

My personnel office escort puffed up his chest and in a squeaky little voice tried to sound commanding as he pointed to the group with a large gesture, "Why you? Why should the rest of us leave?"

His voice barely carried over the din of the other voices, but I had no such problem. "Because my brother is a cop and I know what I'm doing. Honest, Mr. Schnitzer, I have experience with this. I'll explain it all later."

Surprisingly enough, my b.s. worked. Shock does strange things to people's behavior and they obeyed me. Mom always said that confidence is a great leadership tool.

Actually I sounded more confident than I felt. As the

oldest of six kids, being bossy had become my survival skill. However, I was still nervous around a dead body. And I didn't want to tell anyone that even though I really was a cop's sister, my knowledge of crime scenes came primarily from reading psychological thrillers.

After everyone left, some of them a bit ungraciously, a mewling noise caught my attention. Lying on the floor near the door was the woman who had greeted me that morning at the reception desk. She was crumpled into an almost fetal position, crying softly, and looked nothing like the receptionist who had met me earlier. Then, her nametag had blazed proudly on her chest and the glare careening off her overly coifed helmet-head had almost matched the blinding light from her teeth. A 180-degree turnaround in less than an hour.

She was pretty in a brassy sort of way, even in her current disarray; her red-lacquered nails matched the crimson I remembered seeing on her large expressive mouth. Maybe she was younger than I was, but not by much. She looked like a person from the wrong side of town who worked hard to become someone who was no longer a social outcast.

My take was she'd never make it into the big time in Quincy, but she wouldn't get the cold shoulder in nice restaurants either.

Her voice had a slight drawl to it. The uninitiated might think she was from the south, but my bet was that she was a River Rat who crawled up to dry land. In our town in West Central Illinois, the wrong side of the tracks meant you had one foot in the Mississippi River and the other foot in mud.

Anyway, this poor wretch on the floor bore little resemblance to that perky confident employee from a scant hour ago.

The woman I'd asked to call the police returned and together we knelt to check the person on the floor. In the midst of this, we introduced ourselves, and I apologized for asking her to make a call to those already on their way. My helper was Marian Dougherty, another therapist, and a tall one at that. The woman acting as a doorstop was Gwen Schneider. We gently raised Gwen to her feet and walked her to a chair in the hallway. I asked Marian to stay with her while I checked on the crime scene.

Marian started to talk, "Why do you need to check... okay, never mind. It's because your brother's a cop and you have experience in these kind of things."

I grinned and nodded.

Her eyebrows rose again, but this time she almost smiled as I walked back into the other room.

The office was eerily silent, although the echo of Gwen's crying seemed to remain. Carefully, I closed the door behind me. I wanted quiet but didn't want to obscure any fingerprints.

Before I did anything else, I needed to stop my heart from galloping out of my chest. I closed my eyes and took a few deep breaths, practicing an abbreviated relaxation response. I pictured myself with Brad Pitt on an otherwise deserted beach. When that failed to calm me, I pictured myself alone in the same place. As my breathing slowed, so did my pulse.

Calm and thinking clearly now, I decided to look around while I was waiting for the police to arrive. Burns was lying on his back in front of his desk with his face turned toward the door. His arms were extended about shoulder level and he looked like his swan dive was aborted into a back flop. I couldn't see what caused the bleeding. It looked like it came from his neck or his head. The blood was starting to congeal in the large pool under his head, and I noticed a weird irregular blood spatter around the room. The pattern looked like a drunken circle, haphazardly touching desk, walls, carpet, and chairs. Did I only imagine the metallic smell? Suppressing the urge to touch him, I backed away. The Good Samaritan who'd checked Burns' pulse and pronounced him dead had already moved him a bit and I didn't want to add to the evidence disarray.

I observed what I could. If I were lucky, the police would ask me for information and I'd be able to supply it. My brothers were always saying I acted like I wanted to be a cop. I'd prove to them I knew how to maintain the integrity of a crime scene.

Only yesterday I had finished reading *Bipolar Passion.*

The hero had managed to shoo everyone out of the murder room and kept the clues intact. The police heralded him for his astute work and he then proceeded to solve the crime. I was certain I could do the same.

I walked over to the open window, which overlooked the back yard. Wondering why it was open in January, I peered outside. There didn't appear to be anything else out of the ordinary. Except for footprints leading away from the building. In the snow, those footprints glistened. From where I was standing, they appeared to be average size. Heck, I really didn't know what I was looking for, but I thought the cops would like that I noticed some stuff. At least I'd be able to tell my brothers of my astute observation skills.

Finally, the police arrived, and when I saw the officer, I prepared for his inevitable snort.

"What in the hell are you doing here?" he asked.

"I work here; I just started this morning. Don't you remember that I came here for an interview last week? I thought you were one of the smart ones in the family."

"Damn it, Sam, you know what I mean. What are you doing in this room?" As Rob spoke, he walked slowly toward the body. It's funny how quickly a person—in this case, Dr. Burns—becomes "the body."

"I came in with a group of people after we heard a lady scream. You should be thanking me. I got everyone out and preserved the evidence."

"Are you sure you didn't touch anything?"

Typical little brother, second-guessing me. "Of course I didn't touch anything. Well, except the door, but I was careful. See, Rob, I'm looking you straight in the face. You know I can't lie when I do that."

Rob grinned and tried desperately to hide it. He was such a little cutie, almost like a kid playing cops and robbers. His dark brown hair had just a hint of red in it and it complemented the ruddiness in his cheeks.

"That won't stand up in court."

"Yeah, but it's true anyway."

A detective walked in at that moment and I knew Rob would have to turn over the investigation to him. Rob's time in the sun was over. The new arrival wore a stereotypical rumpled suit, Quincy's own Columbo. He was medium height and his salt and pepper hair barely covered his balding head. Smugly I noticed a bit of a strain where buttons joined the edges of the jacket, but had to admit he looked in pretty good shape for his age.

I knew his age—40-something, same as mine.

"Hey, Sam, long time no see. I heard you moved back to town. How are ya?"

"Fine, George. Did you notice there's a dead body in the room?" It was all right for my brother and me to be irreverent, but I wouldn't tolerate it from Butthead George Lansing, the meanest kid ever to grace the detention room of St. Francis High School. I guess I should call him "Detective Butthead." Luckily I believed in miracles, because that's the only explanation for George's success on the police force. Although he was a rotten kid, I heard he was a decent cop. He'd have to prove that before I'd believe it.

For now, I'd be cordial, but that was it.

Butthead got right down to business. "Rob, will you inform the other staff members that I want to speak to them individually, and tell them not to talk to each other about what went on."

"Sure thing."

"And send the coroner to me as soon as he arrives."

Rob nodded as he exited. I don't think George noticed Rob's quick wink to his big sister.

"So, Sam, what are you doing here? And don't say you work here, I mean what are you doing in this room?" He paused. "And why are you grinning?"

"I just noticed you called Rob by his first name. Guess you don't want to call him 'Officer Darling' in public."

"Yeah, right. So what are you doing in this room? Nosing around?" As he questioned me, he herded me into the corridor. I didn't protest. Being in the presence of a dead body was starting to get on my nerves, and I didn't want Butthead to notice.

From his questions, it looked like Butthead knew me

pretty well. That was one more reason I didn't like him.

"Well, Butthea... I mean, George, I came in here with a lot of other staff when we heard a scream. One of the typists, I heard someone call her Doris, was standing in the doorway. Those files were scattered around her on the floor. As we crowded into the room we may have stepped on them. When I got inside the office I saw Burns just like you see him. Someone checked his pulse—it was a male in a white coat—and decided not to do CPR. He must be a doctor because he pronounced Burns dead. But he was the only person to touch the deceased. Gwen Schneider, the receptionist, is the woman sitting on the chair in the hall. She was crumpled on the floor in here crying. I don't think she was there when we came in, though. I kinda pushed the group forward into the room and she probably fell then. I told everyone to get lost and I maintained the integrity of the scene until Rob, I mean Officer Darling, arrived." The least I could do was treat my brother respectfully in front of Butthead.

Nearly twenty-five years after graduating from high school and my animosity toward him had not diminished. No reason to be nice to him. The jerk stood me up on prom night.

What a tool. He didn't deserve my forgiveness. Maybe someday I'd be magnanimous, but the time wasn't right for forgiveness yet. The time was right for moral superiority and looking down on him as the low-life slug that he was.

I couldn't help myself. "I know more." I kept my voice low so Gwen and Marian didn't hear.

George raised one eyebrow. "What do you mean you know more?"

"I know more but you didn't ask me the right question."

"Dammit, Sam, I didn't get a chance to ask you many questions. I asked you one and you started babbling."

I'd show him. "Okay, since you think I'm babbling, I won't tell you what else I know."

"Dammit, Sam, this isn't a game of Twenty Questions. Someone died here."

"I know. And my name is Sam, not 'Dammit, Sam.'"

He wasn't amused. "Tell me what else you think is important."

I decided to cooperate, even though he wasn't good at this question thing. "When I walked into his office for my interview last week, I heard him talking on the phone."

"And…"

"And he said something like, 'I'll have something for you next week.' And then 'Leave me alone.' I didn't think much about it at the time."

"Do you know who he was talking to?"

"Nope."

"How did he sound? Was he calm? Did he look nervous?"

I looked at Butthead a moment before I answered. "I don't really remember. What he said stuck with me because I thought it was a little unusual, but I don't think he seemed upset or anything like that."

"Okay, you can get back to work. I'll let you know when I want to talk to you. Thanks for your help in the investigation."

I wanted to wipe that stupid condescending grin off of his face. If it weren't for me, there would still be a bunch of people in the room, gawking and carrying on. Why was he treating me like excess baggage? I would not be dismissed this easily.

Not bothering to return his smile, I started to leave the room, but then had an idea.

"Hey, George, why don't you interview people in the kitchen? It's a comfortable room. When Dr. Burns gave me a tour I noticed it's isolated from the rooms where the patients will be."

"Thanks. Maybe I will."

Now it was my turn to grin. My brand new office conveniently adjoined the kitchen. I wasn't being nosy; I just wanted to help.

Okay, I was being nosy. But I still wanted to help. Maybe the cops didn't want my opinion and expertise, but darn it, I had a lot of experience with people. Plus I had my "vibes."

My brother, Rob, knew about my "vibes," but I don't

think Butthead suspected. Over the years I'd begun tuning in to the strange bodily sensations I experienced sometimes. I'd get headaches or dizziness or neck spasms when I encountered something evil or maybe just weird. My body was kicking into overdrive and I knew Burns' death was not an accident or suicide. I decided to use these vibes to help me solve the murder. I figured it would be the way to keep my job. If I solved the mystery, the new boss of the psychiatric clinic would certainly reward me with job security.

In the meantime, a little eavesdropping couldn't hurt. I'd listen a while, do some investigating on my own and then pass the information on to my brother. I was just trying to be a good citizen and to keep my job… and just possibly make Rob look smarter than Butthead.

TWO

Before Butthead began interviewing staff, I decided to get settled into my office. Being next to the kitchen was a real bonus for me and my appetite. The office was full of furniture, but lacked a personal touch. I'd remedy that at the earliest opportunity. And it was small compared to Dr. Burns' mega-office, but it was cozy and it was mine.

I sat in my wonderfully overstuffed desk chair, propped up my feet on the oak desk, and looked around, giving myself a metaphorical pat on the back. Moving from government to the private sector was a bright idea.

Muffled voices from the hallway tempted me to open my door and look. Two bored-looking men wheeled Dr. Burns toward the front door. At least, I hoped it was Dr. Burns under the navy wool blanket. One death was plenty, I didn't think I could personally cope with two. I moved to my front window to continue watching as the men loaded the body into the back of the generic funeral home station wagon.

I stood there a few moments after the car left, thinking

about the man who'd hired me and how quickly his life was snuffed out.

My mind wandered to my pleasant surroundings. I was happy to note there were no drapes on my windows. Long, narrow, and curved at the top, the windows were discreetly clad in cloth-covered shades that matched the appealing wallpaper.

A loveseat and matching chair, empty bookshelves, and an end table rounded out the furniture. Behind my desk was a tiny marble fireplace. Next to it sat an oak filing cabinet that I hoped to fill with case notes on exciting and curable patients.

I could live in this room. All the place needed was my stuff. I'd take care of that tomorrow. Assuming I'd still have a job tomorrow. Burns just died, but I imagined the clinic would go on functioning. At least that was my fondest hope.

Coffee, that's what I need to complete this cozy picture. Coffee. Taking one last survey of the room, I headed for the door next to the fireplace that led to the kitchen.

I found a clean mug, filled it, and returned to my office. I decided to re-arrange my furniture a bit, thinking that the desk and chair would look perfect closer to the kitchen door. My chair fit snugly in a little alcove, about three or four feet from the servants' door which led to the most important room in the house.

I settled in, deciding I needed a little quiet time, time to meditate. I wondered what Clancy would say when I told her about today's happenings.

Clancy was my best friend. And my dog. She was a cross between a yellow lab and a chow. At first glance she appeared a regular mutt, but there was much more to her than the mane-like ruff and gorgeous dark eyes. She had excellent nonverbal communication skills and our connection bordered on the psychic. I told her everything. She responded in kind.

Soon I heard voices coming from the kitchen and had no choice but to listen.

B.H.'s voice rang crystal clear as he began asking questions. I couldn't call B.H. by his given name of George, because I was still mad at him. But at least I decided to be mature and call him B.H. instead of Butthead.

My chair moved closer to the door, almost of its own volition. I smiled, thinking I had the best seat in the house.

B.H. began in his best cop manner, "Tell me what happened this morning in your own words."

An unidentified female voice answered. "I knocked on Dr. Burns' door because he told me he wanted to sign the case notes I'd been typing. When there was no answer, I decided to put the notes on his desk where he could find them later." I moved a bit closer at this point because she— I guessed it was Doris—started sniffling a little and it was hard to understand her. "Then I walked in and saw him on the floor bleeding. I screamed and I guess I dropped everything I was holding. That's all that happened until everyone else came in and then that new lady, I think her name is Pam or Sam or something, started bossing us all around and made us leave."

It's really amazing to me how some people can misinterpret someone else's decisive actions as bossiness. Well, obviously, Miss Doris had some unresolved authority issues that she needed to deal with. But unless I wanted to be accused of bossiness again, I probably wouldn't tell her about it.

B.H. continued, "Did you hear anything this morning that sounded suspicious or unusual?"

"Uh-uh." Which I presumed meant "no."

"Has there been anything else going on that was unusual?"

"No, not really (sniff, sniff). But that new guy in town that started the private investigating agency—what's his name… Mick or Mike or something?"

"Michael O'Dear?"

"Yeah, I guess that's his name. Anyway, he was here this morning and saw Dr. Burns, but I don't know why."

It's unfortunate that vibes don't travel through walls and doors. I couldn't get a feel on whether she knew anything else or not. And who was this O'Dear guy? A private detective in Quincy? I wondered why he visited Burns this morning. Was it detective work or a psychiatric visit?

B.H. continued with the questions, "How long have you worked here? Did you get along with Dr. Burns? What time did you arrive this morning? Describe what you did from the moment you arrived until you found Dr. Burns. Did Dr. Burns have any enemies that you know of?"

What I got from the answers was that Dr. Burns wasn't in the running for Nice Guy of the Year Award. I overheard "crabby," "aloof," "overbearing," and "distracted." I was almost glad I hadn't gotten to know him.

Too bad B.H. didn't need my help in the room. Maybe he wouldn't notice if I went in and made a fresh pot of coffee.

He did notice. With the same stupid grin on his face, he stopped the conversation until I made the coffee, waited for it to finish brewing, poured myself a cup, and walked out of the kitchen. A full ten minutes. He was good.

B.H. repeated the same conversation with other staff members, but elicited no new information. Several of them remarked on my ability to take charge of a situation. Perhaps they phrased it a bit differently. I recall hearing the word "bossy" a few times, but resolved that I wouldn't be bothered by the remark. People just needed to get to know me a bit. They'd come around. Listening to them was getting to be boring; the same information was repeated time and again. I was patient however, and soon my persistence paid off. Miss Gwen Schneider arrived for her interview.

By this time, my ear was firmly implanted in the door.

"Miss Schneider, can you tell me what happened this morning in your own words?"

"Boo-hoo, sob, sob, slobber, snort."

The interpretation being, "I know plenty, Bub, but I'm too broken up right now to talk about it."

Through the wall I couldn't get a feel for whether she was upset because she loved him or because she killed him. Or maybe something in between. And I didn't know whether to feel compassion for her or antipathy. Or maybe something in between.

Despite her slobbery sobs, I heard her say that when she walked into Burns' office with the rest of us, she was overcome with grief. She said she fell to the floor and didn't recall anything else until "that bossy lady told Marian to take me into the hallway."

Decisive. Decisive.

It looked like it was time for another cup of coffee.

Without glancing at B.H., I slowly ambled to the coffeepot. When Gwen continued crying, I put my mug on the counter, walked to her, and placed my hands on her shoulders. Looking in her eyes, I asked if I could help. She shook her head, but absolute misery just poured off of her. She was in so much pain. At that point it didn't matter to me whether she'd killed him or not, she was really suffering. I let my hands slide around her and hugged her to me. She resisted for a brief second and then literally collapsed onto me. Her sobs shook her body for several minutes. I was very focused on her and didn't notice until later that B.H. kept silent and didn't interrupt.

When she started to regain her composure, B.H. looked at me and mouthed "Take her out of here." I was glad to oblige and it wasn't entirely done out of the goodness of my heart. This seemed like a good opportunity to tune in to her, ask some questions, and see what was going on.

We left the kitchen and went into my office. I guided Gwen to the loveseat and sat beside her. For a while she continued to sniff and cry into a tissue I'd given her, and then looked at me suspiciously.

"What do you want?"

"Nothing really. I saw that you were hurting and wanted to help."

She half-smiled. "I'm surprised."

"Well, I am a social worker. It's kind of built in."

She started snorting and sniffling again. "I don't deserve your sympathy. I don't deserve anything but jail. I didn't mean to, but…" the snorting sound effects continued.

Aha, here was my chance. "You didn't mean to what, Gwen?"

Before she could regain her composure to answer me, I

suddenly felt someone was in the room with us. I repeated my prompting, "You didn't mean to what, Gwen?"

Too late. She'd controlled her blubbering and wasn't going to give me anything.

The feeling that someone was with us remained.

My footsteps were slow and quiet as I inched toward the kitchen door. I recognized the same heavy breathing on the other side that I remembered from the back seat of a '65 Chevy during high school. With a jerk I pulled the door inward, and just like in a Charlie Chaplin movie, in fell B.H. himself. When I saw him lying there, it did wonders to temporarily appease the revenge mentality I felt. However, he didn't even have the good sense to look embarrassed.

"Miss Schneider, I'd like you to accompany me to the police station. We need to talk some more." He stood as if nothing had happened.

Guiltily and hastily, I blurted, "Gwen, I promise I didn't know he was there. Besides, I know you didn't kill Dr. Burns."

"But…"

"It doesn't matter how I know, I just know." There's no way in the world I could try to explain to this grieving woman and Detective Butthead that Gwen didn't "feel" guilty. "Get yourself a good lawyer, and I'll stay in touch."

"Now, Miss Schneider, there's no need to get a lawyer. I

just want to ask you a few more questions down at the station. You are not being accused of anything and you are not under arrest." Butthead did the best he could to intimidate me. He glared.

I glared back. He was a rank amateur. As the oldest of six kids I had the "sister look" down pat. I could silence a mortal at thirty paces. He pretended it didn't bother him, but he didn't fool me. I knew he was cowed.

As they left, I resolved to find out everything I could about this case. Gwen obviously knew more about the murder and certainly felt guilty about something, but I knew she wasn't the killer. So my quest was to find the one who did the deed.

I felt up to it. The odds were that no one would fire me or lay me off until well after the funeral when the business affairs were settled. Until then, no one would realize that I didn't have any work to do.

Heck, half the office probably didn't even know I was hired. Still, I'd heard that Dr. Burns liked to assign patients to new staff members himself, so I didn't have to worry about being asked to do any actual work for at least a few days. I thought I could earn my salary by looking for who killed the boss. Maybe people would be so impressed that I could keep the job. Who knows? But as my son would say, "Yeah, and maybe pigs will fly out of my butt."

On that note, I set to work. At least I thought about

setting to work. It was quitting time.

My first day on the job was certainly eventful. My main concern now was to solve this case, prove to be indispensable and keep my job.

THREE

"No, no, Paolo. I can't stay with you. I belong to the world."

"Cara mia, stay. I will treat you like the queen that you are. The world will survive without you, but I will not." He began kissing my fingers and slowly and deliciously moved up my arm until he got tantalizingly close to my open lips.

I was torn between pretending hesitancy and following my heart… and my body.

Brrng, brrng.

Shoot!" The phone jolted me awake, and I was not in a good mood. Giving up Paolo wasn't fun; he was the best dream man in a long time. Before I picked up the phone I glanced at the sturdy athletic watch on my wrist. *Six A.M.?*

"Yeah." It wasn't my most clever opening line, but it would have to do.

"Sam, this is Jenny. We got a problem in the ER and need a counselor. I see that you're on call. Rise and shine."

"Is this your idea of a joke? I just got hired yesterday. Couldn't be on call yet."

"Get in here, sis. We need you. You know I wouldn't lie to you. The on-call sheet says you are the designated hitter, so come on."

"Yeah sure." Clever retort. When it came to my younger sister, I was always quick with the witty dialogue. "Okay. What do you need?"

Jen was actually Jennifer Darling Vu, Director of Emergency Services at Bay General, the local hospital, and married to Dr. Manh Vu, a pediatrician, originally from Vietnam. We were happy to have him in the family for a lot of reasons, not the least of which was that he provided free pediatric care to the growing family.

Being the oldest of six was both a gift and a curse. I loved the gang and their assorted spouses, significant others, and kids. I also resented the fact that I'd had to get a divorce in order to have a bedroom to myself.

Jen interrupted my ruminations. "We have an ER full of drunks and I think we need a crisis intervention specialist, rather than calling the police. Can you come in and help?"

"Sure, be there in a few minutes." As I hung up, I actually felt pretty good. Jen asked me for help very infrequently and I was glad to oblige. Before I had applied at the clinic, Jen told me that Doctor Burns negotiated a nice little contractual relationship with the hospital, so that the psychiatric division of the clinic provided emergency crisis intervention and therapeutic intervention on an as-needed basis. The on-call therapist did the initial assessment and determined if the psychiatrist needed to be called. Illinois was one of the states where licensed clinical social workers were allowed to practice independently and even receive insurance payments.

I dressed in jeans, T-shirt and wool sweater. Quincy was cold in January, especially this early. I put on boots and a parka, grabbed my phone and keys and started to leave. It felt odd that there was no one to tell that I was going out. My divorce was a thing of the past, but I was used to having my children around. Their departure was too recent for my solitude to be very comfortable. Adam was a junior at the University of Illinois, and Sarah was in her first year at the same school. After the holidays, they had both gone back to school early because of their commitments, and, I suspected, because of their respective love interests.

As I left, I made sure the answering machine was plugged in. Then I realized I did have someone to notify. Clancy had been following me around ever since the phone rang. She had been sleeping on my bed, and when the phone rang she raised her regal head and gave me her "get off your butt" look.

I crouched down to her level. "I need to go to the ER. I promise I'll be back in time for your morning run. And remind me to tell you about my dream. It was a corker."

I could tell from the doubt in her eyes that she didn't

believe we'd still do the run and consequently felt neglected, but I didn't have time to deal with her hurt feelings. The drunks needed me.

As I left my home, the porch light went on in my landlord's house.

"Darn it." I tried to hurry to the garage door, hoping to avoid being spotted by the bane of my existence.

"Sam, oh Sam. What in the world are you doing leaving home at this time of the morning? Surely your new job does not require these hours?"

There she was. Loud, flower-endowed housecoat. Bright pink curlers surrounded by a garish scarf. Eyes squinting in spite of her glasses. Nose sniffing the air, trying to smell God-knows-what. My landlady. My nemesis. My Georgianne Granville.

This is not the neighborhood of my youth. I grew up about six blocks away in a decent working class neighborhood. We always walked by the "rich" section wondering what the lives of the inhabitants were like. Since my recent return, I now knew how the inhabitants lived, because I was one of them. Well, sort of. I rented one of the carriage houses in the ritzy section. It was nice, cozy, and had a great mailing address. I rented from the eccentric Georgianne Granville, one of the "grande dames" of the town. She was in her 80's now but was still a frequent subject of the society pages in the local paper. I wondered how her husband, Gus, tolerated sharing the same house with her.

"No, Georgianne, these are not my normal working hours. I just got a call from the ER and I need to hurry. Sorry I don't have time to chat." *Exit, Sam. Now. Hurry.*

"But, Sam..."

"Bye-bye. Say 'hi' to Gus for me, will you?"

A narrow escape. Getting ambushed by Georgianne sometimes meant hours of entanglement, but I've improved in doing the "Ditch Georgianne Dance" in the short time I've been back in Quincy.

One of the benefits of living in a small city is that it doesn't take much more than 15 minutes to drive anywhere. I walked into the ER less than 20 minutes after I was abruptly awakened.

I hurried to the triage area, where patients were being evaluated as to the severity of their needs. There is usually an air of excitement in the ER and my adrenaline always starts flowing when I arrive. I've been in emergency rooms many times, sometimes to meet Jen for lunch, sometimes when my children or I needed emergency help, or many times in Chicago because of my job with the Department of Children and Family Services. When a child was injured because of abuse and neglect, one of my duties was to meet them and the family at the emergency room and make some immediate decisions as to the placement of the child and siblings.

I waited while a secretary fetched Jen. As I looked around the ER, I thought of the many reasons I had decided to return to Quincy and change jobs. During my interview, when Dr. Burns asked me why I left DCFS after fifteen years, I found it hard to answer.

I didn't know which answer to give him. The one that said I'd been imagining the pleasures of working with people with short term neuroses—people who had hope for the future? Having worked for DCFS in Chicago, I was a bit discouraged about my inability to make a difference in people's lives. Should I have told him that I finally completed my master's degree and returned to my hometown ready to change jobs?

What would he have thought if I had told him that there were times when I was almost convinced I had actually helped some folks, but that was the exception, not the rule? Or if I'd mentioned how many midnight calls I'd made to homes where kids were screaming, parents were screaming, neighbors were screaming, and I was screaming? Taking kids away from their parents, even for one night, was one of the worst jobs imaginable. Far worse, however, was interviewing families after a child had been killed through abuse or neglect.

Should I have told him I wanted to change jobs because I didn't think it was a sin to want an easier job and make good money?

Why then did I feel guilty about this career change? It wasn't like I was selling out or anything. I wanted to work with people with insurance. No big deal.

And I wanted to stop dreaming about those kids.

The noises of the emergency department brought me back to the present.

So much for my fantasy of dealing with patients in a nicely appointed, clinical office. I was hired yesterday and here I was… in the ER again.

I wondered why the Clinic hadn't notified me that I was on-call. I remembered Marian Dougherty mentioning that she was the on-call therapist for the week. Resolving to clear that up later, I found my sister holding emesis basins for two different patients. She handed one to me, said something about making myself useful, and began filling me in.

I couldn't pay attention to what I was doing. Watching someone vomit is not my idea of a good time. Instead, I looked at my sister. Jenny was a year younger than I and ten years more mature. She was short, blonde, and thin, and managed to look good in the ugly green scrubs. If I didn't love her I would have hated her.

Most of my sibs were in helping professions, with the majority in the medical field. I was a notable exception to the medical sibs, based primarily on my inability to deal with anything coming out of any orifices of the body. Consequently, it was difficult for me to listen to Jenny. The gagging noises I made drowned out much of the conversation. I was able to gather that there were fourteen patients who were not only inebriated but had probably gotten into some rotten homemade elderberry wine and most of them were violently ill. I still didn't know why she needed my help as the patients seemed much too busy throwing up to be causing any major problems. Finally, Jen asked me to step into one of the treatment rooms with her. Handing the emesis basin to a grinning EMT, I followed her into Treatment Room #3. I began to get a bit suspicious as Jen lagged behind me and pushed me into the room ahead of her.

"Surprise." "Congratulations." "Welcome aboard." My eyes could barely see everyone, because of the tears that suddenly spilled onto my cheeks. There was Ed, Pete, Jill, and Rob. With Jen behind me, the whole family crew was there.

"I can't believe you guys set me up like this. It's so early in the morning that it's practically the middle of the night."

Jen moved into the center of the crowd. "It's the only time we could get everyone together."

It was a wonderful surprise and I continued to grin as I looked around at them. Most of us looked alike and were obviously siblings.

Jenny was around five feet tall, with short no-nonsense dark blonde hair. Ed was tall and rangy. He had remained a towhead, and his hair kept falling into his eyes, just as it had when he was a kid. The tallest of the six, Pete had wheat-colored hair that curled in waves around his ears. Those curls had always made me jealous when we were younger. Jill wore her ash blonde hair in a ponytail today. Most of the time she wore her long hair up on top of her head, in a misguided attempt to look older. Rob was the only non-blond. His dark brown hair shone with a hint of red in it.

And wonder of wonders—everyone was getting along. This was one for the record books.

Most of the gang worked at that very hospital, which we affectionately dubbed "Darling Memorial." Mom and Dad had figured that we owned most of it anyway since all of us were born there.

Jen quickly poured the punch, cut the cake, and then cut out of there to get back to work. With a breezy, "Love you," she headed back to the inebriated masses. I visited with the rest of the crew until we heard a scream coming from the waiting area. Wondering if this was the continuation of my surprise party, I led the sibs out to see what was going on.

We came upon a scene straight from "COPS." A young man paced in the waiting room, holding a gun and waving it haphazardly—now at the ceiling, now at frantic bystanders.

"This damn place don't care about people. All they care about is money. Nobody here gives a damn. We ought to close it down. Everybody get out; don't give them no more money." He started weaving as he gestured. "What happened to Dr. Burns is gonna happen to a lot more doctors around here."

Ed, Rob and I all made a move to deal with the situation. I guess it really was Ed's place as Director of Hospital Security. But Rob was a cop and was technically on duty all the time. I was going to intervene because I was pretty good at crisis intervention, and since I was fairly codependent I was always eager to help.

The three of us were doing our variation of a Three Stooges routine when a man walked into the waiting room, calmly approached the dude, did a modified karate chop to the wrist and grabbed the gun before it hit the floor.

I was impressed. I was more than impressed; I was staring. The hero was a giant, muscled god. Every wannabe surfer girl's dream.

Rob identified himself as an off duty cop and took over. As he held onto the miscreant he turned and said, "We're going to need a statement from you, Mr.—uh I didn't catch your name."

"O'Dear. Michael O'Dear."

Aha. The private eye who visited Burns yesterday morning.

O'Dear glanced around the room, his eyes finally lighting on me. I managed to fluff my hair and wet my lips before I realized what I was doing.

I smiled and stuttered, "Sam Darling."

His smile drew me a step closer. "My name's Michael, but you can call me 'darling' if you want." He handed me a business card.

"No, my name is Sam Darling." Why couldn't I wipe the idiotic grin off my face?

I tore my gaze away from him and decided to do my bit to help. I started to gather the witnesses in order to interview them.

"Sam, if you want to be a cop, why don't you be one?" Ed said. "And if you don't want to be a cop, then let us handle it. I'll take care of the details here. Go home and get some rest."

I agreed but without much spirit. It's really hard to be the bossy older sister when your brothers keep insisting on taking over.

I discreetly turned my eyes to O'Dear and found that he was still looking at me. My mirror often lied to me and told me I didn't look my age and that my smile and eyes were gorgeous. I didn't believe my mirror. However the way the god looked at me made me think he believed it.

Oh, God, please let him be single. Please let him be straight. Please let him like me. Please let him carry me off to his villa in Spain. Oh, God, please let him…

His smile broadened. His easy confidence when he winked and grinned made me feel like a country bumpkin.

As he walked away, his smile seemed to linger. Not in a Cheshire Cat kind of way, but in a Prince Charming kind of way. I imagined him climbing into a chariot with a surfboard attached and heading for the nearest beach. That would be Hogback Island in Quincy Bay, which diminished the romance of my fantasy.

He intrigued me. Then I glanced at his business card and was reminded of his name.

Yeah right. We'll fall in love, get married, and my name will be Sam Darling O'Dear. Not on your life.

"Hi ya, Sam."

Just my luck. Why would B.H. be the cop to show up? Doesn't he ever go home?

I greeted him. It wasn't a frosty greeting; after all, Michael was still within hearing distance and I wanted to make a good impression on him. At the sound of the detective's voice, Michael walked back to our area.

"Michael, this is B.H. Lansing, a detective with Quincy Police Department. B.H., this is Michael O'Dear."

B.H. shot a confused look at me as he shook Michael's hand. "The name's George Lansing."

I shrugged as they talked for a few minutes, mostly about Burns' murder. B.H. ended their short conversation with, "I understand you were meeting with Doctor Burns shortly before he died. I'd like to speak to you about that later this morning."

They agreed on a meeting time and place, then B.H. wandered off, following Rob and the guy who provided such cheap entertainment for the ER.

My curiosity, as usual, got the better of me. "I do have a question before you leave." Michael arched his eyebrows and nodded. "What are you doing in the emergency room this early in the morning?"

Chuckling, he said, "I was about to ask you the same question. Maybe we could get together some time and talk about it."

"Okay." The stupid grin on my face was probably going to stay there for a long time. I tried to get rid of it, but no such luck. I was stuck with it.

I couldn't help but think that the guy who stood me up just met the guy who's gonna take me out. There's a certain symmetry to that.

FOUR

When I got home from the hospital there wasn't time to do the things I'd planned: take a leisurely shower, eat breakfast, and pick up my junk scattered around the house. Those chores could wait. There was one task I couldn't put off. The first thing I saw when I walked in the door was Clancy, standing by the couch with her leash in her mouth, holding me to my part of the bargain. When the kids and I brought her home as a puppy, she promised to be faithful, protect us, be there when we were lonely, and in general, just be cool. In return I promised to walk her and feed her, things she reminded me to do on a daily basis.

The morning walk was always a special time for me. Clancy knew where we were going and led the way to the park down the street. I didn't have to think about any of the details. She stopped at every street corner and looked both ways and then pulled me across when it was safe.

The scenery along the route was beautiful. Much of this neighborhood was on the National Historic Register and rightly so. Today Clancy and I walked by the Clinic. At this time of day it really looked like the mansion that it was. Built by one of the trade barons in 1880 when most of the town was making money hand over fist, it was one of the masterpieces on this street. The builder of the mansion, Jeremiah Woodson, one of the founding fathers of Quincy, started out in poverty, but through judicious use of a boat he owned, eventually parlayed a small nest egg into a remarkable fortune. In those days, there were many like him, and most of them built their homes on Maine Street and those surrounding it. The Clinic was the diamond among many jewels.

I was fortunate that I lived on such a street and that I had Clancy as a tour guide.

When I first saw Clancy at the Humane Society, I felt her sadness in a physical way. I found it hard to explain, but her pain was palpable. She was lonely and she was scared. I chose her immediately, with no objection from my kids.

Since the moment Clancy came into our lives, she has been my closest confidante. She understands me better than anyone else in my life. She also accepts none of my b.s.

I didn't fear the snow and ice because Clancy took care of the mechanics of the walk. All I had to do was go along. This was my thinking time. I solved many of the world's problems during these morning walks. Too bad I wasn't so successful in solving my own problems. They weren't monumental, but they were constant. Clancy's heard them all. "You know, Clancy, social workers don't earn huge salaries, but things are really looking up now that I'm at the clinic. And the cost of living is a lot less here in Quincy than it was in Chicago. I think things will improve in the money department. Maybe I'll be able to buy you the gourmet dog food." Clancy responded positively to that idea; her tail went crazy. I wished all of my problems could be solved so easily.

My other problem was a lousy love life. Lousy? It was nonexistent. I'd been divorced from Alan for several years, and had had a few dates, none very serious. Clancy stopped and looked at me. "Okay, Clancy, I didn't realize I said that out loud. One of these days I'll find Mr. Right. Heaven knows I've been successful at finding Mr. Wrong. Maybe I'll just reverse my tactics. That ought to work. Yeah, I know I'm just talking; this is Fantasy Island. Right?" I felt embarrassed verbalizing this stuff. I was a feminist before the word was invented, but when I fantasize, there is always a Mr. Right. This morning he looked alarmingly like Mr. O'Dear.

During this walk, however, my thoughts drifted mostly toward THE MURDER. In my mind, it was always capitalized. THE MURDER. My first. I was intrigued.

"I know I should be sadder about Burns' death. I'm a social worker. I almost feel guilty that I don't feel bad enough. I didn't know him though, and when I met him last week for my interview there was something about him that gave me the creeps. Even though he was smart enough to hire me, I couldn't make myself like him."

We crossed a busy street. It only momentarily stopped my babbling.

"Well, I don't know why I didn't like him, but his eyes were cold. When he noticed me staring, they got warm again. It was weird. So I'm sad that a human being is dead, but I feel no real loss of Dr. Burns. Does that make sense?"

Clancy nodded, then headed back to her job of leading the trek.

There was one good thing about this murder investigation. It would take my mind off the empty nest at my house. "God, I miss the kids. They're growing up so fast and pretty soon they'll be gone for good, instead of just away at school." Clancy looked at me with empathy. I stooped and patted her as I continued, "Well, I'll never really be alone. I've got you and the rest of the clan. Even though I live by myself…" A low growl emanated from Clancy, "Oh, sorry, girl. Even though you and I live by ourselves, we're never really alone. Relatives are always stopping by, and we get invited over to their homes a lot. Moving back here was definitely the right thing to do."

I'd missed the support of the family over the years, especially when Alan left me. I loved Chicago, but Quincy was still home. Besides the sibs and their spouses and kids, there were myriad aunts, uncles, and cousins. Sometimes they got on my nerves, but it was neat to be a member of this club. Even though the membership list was so long it appeared that anyone could be a member.

I also told Clancy about the "John Doe" from the ER. "What do you think is going on with him? What possible reason could he have had for threatening people like that? Did I tell you that he said other doctors might die like Burns?" She pondered that one for a bit. "Why am I so worried about him? It's not like I'll ever see him again."

Clancy gave me her "hey, stupid" look.

"Okay, he did threaten other doctors. Maybe I will see him again. Wonder if he had anything to do with Burns' death?"

Her eyebrows raised as she thought about that notion.

"Nah, Clance, he didn't feel guilty to me. He just felt ill. There's a difference."

And why did Michael O'Dear's face keep popping up in my mind? The last question I didn't verbalize. I didn't want Clancy to hear me thinking so much about a man; she might lose respect for me.

I chuckled as I realized that all of these questions made my life sound like a commercial for a soap opera. But, anyway, I found myself looking forward to seeing O'Dear again a lot more than I wanted to admit. Clancy scooted out of my way as I tripped on a curb. I caught myself before I landed face down in the snow. "Guess I'm a little preoccupied."

I swear she chuckled.

We finished our walk at a brisk pace. After returning home, I got Clancy her food and water, showered and got ready for my first real day in the office. I didn't have much time to learn about my job or do any work yesterday since Dr. Burns' murder overshadowed my appearance as the new kid on the block. I'd spent most of yesterday sitting in my new office with my ear to the door.

Today I would settle in. I filled my briefcase with framed pictures of the kids, my license to practice as a clinical social worker in the state of Illinois, and a small plaque painted by a friend that said, "God has entrusted us to each other." Those would fill my desk until I messed it up with files and books.

I also put a few boxes of books by the front door, ready to go into my car. Those would fit nicely into the built-in bookcases in my office. I was excited about going to work, although I was bummed about my boss being dead. Since I had a choice, I decided to go with the excitement rather than dwell on the sad stuff.

Everything was ready but my all-important outfit. After I poured a cup of coffee, I wandered into my walk-in closet. Actually, it was a climb-in closet. It was piled almost to the ceiling with "stuff," things I'd been promising myself I'd put away as soon as I had time. I moved aside the Scrabble game and old Rolling Stone magazines and took out my good suit. It had seen me through a lot of tough times, but I wore it the other day for my interview. Would the other staff members recognize it? Would it matter if they did? Didn't I have anything better to obsess about?

I wore the suit.

I said good-bye to Clancy and left home feeling a bit ambivalent. On one hand, I had optimism and hope in my heart for my newly organized future. On the other hand, I was saddened about Burns' demise. It was difficult sorting out the emotions.

Because of all my paraphernalia I decided to drive to work again. The trip was a short one, and I arrived around seven, a full hour before I was required to be there. I describe myself as an on-time employee. My family would call it compulsive behavior.

Schnitzer hadn't given me a key yet, but I had a feeling Gwen Schneider would be there early and would let me in.

The first part was correct anyway. She was at her desk. I peered through the glass door, like a little kid waiting for the toy store to open. I rapped gently at first, but finally ended up pounding with both fists when I got no response to my polite approach. Somehow I knew she heard me. Even through the glass, I could sense her nasty attitude toward me. I couldn't figure out why she disliked me already. When

I came for my interview and was a visitor, she treated me like royalty. And yesterday, after Burns' murder, she even allowed me to comfort her. Normally people had to work with me a few days before they didn't like me.

Could she be jealous of me? Nah, it must be something else. Maybe she was embarrassed that I saw her at her worst in Burns' office. She was the first person I could accurately describe as a blithering idiot. Not a professional description, but accurate all the same. I was going to find out what was going on with her. In the meantime, I would dazzle her with kindness—and maybe b.s. She wouldn't be able to stand it.

She finally deigned to acknowledge my existence. As she walked slowly and deliberately toward the door, her hips swayed as if she meant business, but her hair didn't move at all. She'd cornered the market on hair spray. When she opened the door, she flashed her pearly whites and said, "Good morning. Were you waiting long?"

"Yeah, I was." I thought lying was a waste of time, and besides I wasn't very good at it. "Why wouldn't you let me in?"

"I didn't hear you." She apparently thought that she was good at lying. Her eyes betrayed her. "Would you like some coffee?" Her smile didn't falter, but the rest of her body language gave a little bit, and her eyes were glistening as if she'd been crying. She turned to the coffeepot behind her desk. My vibes must have been taking a break, because I didn't get any strong emotions emanating from her other than sadness. Why wouldn't she let me in if she was just sad?

I decided to be noble and forgiving. She had a hard time making eye contact, but I didn't. I walked around her desk and touched her on the shoulder. "Gwen, I know that Dr. Burns' death was hard on you. I also know you probably spent most of the night at the police station getting grilled. Whatever is going on with you, I am not your enemy. I know you didn't kill him and I'm willing to help you."

She nodded and started sobbing. She ran toward the bathroom. I started to follow her, but figured I'd done enough damage already.

I picked up the coffee that Gwen had poured for me and I meandered to my office. Meander is the correct word because I took a few wrong turns. The scenic route. Instead of turning left from the waiting area, I accidentally went right and then left and I walked past a conference room and several smaller offices. When I reached the back of the mansion, I continued left, making a circle through the building. This route took me past Dr. Burns' office.

I fought the urge to look around the crime scene.

After Burns' office came the kitchen, then my office. My very own office. I didn't share it with anyone. That was so cool.

I put down my briefcase and purse, went back out to my car two more times for the boxes of books, and finally did a very important, symbolic act. I rummaged through my briefcase full of stuff and poured the coffee from the clinic mug into my own mug. My sibs gave the mug to me on the occasion of my employment by DCFS. It said, "Just take it one, gigantic, earth-shattering crisis at a time." The cup appeals to my smart alec side and survived fifteen years with the Department. It remained my talisman.

Throughout the morning people kept poking their heads into my office and welcoming me. As expected, the big topic of conversation was the murder. Everyone had a favorite villain. It made for pretty interesting conversation, and I didn't have anything better to do. I probably would have a few days of light duty before I got some patients assigned to me.

Besides trying to catch all the available gossip, I used this time to study policies and procedures. I really wanted to learn the important things about the company—like how many vacation days I got per year, how much sick time, personal days, all of the vital stuff.

I wondered when B.H. would be back to question the rest of the staff. Marian Dougherty came by my office and asked me to join everyone in the kitchen, which doubled as the staff lounge. She introduced me to others I hadn't met. In this office, most staff members were counselors, social workers, and psychologists. There were also a few nursing personnel. Most of my co-workers seemed friendly enough, and since I took charge yesterday, they all continued to ask me questions. I pretended I knew a lot more than I did.

I used all my knowledge garnered from *Bipolar Passion* and *Schizoid Revenge*, my latest forays into reading psychological thrillers. Although my favorite books dealt primarily with the mental illness angle of murders, they also had incredible details about crime scenes and police procedures. Everyone seemed impressed with my knowledge, and I hoped that changed their minds about my bossy demeanor yesterday.

When Gwen Schneider entered the room, a chill entered with her. Earlier Marian told me Gwen worked for Dr. Burns for almost the entire time he was in practice. I knew there was more to her than met the eye, but vowed to let it drop. Or at least I vowed to try to let it drop. Being nosy is a genetic disorder I inherited from my mother. There is no cure.

I tried to observe my surroundings instead of staring at Gwen. This kitchen was huge. Most of the appliances were ultra modern but were in muted tones that blended in well with the Victorian surroundings. We all sat around a butcher-block table that was large enough to seat my whole family. I wondered idly how they moved it to clean. Three of the walls were covered in a yellow washed paper. The fourth wall was natural red brick. Homey and inviting.

No matter how I tried not to look, my glance kept

moving to Gwen when I thought no one would notice. She was antsy, unable to sit still, but I didn't feel the same amount of animosity as earlier. Her energy was really disorganized. Almost chaotic. Even though I noticed things like this, I didn't know what to make of it. My gut told me that Gwen Schneider was in major hot water. Or maybe not. Maybe she was mentally ill. There I went again. I decided to go with my feelings that she was in big trouble. Of course, anybody who knew she spent last night being questioned by the cops would know she was in trouble. *Nothing like going for the obvious, Sam.*

FIVE

Okay, perhaps I'm not the most tactful individual, and grace is not my strong suit, but you'd think I'd be able to ask people questions without them thinking I'm trying to dig up some dirt. Apparently not.

So, armed with good intentions and gut instinct, I began my quest for the villain. I decided to hang out in the kitchen because sooner or later everyone passed through there. Also it was close to the scene of the crime, and I knew that curiosity would get the better of everyone eventually. They would all feel the need to get close to where it happened. Burns' office itself was taped off with the yellow pre-printed crime scene tape. For some reason, that surprised me. I almost expected generic masking tape, on which someone might have written, "Do not enter. Crime scene." I guessed the QPD had more professionalism than I thought.

Even so, murders were rare, and part of the reason I moved home. The last murder I recalled happened when I was a teenager. "Old Lady" Tippins beat the hell out of "Old Man" Tippins one too many times and he died.

Immediately upon being notified of his death, she also died. Which just goes to show you that love comes in a lot of varieties, and there is no age limit to the *Romeo and Juliet* theme.

I sat in the kitchen waiting for the unsuspecting staff members to wander in. The first one was Marian Dougherty. She gave me a sideways glance as if she knew I was going to fire some questions at her. Discretion would be my watchword.

"How's it going, Marian?"

"Uh, okay." She fiddled with the faux pearls around her neck, eyes darting everywhere but in my direction. She seemed like a nice enough person, and had sincerely welcomed my arrival. I'd heard Marian was a decent therapist and a genuinely caring individual. She was about my age, a bit overweight, with reddish sun streaks in her almost black hair.

"Is your work going well?"

Her reticence vanished. It was as if she was ready to talk and I was the lucky person who happened to be there at the time the dam burst.

She sighed and said that it was hard doing therapy when her mind was elsewhere. She asked if I thought we could legitimately cancel appointments because of Dr. Burns' death.

"Who's in charge of the therapists?"

"No one now. Dr. Burns supervised all of us directly and there's not a middle manager on the behavioral health side."

She and I both came to the same conclusion. We would suggest to the rest of the therapists that they evaluate all of their patients and cancel the appointments they thought were appropriate. There might be a few people with problems so acute that it would not be in the patients' best interests to cancel. We figured that whoever was in charge of the clinic would surely close the whole office for Dr. Burns' funeral and appointments could be shuffled if necessary for that occasion. Today was Thursday and the funeral would probably be Saturday or Monday, depending on the wishes of the family. We'd probably find out more about that tomorrow.

So, now that she was trusting, I got to the meat of the discussion. As she innocently poured a cup of coffee, I pounced.

"So, this was really a surprise, huh?"

"You think people get murdered in Quincy every day or something? Of course it was a surprise. Dr. Burns was a dear man." Marian added teaspoon after teaspoon of sugar to her coffee. "Well, maybe not a dear man, but a good man. Well…"

I got the picture. And filed it away in my brain for later retrieval.

She continued. "Anyway, my paycheck never bounced.

He sure knew how to run a business. I'm going to miss him. At least I'll miss him sometimes." She stirred her coffee without looking at it, unaware that the hot liquid sloshed over the sides of the mug. "Well, to be honest, he could be a real jerk, but no one should have killed him. Nobody deserves that. I always thought there was more to Gwen than met the eye, but I didn't think she would kill him."

Whoa, the verdict was in, even before Gwen had been arraigned. She hadn't even been arrested. In fact, she was still sitting in the reception area, trying to muddle through.

The joys of small town living. Probably everyone in town was by now debating her innocence or guilt. Since people love a good scandal, the majority was probably convinced of her guilt.

I decided to probe a little more.

"What makes you think Gwen killed him? Had there been trouble before or something?"

She hesitated and looked around before answering. "You know they were having an affair. And I'm not one to gossip, but Gwen never married and she worked late a lot and Dr. Burns worked late a lot and Gwen always has expensive jewelry and her mother stopped talking to her and she never goes to the Christmas party because Mrs. Burns will be there, and…" At this point she stopped to take a breath and I was glad. I had begun worrying that she would keel over, her face was so red. I started talking before she could go again.

"That's very interesting," *and juicy,* "but if they were having an affair, why would Gwen kill him? That's kind of like biting the hand that feeds you." I was quick with the clichés.

"I don't know why she would kill him, but I heard she confessed right in your office." *Damn those heating grates.*

"She did not confess. Please tell everyone that. And I don't think she killed him. I can't reveal my source right now, but I trust the truth will become evident to everyone very soon. In fact, a trusted investigator is on the case even as we speak." It wasn't my fault that Marian probably assumed that the trusted investigator was Michael O'Dear instead of me.

Thinking of his name reminded me that I was eager to see him again. Maybe I could weasel some information out of him, but I had to have a plan. For now I had a witness to milk for information. Maybe I mixed my metaphors a little, but I was getting excited. And that feeling was one I hadn't experienced in quite a while.

I continued, "I only knew him a few minutes before he died, so I didn't form an opinion of him."

Marian raised her eyebrows in disbelief.

"Okay, so maybe I have an opinion, but I want to hear more of yours. What did you mean, 'he could be a real jerk sometimes'?"

Marian hesitated. "I probably shouldn't be telling you

this, but he wasn't a very good psychiatrist. Great businessman, poor therapist. Over the years I've taken several of his former patients—after all there's not another clinic for them to go to—and they're almost pathetically grateful that I listen to them. Apparently, Dr. Burns was pretty directive. I've even heard him described as manipulative."

I certainly didn't get this personality profile in the few moments I'd known him. This was some good stuff. I tried for more but Marian was finished with her sharing.

She left the kitchen soon afterward when she realized that I was not going to say anything interesting. I waited for the next victim.

Soon Doris walked in, took one look at me and walked out. I felt pretty put out about it, but figured that Marian must have passed the word about my prowess as an interrogator.

There weren't any evil vibes surrounding anyone in the office, so I decided to take my quest elsewhere. First, I called one of my favorite human confidants to see if he was available for consultation.

He picked up the phone immediately. The sound of his voice always made me smile.

"Pete, Sam."

"Hi, Sam, what's up? Something important to talk about?" No beating around the bush with Pete. He cut right to the chase. I think he's the only other one of the siblings who was psychic too, but it's not something we talked about. I just know that Pete and I have always used shorthand language with each other. We finished thoughts and sentences and sometimes the others felt left out. Of course, like any dysfunctional family, we all finished sentences for each other and talked over each other, but this was different. It was special.

Pete was the head nurse on the cardiac care unit at the hospital. Like me, he had recently returned to Quincy. For a number of years he served as both a priest and a nurse at a mission in Maui. We teased him that being stationed on Maui was kind of defeating the purpose of making the sacrifice to be a missionary. We didn't tease him too much though, because all of us were able to take a cheap vacation at one time or another, courtesy of Father Brother—Pete's nickname. For reasons known only to Pete, God, and me, he was on sabbatical and had come home for a while. And he was extremely successful at the job he chose. He had a special compassion for people that was beautiful and rare. He was indeed a great gift to all of us. Of course, we wouldn't be caught dead saying that to his face.

"Yeah, it is important. Are you free? Can we get together?"

We made arrangements to meet in a half hour at The Dairy, a favorite family gathering place. The location was ideal, as it was between our family home, the church, and elementary school. Besides, it had a table big enough to accommodate all of us.

I arrived twenty-five minutes later and met Pete as he was walking in the door. After a quick hug, we moved to our favorite table even though there were only two of us today.

Pete's Irish cable-knit sweater, worn over a green turtleneck, complemented his curly blonde hair. He had a great profile too; one of the few who didn't inherit the family pug nose. Females in town called him "Father What-a-Waste."

Marge, the waitress, nodded and we knew she'd bring over two black cows—the Midwest equivalent of a root beer float.

"What's up?" he asked. As usual, Pete didn't waste time.

I really loved this man. When he was born, he'd already had a glow about him that had not diminished. As a five-year-old I had remarked upon the glow. Well-meaning aunts quizzed me about it. They thought I was either hallucinating or having religious visions, neither of which was acceptable in their view. They would have preferred the religious visions, but even that would have raised eyebrows. So I stopped remarking on the things I saw and felt. Mom and Dad knew, or suspected. I think Mom may have had a bit of the "feeling" herself. Or at least I like to think she did.

"I need to talk over some things. My boss was murdered

yesterday." I waited for an exclamation of surprise and was disappointed when it didn't appear. I had forgotten that the murder had happened over twenty-four hours ago. I hadn't seen a newspaper or listened to the news. Surely people as far away as Marblehead, a distance of six miles, knew and also probably knew who did it. Well, doggone it. I didn't know who did it. And I wanted to prove everyone else wrong.

"Gwen didn't do it, Pete."

"If you say so, Gwen didn't do it. Now let's talk about who might have killed your boss."

And we set to work.

SIX

Pete and I talked for a long time, but we didn't come up with any likely suspects. I knew it was time to stop when we started giggling over probable candidates like the butler, the upstairs maid, our sister Jill, Butthead, and Dr. Burns himself. We said goodbye and made plans to get together soon to continue the discussion. I knew I could count on Pete to keep things hush-hush. I certainly didn't want Ed and Rob to find out I was working on the case. And, above all, B.H. could not know. My greatest thrill would be to solve the case, give some credit to my brother, Rob, and leave B.H. in the dust.

My hostility toward B.H. was probably juvenile, and I even felt guilty about it, but I wasn't ready to give it up. He'd broken my heart.

I arrived home a few moments later to an angry dog. Over my profuse apologies, she got her leash and then waited impatiently for me to check my messages before we left for the walk. I had one message. From Michael O'Dear, asking if I'd go out to dinner with him on Friday. I couldn't wipe the smile off my face. At the end of his message he asked if I had heard that Gwen Schneider had killed Dr. Burns. He sounded smug. But he didn't have the knowledge I had. I knew she didn't do it. I knew it for a fact, beyond a shadow of a doubt. Of course I had no proof, but I wasn't going to let a small thing like that stand in my way. I just needed to find the killer.

I called Michael's number immediately, told his machine that Friday would be fine, and that I'd be ready at seven. It was hard sounding sophisticated while doing a happy dance around my living room.

I smiled at Clancy as I tried to make up with her. She is my significant other and I couldn't afford to have her mad at me. She finally gave me one of her "okay, you're only human" looks and handed her leash to me. I accepted it gratefully and we headed for the park.

This part of the city had a lot of parks. In fact, many of the lawns were large enough to qualify as well. I put myself on automatic pilot and concentrated on the case. I had never met Mrs. Burns but planned to see her at the funeral home. Other staff told me she was a nice lady, but they said it in a way that seemed they didn't quite mean it. I also heard she was a beauty and quite a bit younger than the doctor. I was anxious to meet the woman who had been married to the enigmatic Dr. Burns.

Clancy and I walked for over an hour and both of us got

nice and sweaty. That felt great while the blood was still pumping, but it soon chilled me to the bone. I wanted to hurry into the carriage house, but saw Mrs. Granville's curtains move as I started to pass.

"Clancy, she saw us. Act sick, so I have an excuse not to talk long." Clancy immediately obliged and hung her head as she stuck out her tongue.

"Oh, Ms. Darling, may I speak to you a minute?"

Smiling my phoniest smile, I approached her verandah. Other people would have called it a porch, but to Mrs. Granville it was, and would always be, a verandah.

Georgianne Granville had on her usual evening attire: a quilted bathrobe, pink fuzzy slippers, and pink plastic curlers that were covered by a diaphanous scarf-like apparatus. With all her money, I wondered why she didn't have better taste in at-home loungewear. She pulled herself up to her full 4'10" and spoke to me as if she were Queen Elizabeth II on her balcony.

"Ms. Darling, I saw a man looking around the carriage house today while you were gone. I hope you don't plan to have people lollygagging around while you are engaged elsewhere."

"No, Georgianne. My plans don't include the lollygagging of people around my house. Did you see what he looked like?"

"Well, I wasn't really looking." She couldn't see me roll

my eyes in the dark. "But he appeared about twenty-five to twenty-eight, dark hair, a little shaggy around the ears, he had on a brown corduroy jacket with the patches on the elbows. So outré, don't you think? And he was looking very suspicious. But as I said, I really didn't get a good look."

That didn't describe any of my brothers, Michael O'Dear, or B.H. Lansing. Aha, as they say, the plot thickens.

"Well thanks for telling me. By the way, how is Gus today?"

"He is still very ill and unable to have visitors."

Just then a booming voice echoed out of the open door, "Sam, is that you? Come in here and see me, girl."

Ignoring Georgianne's grimace of distaste, Clancy and I both bounded up the stairs and into what Georgianne called the parlor. Lying on the couch was one of the nicest men ever to grace this earth. Unfortunately, he probably wasn't going to be gracing it much longer. I thought he would probably live a long and healthy life if it weren't for his wife. But maybe that's too cruel. Some people enjoy sparring with their partner, it keeps them lively. I know I enjoyed it too, until I discovered that my husband was sparring with someone else at the same time. Sparring outside of marriage was against my personal belief system.

What Georgianne knew and didn't like was that I had known Gus for many years, ever since I was in elementary school. I had been brave enough to not only walk past the rich people's houses, but also to dawdle a bit. One day, I came upon a gardener, working in a flowerbed at the Granville's. He was singing WWI and WWII era songs in a booming baritone. I joined in. He was surprised that someone my age would know these songs. I later told him how my mom had taught me songs from her youth and from her own mother's youth.

I began helping Gus the gardener nearly every day after school and he taught me many more songs. It was fun singing and playing in the dirt. I'd run home right after school and change into my blue jeans. Gus always wore overalls. In the summer he wore an undershirt and the other seasons he wore comfortable old flannel shirts. I began asking him questions about the rich people who lived there. He told me that money wasn't everything. And I said I wouldn't know, never having had any. So he started paying me a quarter every time I helped. Eventually he revealed himself to me as Gus Granville, the owner of the home. Well, actually he said his wife owned it and she let him live there. With that, he laughed the loudest, most beautiful laugh I'd ever heard. He laughed until he cried. I did too, although I didn't know what I was laughing at.

I kept in touch with Gus over the years, stopping by whenever I was in Quincy. He cherished pictures of my kids, attended their baptisms, and grieved with me over the death of my parents. He grieved again with me when my husband left. Other than my family and Clancy, Gus was the best friend I'd ever had. When I returned to Quincy, I bunked with Jen and her brood for a few weeks while I looked around for a place to rent. When Gus found out I was looking, his eyes twinkled and he said he had just the place for me. He put on his overcoat and boots and took me out back to the carriage house. Like a proud artist, he pointed at it, wanting me to love it as he did.

"Don't tell the Missus I told you this, but we've had a few spats over the years. When we were young I decided I didn't want to get mad and leave, but I needed a space to call my own. So I converted the carriage house into an apartment. Lately, I haven't felt the need or the energy to use it, so it's empty and would be perfect for you. Please take it."

I said "yes" without even looking at it. Knowing it would bring such joy to Gus and such agony to Georgianne were enough reasons for me. When I went inside, I knew my instincts were correct. There was a small kitchen downstairs, with a nice sized living room, small dining room, and large master bedroom and bath. Upstairs were two small bedrooms and another bath. It was just what I wanted and needed. There was room for the kids when they came home from school, but my personal living space was all on one floor. I moved in the next day, converting the dining room into my office. My brothers and sisters were huffing and puffing, but we got the job done. I was very happy in my new home and even happier with one half of my landlord couple.

When I tuned back in to the conversation, Georgianne sniffed her distaste and continued a diatribe already in progress, "… I insist. Please take your animal outside and tie it up. We cannot have animal dander in the house. My husband is ill and his breathing will be compromised. Surely you don't want to be responsible…"

Gus interrupted, "Leave the girl alone, Georgie. Go ahead, Sam, tell me what's up."

Georgie? I managed to avoid a fit of the giggles and went on. "It was really something. No sooner had I started my new job, than Dr. Burns was killed. I was still in the personnel office filling out forms when I heard the scream."

Gus responded that he'd heard details from his neighbors already. "I probably knew almost as soon as you did," he chuckled.

I asked him if he had known Dr. Burns well.

Gus sat up so I could join him on the couch. "I wouldn't say I knew him well. I did know him for a lot of years. Hell, this is a small community and we lived in the same general neighborhood."

"Did you like him?"

Gus laughed again. "I didn't care much for the old fart,"

he became serious, "but I'm sorry he was killed."

"Please don't use such vulgarities." Georgianne reminded us she was still around. "I'm sure you can convey your meaning in a more refined manner."

"Sure, honey." Gus said to his wife, and then turned toward me again, "I didn't care much for the old bastard, but I'm sorry he was killed."

He cocked his head to look at his wife, "Is that better?"

That did it. The laugh that I'd been able to suppress finally forcibly exploded. "'Scuse me."

Gus smiled and Georgianne pouted. I liked that.

I asked Gus if I could bounce some ideas off him. He brightened up.

"Sure. I'm bored stiff cooped up in this house all the time."

"Okay, here's what I want to know. Even though you don't get out much I know people visit you all the time. So do you know if anyone hated Dr. Burns?"

Gus laughed. "If anyone hated him? It'd be easier to list the people who didn't hate him. There weren't many of those."

"Well, he did give me the creeps. But why did everyone dislike him?"

"I dunno. He seemed to have everything but always wanted more. Then when his wife started making so much money, I think he got a little jealous."

"Wait a minute. What did his wife do to earn a lot of money?"

"Guess you haven't heard about it since you've been gone so long, but Carolyn Burns is actually Felicia Greene."

"Whoa. Burns' wife is Felicia Greene? I don't believe it. I've read all her books."

"Yep. She's quite a bit younger than Burns and rumor has it that she got bored one day and just started writing. Surprised everyone when she got published. Burns didn't fuss too much about what he called 'her little hobby,' as long as it didn't infringe on his life. His only input was to insist that she use a nom de plume so no one would know his wife was a novelist."

"This is unbelievable. Her books are my favorites. I mean they have everything in them—murder, sex, intrigue, mental illness. She's got the workings of the mind down pat. Was she involved in the mental health field too?"

Gus chuckled before he spoke. "I don't think Carolyn Burns worked a day in her life before she began writing. Wait until you meet her and then tell me what you think."

I pictured Mrs. Burns as middle aged and dumpy and thought she must have used someone else for the author's picture on her book jackets. After all, Dr. Burns was in his sixties and the young woman pictured as Felicia Greene certainly couldn't have been married to him. I'd heard

Burns' wife was younger than he was, but there were limits to my imagination.

"Ms. Darling," Georgianne again, "my husband needs his rest. I think it's time for you to be going."

"Sure thing, Georgie," I loved calling this formal, cold woman by her nickname.

As I kissed Gus on the cheek he said "No need to rush off," but his tired eyes belied his words.

"I've got a lot to do. I'll see you soon though."

Gus replied, "I think I'll feel well enough to attend the funeral. It's likely to be a real shindig and I don't want to miss it. I'll see you there."

Clancy and I entered our home just as the phone was ringing. When I answered it, two youthful voices said, "Hi, Ma." It was Adam and Sarah calling from school. I'd called and told them about my boss's death and they wanted to know how I was holding up.

"I'm fine. I'm sure sorry he was killed. It was really a bad experience for everyone, and I imagine his wife is devastated. I haven't paid my condolence call yet, but I'll meet her soon."

"Mom, you seem way too excited. What else is going on?" Sarah knew me too well.

"Well, I just thought I'd look around a bit and see if I can help your Uncle Rob solve the case." Surely my kids couldn't object to that.

"Mom," Adam's turn, "remember, you're a social worker and not a cop. Leave the detective work to Uncle Rob and his coworkers. Stay out of it. We don't want anything to happen to you."

When did my lovely son turn into a man? "Listen, you guys, I'm fine. I'm not doing anything stupid and I can take care of myself. Remember who the parent is here. Now, be good little kids and get back to your homework."

We spoke for a few more minutes and after I hung up the phone, I kept thinking about them. It hadn't been easy after the divorce, but all in all the kids turned out fine. I was so proud of both of them. I also loved the fact that they were at the same school, and was grateful that they had each other while they were gone.

I made dinner for Clancy and me. In the past I had been a firm believer that dogs should only get dog food, but ever since Clancy and I have been alone, I've changed my mind. Many times, she and I have shared the same meal. I'm a vegetarian however, and Clancy didn't used to be, but she's almost converted; she does have her limits and draws the line at tofu. I warmed up leftover vegetable lasagna and put some in her bowl along with some canine morsels. I poured myself a glass of Sauvignon Blanc and sighed contentedly. Sometimes life was really good.

I had just finished my meal and was making a pot of decaf, when I heard a light tapping on my door. I opened it without looking to see who it was. Another bad habit from my childhood, but it's one I had a hard time breaking. It took a moment for my eyes to adjust to the darkness; then I noticed a man standing there. He was hiding in the shadows, and rocking back and forth on his heels.

I said, "Can I help you?"

A sad voice asked, "Are you the new lady at the clinic?"

I answered in the affirmative.

"Are you Father Brother's sister?"

Again I answered affirmatively, and then added, "Well, I used to be; I mean he used to be. Well, yeah."

"I know him from the hospital and he told me about you. I need to talk to you. Can I come in? Please?"

The "please" did it. I didn't know too many bad guys who would look and sound so sad and who would say "please" when they wanted to enter a house. So I stepped aside for him to enter. Besides, Clancy was still eating—a sure sign the stranger posed no threat to me.

As he walked into the living room, I thought he might be the person that Georgianne Granville described. When he stepped into the light I also noticed that he was the "John Doe" from the ER earlier in the day.

The first thing I said was, "Tell me your name." I was tired of this "John Doe" thing.

He looked surprised at my directness, but answered, "Charlie Schneider."

The puzzle pieces were multiplying, but a few were starting to fit. "Any relation to Gwen Schneider?"

"Yeah," he said, "she's my sister. That's why I'm here."

"Well, I thought it also could have something to do with the incident this morning in the ER. I saw your fascinating performance and since I'm a therapist and occasionally accept private patients, I thought you might be here for some counseling."

He gave me a look he could have learned from B.H. or Clancy. I decided to mind my manners and not glare back. Clancy didn't have any such reservations, however. She decided to acknowledge his existence by staring. Charlie didn't notice.

"Can I sit down? I'm kinda tired."

I offered him a seat and I joined my dog on the couch. "Why don't you just tell me what I can do for you?"

He glanced around a little before looking me straight in the eye, and said, "They arrested my sister tonight for murdering Dr. Burns, and I know she didn't do it. She told me you said you would help. Since you're Father Brother's sister, I thought I could trust you. I don't know who else to go to, so here I am."

He made perfect sense to me, and that was scary. I quickly reassured him, "I know she didn't do it, Charlie, but I don't have any proof."

"I'm your proof," he blurted. "I did it."

The corpse was barely cold and I'd already solved the murder. God, I'm good. Even Clancy was wagging her tail.

SEVEN

So I was sitting in my living room with my dog and a confessed murderer. And what did I do?

"Charlie, would you like cream in your coffee? How about another piece of pie? You look like you could use something more to eat."

I wouldn't let him talk while he was finishing the leftover lasagna, garlic bread, and pie. This was every mother's dream—someone who really appreciated a good meal. I didn't think it necessary to tell Charlie that the lasagna was made by Mama Manicotti in a sterilized kitchen and that the pie was frozen before I popped it in my oven. He gulped down two cups of coffee as if he were freezing. As he let out a very satisfied belch and wiped his mouth with his sleeve, I realized this guy was probably not the brightest porch light on the block. I also knew he was innocent. My vibes were dormant; there were no errant physical sensations. And it made me mad that he felt he had to confess. This guy was as innocent of murdering Dr. Burns as I was. It was obvious that he was trying to protect his older sister, Gwen.

I decided to try to get a little more information. "Charlie, will you tell me what was going on with you in the ER this morning?"

He looked sheepish; his unstructured hair fell into his eyes, a shield protecting him from the world. "Yeah, they make me so mad in them damn hospitals. My wife and little baby was hurt bad a couple years back in a car wreck and we didn't have no insurance and they took 'em to the hospital and they both died there." Charlie had a hard time maintaining eye contact; his eyes darted back and forth from the plate to Clancy, scarcely alighting on me. "They're still sendin' me bills. It's like they don't know there's human beings on the receivin' end of them bills. Every time I get one of 'em, I get a little crazy. But Dr. Burns said I wasn't crazy. He called it something else, like post dramatic stress."

More information. Charlie was seeing Dr. Burns professionally and was diagnosed with Post-Traumatic Stress Disorder. He would be a perfect candidate for the villain. PTSD, mood swings, the victim was screwing his sister—literally, and the hospital was screwing him—figuratively. Too bad he wasn't guilty.

"Charlie, will you answer another question for me?"

He nodded.

"Did you get arrested this morning for what you did at the hospital?"

"Yes, ma'am, I did. But they know'd me down at the

police station and they let me out until the court day. My lawyer said it'd be awhile. Heck, I'll be in jail anyway for murder, so this thing won't count for much extra."

"Why are you saying you killed Dr. Burns, when I know you didn't?"

"I did too kill him."

"Okay, why did you do it?"

"Just cause I wanted to, that's why."

"So you killed him because you wanted to. How did you do it, Charlie? What did you do to him?"

He stuttered a bit, unable to come up with a plausible method. I was convinced that neither of us knew how Burns had been killed, but I knew more about it than Charlie did. I'd seen Burns dead.

"Sorry, that's not good enough. I know positively that you are innocent. Unfortunately, I can't reveal my source at this time." I was getting tired of saying that. "What's going on?"

"Well, they got my sister and she didn't do it neither. I thought 'cause I'm such a screw-up anyway and I don't have nobody but her, that I oughta say I did it. That way she'd get out."

"Don't worry, Charlie, she'll get out anyway. I'm going to help her by finding the real killer. Now the best thing for you to do is to take good care of yourself and make sure you visit her a lot."

He nodded. After crossing our fingers for luck, and pinky swearing that we wouldn't tell anyone else about me working on the case except Pete, otherwise known as Father Brother, we parted company for the night.

I felt absolutely drained, but I also felt such an adrenaline rush, it was hard to settle down. "Clancy, how about an extra outing tonight? I feel like running a little."

She returned with her leash even before I finished my sentence. I put on my boots and parka and we started out. The snowy night was so bright that I could see clearly. The ground was already covered and flakes were once again falling. I couldn't run much because of my boots and because of the snow, but I knew I had to try, or I'd never be able to sleep.

We started jogging around the big house, but then hit a patch of ice. Clancy skidded; I let go of her leash and windmilled my arms trying to avoid the inevitable. No such luck. With a giant thud I fell flat on my butt. Luckily I had enough padding so I suffered no injury. And because there were no witnesses other than Clancy, even my dignity wasn't damaged. I laughed so hard that I couldn't get up. Clancy was laughing too. We couldn't stop. The guffaws were flying from both of us. The Granville's light went on and I knew that Georgianne would soon be on the back porch with a shotgun, looking for the intruder. I still couldn't get up, so I belly crawled next to her house so she wouldn't be able to see me. Breathing heavily, I pulled Clancy close and begged her not to make any noise.

Sure enough, "Who is it? I've called the police. You better get out of here."

I could just picture her hair in curlers and a gun in her hand. Gus, long weary of his wife's eccentricities, would be snoring happily upstairs. After a few moments, she went inside and I was able to limp back to my house, dragging an unwilling Clancy with me.

"I know I lied, Clance, but my energy is gone now and I can't run. Besides, I'm literally freezing my butt off. Would you like some hot tea and cookies?"

The bribe worked. We drank. Then we slept.

An early phone call the next morning from Schnitzer in the personnel department notified me that the office would be closed until after Dr. Burns' funeral on Monday, so I had the whole day to myself. I could clean house, solve the murder, or think about going out with Michael. I chose Door #2 and decided to do some sleuthing.

First things first. I called Angie, my brother Ed's wife.

"Darlings." She loved to answer the phone that way.

"Angie, hi, this is Sam."

"Oh, hey, I heard about the tragedy at your office. So sorry about it. And to think the murderer was right under your nose. She worked for him for almost twenty years, I heard."

"Yeah, yeah, yeah, but that's not why I called. I want to make a call on Mrs. Burns and I either need to pick up a dish from the deli or call upon my favorite sister-in-law to see if you have anything freshly baked just laying around."

I could hear the grin in her voice. My family was used to covering for me at potluck dinners and carry-ins. "I'm your only sister-in-law, and it just so happens I've made two bundt cakes. And you can have one. Good timing, sis." Angie was an only child and has certainly adapted well to the vagaries of a big family. She knew how to go with the flow.

"Thanks, Ang, I'll pick it up in a little while. I owe you." I couldn't begin to count the number of times she rescued me. God help me if she ever decided to keep track.

"I know you do. Can you babysit for Skeeter tonight so we can go to the game?" There was no need to tell me which game. St. Francis University had a superb basketball team and the entire town attended the games.

"Love to but I can't. I think I have a date. Don't laugh. I really do. But next time you need a sitter, you got one. See you in a few minutes."

After hanging up the phone and also saying good-bye to Clancy, I stopped to speak to Gus for a while. I'd seen Georgianne leave a few minutes earlier.

"Hi ya, gal." Gus was genuinely glad to see me.

"I want to run a few things by you." He nodded and put

on his "business" face.

"Right after we discovered Burns' body, I saw his receptionist sitting in the corner of his office, sobbing. A little while later she said, 'I didn't mean to do it, but…' and then she started sobbing again. It sounds like she was trying to confess, but I don't think she did it. The next day she acted really weird when I arrived at the clinic. Pretended she didn't hear me knocking, and then acted phony-sweet to me. I can't say I like her, but I'm convinced of her innocence."

Gus didn't bother asking me how I knew Gwen was innocent. "Maybe she's just in shock. Finding Burns dead like that would be enough to make anyone act a bit goofy. Why don't you give her a few days and see how she behaves?"

"And I'm the one who's the therapist? You're right. Her behavior is consistent with people who suffered a traumatic event."

I thanked him, gave him a peck on the cheek, and made my getaway before Georgianne's return.

I drove the few miles to Ed and Angie's. As I pulled into the driveway, I couldn't help but smile. The lawn could not be described as "neatly manicured." In the past it had been littered with bikes of various makes, colors and sizes. Now most of the kids were older and drove cars, but the yard still held reminders that a large family lived there.

Ed and Angie had committed the big "no-no" and so they got married immediately after graduating from high school. Alice was born a few months afterward, then Susan, John, Robert, and fourteen years later the ever popular Skeeter.

Skeeter met me at the door. He was dressed in bib overalls and a long sleeved T-shirt. Perched on his head was his favorite baseball cap that said, "Cute." He was cute; in fact he was downright adorable. He was adept at walking; and he smiled and drooled at the sight of his Aunt Sam. We had a great rapport, and spoke each other's language. Even though I was in a hurry, I couldn't resist crawling around on the floor with Skeeter for a few minutes.

As someone with a "favorite Aunt" status, I always bought kids toys that I liked. That way I had something fun to play with when I visited them. So Skeeter and I played with a talking truck for a short time.

Angie hollered from the kitchen, "Sure you don't want to stay for lunch? Ed'll be home in a little while."

"I'd love to, but I can't. Gotta visit Mrs. Burns." I grabbed the cake, hugged and thanked Angie, scooped up Skeeter, and promised to spend more time with him as soon as I could.

Then I drove back to "my" section of town. The Burns' home was a conglomeration of styles, a white quasi-Spanish-Moorish-Victorian-Tudor-Queen Anne home. It was built in 1887 and was one of the showplaces of Quincy. It was a favorite in the annual "let's show off our homes" tour. I'd never been inside, and was kind of looking forward to it, wondering how anyone could live in such a hodgepodge house.

I rang the bell and tidied myself up a little, brushing off stray Clancy hairs from my coat. A stiff looking guy in a black suit with tails opened the door. It couldn't have been a butler, but it was. A bit pretentious, even for this section of town. I swear he would drown if it started raining, his nose was so far in the air.

He said, "May I help you?" and I introduced myself as an employee of Dr. Burns. It didn't seem important that I tell him the employment was for less than an hour prior to Burns' death. Anyway, he let me in and took my coat. As he opened the closet, it was apparent that my coat, like me, didn't quite fit in. Choosing to ignore this, I followed the sound of voices.

The room I entered must have been the drawing room. It was too overdone to be called a living room, or even worse—a family room. It was enormous, but it was hard to tell a lot of the details, because it was literally brimming full of people. I looked around for Mrs. Burns. Although we'd never met, I recalled seeing her name in the society pages along with Georgianne's. The only photographs I'd seen were the ones that appeared on the back covers of her novels, but I didn't believe those pictures, which showed her as young, brunette and pretty.

I saw a few people that I recognized from the neighborhood, and grinned when I noticed Gus sitting on a sofa, holding court. He had always been a popular guy, and was even more so, now that he no longer got around much. Georgianne always discouraged visitors, but they kept coming anyway. Once you knew Gus, you found it hard to stay away for too long.

I placed my cake on a table in the hall. Joining Gus on the couch, I took advantage of the momentary lull in his entourage.

"Hi. You feeling better?"

"Of course, Sam. I always feel great when I see you."

My blush lit up my face like a neon sign. *I wish I took compliments better.*

"What's everyone doing here? In my family, we have the wake the day of the funeral. Why are they holding the party of the century before the funeral, with Burns hardly cold?"

Gus smiled, "I think everyone is a little curious. Murder and mystery are scarce in Quincy. No one wants to miss out on anything." At that he glanced around to see if his wife was nearby. "Including Georgianne. I must admit it didn't take much convincing to get me to come. I'm curious too. Not much excitement in my life. Thought this might be interesting."

I hugged him and stood. "Well, I need to express my condolences. Can you point out Mrs. Burns to me, please?"

As he pointed, I gasped. There, talking to my future date, was one of the most gorgeous women I had ever seen. Much more beautiful in person than in pictures. At the same time, a wave of revulsion washed over me, unlike anything I'd ever experienced. Even if I wanted to second-guess my ability, I couldn't at that point. I was literally doubled over with psychic, painful vibes. The woman made me sick.

Michael rushed over and Mrs. Burns arrived at the same time. They both grabbed me. And I fainted. Yes, I swooned. Not only was I in the presence of all of the money in the city, but this was the first time Michael had touched me—and I passed out. I wouldn't know what class was if it bit me in the butt.

Michael and Mrs. Burns helped me into an adjoining room. With my keen observation skills, I guessed it was the library. Hundreds of books lined the walls. I reclined on a chaise lounge, and Mrs. Burns immediately placed a cover over and around me, probably not from any sense of care, but because she didn't know what to expect from me next, or maybe so I wouldn't touch her fancy-schmancy furniture.

I tried to be gracious. "Thank you very much, but I'm fine now. I am so sorry, Mrs. Burns." It was hard to be nice when this woman made me dizzy and sick to my stomach. I'd never had such a powerful negative reaction to a person before. If this was what tuning into my psychic abilities would do, then I thought I'd pass.

Normally I'd just get a crick in my neck or a dizzy, light-headed sensation. This was an entirely too drastic reaction. The only possible explanation was that Mrs. Burns must be the murderer.

"No need to be sorry, dear." Dear, indeed, and this from a woman who either was twenty years younger than me or else had extensive work done on her face and body. I hoped it was the latter. There must be something in the rulebook that states a widow cannot look so sexy at her husband's wake. At least there has to be a paragraph somewhere that says they can't wear skintight black wool crepe dresses. Especially in front of my soon-to-be date. She continued to be solicitous, "Are you sure you feel well? Is there anything I can get for you? There are a few doctors in the other room. Would you like me to find one for you?"

After saying, "No thanks," I reclined and panicked. Panicked and reclined. The panic subsided somewhat, but the reclining didn't. Now that I was more accustomed to being in the presence of a murderess, I was feeling better physically, but still couldn't figure out what to do. I needed to get rid of her so I could talk to Michael.

"I'm sorry to bother you, but could you please get me a club soda?"

She didn't look like she wanted to leave me alone with

Michael. Maybe she had designs on him. God knows, he was good looking. But he was mine. Or soon would be, as soon as I sat up and started charming him.

Anyway, ever the dutiful hostess, Mrs. Burns slithered out of the library.

I shot into an upright position. "Michael, she did it!"

"No, she didn't, Sam. All she did was touch you. You passed out. It wasn't her fault."

"No, I don't mean that," trying hard to sound competent, "I mean she killed her husband."

Did he have a glint of amusement in his eyes? Or was it a patronizing look one gives a child? Or maybe, he just felt a little woozy himself because of my mesmerizing effect on him.

"What makes you think she killed her husband?" The detective in him couldn't resist asking questions.

With that he put his hands on my shoulders and gently pushed me back into a reclining position. He stroked my hair and I melted. Again. Tingles everywhere. And a dangerous remnant of dizziness.

"Well, I can't really tell you my source. Just trust me. I know it and I'm not wrong. Believe me, Michael, I'm not making this up. Please…"

My pathetic whining must have done the trick. Michael took my hand, looked into my eyes and said, "God, you look horrible."

Then he smiled, and I couldn't be mad at him. "Yeah, I know I look bad, I just fainted; but that doesn't change the fact that Mrs. Burns killed her husband."

"Carolyn didn't kill anyone, Sam." Carolyn? Since when was my soon-to-be-beloved on a first name basis with a murderer?

"Michael, she did, and I'll prove it." At that, Mrs. Carolyn Burns returned with my club soda and smiled at us. Actually she was probably smiling at Michael. See that's what makes me mad about cute guys. He didn't do anything wrong and already I'm mad at him. Haven't even had our first date and I'm jealous. That really steams me. Why did he smile back at her? Does he always smile so broadly at murderers or just beautiful women? Or was he just covering so she wouldn't suspect that I suspected? Just being in the same room with her was getting to me.

"Thanks, Mrs. Burns, but I need to go home. There's a bundt cake on the hall table. That's for you. Gotta go. I'll be back for the funeral Monday. Bye. Oh, I meant to tell you I really like your books."

With that I tried to get up. I looked at the smiling Mrs. Burns and felt dizzy. As I stumbled against Michael, Mrs. Burns put out her hand and touched me and I—omigod, not again—the room started spinning and soon I did too. The last thing I saw was a delicate Asian vase on an end table. It got closer and closer to me as I fainted. Her eardrum-bursting shriek brought little satisfaction but it did rouse me from my faint. She must have thought I was going to break a precious possession in this pristine palace. Michael apologized to her, said he would see that I got home, and waltzed me out the door. As soon as we were away from her I immediately felt a little better, but I didn't look better.

"Come on, let's get you home."

Embarrassed, I said, "I feel fine now, I promise. I can make it home. Besides, you're all dressed up, so you probably need to go home and change into comfortable clothes before you pick me up for dinner."

"Dinner? Sam, you must be kidding. You just fainted. Twice." He paused. "Are you sure?" I didn't think I liked the amused tone, but I was willing to overlook it for now. Besides I was too embarrassed to say very much.

"I promise I'm fine." I looked him in the eyes so he would know I was telling the truth. Then I remembered, he didn't know that about me. In fact he didn't know much about me at all, and vice versa. I surely wanted to remedy that. Very soon, in fact. "Go home and change. Give me a few hours. I'm kind of tired, so I think I'll take a short nap, then clean up and I'll be ready by seven."

He still didn't look convinced, but walked me to my car. "Okay, I'll see you at seven, but if you change your mind or if you start feeling bad again, give me a call."

With that he helped me into my car and patted the hood as I drove away. I looked into the rear view mirror and once again thanked my lucky stars that I had a date with him tonight. But nothing serious, I reminded myself. Especially, no marriage. I refused to be Sam Darling O'Dear. Of course, I guessed I could keep my maiden name. When I married Alan, I did just that. His last name was Wonder, so I certainly didn't want to be Sam Darling Wonder. So I've been Sam Darling all my life. Guess I could keep that up when Michael and I got married.

This fantasy was certainly far out. Michael and I hadn't even experienced our first date and already I had decided to keep my maiden name. I better be careful and not blurt out this insanity in his presence. That would scare him off for sure.

It took all of two minutes to arrive at my castle. As I dragged myself in the door, Clancy gave me "the look."

I stripped off my wrinkled clothes and left a trail to the bathroom. I took a two-minute shower and then left a message with my wake-up service. "Listen, Clance, I don't have time to talk. Wake me up in an hour."

She didn't. But something else did.

EIGHT

Through a daze I felt the pain begin. It started slowly and then hit in large waves that pushed me toward consciousness. I resisted opening my eyes but someone kept slapping me. I raised an eyelid, so I could see who would receive my revenge. Georgianne Granville! The old witch. I tried to slap her back, but couldn't move. Why in the world was she hitting me? Why was I lying in the snow?

"She's awake."

I opened another eye. Gus and Michael knelt by me with looks of concern on their faces. Was this how Dorothy felt in the "Wizard of Oz," when she woke up with a horrible headache and memories of a fantastic dream? But the wicked witch wasn't dead, she was here. And she was slapping me. Or at least one of the wicked witches was here. I was sure there were more. Part of my dream included a beautiful witch who was after my intended boyfriend.

"What happened?"

Gus smiled down at me, "Don't worry, honey, everything is going to be fine. You're just lucky no one lit a match. The carriage house'll be fine as soon as we air it out."

Air it out? What was he talking about? I knew that I probably had "nap breath," but I'd showered before I went to sleep and planned on brushing my teeth before my date. I suddenly remembered that I was nude the last time I looked. Unfortunately my head refused to move and I couldn't check the status of my clothing.

Michael looked at Gus, "Let's move her into your house, okay? We need to get her off the ground."

"What happened?"

"I suppose you can take her into my home, but I hope it won't be for long. Mr. Granville needs his rest you know, too much excitement can lead to…"

"Georgianne, quit jabbering and open the damn door."

Jeez, I would have paid money for this.

"What happened?" I was feeling a bit redundant by this time. It appeared that I was the star of this melodrama, but no one was paying attention to me.

"What happened?" I yelled, or more correctly, I tried to yell, but my throat hurt and my voice sounded like it used to after a night of beer and cigarettes. I felt like crap, too.

"We'll tell you everything in a minute, Sam. Right now, we're going to take you into the Granville's house. I guess we should take her dog, too." Michael glanced at Gus for permission. He probably already knew that Georgianne wouldn't roll out the welcome mat for Clancy.

"Clancy. Where is she? What happened?" That took my remaining energy and was all I remembered until I woke up on the Granville's sofa. Jill was hovering over me, playing doctor. Okay, so she is a doctor, but she's my kid sister and it's hard to take.

"What happened?" I'm nothing if not persistent. Stubborn might be a more apt description, but I was entitled to know what in the hell was going on.

Jill decided to treat me like a grown up. "There was a gas leak or something in your home and you breathed a lot of fumes. I want to take you in to the ER to check your blood gasses, run some other tests, and to keep an eye on you for a while."

Jill looked so cute and grown up with the stethoscope around her neck. Was this competent young physician my baby sister? I decided she was serious and I better obey.

"Where's Clancy?" With that I noticed that the kisses being planted on my face were not a gift from Michael as I'd fantasized, but came from my faithful companion. Clancy seemed no worse for the wear.

"How did I get out?"

Now it was Gus's turn. "That was the darndest thing, Sam. I heard Clancy barking real loud, like she does when strangers come to your door. So I looked out the back window and didn't see anything. She was still barking, so I put on my coat and went out. At the same time this nice young man was approaching your house and we both smelled gas. Lucky I had my keys with me. I unlocked your door and we saw Clancy lying on her belly barking like crazy. This young man opened windows while I followed Clancy to you. I found you on your bed, passed out."

"My clothes?" I stammered, hoping against hope that Michael hadn't seen me nude. If I was passed out that meant I wasn't holding my stomach in.

Gus reassured me. "Don't worry, honey, I wrapped you in your grandma's quilt that was on your bed."

I glanced down, saw the quilt and felt better. Then a scream escaped my raw throat, "Eeeeyuk."

"What?" The word came from everyone at once.

"Eeeeyuk. Georgianne's housecoat. Eeeeyuk." How could they do that to me?

Georgianne seemed oblivious to my distaste. "I assumed you'd want to be modest under the quilt, so when we brought you inside I volunteered the use of my dressing gown."

I stammered my thanks, and tried to figure out how to ditch the robe as soon as possible. And to think Michael was looking at me, in clothing that clashed with every single fiber of my being.

Again I returned to the subject of my housemate, "How did Clancy survive? She weighs a few pounds less than I do."

Michael ignored my slight exaggeration. "She was

splayed out on the floor by the door. Almost looked like she'd been through some military basic training and knew to stay low to the ground."

Gus continued the saga, "We brought you outside and I turned off the main gas line. Georgianne called Jill. You always tell me she's the best doctor in the city. After you came around, we carried you in here. Jill arrived a few minutes ago."

I smiled in spite of it all. So did Jill.

"I appreciate everyone's concern but I'm not going to the ER."

"Oh yes you are." Jill again.

"Oh no I'm not."

"Oh yes you are." Michael's turn.

"Oh no I'm not."

"Oh yes you…" Gus and Georgianne began in unison.

"Oh no I'm not… to infinity."

"Infinity plus one," chimed in Jill. "I win and you're going to the hospital."

"But I've got a date with Michael." This in a whining voice from the pathetic loser, me. No one heard me, or if they did, they ignored my protestations.

Finally, I decided fighting was futile. If Jill wanted me to go to "Darling Memorial" then I would.

I turned to my friend. "Gus, would you keep Clancy for me? She'd feel better close to home."

Gus said yes immediately and ignored his wife's malevolent stare. I knew he'd pay for this later, but was grateful that he dared go against Georgianne. That was true friendship. Clancy would be one less thing I'd have to worry about now.

Then I remembered Michael. "Michael, our date…" Now I was almost blubbering. Can you beat that? Not the least bit upset that I almost died, but that I was forced to miss the big date.

"That's okay. I'll cancel our reservations. I'll go with you to the hospital and I'll grab something to eat there."

I decided to be unselfish. "No, I wouldn't wish hospital food on a friend. Call me later tonight. I'm sure I'll be home before bedtime. We'll talk." I still wanted to find out some things, like what he'd been doing at Burns' office, in the ER, and at Burns' house with Carolyn.

He finally agreed with me, pecked me on the cheek and left. Our first kiss and I felt sick. Plus smelled like gas. I just knew he'd come back for more.

Jill drove as she did everything else—confidently. "Put that blanket around you. Just relax and don't try to sit up straight. We'll be at the hospital in a few minutes." I smiled in spite of my headache. This was a nice change of roles for me, the nurturee rather than the nurturer. I could get used to this.

Jill took charge when we got there. She quickly drew

blood, not waiting for a medical technologist to arrive. When she was assured of my comfort, she left.

As I was waiting in the treatment room for the results of the tests, the door opened and *he* stood there showing concern. My un-favorite detective, Butthead.

His suit looked the same—rumpled, but decent looking. I idly wondered who picked them out for him. Was he married? Who would have him? What did I ever see in him? Why was I asking myself so many questions?

Looking like a Columbo who was losing his hair, he began, "I heard you had some trouble at your house. You okay?"

"Yeah, what are you doing here?" I turned the tables on him, because I recalled that this was virtually the same question he asked me when we found Dr. Burns dead on the floor.

"Don't get all defensive on me. Gus called me because he was concerned about the supposed gas leak at your house. Gus prides himself on running a tight ship, so he was upset, not only at you being in danger, but also because he was sure that the house was safe. I called Central Illinois Public Service, and they sent out a technician to check. There was a gas leak behind your stove, but there's a possibility that someone tampered with the line. There were a few suspicious holes in the pipe. Feeling suicidal, Sam?"

God, I wanted to wipe that grin off of his face. "You

know, I'm feeling more homicidal than suicidal."

He ignored my clever jibe. "Do you know anyone that might want to see you dead? Or maybe just scare you?"

"No. There might be a few misguided souls who might not like me, but I don't think anyone would want to kill me."

He smiled that smile again. Why did he make me so mad after all these years?

He made a feeble attempt to grasp my hand, which I evaded with the skill of a commando.

"This is a serious matter." He tried to appear unaffected by my rebuff. "There's a good chance someone tried to kill you, or at the very least make you sick. I want to talk to you again tomorrow when you're feeling better. In the meantime, the gas company is working on the line and it should be fixed by morning."

Jill entered at that moment and piped in, "She can stay at my house tonight, Detective. She seems fine, but I want to keep an eye on her anyway." She went off to call her husband, Ben.

After she left, B.H. turned toward me and asked, "I'd like to ask you a personal question."

I had a horrible headache, but figured a little more agony wouldn't do any harm. "Sure."

"What's this B.H. stuff?"

I was too tired to beat around the bush. "'B.H.' stands

for 'Butthead.' I thought it was more respectful to abbreviate it, so I don't embarrass you in public."

"Butthead, huh?" The smile didn't falter for long. "You sure know how to hold a grudge, don't you? You know, I didn't stand you up on purpose. Prom night was kinda important to me too. I just…"

I interrupted him; "I'm not interested in your pathetic apologies. You stood me up. You didn't call. You didn't attempt to explain. I think that says it all."

His usual cool disappeared. He looked decidedly uncomfortable. I felt great. He eyed me one last time, then turned and headed for the door. He glanced back and in a more businesslike tone said, "I'll be in touch tomorrow." With that, he was gone.

See, that's another thing I hate about men. He was the Butthead, but I felt guilty. My short-term elation at his discomfort was just that. There was a murderer still on the loose and here I was, laid up.

After arriving at Jill's, I still felt bad and decided to take a nap. A fitting ending to an overly-eventful day.

NINE

I awoke the next morning to kisses. "Clancy, cut it out. I'll take you outside in a minute." Then I heard giggles that were decidedly un-Clancylike.

Jill's kids were attacking me with smooches. Jack and Marty were four and three respectively, and were bundles of energy. Jack had his mother's fair complexion and blonde hair and Marty was the spitting image of his father, Ben, with dark hair and dark eyes. Together these two kids looked like a salt and pepper set, delightful and complementary.

"Ready for breakfast, Sam?" Ben grinned at me from the kitchen doorway, brandishing a pan and spatula. A wisp of dark hair fell over his eyes. Attired in a "Kiss the Cook" apron that fit nicely over his jeans and T-shirt, he looked every inch the strong man that he was.

"Did you make your special pancakes?"

"Yep, and we got coffee and juice, too."

"Count me in." A healthy appetite was something I could always count on.

I allowed the kids to tug on me and to help pull me up from the couch and lead me to the kitchen. This was a very comfortable home. I'd been here many times, primarily because I was Jill's godmother and in our family, we took that role seriously and it was a life-long relationship.

Jill had the good fortune—and good sense—to marry a great guy. Ben was a plumber and was struggling to start his own business. He had worked for other people while Jill was in medical school, and now it was her turn to provide the major financial support while his company was in its infancy. When they were both at work, the kids stayed at Angie and Ed's. Angie provided daycare for the family. It worked out well for everyone.

Jill was already at work, so Ben said he would drop me off at my house when he took the kids to Angie's. It was Saturday, but both of them had non-traditional work schedules.

I enjoyed the breakfast and ate much more than was wise. I was wondering if I dared ask for one more flapjack when my phone interrupted me. It was Gus.

"Your house is ship-shape again and Clancy is panting for your return." It was comforting to know someone was.

Later, unlocking the door to the carriage house, it just seemed different. I normally felt so secure there. It was home. How dare someone invade my world with such potentially deadly results? Hating myself for being so weak,

I felt the need to check each room, closet, and under every bed.

I began in the living room. Feeling foolish, I checked in Grandma's armoire. It was stuffed with junk, just like always. No bad guys. There was a small coat closet in the front hall. Nothing there.

On to the dining room, my office. No closets, nothing anyone could hide in. I smiled at the stack of unpaid bills on my desk. They seemed a bit inconsequential when I thought about my close call last night.

The kitchen beckoned, a room with which I had a love/hate relationship. I loved the food and hated the work. No place for a nasty person to lurk, except for the almost bare pantry. Empty. Of people, as well as food.

I turned and made my way down the short hallway to my bedroom and bath. Lots of cubbyholes and hiding places back there. I'd never been a particularly cautious person nor easily frightened, but I felt my heart rate increase. I flicked on the light switch, opened the curtains and before I could talk myself out of it I flung open the closet door and the bathroom door at the same time. I jumped out of the way immediately, just in case someone was waiting to pounce. No one pounced. I looked under the king-sized bed. No monsters there either.

A search of the two bedrooms and bathroom upstairs also revealed no bogeyman. The upstairs bath was the hardest room to search, as the music from *Psycho* and *Jaws* both played in my head at the same time.

Satisfied, I re-locked the door and slowly walked across the back lawn to Gus and Georgianne's.

Clancy greeted me in the expected way, with disdain. How dare I leave her overnight, even with someone as nice as Gus? Not to mention forcing the indignity of Georgianne on her.

I whispered, "I'll make it up to you," and thanked Georgianne for her kindness. She harrumphed, but grudgingly said I was welcome.

Gus insisted on escorting me to my house. I didn't let him know that I'd already checked it for goblins.

Clancy ran around smelling every piece of furniture and hidey-hole, just to make sure everything was okay in her fiefdom. As she bounced around, Gus whispered, "Do you think it's wise to stay here by yourself?"

"There's no need to whisper, Gus. I don't have secrets from Clancy. Besides, I'm not alone. Clancy's here and remember, she saved my life yesterday. I'll be fine, I promise. And you're just a back yard away. I swear I'll call you if I need help."

Gus finally agreed and listed several ways to contact him. He talked about bells, whistles, lights, signals, and finally agreed that the phone would be adequate until he could install an alarm which would buzz in his home if I punched

WHO KILLED MY BOSS?

a panic button that would be hooked up in several places in my house. As he turned to leave, murmuring about watts, wires, and what not, he appeared livelier than I'd seen him in years.

"I may be wrong, Gus, but you seem to be feeling a lot better. Lots of energy."

"Well, it's surprising, but with Dr. Burns dying and you almost dying, it's kind of exciting around here. I don't want to miss anything." With that he hugged me and exited.

I wanted to crash for awhile, but thought I'd check my messages. I wasn't surprised to find the message light blinking frantically.

Beep. "It's Jen. Jill told me what happened. If you need anything let me know. Love you."

Beep. "Sam, Ed. Glad you're okay. Angie sends her love. Talk to you later."

Beep. "I'm praying for you." Pete. "Call me when you can."

Beep. "I know I just saw you a few minutes ago," Jill's maternal voice made me smile, "but I wanted to make sure you were all right. Don't forget to come into the office on Monday."

Beep. "Sam. Rob. Glad you're okay. Don't worry about Dr. Burns' killer. We'll get him soon. And if someone did sabotage your gas line, we'll find him too. Take care."

Beep. "Hey, Mom." Sarah. "Aunt Jill told us you were

okay, so we're not worried. We both want to know how you get yourself in these messes. Sometimes I feel like the Mom instead of the kid. Adam sends his love too. We'll call again later. Get some rest."

Two final messages.

Beep. "Sam, this is George Lansing." B.H. "I'd like to come by your place around three if that's okay. I want to talk about a few things. See ya then."

Beep. "Hello. This is Michael O'Dear. I hope you're feeling better. I'd like to stop by later today to see you. Maybe we can have dinner. Give me a call when you get a chance."

It looked like I would be spending as much time with B.H. as with Michael. Yuck. Maybe I could make an appointment with the honorable detective and then not show up. Fitting revenge after all these years.

Clancy kept looking at me, as if I weren't keeping my end of the bargain. "I promise we'll walk later, Clancy. Georgianne said that she hired someone to take you for a long walk and you were gone over an hour. So don't try to make me feel guilty for not going. We'll go out later. I need to rest." She halfheartedly accepted this compromise, but I had a feeling I'd pay for it later.

Before climbing into bed, I left a message for B.H. saying that 3:00 would be convenient. Same message for Michael, although with more warmth in my voice, and a different time. I told him to come by around 7, and we could go to dinner. Then, last but not least, I sent an email through my on-line service for most of my sibs and my kids—the most common way we stayed in touch. Confident that I had tied up the loose ends of my life, I turned up the heat, removed all my clothing, and climbed into bed. One of the nurturing things in my life was Grandma's quilt, guaranteed to make the scary things disappear.

When I woke up two hours later, I was famished. There were still a few more hours until B.H. would arrive to interview—or interrogate—me, so I decided to go to the market for some groceries. I put on my gray sweatpants and navy St. Francis U. sweatshirt, pulled on my boots and parka and was ready to roll. The nap had soothed my soul; now I needed something to soothe my stomach.

Clancy climbed in the car too, temporarily satisfied. This did not count as a walk, but at least it was an outing. Backing out into the alley—a horrible term for this upscale neighborhood—was always a precarious chore at best. It was difficult to see in either direction because of the many trees and bushes and because of the carriage house itself, built flush with the alley. When the trees were winter-bare I could see a little better, but not much. So I did my usual back-up, glancing in both directions and then flooring it. It had snowed and then warmed up a bit, so the asphalt road was slick, and I slid around a little.

Clancy yelped.

"Hey, leave me alone. You're the one who wanted to come along."

I'm a confident driver. That doesn't mean I'm competent, just confident. I drive with alacrity, with aplomb, with speed. Normally I drive quickly through the alley, because other than the occasional garbage truck, traffic is sparse. There was no problem as I accelerated toward Sixteenth Street. The problem was stopping.

I saw the garbage truck a split second before I heard it. I stepped on the brake and felt the pedal depress all the way to the floor. I don't remember which I said first—"Darn it," or "Sorry, Clancy." Then blackness.

This was getting pretty old and so was I. My body felt like it had been run over by a truck. Not far from the truth. I opened my eyes and saw Jill's face looking down at me.

"We gotta stop meeting like this, Dr. Jill."

"Sam, just relax. You're okay. Your car hit a garbage truck in the alley. The truck driver is fine too. Any more questions?"

"Yeah, but I can't talk now…" I slept.

When I woke up she was still there.

I continued the conversation, "Yeah, I do have one question. Who messed up my car? I bet if you look you'll see the brakes lines are cut or something."

A grunting sound came from the corner. I tried to move

my head but it hurt too much. Sooner than I would have liked, B.H. sauntered into view.

"You okay?" He actually looked like he cared. Good actor.

"Yeah, I'm fine, if you don't count the sledgehammers going full bore into my brain. Where's Clancy? She okay? Did you check the brakes on my car?"

"Clancy's fine. Gus has her." He looked a bit sheepish. "And actually we didn't check your brakes. We didn't suspect foul play, so we arranged for your car to go to the body shop. Well, anyway, I thought I'd help and I had the body shop pick up your car." He had the good grace to stop talking when I gave him the look.

"Darn it, B.H., someone sabotaged my car. The brakes didn't work. It wasn't just the ice and I wasn't speeding. Well, not much anyway. You can just tell the difference. Somebody screwed with my car and now we won't be able to tell."

"I'll call the shop right away, Sam. And remind me not to do anything nice for you." With a meager grunt, he left. I'd have to tell Georgianne to give B.H. "harrumphing" lessons. He wasn't nearly as talented as she was in that regard.

I looked at Jill. "If he didn't suspect foul play, then what was he doing here?"

"He heard the ambulance call over the radio and came

in to see how you were. He was here as a friend, Sam, not as a cop."

That motherly tone crept into her voice again. If I was the older sister, why did she always use that tone with me?

The doctor persona replaced the motherly/sisterly one. "I want to keep you overnight. I don't think there'll be any complications, but this wreck, coupled with the gas incident yesterday, has really assaulted your body. You need a night of uninterrupted sleep."

Of course, I didn't like the idea. I wanted my date with Michael and I was going to have my date with Michael.

"I'm sorry but I just can't stay. I've got too much to do."

"You're staying and there'll be no discussion, argument, or whining. You were unconscious twice in less than twenty-four hours. That's hard on anyone, but at your age…" She was smart enough to stop before she finished the sentence.

"Okay, okay." I knew when I was licked.

"Oh, by the way, that Michael guy called and said he'd drop by later to see you."

Satisfied that she'd cowed me into submission, Jill left to tie up some loose ends on her shift. That gave me time to think about what was going on. What *was* going on? First, I got the job I wanted. Then immediately after hiring me, my boss was killed. Two people basically confessed, Gwen and her brother, and I was convinced neither one of them was guilty, although Gwen was sitting in jail. Then the next day, I went to Dr. Burns' house and met his wife, Carolyn. My bodily reactions convinced me she was the killer. I fainted, went home, inhaled gas, went to the ER, spent the night at Jill's, came home, got in a wreck, and ended up at the hospital again. Gee, what's wrong with this picture?

Someone had killed Burns and now, for all intents and purposes, someone had almost killed me. Were these things related? Or was this a completely different murder scheme? All of this was severely trying my patience, not to mention my mental capacity. So I did what any sane woman would do. I forgot about "whodunit" while I tidied up for Michael's visit.

TEN

My face was bruised, my mouth felt like Clancy's smelled, and I was tired, tired, tired. I grimaced at the mirror in the sterile hospital bathroom. Combing my hair was a real chore. Each brush stroke caused my teeth to grit, causing my head to hurt, causing my teeth to grit, causing my head to... I was getting dizzy from even thinking about the cause and effect of the situation. Luckily, I kept my hair short—I kept it blonde, too—so I didn't have to spend much time on it. I decided against makeup, as I didn't want to look as sluttish as Mrs. Burns. Today, slamming her didn't feel as good, but I couldn't stop.

I had just finished gently brushing my teeth and maneuvering my way back into bed when Michael peeked around the door. The sight of him brought with it lightheadedness. Ah, romance. He had a grin on his face, a bouquet in one hand, and champagne in the other. As his grin broadened, he motioned to someone in the hallway to follow him into the room.

As I sat dumbfounded, a waiter walked in pushing a table

laden with food. I'd forgotten how hungry I was, but soon remembered as he lifted the lids off trays of pasta primavera, antipasto, garlic bread, and salad. One of my favorite meals and it was catered by one of my favorite restaurants, the Rectory.

"I figured the hospital would be trying to force feed you a bland diet, so…" Michael grinned, as proud of this maneuver as if he had executed a perfect "10" on the parallel bars. And he deserved to be proud. A fantastic coup—he captured my heart and my stomach with the same feat.

I watched as the waiter, with a goofy grin on his face, took the covers off the platters and set up the table.

This was virtually a dream come true for me. A man, handsome and intelligent, actually liked me. A man, romantic and kind, sat on my bed and was about to kiss me. Women have killed for this scenario. I moistened my lips, closed my eyes, prepared for the pucker, and wouldn't you know it—the dizziness intensified.

"Michael, help."

He leaned toward me. Just in time. The good part was that I didn't have far to fall.

This scenario could have come straight out of a romance novel. I actually swooned. Michael did give me a nice place to land though.

"Are you all right? Should I call the nurse?" He helped me lie back on the pillows.

I tried pathetically to sound romantic, "No, I'm fine, just a little lightheaded. Probably from the accident." I smoothed my hair and puckered my lips again.

Michael didn't succumb to my womanly wiles. "Guess I better go if you aren't feeling well. Should I leave the food?"

I didn't know which I wanted more—Michael or the pasta. After a brief internal struggle I knew I wanted both. "Michael, don't go. We can still enjoy the food. I can't believe you did all this for me. I'd really like you to stay."

He reddened a little and said, "I hate to admit this, but I don't like hospitals. Don't take this personally, but I think we ought to postpone our meal together until you're better."

Drat. There I was, reclining in bed and I still couldn't get a kiss out of the guy. Of course, I was bruised and had on the hospital-gown-from-hell, but I wanted him to stay.

Michael spoke to the waiter, "How about leaving the food for an hour or so?" He handed the young man a folded bill.

"Sure thing, Mr. O'Dear." As he turned to leave, I swear the waiter winked at me.

I batted my eyes at Michael, but it didn't work. He took both my hands in his and said, "I'm sorry you don't feel well. But it was good to see you just the same."

Michael leaned over; I closed my eyes and prepared for the inevitable. Instead of giving me the passionate kiss I'd fantasized about, he planted a light one on my forehead. Right on a bruise.

The dizziness returned, but I didn't tell Michael.

Before he left, Michael pulled the table over to my bed, and he helped me sit up with my feet dangling over the side. His smile as he exited gave me almost as big a thrill as the feast before me.

As I ate I pondered my latest calamity. Why in the world was my equilibrium in such a state of upheaval around Michael? I really liked this guy, although I hardly knew him. And I desperately wanted to know him.

It seemed strange that every time I was near him I got dizzy. Maybe I was just scared of a relationship. Maybe I had Meniere's disease. Maybe I was allergic to Michael. Maybe I was obsessing again. So I pushed the tray aside and slept.

It had been years since I'd been in a hospital for an overnight stay. It was almost comforting that so much of the routine was the same. A smiling, nurturing nurse woke me up to give me a sleeping pill. Something clanging in the next room woke me again. Although the plastic bedpans were quieter than the old metal ones, I pictured some sadistic person in white making them clang anyway. Then a much too perky nurse roused me as she checked my blood pressure. I needed to get home so I could rest.

When I woke up the next morning, the restaurant table was gone. The waiter must have been much quieter than the nurses.

It was Sunday. I told the charge nurse I wanted to go to Mass. An aide helped me dress and insisted on delivering me to the chapel in a wheelchair. I insisted that I walk. I won.

Over the years, there'd been many changes in my life, but attending Mass wasn't one of them. Our parents had instilled that faith in us, and I felt connected when I was in church. Connected not only to people all over the world, but also to my ancestors.

As I walked into the chapel, I noticed Pete was already there, arranging things on the altar. He was on the night shift this weekend and was just coming off duty. Pete was still a priest in good standing, but was on a temporary leave from his priestly assignment. He was allowed and even encouraged to use his "priestly faculties" and often helped out at the hospital with Mass and bringing Communion to bedridden patients. I dearly loved going to Mass when he was the celebrant. What a blessing to have a brother who was a priest, and a friend, too.

"Father Brother." I smiled when I thought about how he got that name. When Pete was ordained, Rob was a teenager and didn't like the idea that everybody was calling his brother "Father." I tried to explain, but Rob started crying. When we asked him what was wrong, he said, "I don't want him to be my father, I want him to still be my brother." At that, Pete put his hand on his little brother's shoulder and told him, "I'll be your brother and I'll be Father, too. You can still call me Pete, okay?" And Rob said, "Hey, you can be my Father Brother." That's how he got the name. And it stuck.

Pete hugged me gently during the sign of peace and flashed a grin when he gave me Communion. The Chapel only held a handful of people, so the service was short.

During the closing hymn—which Pete led in a booming, slightly off-key baritone—he looked toward me and raised an eyebrow. That was the sign he wanted to talk.

After another gentle hug Pete said, "You're looking pretty energetic for someone who's been gassed and hit by a truck."

I thanked him, took his arm, and asked if he'd walk me back to my room. The bravado I'd shown by coming here without a wheelchair had been replaced by a painful exhaustion. I ached everywhere.

Pete adjusted his pace to mine. "What's up with the murder investigation?"

"Nothing much. I know Carolyn Burns killed her husband," I looked at Pete to see if he would make fun of me, "but I think she had an accomplice."

Pete didn't say anything, but he placed his hand on top of my own.

I continued, "There's something about her books that bugs me. They're good; maybe they're too good. I mean, she's not in the mental health field, but she writes as if she is. And Dr. Burns didn't seem like the kind of guy who would have helped her with those details. I looked and the acknowledgements in her books didn't thank anyone for helping."

Pete pressed the button to summon the elevator. "What does Rob say?"

"I think he's been avoiding me. You know he doesn't want me involved in the investigation."

"You can see his point, I'm sure." He held the elevator door open for me. "You really don't have any reason to be snooping."

"Now you're turning on me too?"

"Nope," he gave my hand a squeeze. "I just don't want you getting hurt. And I don't want you to get in Rob and George's way. I was wrong to encourage you earlier, Sam. It appears someone broke into your house and tried to kill you. I don't know what I would have done if they'd been successful."

My anger dissolved into mush. I couldn't stay mad at Pete. We left the elevator and strolled to my room in a companionable silence.

After Pete left I waited for Jill to discharge me. I felt sore and knew that was just temporary. But I was still pissed off that someone had tried to kill me. Why in the world would someone want to see me dead? Tampering with the gas line in the house and the brake lines in the car had an almost deadly symmetry to it.

Since I hadn't planned on a hospital stay, I hadn't packed any of my books. To kill time, I settled in a chair, turned on the TV, and numbed my mind with the Beverly Hillbillies.

My enjoyment ended abruptly when my own private Jethro walked in.

"How ya doin', Sam?"

I kept my attention on the television. I mumbled, "What do you want, B.H.?" What was wrong with me? Why was I so mean to him? My tendency to hold grudges was my least favorite attribute.

"Wanted to see how you were doing, and also let you know that we got Dr. Burns' autopsy results. Just what we thought. He died from the blood loss from something sharp that someone stuck in his neck. Something like a knife or a scalpel. Hit his jugular vein and it was just like Niagara Falls. Swoosh." He accompanied his narrative with suitable charades, hands scraping across his neck and face grimacing as he mimicked the death throes.

He finally got my attention and I smiled without wanting to. "You sound absolutely gleeful."

"Sorry." He behaved long enough to look uncomfortable. "Interesting thing. The killer knew how to use the instrument. It was a precise cut. Rather than sideways, the cut went up and down the vein. Very effective.

Very lethal. Messy too."

I didn't say anything, but the wheels were turning. B.H. said the cut was messy. I wondered how the murderer got out of Burns' office without leaving a bloody trail. I remembered that the footprints in the snow leading away from the window were clean. No blood outside. Had the cops thought about that?

I'd find out. "You said the cut was messy. Do you think the murderer was covered in blood?"

"None of your business." He dismissed my question quickly. "Anyway I want to talk to you about your mishaps."

"Yes," I tried to sound open, but failed. My basic distrust of B.H. kept leaking through. I'd figure out the blood angle on my own.

"Tell me why you think your car was sabotaged." He jerked me back to the present with his question.

"What do you mean, 'think'? It felt like the brake lines were cut or something. They went out. Slammed all the way to the floor. I know someone messed with them."

He tried to sit on the edge of my bed, but I moved my leg there so he slipped off. He recovered quickly and continued the conversation. "When you said the brakes went out you were right. They were in bad shape, but show no signs of tampering. I spoke to the mechanic myself."

"But…"

B.H. held out a hand in a "stop" fashion. "And before you tell me that the mechanic was in on the plot to get you, I want to tell you that the mechanic is your cousin, Bobby."

"Well…"

"Do you have any other reason to think your car was tampered with? Did anyone threaten you?" B.H. sat in the only chair available.

"Well, no, but since I'm on the trail of the murderer, I'm sure someone is after me, and…" I didn't want to let him in on my certainty that Carolyn Burns committed the crime.

"Rob and I told you to stay out of it and let us handle the case. You're a social worker, not a cop."

This was beginning to get boring. Everyone kept telling me what my job was.

"Well, listen here, what about the gas in my house? You said that was deliberate."

The stop sign went up again. "The man from the gas company said the line *might* have been cut. 'Might have been cut' is a long way from 'was cut.'"

"Don't you dare give me the 'talk to the hand' sign." I threw a pillow at him and instantly regretted it for two reasons. First, it hurt like hell and second, it only made him chuckle. "You think you know everything. Just get out of here."

"Uh-uh. Not until you tell me what you know about the murder."

I relented a bit. "I'll tell you what I know if you tell me what you know."

He grinned. "Didn't we say that to each other in fifth grade when we found out how babies were made? I went into the 'guy' movie with Fr. MacGregor and you went to the 'girl' movie with Sr. Mary Francis."

I scowled. "Yeah, I remember. And it wasn't long after that you said, 'You show me yours and I'll show you mine.'"

"You never did show me."

I was triumphant. "And I never will."

"Seriously, Sam. I need to find out what you know and what you think you know. And I promise I'll tell you what I can. Deal?"

"Yeah, uh, okay." I sighed. Loudly.

"Oh, I guess you don't feel too good, huh? Maybe we can talk later. How about tomorrow? Maybe we can have dinner or something."

"Yeah, right. And I'll wear my prom dress."

"Sam…"

I sighed again and added a groan for good measure. "Okay, that was a little much, I admit."

He took that as a dismissal and left.

My last conscious thought before I dozed off again was that I'd have to figure out how the murderer escaped being bloody. My dreams were a kaleidoscope of prom dresses and bloody scalpels.

ELEVEN

Jill discharged me late Sunday afternoon with admonitions to be careful. I refused her offer of a wheelchair to the parking lot, but lost that battle. She passed me to a smiling aide with a shiny wheelchair. And before I could murmur much more than "good-bye and thanks," I was whisked away faster than you could say "Indianapolis 500." We quickly reached the parking lot and when the aide asked which car was mine, I didn't know. B.H. had gotten a rental car for me while mine was being repaired. Nice gesture, and it almost started melting this cold, cold heart. I looked on the key chain and noted the rental was a generic little sedan. New. Automatic. No character. This car was nothing like my baby. I had a '68 Volkswagen Beetle. A classic. With character. After a row by row search, we found a license plate that matched the one on the key chain. Even though I was unimpressed with the vehicle, today my poor muscles could appreciate the power steering and automatic transmission.

I drove home, picked up Clancy from Gus's house, and spent the rest of the day alternating between resting and apologizing to Clancy. She must be a Catholic dog; she's got the guilt trip down pat. I did manage to take her for a short, and slow, walk. After that tiring exercise, I slept. And slept.

I woke up at 8 AM on Monday to a dog with a leash in her mouth. "Okay, girl, I've got time for a short walk and that's all. I've got a funeral to go to."

Clancy didn't argue the point. She waited patiently while I donned my sweat pants and jacket.

We walked a few blocks west on Maine Street. I was grateful the ice had melted on the sidewalks. There was still some snow on the lawns, forming a perfect frame for the Victorian mansions on our street.

"Thanks for walking slowly today, girl. I'm still stiff from the accident. But you don't seem to feel any bad effects." I swear she started limping. "Nice try, but you won't get any sympathy from me."

After turning around and re-tracing our steps, we reached our little corner of heaven about 20 minutes after we began.

"I promise a longer walk tomorrow. And I'll try to go a little faster too." We both smiled. "I've got to get ready for the funeral. I wouldn't miss this show for the world."

As I unhooked Clancy's leash, I continued, "Even though B.H. said no one is out to get me, I'm not convinced that the gas line and my car wreck were accidents. I have a feeling about this and I'm going to trust my instincts."

Clancy jumped on the bed and watched while I gingerly climbed into my closet again, looking for the perfect outfit. Classy, yet understated. Demure, yet attractive. I knew Michael would be at the funeral, and if I could hold my vertigo long enough, I'd find out what his connection was to Dr. and Mrs. Burns.

I found I couldn't concentrate on clothes yet and turned to my confidante. "I can't believe that Felicia Greene is Carolyn Burns. Doesn't that just jerk your chain? My favorite novelist is my least favorite villain. How can I love those books so much and hate the author? Doesn't seem logical."

I continued the conversation thread, although silently. Carolyn's books were psychological thrillers, dealing with psychotic and mentally ill murderers. I smiled as I contemplated Carolyn Burns as the model for all the villains in her books. I thought about re-reading her books, trying to get inside her criminal mind. I left the bedroom and semi-limped through the house, gathering up Felicia Greene's books as I went. They formed two good-sized stacks next to my bed; but looking through them would have to wait. I needed to get back to the important business at hand—what to wear.

The only decent thing I had was my power suit. I certainly didn't want to wear it again. Just because it was the only good thing I owned didn't mean I wanted people to know it. I got creative. I took an old black cocktail dress and added a black blazer. Looked pretty good. And fit my criteria: classy, understated, demure. Michael would be an idiot not to be attracted to me.

I drove to the church for the funeral Mass. The majority of people in Quincy are Catholic. Even bad guys. As I arrived I was surprised to note that the parking lot was nearly full, although it was early. Like most in my family, I'm compulsively early. Always want to get a good seat.

The church was pretty full, for a Monday, and for a funeral Mass. I found a seat toward the front. I wanted to see the action. None of my family was there, so it was easy to find a solitary seat.

I knelt to pray and felt someone looking at me. Across the aisle I saw a grinning Gus. I nodded and discreetly waved. Georgianne was sitting regally beside her husband. I nodded to her also, while keeping a nonchalant expression. It was hard not to laugh, though. She pictured herself as one of the ruling class and pompously looked down her nose as much as the Burns' butler.

Right before Mass started, Carolyn Burns was escorted up the aisle by none other than Michael O'Dear. Luckily, I'd prepared myself for the shock, so only felt a distant dizziness and wasn't in danger of getting sick. I think I'd be too scared to do that anyway, remembering the ridicule afforded to those kids who fainted or hurled in church during my school years.

"Hi ya, Sam."

He was making a habit of interrupting my pleasant thoughts. It was no surprise that he couldn't even leave me alone when I was praying, or almost praying.

"Hey, B.H." I'm nice in church.

He leaned over and whispered, "So, you goin' out to the cemetery?"

"Yeah."

"So you goin' to Burns' house?" He tried to enter the pew.

"Yeah." I didn't let him.

"Can I go with you?" He tried again.

"No." I didn't budge, ignoring the stares of those around us.

He stopped whispering. "Sam, let me go. I need to go, but can't go as a cop. Everyone would clam up. I gotta go with a friend. C'mon."

"Okay, but two things. Number one, you must tell me some of the stuff you know."

"And two?"

My voice finally rose above a whisper. "Number two is you can't, under penalty of death, pretend you're my date. Got it? That is vitally important."

He grinned. "Afraid O'Dear will get jealous."

I didn't let him make me mad. "Yes or no?"

"Yes, but it looks like O'Dear is pretty busy with Mrs. Burns."

"Getting smart with me will not get you invited." I returned the intimidating look of a dowager in front of me.

"Okay, Sam. We're just old friends and that's the way I'll play it."

"Okay." I tired of being mean, finally relented, and allowed him to join me in the pew.

I resumed my reverent posture. It wasn't entirely for B.H.'s benefit. I was praying that Michael would like me best.

B.H. and I called a temporary truce and stood, knelt, and sat on cue. I found it hard to concentrate during Mass and wondered if Carolyn would like to trade "dates" with me. B.H. could be her bodyguard—they deserved each other— and Michael could sit with me. Of course, I didn't act on my impulse. The ghost of Sister Nicholas was a strong presence in that church and I could just picture her with hands on her hips, threatening me with eternal purgatory if I didn't pay attention during Mass.

When the service ended, Michael and Carolyn walked down the aisle following the casket. Michael saw me and mouthed something. It looked like, "I love you, Sam," but I couldn't swear to that. Maybe I was fantasizing again. Maybe what he really mouthed was, "I want to talk to you."

The town's Catholic cemetery was only a few miles away. In small towns, distance is measured by miles and not by minutes. You know that if the distance is ten miles and you drive 60 mph it will take you ten minutes. If you drive 30 mph it will take you twenty minutes. It's simple in a location that has no real rush hour. In fact, rush hour in Quincy meant we all drove fast to miss the train at the crossing and also miss all the tractors on the highway.

We got in my car.

"Listen, B.H., I never really thanked you for taking my car to the shop and getting this car for me."

"You still haven't."

"Okay, thanks." That was hard.

"See that wasn't so bad was it? You're welcome."

"Put your seatbelt on or we won't go anywhere." I used my best "mommy voice" for this.

He complied and sarcastically thanked me for caring about his well being.

I pulled into line behind a Mercedes. "We've only got a few minutes. I really want to talk to you."

"Hey, that's my line. I need to talk to you too. I want to find out what you know…" He relaxed into the generic seat of the generic rental.

"And tell me what you know."

"And tell you *some* of what I know."

I relented. "Okay, here's the deal. You and I can go to dinner tomorrow night. You buy. Separate cars. Don't tell anyone. No touching."

"Deal. Let's go to The Rectory."

The Rectory had nothing to do with the church. It was a popular restaurant and watering hole located close to St. Francis University. Stained glass windows were the closest it got to church related matters. Most of the students from SFU hung out there. The downside was that it was in my old neighborhood and I was sure to see people I knew. The upside was that it had the best onion rings in town and cheap beer.

"I'll meet you there. Six o'clock, tomorrow night. Now that's Tuesday, George."

"I know, Sam. And thanks for calling me George."

Like he cares. He hadn't objected to my calling him B.H. And he kept acting like a Butthead.

At that moment we pulled up behind the line of cars at the cemetery and Michael came over to the window. I didn't have the opportunity to tell B.H. that I'd called him "George" accidentally. But if it made him feel better, I would continue. Maybe I could get more information from him that way.

I spent a few minutes smiling at Michael as I struggled to get the window down. It wouldn't budge. I felt stupid and was sure that Michael did not find my struggle attractive.

"You have to have the engine running to use the automatic windows."

"Shut up, George."

I stopped bothering with the window and opened the door. Michael seemed glad to see me and the feeling was very mutual. I explained to him that George just needed a ride and then patiently waited for him to explain why he was with Carolyn Burns. He didn't.

"Michael, why are you with Mrs. Burns?"

"Carolyn asked me to accompany her. She has no family and since the murderer is still at large, she feels a little uncertain and alone. So she hired me to be her bodyguard as well as investigate the murder. Any more questions?"

God, he was gorgeous.

"No, just curious. But I told you she's the murderer. And I need you to believe me. She killed her husband."

George leaned over the console and said, "Sam thinks she knows everything about the murder. In fact she…"

I slammed the door in his face without acknowledging his childish taunt.

Michael seemed interested. "How do you know that?"

"I just know and I can't tell you why. At least not here. I'll tell you later. Tonight. Do you think we can have dinner, after the thing at Burns' house?"

"That sounds like a good idea. I'll see if one of my men can take over. Right now I need to be with Carolyn. See you at her house later?"

I smiled and nodded. I also tried to control the dizzy

feeling that the thought of Carolyn Burns brought on.

After Michael left, George got out of the car with another stupid grin in evidence. He had quite a repertoire of ignorant looks.

I wanted to be silent, but couldn't. "What?"

"What do you mean, 'what?'"

"What are you grinning at?"

"Nothing," he lied. "Just smiling."

George and I walked over well-tended graves and settled at the edge of the large crowd. He watched everyone and I watched Michael. And Carolyn. I mean, I'm a nice person and normally I'd feel sympathy for a woman whose husband has just been killed. But, my God, she killed him and I couldn't feel any sorrow for her. Not only did she kill her husband, but she was also trying to steal my boyfriend. My potential boyfriend anyway.

The burial was strictly by the book. Almost everyone from the church was at the cemetery. I didn't know if they were there out of respect for Dr. Burns or because murders were rare in Quincy.

The priest said lots of familiar phrases. "Pillar of the community." "Quincy's loss." "Sympathy to Mrs. Burns." "Meet in heaven." And so on. Heard it before. Too many times.

It was cold. The wind whipped around the tent and people huddled together, whether from grief or from the cold, I couldn't tell. I snuggled down into my coat and thought about how Burns died. Sliced in the neck with a scalpel. It was an ignominious end for a doctor.

The memory of Burns' phone conversation while I was waiting in the hall for my interview suddenly surfaced and caused me to hit myself in the forehead. I grimaced as I made contact with a still-tender spot. "Damn!" Heads turned to stare at my outburst. "Sorry," I whispered to no one in particular.

I swear George chuckled. It was almost enough for me to call him B.H. again.

My interview with Dr. Burns had interrupted a phone call. Who had he been talking to? He said, "I'll have it for you next week." After a few moments he'd blurted, "Leave me alone or you'll be sorry." That didn't sound like something he would say to his wife.

I was sure she killed him. Absolutely one hundred percent sure. But that didn't mean she had done it alone. She could have had an accomplice. Maybe that's who Burns had been talking to that morning. I'd mentioned this to George right after the murder, then promptly forgot about it. I wondered if he remembered. I'd bring it up again tomorrow night, after he gave me some tidbits.

After the burial, George and I joined the many cars heading out to Burns' house. The sedan seemed out of place amidst the Mercedes, BMWs, Range Rovers, and Porsches.

Earlier I'd thought that the nondescript car would be ideal for a stakeout. But not in this crowd. It stood out like a Darling at a Debutante Ball.

We got to the house and went inside. I didn't even hesitate as the butler took our coats and led us into the drawing room. I was getting used to this.

George tried to take my arm. "No way. Remember our deal. I said you could come with me and we'd walk in together. We're here now and you're on your own. And I specifically said 'no touching.'"

"Sorry, Sam. Guess I forgot your rules." Was he being sarcastic or sincere? I couldn't tell and I didn't care.

I separated from George at the first opportunity and looked around for Michael. He and Carolyn Burns were conspicuous by their absence. I wanted to talk to him, and look at him, so I started nosing around. I had a cover story all prepared. If questioned, I'd say that I was looking for a bathroom. That wasn't original, and perhaps I didn't think it through very thoroughly, but I thought it would work. After all, we were at a wake and people certainly wouldn't suspect me of any nefarious activity. So I ventured into the kitchen. No one there. I grabbed a few snacks off a silver tray and went up the back stairs.

At the top of the stairs lay two small bedrooms. Probably servants' rooms originally. One was made into a sewing room and the other contained a treadmill, stair stepper and weights. The far wall was covered with a floor-to-ceiling mirror. I bet Carolyn Burns spent hours staring at herself.

Next was a bathroom. After that, two doors on either side of the hall led to two larger bedrooms, both a little too frou-frou for my taste. At the far end, past the front staircase, was a closed door. Probably the master suite. It looked like it took up the whole front of the house.

As I stood there wondering if I should go inside, I heard voices. Those voices needed listening to, so I volunteered.

No one was around so I pressed my ear against the door.

"Listen, if you just keep your mouth shut, nothing will happen. There is no proof and there won't be any proof. Just shut up and we won't have any problems." That sounded like Carolyn. Sure didn't sound so refined and uppity now.

"Mumble, mumble."

I'd heard that mumbling voice before. Who was it?

"I beg your pardon, Ma'am. May I help you?"

The butler.

"Yes, I was looking for the bathroom."

"It's down the hall, Madam. Would you like me to show you?"

"Certainly not." I tried to "harrumph" but couldn't quite pull it off. So I sashayed to the bathroom.

TWELVE

I avoided George but noticed he managed to speak to a lot of people and apparently didn't ruffle any feathers. Being from Quincy had its advantages. He was "one of us" and could get away with being a guest—and a pest— without attracting undue attention.

Once I found Gus, he made my visit palatable. We sat on a couch and he entertained me with stories about our fellow guests. He speculated on possible suspects and motives. I wasn't ready to let him in on my absolute assurance that Carolyn did it, but I did want to know what he thought.

"Who do you think killed Dr. Burns?" I tried to make the question sound innocent.

"Well, I've been thinking about it and he wasn't a very popular character. He's been involved in some shady business deals and…"

I interrupted, "Shady business deals? What kind?"

Gus continued as if I hadn't spoken, "… he's treated lots of folks pretty badly. I've heard complaints about his therapy practice too, but for years he was the only game in town." He moved on to another thought. "You told me you don't think Gwen Schneider did it. Have you changed your opinion? Everyone's talking about how she confessed to you."

"I'm sure she didn't do it. For lots of reasons, including that she didn't have a motive. She and the doctor were close. Very close." I raised my eyebrows and elbowed Gus in the ribs so he would understand my meaning. "Also her brother Charlie confessed and I'm equally sure he didn't do it."

Gus grinned at my hint, but then became serious when he asked, "Why are you so sure that Charlie Schneider didn't do it?"

"I'm just sure. Let's talk about something else; what did you mean Burns was involved in shady business deals?"

Gus bit into a mini-quiche, chewed for a moment, swallowed, and took a sip from his beer before answering. "Nothing in particular, just heard some things that told me he wasn't on the up-and-up. Insider trading, prescriptions for friends without examining them, things like that."

That wasn't worth waiting for. Then the conversation took a turn for the worse when he changed the subject to Carolyn Burns.

"You've read her books, right?"

"You know I don't read trash." I said it with a straight face, but Gus is not easily fooled by my fabrications.

"You already told me you've read her books. And just because you don't like her, doesn't mean her books aren't worthwhile." He smiled at me as one does at a much-loved, but errant child.

"Okay," I grudgingly admitted, "I've read a few…"

Gus stared at me, unbelieving and silent.

"All right, I've read all of them. I didn't like them much."

The maddening silence and stare continued.

"God, Gus, stop with the third degree, will you? I read them all and I liked them all, but that was before I knew Felicia Greene is Carolyn Burns." Blecch! I still shivered at the thought that Carolyn Burns wrote the books that had been scattered all over my house.

An idea struck and I almost pounded on my fellow crime solver. "You know, one reason I like the books so much is that they're realistic. I mean the criminal mind with its emotional disturbances… it's almost as if the author was either a therapist, a criminal, or crazy herself." Two out of three wasn't bad.

"You think she killed her husband?"

Hesitantly I nodded, not sure of exactly what to say.

"You think she's crazy, Sam?" Gus's raised eyebrows and squinted eyes showed he obviously didn't.

"Maybe not crazy, but she's evil. She had to have an accomplice and that accomplice must be a therapist or psychiatrist."

Gus didn't bother to swallow his current canapé as he blurted, "An accomplice in writing the books? Or in murder?"

I thought for a second before answering. "Maybe both. Someone had to help her with the details in the books. And she doesn't have a medical background, so how did she know to slice the vein lengthwise?"

Gus replied, "Hearing all that, it would seem more logical that she didn't have anything to do with the murder."

"You surprise me, Gus."

He put his arm around my shoulder. "Now, I'm not saying you're wrong. I'm just suggesting you keep your mind open to other possibilities."

"Yeah, yeah. But she did it. Really she did. She is just evil."

"Do your feelings about Carolyn Burns have anything to do with your young fellow?"

I immediately and adroitly changed the subject again. Gus followed suit; after all he was my friend. He took my mind off Michael and Carolyn for a while. I sat and basked in his wit and warmth.

Finally my patience was rewarded and Michael approached me.

"Hi, Sam. Gus."

Gus echoed my hello.

Michael's look made me smile. "Can we talk for a minute?" I nodded. "We can go in the kitchen."

Of course, I'm sure Carolyn never goes in there. "Sure, Michael. Gus, I'll see you at home." I winked at Gus as I walked away.

Michael led me into the kitchen. So far, so good. I was only feeling a slight dizziness. And except for ingesting a couple slugs of pink stomach-soother, I hadn't eaten anything except the snacks I grabbed on my reconnaissance mission.

Michael turned as he spoke. "I know you have a lot of questions. And I do too. Can you hold them until dinner tonight?"

"Yeah, I guess. But this time, we're going to dinner even if I'm in a cast from head to toe."

"I agree. It certainly appears that the fates are conspiring against us. How about if we go for an early meal? I'll follow you home from here and pick you up right away. That way there'll be no chance of anything new happening to you."

"Sounds good to me. By the way, where've you been the last hour or so? I looked for you."

"Oh, you did?" He grinned as if he found that thought appealing. "I was around. We've just installed a new security system and I was checking it out, plus I was meeting with one of my associates about taking over for me tonight."

"Oh, I thought you might have been with Carolyn."

"No, in fact I haven't seen much of her since we got back from the cemetery." He stepped aside as a bejeweled and bewigged matron passed by. "Why did you think I'd be with her?"

"Dunno. Just thought, since you're her bodyguard that you'd be with her." I moved as the woman realized she was in the kitchen of all places and beat a hasty exit.

"Well, we decided she'd be safe here. I think she wasn't feeling well and went up to her room."

"Is that the big room at the front of the house?" I gestured in the general direction.

"Yeah, it's the master suite, why?"

"Just curious." I promptly changed the subject, because I didn't want to discuss my nefarious activities with him.

While Michael continued talking about the wonders of the new security system, I was thinking about those voices coming from the bedroom. The talker was Carolyn, I was pretty sure of that. She didn't give me any hard evidence that she was the murderer, but she did talk about someone keeping their mouth shut and "proof." I still couldn't figure out who the mumbler was. Did I actually think it might have been Michael? Impossible. He was a nice guy and I had no reason to suspect him. Any guy who liked me couldn't be all bad. Besides, he was too gorgeous to be a crook.

"Are you ready to go? You don't seem too interested in hearing about my work."

I tuned back in. "I'm interested; just getting hungry. I haven't eaten much today. And yes, I'm ready, but I did want to express my condolences to Mrs. Burns. Why don't you get our coats and I'll see if she's available?"

He agreed and went off in search of the butler.

I climbed upstairs, as fast as I could, intent upon checking Carolyn's bedroom. The door was opened slightly. There was no one else in sight and hopefully Mr. Stiff Upper Lip Butler was busy getting our coats.

I accidentally nudged the door with my foot. At least I hoped it looked accidental, in case anyone was watching. As I peeked around the corner, I gained confidence. After all, this wasn't a movie or TV. This was real life and no one would hurt me. George had assured me that my car wreck was an accident and the jury was still out on the gas leak. So I felt pretty safe.

The huge bedroom was too opulent for my taste. And almost as big as my carriage house. Off to the left was the bathroom. I didn't see or hear anyone, so I stepped inside.

The ornate and fussy furniture looked like it was lifted directly from Buckingham Palace. I smirked as I pictured Carolyn lounging on the brocade-covered furniture in an overly dramatic pose. The red velvet was cloying and I almost choked at the ostentatious décor of the room.

I took a few more steps inside. The room was obsessively neat. Mine would be neat too if I had the servants she had.

There didn't appear to be anything out of the ordinary—at least for that house.

I opened the gigantic walk-in closet. My bedroom could easily fit in it. Women's clothing, shoes, hats, bags and general "stuff" filled the entire area. I wondered where Dr. Burns' clothes were. Surely Carolyn hadn't disposed of them already. I didn't see another closet, but perhaps he'd used one in another bedroom.

"Ms. Darling, may I help you?"

Carolyn Burns poked her head around the corner and seemed happy that she caught me off guard and red-handed.

"I was just looking for the bathroom. Is this the only one up here?"

"Come now, Ms. Darling. Isn't it just possible that you were snooping? Isn't that a bit rude? To be snooping through the bedroom of a grieving widow?"

I knew I was right. Carolyn Burns was a smart-alec. Maybe that wasn't incontrovertible evidence that she was a murderer, but it sure helped point the finger.

"I'm sorry you feel that way, Mrs. Burns. I wasn't snooping. I just have a lousy sense of direction." It was a clever line and it was delivered with no eye contact.

"Then I apologize. I'll be happy to show you to the other powder room."

"No need. I don't have to go anymore. So I think I'll go home. I have a date with Michael, you know." I couldn't pass up the opportunity to rub it in.

Carolyn looked uncomfortable and a mite jealous. Of course, I was delighted with that.

I exited, with a lot more aplomb than I felt. This woman made me sick—figuratively and literally. I felt so dizzy that I almost needed the use of her chaise lounge myself. These vibes of mine were a pain in the butt. They'd never been this bad before. Maybe that was because I'd never met a murderer before Carolyn. The room spun around every time I was near her and only slightly less so around Michael. It made no sense to me that I felt the same way around Michael as I did around Carolyn. There's no way he was involved in the crime; I just knew it. I wondered why I felt so unsteady around him.

Rather than dwell on that, I chose to ignore it and concentrate on clearing my head. Despite telling Carolyn I didn't need the bathroom, I found it and did a mirror talk.

"Listen, Sam, don't be a wimp. You know Carolyn is the murderer because of your physical reaction toward her. Go with those instincts. Believe them. Now stop being a dizzy blonde." That made me laugh and I suddenly realized that I was making a lot of noise and quickly flushed the toilet, hoping that would cover my indiscretion.

"And yes, she's beautiful… but Michael likes you. She's just a business arrangement to him." I batted my baby blues at myself and felt more confident.

Well, enough introspection. It was time to let Michael follow me home and for us to finally go on our date.

Gus was already gone, so there was no one else I needed to speak to. I garnered my coat from Michael and we started out the door. I had the feeling I was forgetting something, but couldn't figure out what it was.

"Hi ya, Sam. Forget something?" George grinned.

I glowered. "Go get in the car."

I turned to the guy who mattered. "Michael, I need to drop George off at the church. That's where he left his car. I'll meet you at my house in about fifteen minutes. Okay?" My glower turned to a glow.

"Sure. See you in a few minutes. Bye, Detective. Good to see you."

"Yeah, you too, O'Dear."

After Michael turned away George spoke again, "By the way, O'Dear, I'd like to get together with you tomorrow and talk about the case. I heard you tell Sam that Mrs. Burns hired you to protect her and also to investigate the murder. I want to hear what you know."

Michael turned back toward us. "Sure, Detective, I'd be happy to meet with you. Maybe you can help me too."

I really didn't want to talk to George during the trip back to the parking lot, but I wanted to get information from him. Short of giving him mind-altering drugs, the only way I could milk his brain was to talk to him.

"So, George," I turned and smiled, "did you find out anything?"

"WATCH OUT!"

I swerved, missing the car in front of us by inches. My smile disappeared.

"So, did you find out anything?" My eyes were glued to the road; my hands gripped the steering wheel.

"I found out that Dr. and Mrs. Burns didn't share the master bedroom. He used one of the guest rooms."

"Oh, I knew that. His clothes weren't in the closet in the master suite." I didn't care that I sounded smug and self-satisfied.

"So what were you doing in Carolyn's bedroom?"

"Using the bathroom," I lied, not hard to do with my eyes on the road. "What else did you find out?"

"He had a sweetie on the side."

"Everybody knows that. Gwen Schneider."

"Nah, I mean besides her."

I turned my head and stared at him. I didn't want him to see my surprise—or get in a wreck—so I quickly faced forward again. Maybe I needed to delve a little more at work tomorrow.

"Who's the other girlfriend?" I tried to sound nonchalant.

"I don't know, but apparently she's fairly new."

"Okay, I'll find out for you, if you want." I stopped the

rental next to his unmarked police car.

"Sure, yeah. Well, here we are. Don't forget, Sam. We'll talk more at dinner tomorrow night. I'll see you at six at The Rectory." George opened the door.

"I won't forget. You'll recognize me as the one wearing a bunny fur and wrist corsage."

"Very funny. Thanks for the ride. I'll see you tomorrow."

After he shut the car door I thought that George was the last person I wanted to concentrate on right now, but his face kept popping up in my brain as I drove away. I wondered why he was being so nice to me. I also wondered what he wanted. The good news was that he said it was okay for me to find out who Dr. Burns' new girlfriend was. For now though, I needed to just forget about good old George Lansing as I had other fish to fry.

I wished I had time to bait the hook a little better, but Michael was already parked by the carriage house when I pulled up.

"Hi." His smile lit up his face and my hopes.

"Hi. Come on in. I need just a minute to freshen up." Was that me who said "freshen up?" I'd never said those words before in my life. "I also have to take Clancy out for a few minutes."

Clancy vacillated between being happy to see me and glaring at me because I'd been gone for the day. She gave in and got excited. When she wagged her tail, her whole butt moved from side to side in what I called the "Clancy Rumba." It was cute and endearing, making me remember another reason we adopted her.

"Nice dog," Michael said as he hunkered down with his palm outstretched.

"Thanks. She's a member of the family."

Clancy sidled over to Michael and began sniffing him. Finally she lay down in front of him and rolled onto her back, allowing him to scratch her belly.

I laughed, "I'm afraid she has no shame."

"That's all right with me," Michael replied, "I love dogs."

"Would you like a drink while you're waiting? I'm afraid all I have is beer and wine."

"I'll take a beer. Why don't you do what you have to do and I'll help myself."

He and Clancy were still involved when I left the room.

It only took me a moment to "freshen up." I decided to wear the same outfit I'd worn all day and only needed to refresh my make up and run a brush through my hair.

By the time I returned, Michael was sitting on the couch drinking a beer and Clancy was sitting in front of him with a look of adoration on her face.

"C'mon, girl. Let's go outside."

She beat me to the door. I heard Michael laugh at her behavior. That made me like him even more.

Clancy didn't need a leash to go outside. She was trained

to stay in the yard. She also was trained to "use the facilities" on all of Georgianne's plants. An immature move on my part, I knew, but by the time I thought better of it, it was too late to change Clancy's behavior. Since it was January, Clancy's choices were limited and she chose a small evergreen by Georgianne's back door.

I filled Clancy in on the latest goings on while we were outside, hoping that this would appease her a bit. She appeared interested but I could tell that she thought she should be my crime-solving partner rather than Michael or Gus.

Clancy finished her business and looked at me expectantly. "Good girl, Clancy. C'mon, let's go in."

She wasn't excited about returning inside and I finally pushed her a little with my knee, urging her through the door. She looked at me, sniffed, glanced at Michael once, turned on the charm to get one more scratch from him, and then went to her bed. I used to think it was my bed, but actually we shared it. However, I was sure that Clancy thought it was hers and that she allowed me to share it with her.

"Okay. I'm ready."

"You look great."

Hating the flush I felt on my cheeks, I said, "I'm wearing the same thing I had on earlier."

"You looked great earlier too."

I smiled as we put on our coats. It seemed I was smiling a lot tonight.

"If it's all right with you," Michael said, "I'd like to get the business done first. Then we can enjoy our meal and our date."

I agreed that it was a good idea.

We drove in a companionable silence for the few blocks to The Rectory. One of the downsides of living in a small town is that the dining choices are limited. So I'd be here two nights in a row, with two different guys. I definitely thought it was cool, even if one of them was George.

As we walked the half block from the parking lot to the restaurant door, Michael took my hand and said, "There are some things I want to clear up with you. You wanted to know what I was doing at Burns' office, what I was doing in the ER the night Charlie Schneider was acting up, and about my relationship with Carolyn Burns."

My mouth dropped open. Not only was he holding my hand in public, Michael was going to answer my every question, and maybe at some point he might answer my every need. I could hope anyway.

Nonchalantly, I replied, "If you really want to tell me all that, I guess I can listen."

"Please don't play dumb. I like it much better when you are yourself. You are one smart lady, and I like that."

The guy was gorgeous, he was kind, and he wanted to tell me everything I wanted to know. So I guess it was time for me to get dizzy.

THIRTEEN

"Sorry, Michael." I wobbled. "I'm feeling a little woozy. Maybe I need some food."

"Well, just to be safe, I'll make sure we get a small table and I'll sit close so I can catch you if you fall." He smiled. I thought he was kidding, but wasn't quite sure.

Michael pulled open the Rectory's large oak door with stained glass inserts and stepped aside so I could enter first.

"Sam, welcome. It is so good to see you." Anthony, the owner, hugged me so tightly I could barely breathe. His hearty laugh reverberated throughout my body. "And who is this young man with you?"

"Anthony, this is Michael O'Dear, he's new in town." I disentangled myself from my friend. "And Michael, this is Anthony Lasorda. He owns The Rectory and don't ask him if he's related to the former Los Angeles Dodgers' coach. He'll talk all night."

They exchanged pleasantries as Anthony escorted us to a much-coveted table. He then kept us busy with a run down of his large family. This one started college, that one got married, this one joined the army. I never could keep up with his kids' names. It was difficult enough keeping track of my own family.

Finally we were settled, and, after gaining my assurance that I liked it, Michael ordered a bottle of California merlot.

Anthony beamed. "An excellent choice, Mr. O'Dear. If you permit, I will make a special meal for you. It's not on the menu, but you will love it. Are you a vegetarian like Sam or may I put some seafood in your portion?"

Michael admitted he was a practicing carnivore and that any kind of meat or fish would be fine with him. This was the first and only strike against him.

Anthony left to personally prepare our dinners and Michael turned his attention to me. "We said we'd get business out of the way. Are you ready to talk?"

Was I ever. "Sure." It was hard acting nonchalant.

Michael began, "I was at the clinic because I was meeting with Burns. He'd hired me after clinic employees complained someone had been rifling through the patient files in his office. Things were out of place. Nothing had been taken as far as anyone could tell, but things had been disturbed. A file clerk was the first one to notice and mentioned it to Burns. When it happened a few more times, he brought me in. He claimed he wasn't concerned about it though." Almost as an afterthought, he added, "Also some patients were threatening to sue him over alleged improprieties."

"What were they?"

He looked adorable as he refused my request. "You know I can't tell you that. Therapists aren't the only ones bound by confidentiality. Anyway, I took the job and found it only mildly interesting." He almost absentmindedly fiddled with his silverware. "I hadn't really gotten into it much before Burns was killed. So that's why I was at the clinic."

"Okay, I buy that. But why were you at the ER in the middle of the night?"

"I was there because of Charlie Schneider. I told you Mrs. Burns wanted me to do some investigating about the murder." He broke off a piece of Italian bread and buttered it. "I'd heard from some former employees that Burns and Gwen Schneider had been involved in a long-term affair and I was checking her out as a possible suspect. Her brother was a real loose cannon. Half crazy. Burns had told me he was seeing Charlie as a patient as a favor to Gwen. I was following him that night and got to the ER waiting room just in time to knock the gun out of his hand. By the way, I convinced the DA not to prosecute. He's already on probation for some minor offenses, and they're just going to continue supervision, as long as he continues therapy with someone. Charlie's a sad case. He lost his wife and kid at that hospital and has never been the same."

"So far, so good. Now what is the real relationship between you and Carolyn Burns?" I waited expectantly, hoping that he'd give the answer I wanted.

"It's exactly what I told you. She hired me because the murderer is still on the loose and she felt the need for a bodyguard. That's it. She doesn't mean anything to me. I mean, it's kind of cool to have a famous novelist in Quincy. So I've been having fun with it."

I looked at him.

"Close your mouth. It's true. And that's that. Now I'd like to hear what you know. Fair is fair."

I figured I'd better tell him what I knew so we could get to the important stuff, like our date.

Anthony returned with the wine, let Michael sniff and swirl, and poured our glasses full after Michael nodded approval. After we clinked glasses and each took a drink, I answered Michael's question. "I don't really know much. I know that Gwen Schneider and Charlie Schneider did not kill Burns. Charlie confessed to try to save his sister. I don't know why Gwen confessed, but she didn't do it. I'm positive of that."

"I'm probably going to be sorry I asked, but how do you know that Gwen didn't do it?"

I ignored his smart comment, because I was ready to fall in love with him. "Okay, I'll tell you. She doesn't *feel* guilty. Before you start laughing at me, I gotta tell you something about me. See, sometimes I feel things; I get vibes about people. And sometimes I'm right and sometimes I'm wrong, but most of the time I'm right. And I'm 100% sure on this one. Just like I'm 100% sure that Carolyn killed her husband."

"Sounds like you've been reading Carolyn's thrillers."

Once again, I ignored his smart-ass comment. Did he realize just what I was going through to show my interest in him?

"She just *feels* guilty, Michael. In fact, the feeling is so powerful that I get dizzy or sick whenever I'm around her. And it's not the flu or an upset stomach. She literally makes me sick. I cannot stand to be around her. She's evil."

My intense feelings about the woman propelled me into a standing position. My hands were flat on the table and I loomed over Michael.

Michael looked directly into my eyes as he said, "I just don't buy it. I mean, I think you believe it, but I'm not into that stuff."

"I'm not into that stuff either. This is just part of who I am. I've always been this way. Even when I was a little kid I'd get these feelings about people and I'd get twitches and stuff all over my body."

"Twitches?" He tried and failed to suppress a disbelieving grin.

"Yeah, twitches." I sat. "And sometimes dizziness and other times just feelings, just vibrations." I found it hard to explain this to anyone, especially this gorgeous hunk who would now never touch me except to push me away.

He hesitated, then spoke softly, "You get dizzy around me too."

I put my hand on his, then quickly withdrew it. "What I feel around Carolyn is nothing like what I feel around you. I promise."

He relaxed against the back of his chair.

I continued. "I know it sounds crazy. That's why I haven't told many people. I'm telling you because I need you to believe me. Carolyn killed her husband. No ifs, ands, or buts. She did it. Period. End of quote."

"Okay, let's say you're right."

I smiled.

"This is just for argument's sake. Let's say you're right. How in the world could the police arrest Carolyn for her husband's murder without any evidence?"

"Aw, come on, Michael. Cops arrest people without evidence all the time. Don't you watch television? Anyway, what we need to do is find the evidence and then we can turn it over to my brother, Rob, who will notify Detective Lansing and then Rob will be promoted. I'll be vindicated. And you…" I hesitated.

"And I'll what?"

"And you'll believe me." Gee, I almost slipped up there and said, "… you'll fall in love with me." Where did I get this crap? I hadn't felt like this in more years than I cared to remember.

"What did Gwen Schneider say when you asked her why she confessed?"

"What?" I practically stuttered.

He began to repeat his question, "What did Gwen—"

I interrupted, "I heard you. I said 'what' because I can't believe I've not asked her why she confessed. In the beginning everything was moving so quickly and then she was arrested and was in jail. I just didn't think of it."

Michael spoke softly, "See, Sam. You're a social worker, not a cop."

I ignored his statement and continued, "Will you help me?" I tried not to beg.

"Under one condition. That you let me do it. It's my job. You're a social worker, not a cop, not a private investigator. A social worker."

Same song, different singer. Ho-hum. "Okay. I'll stay out of it." I carefully avoided eye contact. Gee, this lying and not looking people in the eye was a lot easier than I had anticipated.

"Let's change the subject, and talk about you," Michael said.

"And you," I added.

I noticed that "you" and "you" didn't add up to a "we," but that only meant it was our first real date. "We" could become a reality.

The rest of the all-too-short evening was delightful.

Michael asked all the right questions about me, my kids, marriage, and family. Since I'm a therapist, I asked open-ended questions. He rewarded me with rich conversation.

No, he'd never been married. Been close a few times. Yes, he moved here recently, liked Quincy, and would like to stay for a while. Born and raised in St. Louis. He learned his skills as a military policeman in the Army. No, he'd never met Carolyn Burns before her husband's murder. She'd found his name in the yellow pages and didn't know beforehand that he'd worked for her husband.

Okay, those aren't the responses to open-ended questions. Maybe I did interrogate him a little, but I was entitled. I'd waited a long time for a real date, and getting together with Michael had proven to be very problematic. Finally, my equilibrium had stabilized, my hair was behaving, and even my mouth was cooperating. Not much cussing tonight.

Then, in a gesture I was eagerly anticipating, Michael touched my hand and leaned toward me. As he did so, I wondered if we were having an earthquake. My balance was disrupted. I nearly fell off my chair, but two strong arms caught me and kept me vertical.

"We need to get you home, Sam."

"No, I'm fine." This time I whined.

"I'm not going to argue with you. It's home and to bed." He meant alone.

FOURTEEN

"**. . .a**s he approached me, I fancied he had ideas about my virtue. His eyes were heated, as was my body. I waited for him to speak, but no words escaped his lips. He merely touched my bodice, and delicately undid the top button, being very careful not to touch the skin underneath. I feared I would swoon, but did not. Instead I looked at him with eyes that were as lustful as his own. A sigh escaped my lips and I…"

DING!

Thank God. It was over. Listening to Mrs. Abernathy was like reading a steamy romance novel.

"Mrs. Abernathy, I'm sorry. Your time is up for this session."

"Oh no, Ms. Darling. I was just getting to the interesting part of my dream. Couldn't we just stretch the time a bit so I can describe the rest? I know you will be able to appreciate it." Her bottom lip quivered as her chest heaved. My heart was palpitating a bit as well. Mrs. Abernathy did a wonderful job of describing her dream. It was amazing that her dreams were so sexual and so vivid. She was a short, rotund, elderly woman wearing a conservative black frock, and she was homely. That was the kindest adjective I could summon to describe her. Her dreams, however, were erotic enough for the letters section of a porn magazine.

"I'm sorry, Mrs. Abernathy. Your time is up for this session." I learned the broken record routine years ago in a not-needed assertive training class. "We can continue next week. Make sure you confirm your appointment with Mrs. Schmitt at the front desk. Good-bye and have a wonderful week."

"But, Ms. Darling…"

I stood and assisted Mrs. Abernathy to the door. "I look forward to talking to you again next week."

"All right. Perhaps I'll write down my dreams during the week to make sure I won't forget any of them." She had a hopeful look in her eye.

"Certainly. That will be fine. 'Bye." Oh, joy. I'd have to listen to her dreams for another hour.

My first patient at my new job. What a disappointment. I had visions of helping people sort out real difficulties in their lives. Instead I got Mrs. Abernathy. I no longer wondered why Marian and the others had grinned at the staff meeting when I received Mrs. Abernathy as my first client. I guessed that she had already been a part of their caseloads and had been passed from person to person.

I could empathize with Mrs. Abernathy because I wanted to note on her chart, Diagnosis: Lonely, Bored and Horny. While I was trying to do a diagnostic interview, she spent the hour energetically describing the erotic dreams she'd been having. When I got to know her better, perhaps I would recommend she try writing romance novels. She might be quite successful.

That reminded me of Carolyn Burns. I was more convinced than ever that she killed Dr. Burns. Unfortunately, my "vibes" wouldn't stand up in court, and I really didn't want to talk about my instincts publicly. It was bad enough that some of my sibs knew. They'd stopped teasing me about it years ago, but most weren't comfortable talking about my gift/curse. Now Michael knew and soon others would find out. This could prove to be embarrassing.

I just had to find some hard evidence.

As I went through the private door from my office to the kitchen, I noticed the closed door on the other side of that large room. It led to Burns' office, which was still off limits to us. "The investigation is ongoing," the press release stated. It was posted all over the office so I couldn't pretend I didn't know.

Since my office connected to the kitchen and the kitchen connected to the scene of the crime, I could slip into Burns' office without anyone knowing. And I wouldn't even feel guilty about it.

I tiptoed across the kitchen. Maybe I wasn't going to feel guilty but I still needed to be discreet.

The door was closed. I crossed my fingers and gently turned the knob. That was impossible to do with my fingers crossed. I uncrossed my fingers and quietly opened the door a few inches and peeked inside. No one there. And the door leading from his office to the hallway was closed.

Before anyone could come into the kitchen and interrupt my sleuthing, I moved quickly into Burns' office and closed the door. The room looked just as it had the last time I was in it, with two notable exceptions. First, there was no dead body on the floor. Second, standing in the corner, rifling through a file cabinet, was none other than Carolyn Burns.

Intent on her evil deeds, she didn't notice me until I spoke.

"So, Carolyn. It's curtains for you."

"I beg your pardon." Even though I caught her in the act, she did a great job of making me feel inept and in the wrong.

"It's curtains for you. You're up a creek without a paddle. You're S.O.L. You know. You returned to the scene of the crime. I caught you."

"Ms. Darling, even though you are speaking in clichés, I have no idea what you are talking about. I have every right to be in my husband's office."

"Not when there's masking tape or scotch tape or something barring the door."

"I wondered if you'd noticed that, Ms. Darling. So what are you doing here?"

Okay, she had me there. "That's none of your concern. There was no tape over the door I used and besides, I just caught you snooping through those confidential files."

This all fit. Burns had hired Michael because someone had been going through his files. I now knew who that someone was. Finally, I was getting the much-needed evidence and the noose was tightening around Carolyn's neck. Well, maybe that was a little melodramatic, but it expressed my sentiments succinctly.

"I was looking for some insurance papers and I notified the new receptionist that I was doing so. Any other questions?" She looked so smug and self-righteous that I wanted to smack her. That would certainly wipe the grin off her face.

"You're looking for insurance papers in the patient file drawer?" Aha, I had her now.

"Oh, no wonder I couldn't find them. I thought this file cabinet was where my husband kept his personal files." How she managed to look so innocent was beyond me.

"All right, Carolyn. I'll check with Mrs. Schmitt in just a moment. In the meantime, I'll notify Officer Darling that you are here."

She merely raised an eyebrow. I guess my brother Rob wasn't enough of a threat.

"And I will also notify Detective Lansing."

"There's no need to do that, Ms. Darling." I found the lever that could move her. "I was just leaving and you can see that I have nothing in my hands."

She had a big purse however. "I'm sorry, Carolyn, but I feel obligated to tell the authorities. I'm sure you understand."

"Why must you do that?" Then she did what many heroines in her books did when they got upset. She sat down and cried. That was the only part of her characterizations I didn't like. It was hard admitting that everything else about her books intrigued me. In fact, they seemed familiar to me and contained good descriptions of people's neuroses and psychoses.

I continued the conversation while slowly advancing toward her. "I already told you when I was at your house. I know you killed your husband. And I also know you had help."

"It's not true." She paused and looked up at me. "How do you know all that?"

It was time for me to sing the same song again. "I just know." I didn't want to tell her how I knew and I also didn't want to tell her that I knew she was too prissy to actually stick the scalpel in his neck.

"Just like you know Gwen Schneider didn't do it?"

"Where did you hear that?"

"You're not the only one Michael talks to." Her smile made me want to pass out. That was just a figure of speech. Oddly enough, this time I didn't feel faint around her. Maybe my anger helped control my dizziness.

For good measure I threw in, "And you cut the gas line in my house and the brake line in my car."

"We did not cut the brake line in your car. That's ludicrous."

I pounced. "You said 'we.'"

She turned away. "I meant 'I.'"

I took another step toward her. "So you admit you tampered with the gas line in my home."

She sighed as she faced me again. "That is so patently ridiculous it doesn't even deserve comment."

"Well, you have fingerprint powder all over your nice black suit." I guess I showed her. I resisted the urge to stick out my tongue and go "nyah-nyah-nyah."

She wiped at the grayish-white powder. Her fingers beat a staccato tattoo on her thighs. She accompanied the beat with "ooh-ooh, ooh-ooh." What a priss.

She was fastidious all right. I wondered if she was around when the blood started spurting from her husband's neck like a full-speed-ahead garden hose. How did she handle that?

As I thought about that gory detail, the door from the hallway opened and a familiar voice announced his presence, "Hi ya, Sam. Mrs. Burns."

"George, I was just about to call you. Carolyn is in here without permission." Oh my God. I'd turned into the very person I despised—a tattletale. This was gross. "And she's going through the file cabinets. Make her stop." I was talking and I couldn't shut up.

George looked quizzically at me, then shook his head as if to clear it of my face. "Mrs. Burns, I've been looking for you. Saw your car outside. Will you please accompany me to the station so we can talk?"

"Does she need a lawyer? Are you going to read her her rights?" I was as excited as a girl on her first date.

He didn't spare a glance in my direction. He was good at this.

"Of course, Officer Lansing. I'll be happy to oblige. Will I need to notify my attorney?"

"We just want to talk. You aren't under arrest. Of course, if you want to have your attorney present, you may. By the way, I understood that O'Dear was providing security service for you. Where is he?"

"Waiting at my home, I presume. I needed some, um, private time, so I left by a side door. These insurance papers are very important to me and I felt I couldn't wait until you declared this area open again. I'm certainly sorry if I broke any rules."

I didn't buy what she was selling. Like I thought she was

really sorry. I understood her quite well and predicted that the next thing she would do was bat her eyes.

Gosh almighty, if she didn't. She batted her eyes at George, and I could tell he liked it. The scum-sucking dog.

"Mrs. Burns, we'll talk about what you're doing here later. For now, let's go to the station. I have some other questions for you."

Carolyn gathered her belongings and wiggled out the door.

I couldn't resist one last jab at her. "Look in her purse. Bet she's got something in there that she shouldn't have."

"Bye, Sam. See ya tonight."

Oh, yeah, tonight. I'd almost forgotten. A dinner with George. I hesitated to call it a dinner date, because it wasn't a date, not a real one. He'd had his chance at a date with me back in the '80s. And he blew it. Big time. One strike and you are out, George Lansing.

He poked his balding head back through the door. "And, Sam. Please leave this room. Now. And I'd appreciate it if you didn't return until we've cleared it. Got that?"

"I understand." I understood, but that didn't mean I was going to do what he said.

As he slithered out the hall door, I exited through the kitchen and snagged a cup of coffee on the way to my office.

I sat in my chair, plopped my feet on the desk, and wrapped both hands around the mug. There's something comforting about the warmth of a mug of coffee. So why didn't I feel comforted?

Why didn't anyone believe me about Carolyn Burns? At least Michael claimed he wanted to believe me. That was a giant leap ahead of George, who just looked at me with that condescending grin of his and sloughed me off as if I were a child. I wondered if my brother Rob had any other information about the case. I also wondered if he would share it with me.

A quick call to the Quincy Police Department told me that Rob was out on patrol. I didn't leave a message.

I took a big swig of the dark rich brew. My next step needed careful planning. Would there be any value in checking Burns' files? Would I know if something were missing?

I wished I could figure out who was in on this with Carolyn. The only people I was sure were innocent were Gwen and Charlie Schneider. Everyone else was up for grabs.

And why did Burns tell Michael he wasn't concerned about the patient files being out of order? Did he think it was the result of carelessness? Or was it something more sinister; was Burns himself involved?

There was something else niggling at my brain. Every time it tried to surface I pushed it back down. I didn't want to think about it. But these few minutes alone were all it needed to rear its ugly head.

Michael. Dear, sweet, handsome, nice butt, Michael. Would I care to examine that I got dizzy almost every time I was around him? Would I care to compare faintness with the times that I was around Carolyn? Both felt the same. The loss of balance was certainly the same.

The first time I had seen Carolyn was at her house on the day after her husband was murdered. She and Michael were talking together. And I felt dizzy. They both touched me and I passed out. As I was getting up from the chaise lounge, they both touched me again. Dizziness again. That had to be a coincidence. Michael and Carolyn were not accomplices in murder. I was sure of that.

Devil Sam: "Just a coincidence. Michael had nothing to do with the murder."

Angel Sam: "You've been dizzy more around Michael than you've ever been around Carolyn. At least look at the possibility that he's involved."

Devil Sam: "Don't bother. He's much too cute to have murdered anyone. Besides it's been more years than you care to remember since you have… you know… had sex."

I had to stop those schizophrenic meanderings. Anyway, Devil Sam must not be too good at what she does if she has such a hard time talking about sex. I didn't think I was the type of morally bankrupt person who would let the possibility of getting laid get in the way of justice.

To distract myself, I decided to catch up on reading some of my professional journals and quit thinking about the case. A boring, but necessary, part of being a therapist is keeping up with the latest research. I couldn't say how much time passed before I heard someone knock hesitantly on the door and open it just a crack.

I looked up to see two well-matched heads peeking around the doorframe. "Gwen. Charlie. Come on in. When did they spring you?" I couldn't believe what I heard myself saying. I sounded like a cop.

"Hi Sam," Gwen said. "They had a preliminary hearing this morning and the judge didn't find enough evidence to bind me over for trial."

She motioned her brother to come into the room so she could close the door. "Officer Lansing couldn't hear everything from the other room — he only heard part of what I said to you. And since you're a therapist, bound by confidentiality, my lawyer made a good case for them not pressing charges against me. He said I could still be picked up again, but I'm free for now."

"Good for you. That serves Officer Lansing right. Eavesdropping is a nasty habit." Surprisingly enough, I was able to say that with a straight face. I was sure glad I didn't have to testify. It would have sounded nuts for me to say that Gwen was innocent because she didn't "feel" guilty.

"I just came by to get my stuff. Under the circumstances,

I figured that I shouldn't be working here. Anyway, I thought I'd leave before they fired me." The sniffling began again. Luckily Brother Charlie was quick with a handkerchief.

I thought this was an opportune time to get the skinny on Gwen's relationship with Burns. "Charlie, would you mind sitting in the waiting room for a little while? I'd like to talk to your sister privately."

He exited without objection. His hangdog expression left a pall in the room as he walked out.

"Why did you confess to me?" I wasn't going to forget to ask this again.

She seemed surprised by my question. "I don't know. I think I was in shock. It was really stupid to say it. Now you and Charlie are the only ones who believe I'm innocent."

I decided to continue the direct approach. "Is it true you were having an affair with Dr. Burns?"

Niagara Falls began. "Yes," snort, slobber, "but he broke it off with me about a month before he died."

Gwen had a real talent for shutting those waterworks on and off. I held my suspicions at bay but knew that she wasn't being entirely straight with me.

"Gwen, is there anything I can do to help you now?" I reached out and put my hand on her arm. No dizziness on my part.

"No, I've got to sort it out by myself. But..." she looked

at the connecting door to the kitchen.

"Is something else bothering you?"

She said, "No," but her eyes kept straying to the door.

I got up and checked, pulling the door toward me. The kitchen was empty. "Nobody there this time."

Then she really started blubbering. "I really didn't mean to, but I did and I'm sorry and Dr. Burns…" More slobbering and more mumbling and not much clear conversation, but her glance kept straying toward the kitchen door.

"Gwen, I can't understand what you are saying. Can you please calm down and tell me what you did and what you are sorry for?" I was getting tired of these half-confessions.

This was getting more and more curious. Why did Gwen insist on confessing to me all the time when I knew she was innocent?

She regained some composure. "Charlie said that you fed him and helped him when I was in jail. I don't know what's gonna happen to him if I leave or if they…" Slobber, slobber, etc.

She really collapsed then and I couldn't get a coherent word out of her. She still couldn't keep her eyes away from the door leading to the kitchen. In between hiccups and blubbering, that is. So acting on a hunch, I got up quietly, opened the kitchen door, walked through that room, and quickly and with lots of force opened the door to Burns' office. A loud thump produced a grunt of satisfaction in me. The thump was the result of Carolyn Burns landing ignominiously on her butt. She lay spread-eagle on the floor. I was sure the position was not unknown to her. The look on her face was worth anything I might have to experience.

The look on her face said, "Guilty as charged."

FIFTEEN

From her new position on the floor, Carolyn grunted her displeasure. I felt a bump behind me as Gwen moved close to look over my shoulder. I tried to behave professionally, since I was on duty and since we were in the office of the dearly departed. I tried, but I failed. The laughter escaped. It felt wonderful to cut loose with a belly laugh. I laughed so hard tears streamed down my face. I laughed so hard I snorted. I laughed so hard I couldn't see. I laughed so hard I couldn't breathe. I laughed so hard that Carolyn and Gwen left without me noticing.

I wondered why they left together, when they should actually hate each other. Maybe it was just a coincidence. Tears were still overflowing from my bout of uncontrollable mirth when I went out to the waiting room to see if Charlie was still there.

"Clara, did you see Charlie Schneider leave?"

"Are you all right?"

"I'm fine." Snort. "Allergies." Hiccup. "Did you see Charlie leave?"

"Yes, he went out rather quickly after Gwen and Mrs. Burns."

"Are you sure they left together or was it just accidental that they went out the door at the same time?"

"I'm quite sure they left together. They were speaking to one another as they left." Even though Clara Schmitt was brand new, she didn't miss a trick. She looked deceptively like a grandmother type, but this lady was sharp. If she said they left together, I guess I needed to believe her.

I didn't call George or Rob, since I'd see George in a few hours. There was only one person on my caseload because of the confusion after the funeral, so I decided to take off early, go home and relax before my dinner with George.

I had walked to work today. The frigid crispness of the January day was just what I'd needed to uncloud my mind. Walking home was even better. The late afternoon sun danced over the ice and snow and brought fanciful notions to my head. I imagined that I was an owner of one of the mansions instead of just a renter. The thought made me walk taller. This was a great neighborhood.

Clancy was waiting at the door for me. Leash in mouth.

"Gee, Clance, can't you give me one minute before we go for a walk?"

The answer was "No." It was comforting to have her in my life, but I could understand why she was upset. Normally we spent a lot of time together, but with my accidents and two dates in a row, it's no wonder she was feeling left out.

I thought about calling Pete, but he had told me he was working evenings this week. The rest of the tribe would be busy at this hour, coming home from work and spending a little time with their families before dinner. I didn't want to disturb anyone just to run my ideas by them. Maybe Clancy would suffice. She was my best bet anyway, at least until I could talk to George or Michael. It seemed like a good idea to solidify my thoughts before I tried to talk to either one of them. Neither was convinced that I knew what I was talking about. And Clancy didn't think I was crazy—at least she didn't tell me so.

"Okay, let's go. I guess I could use the exercise myself. I need to talk about some stuff too. Maybe you could help me." I threw my purse on the couch and opened the door, letting Clancy lead the way. She took off for her favorite haunts with me dutifully following at leash length.

"I'm positive Carolyn killed her husband. But I'm also sure she had help. She's much too prissy to stick a scalpel into someone. Now who was her accomplice?"

Clancy turned and looked at me thoughtfully. She cocked her head in her thinking mode, but didn't say anything. *Gosh, Sam, of course she didn't say anything, you nitwit. She's a dog.*

"Here's the list of possibles. Gwen Schneider. I know she

didn't do it, because she feels innocent. She sure acts strange though. But that's no reason to consider her a murderer. Just because she semi-confessed to me twice doesn't mean she did it. Also, she and Carolyn certainly wouldn't be accomplices in this kind of thing. I do wonder why they left the clinic together though.

"Charlie Schneider. I think he just loves his sister a lot and relies on her to keep him almost sane. He doesn't feel guilty to me either, even though he confessed. He does have a motive though. He feels protective of his sister—she's the only family he has."

"Michael O'Dear. I know, Clance. He can't be guilty. He's too cute and he likes me. The only reason he's on the list is that I'm dizzy when I'm around him, the same as when I'm near Carolyn. So that's the list. I'm sure there are other possibilities. I mean, there's gotta be. Those three are all innocent. So we gotta find Carolyn's accomplice. Or maybe find out more about her. I mean, I could be wrong about her not being able to stick the scalpel in Burns. Maybe she used to be a surgical nurse, or a knife thrower in a circus or something."

Or maybe she's a psychopath. I didn't express that notion aloud; afraid that even Clancy would think it was too much.

On that note, we arrived at the park. I let Clancy off the leash for a while so she could run and tire herself out. I didn't feel like running. All of this brainwork was tiring.

When Clancy came back to me with her tongue hanging out, we headed for home.

The return to our place passed quickly, with Clancy and me taking turns leading.

When we arrived, Clancy went to her corner, got a drink of water, and circled around for a nap.

It was time to decide on the all-important outfit. I climbed into my closet to begin the familiar ritual. What to wear. It was only George, so I grabbed a pair of jeans and a sweatshirt.

As I put them on I let Clancy in on my thoughts, "If I wear these clothes, he probably won't be consumed with desire for me, and then I wouldn't have so much fun being cold to him. So perhaps I ought to dress up a bit more." I looked over my shoulder for her opinion. She agreed.

There really wasn't much of a choice. I had already worn my power suit several times. Last night I wore my black cocktail dress with the black blazer. I had a brainstorm. Maybe jeans, a black camisole and the black blazer. Yes. Cool, sophisticated, and with just a hint of animal magnetism. I didn't want to bowl the poor guy over after all.

It was a clear, crisp night, so I put on some snow boots, placed my shoes in my large purse, found my "good" coat and bade farewell to Clancy.

"Clancy, old girl, watch and learn. I've had two dates in

a row, with two different men. This is something you may never see again in either of our lifetimes." She raised her head and I swore she rolled her eyes. "Okay, don't look at me like that. I know the dinner with George isn't really a date, but it'll look that way to anyone who is watching, so it will still count. Give me a break."

I walked slowly to The Rectory, deliberately arriving twenty minutes late so George would be forced to wait for me. Anthony greeted me effusively at the door.

"Sam, what a pleasure. Two nights in a row. Are you meeting someone?"

"Yes, but I don't see him. Is Detective Lansing here?"

"No, but I do have a reservation in his name for two. Why don't I seat you and I'll stay on the lookout for him?"

"Okay, Anthony. And bring me a—"

"Beer in a long neck bottle, no glass." He chuckled. "Sam, you've been coming in here for a long time. I know what you drink by now."

This felt wonderful. I thought I only moved back to Quincy for the support of my family after my divorce. But I also moved back for this. People who have known me since I was born. People who care about me. There was comfort in being served by a man who knew that I sometimes had wine with dinner, but otherwise it was always beer in a long necked bottle. No glass. Did he suspect the phallic connotations?

The beer arrived quickly. I exchanged my boots for shoes, then I sipped and looked around. The Rectory always had a nice crowd. Some people came for a meal. Some people came for drinks. Some came to ease the loneliness a bit. All came to be catered to by Anthony—a great bear of a man with a heart that filled his entire body.

My mind stayed occupied, just looking around and saying "hello" every now and then to acquaintances. No relatives here tonight.

I finished my beer before I thought to look at my watch. I'd been here over twenty minutes. And that damn George wasn't here. He stood me up again. He did the same damn thing that he did in high school. This was stupid and I was steaming. I slammed some money on the table for the drink. I wouldn't stiff Anthony even though I'd been shafted.

Just as I stood up to get my coat, my glance caught the smiling face of The Late One.

I didn't reciprocate with a smile of my own. "What are you grinning at?"

"I'm happy to see ya, Sam. Why shouldn't I be smiling?"

"You think it's funny that you could stand me up again? You think it's funny that I'm waiting here and you didn't call?"

His smile disappeared, replaced by a frustrated frown and a furrowed brow. "Did you check your voice mail? Did you check your e-mail? I left a message on both since I was gonna be late and I didn't want you thinking I was standing you up."

Feeling stupid was not something I relished, but I did it well. "Sorry, I didn't check. I just assumed."

He resumed his original smiling expression. "I recall you've always done a lot of assuming. We used to say that you'd die by committing 'assumicide.' Why, I remember the time when we were juniors when you—"

I interrupted, "George, I'm not really interested in walking down memory lane with you. It's lonely there."

He looked uncomfortable. "Now that we're middle-aged…" he blanched at my stare, "Now that we're adults, don't you think it might be a good idea to get rid of that stiff-necked pride long enough to let me explain what happened on prom night?"

I lifted my empty bottle toward the bartender and ordered a second beer. Feeling magnanimous, I ordered one for George too. "Okay, explain away." I still wasn't going to forgive him. After all, I was the one who had been left all dressed up with no place to go. My friends had been solicitous, but that didn't relieve the pain of being left with my pink organza formal, bunny fur, and high hopes.

He looked me in the eye and without blinking he began. "I was excited about prom too. Don't talk." He lifted a hand in a stop signal. "Don't talk, Sam."

He stopped me in mid-breath. He knew me well, this old beau of mine.

"I know it's hard for you to sit and listen. Your specialty

is interrupting me and putting words in my mouth." I opened my mouth but couldn't get a word out. "Don't talk."

Shutting up was hard for me. "Don't say 'don't talk' again or I'll explode. I promise I'll be quiet unless you order me to. If you give me a royal command to shut up, then I'm gonna talk. Deal?"

He smiled in spite of himself. "Deal. Now may I get on with my explanation?"

I nodded. And didn't talk.

"Okay. I was excited about the prom too. It's hard for a guy to admit that at any age, but it was especially hard when I was seventeen. But prom was a big deal. Renting that tux, borrowing my dad's car, looking forward to some real making out at the all-night party."

I couldn't help myself. "You wouldn't have gotten to second base."

"I didn't care. Rounding first was enough for me." He grinned again and made me forget that I hated the ground he walked on.

He continued. "I was all set to walk out the door when the phone rang. It was my best friend, Cal. His car was stuck in the mud out on Columbus Road and he wanted me to pick him up. Remember that he lived way out in the country?"

"And...?" I arched my eyebrows. This had better be good.

"And he was my best friend and I was a little early, so I drove out there and found him. He was about twelve miles out of town. Now there are lots of houses out that way, but back then there was nothing, no lights, no houses, no phones, no nothing."

Nothing is what I said.

"His car didn't look like it was stuck too badly, so instead of just giving him a ride into town, we decided to try to push the car out of the mud. And don't roll your eyes at me, Sam Darling. We were kids. Maybe we didn't think it through very well, but it seemed like the right thing to do at the time."

I raised my hand. "May I speak, sir?"

"Skip the sarcasm. It doesn't become you. It might have been cute when you were a teenager. But, now…" He took my beer bottle that I'd been squeezing the life out of and took the last swig.

"Okay," I said, "this isn't about me, it's about you. So cut to the chase. You and Cal decided to push his car out and you probably fell and got all muddy. You are going to use that as a pathetic excuse for not picking me up for prom. Puh-leeze." The waiter delivered the beers just in time. I grabbed mine and took a big gulp.

"Do you want to hear the truth, or do you want to continue making the story fit your misguided notions of what happened? We can play it either way."

183

I stared at the ceiling. I stared at the floor. I stared at the condensation on my bottle of beer. Anywhere but at George. Just before I was going to break under the pressure, he spoke again.

"Okay, you were right. Don't speak. Yes, you were right. I fell in the mud and got my tux completely ruined. I was embarrassed beyond belief and didn't know how to deal with that."

"So you decided to wait twenty-five years to tell me this?"

"That night I was embarrassed and scared and I didn't know how to tell you. I felt so stupid and didn't have enough self-confidence to admit what I'd done. I swore Cal to secrecy. It was too late to rent another tux and I didn't even own a suit. The next day I called and your mom said you 'weren't accepting phone calls from anyone named George Lansing.' I called you every day for two weeks and you wouldn't talk to me. I came to your house, I wrote you letters, and finally, I admitted to myself that it was over. You were so angry that you wouldn't let me explain. Remember that I was a kid too. I made stupid choices, Sam, but so did you. You chose to stay mad all these years, when it could have been over the day after prom."

For a moment, I noticed the sweet guy I had known. I almost felt some sympathy for him, but I quashed it as it was developing in my heart. "Okay, now you told me. Are you happy?"

"Of course I'm not happy about it. You and I had a great time together all through school. That ended the night of prom. I've missed you as a friend. Now that you're back in town, maybe we can rekindle our friendship."

I wasn't going to be that easy, although I wasn't completely against his suggestion. "We'll see. Listen, I really want to talk about the crime. That's the only reason we got together tonight. So tell me what you know."

"You are such an incurable romantic." He tore off a piece of Italian bread and began picking it apart absentmindedly.

Yeah, yeah, funny, funny. "Tell me what you know."

"In a minute." He had a strange look on his face. I wished I could read his feeble male mind. "I'd like you to go first. This is an official police investigation and I can't tell you everything. I'll be glad to share what I can, but you go first."

Was this a trick, designed to find out what I knew without giving away anything? I had a few minutes to think as our food arrived. My favorite meal again, pasta primavera and a house salad. I changed to white wine with the meal, although another beer would have tasted good too. George drove me to drink and that was a fact.

"Okay, I'll tell you what I know, but you gotta promise that you'll tell me some stuff too. Promise?"

Mouth bulging with food, he nodded. I took that to mean he agreed, but with George you never knew.

"Here's the scoop. I already told you that Carolyn killed her husband. Well, you know today I found Carolyn Burns snooping through confidential files in her husband's office. She said she was looking for some insurance papers, but that file cabinet only contains patient folders. You came in and took her downtown, so I hope she told you the truth about what she was doing." I waited expectantly, but he was mum. Not being real comfortable with silence, I continued.

"What you don't know is that a little later I was talking to Gwen Schneider and her brother in my office. I had a feeling something was going on again and for some reason Gwen kept looking at the door, as if she knew something was happening on the other side. The upshot is that I opened the door to Burns' office, knocked Carolyn on her butt, and while I was laughing my head off, Carolyn, Charlie and Gwen left the scene."

He was surprised but not shocked. "Together?"

I nodded. "She came back to the clinic after you let her go from the station. She was snooping through the files again, I bet." I punctuated my accusations with my fork beating against the plate.

"Did you see her snooping again?"

"No, but I bet she was. Why else would she be there?"

"Did you ever think that she might be getting some of her husband's things from his office? Doesn't that make more sense than assuming she was snooping?" He scooped

WHO KILLED MY BOSS?

another mouthful of pasta onto his fork.

"Remember I told you that during my initial interview Burns got a phone call. I don't know who he was talking to, but he got really angry and said something about having something for the person next week. He also said 'Leave me alone or you'll be sorry.' Maybe he was talking to Carolyn."

George took a drink of beer before responding. "Maybe he was talking to Fred Flintstone."

I didn't get caught up in his sarcasm. "George, she did it. That's all there is to it. She did it and you won't believe me."

That stupid condescending look again. God, he made me mad. Just when I was almost ready to begin the long forgiveness process.

"And she left with Gwen Schneider." No reaction. "The widow left my office with the mistress."

God, what was going to make a dent in that Herman Munster countenance of his?

I tried again. "Okay, listen. I get so violently dizzy around her that I sometimes pass out. Really. And you know I'm not a wimp, I'm not the fainting type. These feelings of mine are real. I guess I've never been around a murderer before, so this reaction is a lot more powerful than my usual ones."

"If that's the case, I understand you've been dizzy around O'Dear, too. So, if that's one of the criteria for being a murderer, it looks like he fits the bill also."

"Oh, don't be stupid." I dismissed his notion with a wave of a piece of bread. "Just arrest Carolyn and get it over with. Once you have her in your clutches, I know she'll tell you who her accomplice is. And it's not Michael O'Dear." I wouldn't admit to him that the same thought had been bugging me. Why was I off-balance around Michael so much of the time? It didn't make any sense to me. Just because he was the first guy I'd really fallen for since my divorce, that was no reason for me to be sick. Or was it? I was confused.

"I can't arrest someone on your hunches. Stay out of it. Let me do my work. If Carolyn Burns did it, then we'll find some evidence and arrest her. If she didn't do it, we'll find who did. You'll only get in the way. So please stop. Now, let's enjoy our meal and conversation."

Nice try. Thought he could pat me on the head and I'd shut up like a good little girl.

"Nope, your turn. You tell me what I want to know. This stuff is driving me up the wall. I know she did it, but I don't know how to prove it. Now you hold up your end of the deal. Spill it."

"Well, there's a few things I can tell you. Things that are pretty well known around here."

God, could he drag it out any more? "C'mon, tell me."

"Okay, but remember I'm only telling you this because

it's common knowledge." He wiped up the final dregs of marinara sauce with bread.

Yawn. "Yeah, yeah, I know."

"Carolyn was not Burns' first wife." George took a second to lick his fingers clean and utter a contented sigh. "And Gwen was not Burns' first mistress. In fact, Carolyn was his first mistress when he was married to his first wife." A self-satisfied grin covered his face.

I needed a score card to keep up with this. "Burns apparently had an eye for the ladies. Who was his first wife? And where is she?"

"Her name is Claudia Wolfe Burns and oddly enough, she recently moved back to Quincy."

I know my eyes must have lit up. This woman was Carolyn's accomplice. It all fit. I just needed to meet her and to see how she "felt."

It all made sense now. Claudia was mad at Burns because of Carolyn. Carolyn was mad because of Gwen. And Gwen was probably mad because of the new one, whoever she was.

Claudia Wolfe Burns. That name sounded so familiar. I smacked myself on the head as it suddenly dawned on me that it was the name of the villain in *Bipolar Passion*, one of Carolyn's better books. Something didn't feel right about the scenario, but it did make sense. I needed to get more dirt from George.

George chuckled before I could ask him anything. "Why

did you hit yourself in the head?"

I ignored his question and got to one of my own. "So, why was Gwen released? Tell me the truth. Was it really because you heard her partial confession by eavesdropping, but you couldn't catch all of it?" Now it was my turn to chuckle. I could barely suppress my laughter, remembering how I'd caught him leaning against my office door.

"That's not important," he wiggled out of it. "But I do have some other stuff I can tell you."

"I'll be good, I promise."

He smiled again. "Apparently, some patients were going to sue Burns…"

I interrupted, "I know that. Michael told me."

"Yeah, but do you know why?"

"Maybe because files were lost or misplaced?"

I was just guessing, but it did make sense. It seemed unusual that Dr. Burns had a complete set of patient files in his office.

"Nope. This is pretty hush-hush so I don't know why I'm telling you…"

"Maybe you're captivated by my beauty," I joked.

He got serious. "Something like that."

For a moment he had an almost dreamy look in his eye but quickly shook it away. "Anyway a few patients thought that the descriptions in Felicia Greene's books struck pretty close to home. Some said they recognized themselves as characters."

"Wow, that makes sense. I saw Carolyn at the file cabinet. Did she steal the records?"

"Nothing was proven, and as of now people have withdrawn their suits since Burns' death. I'm going to be talking to them within the next few days though."

I couldn't hold myself back. Putting both my hands on his across the table, I said, "Please, please, please, let me go with you."

He merely shook his head. And didn't remove my hands.

"Okay, I understand you can't do that, but will you please tell me what they say? Please." I knew I was bordering on begging and that it was unattractive, but I was desperate.

"You know I can't promise to tell you anything else. Put the case aside and let's just relax and enjoy the rest of our evening." He adroitly changed the subject as I removed my hands. "Hey, I saw Cal the other day. He heard you were back in town and said to tell you hi."

Cal. Calvin Joseph Wade. B.H.'s partner in crime. His sidekick. His best friend in high school. Which meant he was our constant partner in double dating. And since he had the personality of a lizard and couldn't get up the nerve to ask anyone out, I always had to fix him up with my friends. After one date, they were no longer my friends.

"Ah, Cal. How is he?" Hopefully, George could tell that I really didn't want to know the answer to that question.

He didn't take the hint so we talked about how Cal was

doing, and that led us into talking about old times again.

For a while I quit obsessing on the murder and enjoyed myself in spite of myself, surprising myself.

SIXTEEN

Clancy and I had just settled in for a good round of gossip when there was a loud knocking on the door. Again, I made the mistake of not looking before I opened it. I almost wished it had been the murderer.

In front of me was Georgianne, practically foaming at the mouth. She careened through the door before I had a chance to shut it in her face.

I forced myself to be cordial. After all, the house was in her name and I didn't want to be evicted.

She was not in the mood for friendly banter. "I am tired of people looking in your window all the time when you are gone. You promised me that there would be no further loitering and—."

"Lollygagging."

"Hmm?"

"I promised there would be no lollygagging. I don't think that loitering was ever mentioned."

She started pacing. "Don't you play games with me, young lady. There was a woman looking in your windows, and then another woman, then a man, and then another woman. Tell them to stop it. I cannot tolerate all of this stress. Having to look outside every time I hear a noise, it's hard on my nerves."

"How can I tell them to stop when I don't know who they are? Who are they, Georgianne?"

"I don't know, but make them stop. Your dog barks and I want to calm her down. She's a bit nicer than I thought." At that she stopped pacing and stooped to pet Clancy. "Gus says I can't just use our key anytime I think it's needed. But I told him I thought you'd want me to. So I came out to check on this darling dog and… By the way, don't you think 'Clancy' sounds rather common? She really looks more like a 'Fluffy' or a 'Princess' or perhaps…"

"Georgianne."

"Yes?" She didn't even have the good sense to look a little embarrassed.

"Focus. Tell me about the people who were looking into my house."

"Well, I didn't see them clearly because I don't like to pry. However, the first woman didn't look familiar to me at all. The second one looked remarkably like Carolyn Burns, although what she'd be doing here, I wouldn't even try to guess. Perhaps she's a bit miffed that you are spreading rumors about her being the murderer."

"Back on track, Georgianne. Who was the guy?"

"I'm sure I don't know, although he did look a bit like the one who was here the other night. Remember before the gas leak? And, Sam, Gus and I are so sorry about that leak. We were so sure everything was in tip-top shape back there. We feel just awful about your troubles."

"Awful enough to pay for my hospital bill? My insurance won't kick in for a month." I knew there was a chance it wasn't Gus and Georgianne's fault, that the murderer may have done it, but I couldn't help myself. Georgianne appears and I must say or do something to get her goat.

"Well, I'm sure something can be… now weren't we talking about those prowlers? Let's see the final one wasn't someone I'd seen often. But I think she was that Schneider woman."

Oh-oh, Georgianne looked like she was going to sit down and settle in. I had to stop her at all costs.

"Thanks for the information and I really appreciate your diligence in watching my place. Clancy, kiss Georgianne good-night."

What fun this was. I suppose I should've felt bad about the look of utter distaste and shock that covered Georgianne's face. But, nope, I reveled in it.

I didn't enjoy it however when Clancy kissed her and Georgianne absolutely swooned. I'd have to talk to Gus about what he was doing, or not doing, in the kissing department.

Georgianne got positively goo-goo-eyed over my dog. And it looked like my best friend was returning the favor. They were just lucky that I was too busy worrying about the prowlers and murderers to spend much time worrying about them. Clancy would hear about this treasonous behavior later.

I ushered Georgianne out of the door while listening to her "dear little doggie-woggie." I thought I was going to be sick. But this time I would know the cause.

I closed the door and locked it. "Clancy, I'll talk to you later about your unconscionable behavior. You ought to be ashamed. Right now I've got some important stuff to think about, so go to your room and I mean it."

Clancy went to her room and collapsed on our bed. Even though I couldn't see her, I knew exactly what she was doing. The dog version of "Camille." Dramatic. I'd make up with her later. She needed to feel the sting of my lack of affection for a while.

The parade that passed by my house this evening sounded like an interesting one. Who was the first woman? She must have been disguised or new in town for Georgianne not to identify her. Then Carolyn, Charlie, and Gwen. What a motley crew. I'd call Gwen tomorrow and find out why she was at my house. Carolyn's motive was easy to figure out. She was probably trying to decide how to kill me.

Okay, maybe I'm dramatic too. Anyway, Carolyn was up to no good. Of that I was very, very sure.

After I turned the lights off I noticed the insistent blinking of the red dot on the answering machine. I'd forgotten to check my messages. The first one was indeed B.H. saying that he would be late for dinner. So he hadn't lied after all, what a surprise. There was also one from Jen reminding me of her children's birthday party tomorrow evening. Both her kids were born on the same day, one year apart. It made planning parties quite easy for her.

I slept the sleep of the innocent and woke early enough for a wonderfully long walk. Clancy took this as a sign of amnesty and things were pretty well back to normal with the two of us. I did let her know how I felt about her attention to Georgianne.

"I don't know how you could be so loose with your affection. Remember that you pee on her plants because we don't like her. And you notice that it's *we* don't like her, not *I* don't like her." Then I resorted to a low blow. "Remember who feeds you."

Clancy glanced back at me from her vantage point at the end of the leash. She looked suitably contrite. I had no doubts, however, that she would lavish her fickle affection on Georgianne at the earliest available opportunity. Anything for a belly rub.

At home I toasted a bagel, gave a piece to Clancy and put

peanut butter on my portion. As I chomped I looked around for something to wear to work. Vowing to give in and do some clothes shopping, I dragged out an old pair of khakis, prayed they'd still fit, and sucked in my gut as I struggled with the zipper. I paired the slacks with a big color-blocked sweater. It covered my hips and would be handy in case I split the seam on the pants.

Today was a great day to walk to work. I still didn't have my own car and also didn't have anything to carry to work except my purse. Clancy didn't whine when I said goodbye and I enjoyed the quick walk to the clinic. I wore sunglasses because the glare off the snow from the bright sun was blinding. No complaints though. The sight was mesmerizing.

Clara Schmitt was at her desk when I arrived. She handed a file to me. I actually had a second patient. I took a few minutes to read about Andy Duesterhaus, a thirteen-year-old boy who was described as sullen, moody, and non-communicative. Sounded like my kids when they were thirteen. He'd been referred by the school counselor and so far hadn't been seen by a mental health professional. I planned to do a diagnostic interview and formulate the diagnosis and treatment plan from there.

I had enough time to fill my coffee cup and take one sip when Clara announced that Andy was in the waiting room. Without being seen, I was able to peek around the corner to get a look at him. Andy appeared to be a normal, red-blooded American boy. He oozed contempt for grown-ups, had pierced ears, and his clothes looked like he had picked them out of a rag bin. I welcomed him, walked with him to my office, and offered him a seat. He didn't make eye contact but he sat.

"What brings you here today?"

The usual response from adolescents was something like, "My parents are raggin' on me. They think there's something wrong." Or, "Nothin'." Or even, "My parents made me come."

Andy's response was silence.

I tried a few more opening gambits. And got nothing from him. Not too unusual. The only noticeably odd thing about Andy was that he was clutching a laptop computer.

After talking for a few minutes with no response from the peanut gallery, I turned on the PC on my desk and began fiddling with it. He still didn't speak, but shortly the hairs on the back of my neck stood up because he was breathing on me.

"Way cool." Ah, he spoke.

"Pardon me?"

"Way cool. You're up to level four of *The Thundering Horde*. I've never seen an adult get past level two." I could feel his hands and arms moving behind me.

"I like computers and I like to play games." Not looking

at him yet. Still playing the game. "What level you at?"

"I finished level ten, so I'm done."

"Cool. What else do you like to do?" Still playing my game.

"Playing *Sandblaster* is pretty fun and I kinda like that new game, *Aliens from the Deep*."

"I've never played those. Are they on your computer?" When he nodded, I asked, "Will you teach me how to play?"

I assumed his grunt meant "yes," so I continued. "Do you have those on your laptop or on a PC at home?"

He replied they were on both computers, then said, "Do you want me to show you now?"

Now it was my turn to nod.

He placed the laptop on my desk and turned it on.

I was a willing pupil. Andy was right, these games were fun, but a bit gory.

The "ding" signifying the end of the hour came all too soon, and I didn't feel a bit guilty about earning money for playing games. This was a good start to building a therapeutic relationship with Andy. Maybe next week, he'd even say hello before the computer got turned on.

I had no idea what was going on with him, but at least we were communicating. That was a start.

As I said goodbye to Andy in the lobby, my mind turned to my other task at hand. I needed proof that Carolyn killed her husband and also needed to find her accomplice. This

Claudia Wolfe Burns appeared a likely candidate, but I couldn't imagine her—or anyone for that matter—teaming up with the snooty Carolyn Burns. Carolyn was not the type to have intimate female friends. She was too catty and was also the consummate flirt with men.

I also planned to figure out how the killer got out of the room without dragging blood along.

Before I left for the day I checked with Mrs. Schmitt regarding my schedule. I had three patients scheduled for tomorrow and three more for Friday. Things were looking up.

As I was getting my coat and locking my desk, I suddenly felt like going to Burns' office one more time. I left my things on my loveseat. The tape had been taken off Burns' office door and the police were finished with the room, but I still entered through the kitchen door. It was like my private entrance to the crime scene.

The room looked much the same. Someone had cleaned off the fingerprint powder and the rug had been shampooed. Nothing was going to remove the blood though. I'd seen enough blood in my life, being from a large, rowdy family. The stain was now a dull rust color and formed a circular pattern around a lot of the room, with random splatters branching out. My bet was that the rug would be discarded in a few days.

I wondered who would make that decision. Heck, I

didn't even know who my boss was yet. It was surprising how well the mental health portion of the clinic functioned without a doctor there.

The file cabinet beckoned me. I really didn't want to snoop, but it seemed a shame to pass up the opportunity to look in the drawer Carolyn had pilfered. Of course, I didn't have proof that she took anything, I just didn't buy her statement that she was looking for insurance papers.

This particular cabinet held patient files. Dr. Burns had copies of all the folders, even when others were the primary therapists. At first glance, everything appeared to be in order. Then I noticed Mrs. Abernathy's file was placed after a Jenny Agnew, when it should have been in front of it. There were several others out of place as well, as if they'd been filed haphazardly. I didn't know what to make of this, but filed the information in my brain—in the right order—for later retrieval.

Now seemed like a good time to read a few files. I'd already read Mrs. Abernathy's and even made a few notations myself in the clinic file near Clara Schmitt's desk. I noticed my new notes weren't copied into this file yet. I decided to look at other misfiled records. The first one after Mrs. Abernathy was Alonzo Baron. Then Clare Chaplin and Katrina Ditmeyer. I plucked them from the drawer and took them into my office.

No glaring errors or omissions popped out at me as I

read. But some items in the patient histories seemed eerily familiar. I struggled with an ethical dilemma. It was wrong to take patient files out of the office or to make copies without the client's permission. However I really wanted to compare some of this information with Carolyn's books. If I could prove she used patient files as fodder for her books that would be one step closer to proving she was her husband's murderer.

I thought that I could scan a file and then email it to myself at home. Yet I didn't see that as being any better than making copies. Finally I compromised—I'd make copies of pertinent sections and then swore to myself I'd destroy them as soon as possible. The only other option was to bring Carolyn's novels into work with me and that would seem suspicious.

The copy machine jammed a few times. Of course. But I hurried and completed my task as quickly as I could. It was one thing being nosey, but it was quite another copying files illicitly.

As I returned the files to Burns' office, the matter of the blood spatters caught my attention again. How could someone have killed him and not be covered with blood? I remembered that the window had been open—an obvious entrance and exit, but that still didn't answer the blood question. There probably wasn't a clue to be found since the cops had gone over the room pretty thoroughly. I sat on the floor, right where Burns had fallen, and looked around. A picture of Gwen crouched in a fetal position behind the door flashed in my mind. Was it possible she'd been there the whole time? Nah, she didn't have any blood on her and besides, she wasn't guilty.

Time passed quickly as I lost myself in thoughts, but no solutions poked their heads through my reverie. It was already dark when I rejoined the present. I ran to my office and gathered my things, and practically ran home, hard to do in the dark and snow.

When I finally got home, Clancy got a hurried walk. I knew she was thinking that Georgianne was looking more and more attractive. "Clancy, this isn't a long enough walk, you're right, but I'm late for Rosie's and Annie's birthday party."

At that she stopped her baleful looks. Clancy loved my nieces and nephews, but I couldn't take her with me tonight since Jen's house would be full of people.

I arrived at Jen and Manh's house just as folks were sitting down to dinner.

"Aunt Sam."

"Aunt Sam, look over here."

"Aunt Sam."

"Come here, Aunt Sam. I want to show you something."

"Sit by me, Aunt Sam.

"Wahhhhh! I want Aunt Sam."

Murder, schmurder. *This* is what I really loved.

SEVENTEEN

One family tradition was for everyone to gather for all of the children's birthdays. Today Rosie and Annie were both celebrating. Rosie's real name was Hong, which translates to Rose in English, and Annie's Vietnamese name was Anh, which easily became Annie. They were on the threshold of teendom, but were still recognizable as human beings.

Since Rosie, at twelve, was the elder, she opened her presents first. Mine was no surprise. Money. It takes no thought or planning on my part, but it is also highly prized by the older kids. They especially like the note on the card.

"Oh, Aunt Sam. You didn't forget. 'Happy Birthday, Rosie. This is not underwear money. Have fun. Love, Aunt Sam.'"

Annie echoed her sister's emotions when it was her turn for presents. The kids all loved having so many cousins and aunts and uncles. That translated into lots of money and presents on the appropriate occasions.

I enjoyed being with my family. The noise and chaos

spelled "home" to me. My mind kept drifting to the murder, however. I made sure I had some private time with Pete to let him know what I was up to.

Pete believed me when I said Carolyn was the culprit. He didn't question my gut feelings and he didn't make fun of my certainty. He did, however, make me promise to be careful and not to stick my nose in where it didn't belong. That wasn't a hard promise to make, since I was sure that my nose belonged right in the middle of this murder investigation.

The noise level increased as the kids got out different outfits to put on a dramatic performance. They'd been rehearsing for weeks. Annie put on her father's lab coat and glasses and Rosie pranced around in a discarded choir robe. Marty, one of Jill's sons, was adorable in a disposable surgical gown, mask, glasses, head covering, booties, and gloves. There was nothing of him showing, but I could imagine a contagious grin hidden under the mask. They were discussing ("we're not arguing, Aunt Sam") some of the intricacies of the performance, so I took the opportunity to get some work done.

I caught my sister's eye across the room. "Jen, I'm gonna use the phone. Can I go into your bedroom where it's quiet?"

I thought she said yes, but it was hard to tell above the din. Anyway, her head bobbed a bit, so I took that as an affirmative.

My next task regarding the murder was to contact Claudia Wolfe Burns. I didn't know what kind of scam to use to get her to talk to me so I decided to try an unusual tactic, I'd tell her the truth.

I got the number from Information—for a fee—and she picked up on the second ring. "Hello."

"Hello, Mrs. Burns, this is Sam Darling."

"Good evening. What can I do for you?" Her voice sounded friendlier than Carolyn's.

"I'm employed at the clinic, Mrs. Burns, and—."

She interrupted with, "Please call me 'Claudia.'"

"Thank you, Claudia. I'd like to talk to you about your ex-husband's murder. When would it be convenient to meet?" I decided to give her no choice on whether we met or not, only when.

"I suppose I should be honest. I want to talk to you too. Would it be possible for you to visit my home this evening?"

Okay, I would have told the truth if I'd had a chance. Gee, this was going to be a cinch. I didn't really know exactly what I was going to talk to her about, but I still thought she might be Carolyn's accomplice. How would I bring that into a casual conversation?

It took about twenty minutes to enjoy the show and twenty more to say goodbye to the whole clan.

Driving from Jenny's to Claudia's only took another ten minutes, but that was enough time for me to decide what I was going to do. I was going to tell Claudia my opinion of Carolyn's involvement in the murder. Then I was going to watch her face to see if she was surprised. If she stayed cool, then I might start talking accomplice theories. Otherwise I'd stay quiet about it. I'd play it by ear.

Also, I was going to monitor my sense of well-being. If I got dizzy, I'd know she was in on the murder.

She answered the door with a warm smile. It lit up her surprisingly unlined face. The smile was framed by dark hair with hints of silver. "Welcome." She motioned for me to take off my coat. "I hope it's all right for me to call you 'Sam.' May I get you some coffee or a cold drink?"

I declined. There was so much food in me from the party that I felt I could burst. But I didn't feel sick. Didn't feel much of anything. Maybe my vibes were taking a vacation or maybe the food had calmed them. Could she be the accomplice?

I followed her into a pleasantly furnished condo. Brand new. Paint smell still evident. I sat in an overstuffed chair while Claudia settled on the couch, pulling her legs under her as she nestled against some large pillows.

Deciding to cut to the chase, I said, "Why did you want to see me?"

She smiled. "You certainly don't mess around, do you?" Her smile faltered. "You said you wanted to see me first. What about?"

Suddenly it hit me. "Were you at my home last night?"

"Yes, I thought we could help each other."

Aha. The first prowler.

She continued. "I understand you think you know who killed Martin."

She was the only person who called Burns by his first name. "I'm quite positive I know one of the killers."

Eyebrows arched, she asked, "You think there's more than one?"

"Yes, I do. The killer I have in mind is not the type to slice Dr. Burns the way he was sliced. It was too messy for her to have done the actual deed."

"So you suspect Carolyn."

This was getting interesting. "Yes, what about you?"

"I think there's much more to Carolyn Burns than meets the eye. You might think that I'm just angry at being made a villain in one of her books, but that's not it. Or at least that's not all of it. Martin suspected that Carolyn was involved in some pilfering at the office. Not just recently either, mind you, but for the last several years."

"Pilfering what?"

She hesitated for a moment. "Some of Martin's staff reported patient case records were misfiled. And a few times there were some records missing. They were found later, though—in the file cabinet. It perplexed him."

Some new information, "I knew about the misfiling, but

I didn't know records were missing. What did Dr. Burns think happened?"

"He was sure Carolyn used the files."

I pounced, "For what?" I needed corroboration for my theories.

"Carolyn used patient files to get ideas for her books."

"That's what I suspected too," I confided. "But why didn't Dr. Burns tell the police? It's definitely illegal to use that information."

"I don't know why." Her mouth drew down in a frown, pinching her brow together, forming a downward arrow on her forehead. It appeared she had a suspicion.

I decided to bypass grilling her on that matter, but would come back to it later.

"What's your interest in this? What do you have to gain if the killer gets found, whether or not it's Carolyn? You and Dr. Burns have been divorced for years."

She stood, walked around the coffee table, and sat on an ottoman at my feet. "I don't know you, but I need to talk to someone about this." I put on my most sympathetic face, dying to hear the scoop. She continued, "Have you heard that Martin had a girlfriend?"

"Yes, Gwen Schneider. Although she said they broke up and he was seeing someone else." The light bulb went on. "Was that you? Were you his new girlfriend?"

She looked unbearably sad and began crying. "Yes, when

I moved back to Quincy we went to lunch to discuss some financial matters. One thing led to another and we realized we still had feelings for one another. I loved him. And I want to see whoever killed him get punished."

Did I believe her? Or was she trying to snow me? I wasn't getting any negative vibes from her. In fact no vibes at all. But there seemed to be congruency in what she said and the way she said it. I decided to take her at face value and trust that what she said was true. It seemed she had two major reasons not to murder Burns. One, she loved him and two, she probably received hefty alimony checks from him. If they just began seeing each other fairly recently, he probably didn't make provisions for her in his will. The will. That was something I needed to check out. I'd just bet that Carolyn was provided for handsomely in Burns' will.

Okay, back to Claudia. "Tell me more about Carolyn's using patient files. What made Dr. Burns suspect her?"

"He recognized some of his patients in the books."

"I was under the impression he didn't read her books. That he didn't quite approve."

She looked away. "Martin wasn't entirely supportive of Carolyn's career choice. That's why she used a pseudonym. For a long time he didn't even know she was published. He thought writing was a hobby and that's all. I don't know if he read the books. I just assumed he did because he told me he recognized some patients."

"Tell me more. Why would Carolyn continue taking files once she became good at writing?"

"She was making money with them. Big money." Claudia sat up straight and leaned forward as she looked me in the eyes. "Why should she have to be creative when it was all there, already invented? Every single book of hers had some of Martin's patients in it. She used them as protagonists, as villains, as bystanders. Remember *Bipolar Passion*, the one in which she villainized me? The whole book was based upon one of Martin's patients; he wouldn't tell me the patient's name because of confidentiality. But I bet you could find out. The same with *Anxieties Unlimited* and *Psychotic Mama*. She stole files, copied them, and used them for her books. Martin told me he confronted her and they had a horrible argument."

I wanted clarification. "When was the argument?"

The brow furrow appeared again. "I think it was the day before he died."

"During my interview, Dr. Burns received a phone call from someone. He said something like, 'Don't threaten me, I'll get it to you.' I wonder if that was Carolyn he was talking to."

"It could have been. Although I don't know anything about that phone call. I understand he was killed shortly after hiring you."

It all made sense. It all fit. Carolyn knew that Burns was

going to expose her for the fraud that she was. With Burns dead, her source would dry up, but her royalties would not. At last I had a motive. Now, who was her accomplice?

She cleared her throat, and my thoughts returned to the present. "I said he was killed shortly after hiring you. That's right, isn't it?"

"Sorry, Claudia. I need to think a minute."

I really needed to address Michael. There was a good chance he could have helped Carolyn. But what was his motive? Love? Greed? Carolyn's hefty insurance payment was probably large enough for a 50-50 split to be satisfying.

Of course, I felt silly. I'd fallen for him and I didn't really know him. It was probably just a physical attraction on my part, but he'd also proven to be sweet and kind to me as well. He wasn't very amorous, but I suspected that was because he respected me or because I passed out on him, not because he was a slitter of throats. Well, I'd just have to talk to him and lay it on the line. Perhaps I could delay it a bit, however, until I'd nailed Carolyn.

Now that I knew her motive it was time to spring the trap. But how? They didn't teach us this in graduate school. I'd always been busy learning how to help people. Learning how to trap someone was a whole new ball game.

"Sam." Claudia interrupted my plotting. Her grief was evident. She must have really loved Martin Burns. "I don't know what to do with this information. I think I should tell the police, but I'm afraid I'll get in trouble because I didn't tell them earlier."

Synapses were firing all over the place in my cranium. "I understand your fear. Why don't you let me broach the subject with Detective Lansing? I'm a close friend of his, and I think I can keep you out of it. Okay?"

She was pathetically grateful. "Thank you. Thank you so much. Do you know that Martin talked to me about you?" My surprise must have shown. "Yes, he did. He called me right after hiring you. He thought you would be a fine addition to the staff. That was the last time I spoke to him. And it seems he was killed almost immediately after we said good-bye." Tears again.

I didn't know how I felt about an unpopular guy liking me, but I guessed it was better than the alternative.

Promising to stay in touch, I drove away, well below the speed limit for a change, and tried to sort all this out. Even though Carolyn's motive for murder was clear, I still believed she didn't commit the murder alone. She wouldn't want to get dirty and she also didn't appear to have a background in nursing or medicine. Maybe she knew how to slice a vein from writing her books, but I doubted it.

For the time being I decided to take Claudia at her word, that she was at home when Burns bit the dust. I had no reason to believe her, except that I experienced no twitches, pings, itches, or vertigo around her. I wondered if George knew that Claudia was Burns' new girlfriend. I hoped I was the one who would be able to tell him. Surprising him would be a treat.

Clancy was waiting for me. Even though it was getting late, I took her for a nice long walk, trying to put Burns and his murder out of my mind for the time being. I had jumped headfirst into this murder investigation. No looking before leaping for this gal.

The cold air cleared my head. "Clancy, you won't believe how cute the kids were tonight. You should have seen them all dressed up in their parents' clothes."

The idea hit me so hard I jerked to a stop. Therefore so did Clancy. "Omigod. They used disposable surgical clothing." I described how nothing of Marty showed when he was dressed in scrubs and accessories. I started walking again at a frenetic pace as I put the pieces together. "Those scrubs and glasses and booties are stored in the closet right outside Burns' office. No one keeps rigorous track of how many are used. No one would have noticed."

I slowed down as my lungs started to burn. "So they came in the window, and maybe hid somewhere, put on the scrubs and killed him. They could have put the scrubs in a trash bag and left the same way. If they looked anything like Marty there wouldn't have been any blood on them at all." I wanted to yell "Eureka" I was so proud of my discovery.

Then I thought about some of the other details. "Do you

think George could be right? I mean about the gas leak and the car wreck being accidents."

She looked at me and I got her point. "Well, maybe I was driving a bit too fast for conditions. Hell, okay I probably was."

She smiled. "Yeah, you're right. My own cousin was the mechanic and even he said the brakes were shot. No one messed with them. And the carriage house is old, and so are the gas lines. So no one is after me."

Clancy looked relieved that I finally "got it."

"So then why did I get myself mixed up in this?" She shook her head.

Perhaps my family was right. Maybe I was nosy. Maybe I was co-dependent. Maybe I didn't want anyone to have fun without me.

Clancy and I returned home and she went to bed. Something was stirring in my brain cells and I decided to dig into Carolyn's books. I'd piled them next to the bed. I was embarrassed that I owned them all, because I didn't want people to know I read her kind of literature. And I used that term loosely. Carolyn's books were light, frothy, sexy, and at the same time full of psychological pathos. She was a bestselling author, and I was drawn to her books, even though I looked down my nose at them. I didn't claim to be consistent.

After hurriedly looking through her novels, I found my

answer. I didn't even need the copied clinical notes I'd brought home from the office. I recognized Mrs. Abernathy in one of the books, thinly disguised as Mrs. Abercrombie, a lonely, bored, horny woman with erotic, neurotic dreams. Why hadn't I noticed this before? I turned to my canine co-sleuth, "I wish you could read. You could read the files while I checked the books."

More reading and cross-checking and the truth was evident. Anyone who had access to both the patient files and the books could see it.

I wanted to speak to Carolyn, but couldn't wait until tomorrow. Delayed gratification is not my cup of tea. "Clance, I gotta find out who helped Carolyn kill Burns. Do you have any ideas?" I was only half-kidding. If Clancy could talk, she'd probably tell me all the details of the murder, wrapped up in a bow.

It was too late to call anyone in my family for help. Most of them had little ones and they'd be in bed after the birthday party. The two unmarried ones, Rob and Pete, were both working late shifts again today.

Who could help me? I didn't want to ask Michael, as there was a possibility he was involved. That was a possibility I didn't want to consider, but it was there all the same. It was trying to stare me in the face, but I kept bobbing and weaving so it couldn't. I also didn't want to call George. This was something I wanted to do without official police involvement. Then, when I solved the case, George and my brothers would be more approving of my "meddlesome" behavior.

It was apparent to me that I could solve this and bring Carolyn to justice. I just needed an escort. Clancy could go with me, but she couldn't lend a hand if I needed one. She could lend a paw and a growl however, and that might come in handy. Who else could I ask? Suddenly the obvious answer appeared.

Gus. Gus could help me. Now all I had to do was to talk to him without Georgianne finding out. If I called, she would pick up the extension. It had happened before.

Maybe I'd just go over there and try to talk to Gus privately. It was late, but their lights were still on.

I approached their back door cautiously. "Gus." I whispered his name as I tapped on the door oh so lightly. My luck was not good.

"Sam, what are you doing out at this time of night?" Her curlers followed her voice and her scowl invaded the night.

"Georgianne, I'm sorry to bother you. Can I talk to Gus, please?"

"And your poor little doggy. She's had a busy day and should be getting her rest." Georgianne leaned down to pet Clancy, but this time Clancy was all business. She stood patiently and allowed the pat, but didn't roll over like the fickle companion she sometimes was.

I would not be sidetracked by Georgianne's attempts to win over my dog. "Can I talk to Gus, please?"

"He's not well." She stood up again; apparently convinced Clancy wasn't going to turn traitor. "Surely whatever it is can wait until tomorrow."

"This is important. Is Gus awake?"

Gus's booming voice cut through the gloom on the porch. "Sam, come on in, girl. What's up?"

As we entered the parlor, his wife looked at him with great concern. Even though I thought she was a real witch, it was obvious she loved her husband. She drove me crazy, but she loved one of my best friends. Guess I couldn't hate her as much as I wanted to. And now that she had a relationship with Clancy, it meant she loved two of my best friends.

Now it was time for me to test my courage. I looked Georgianne straight in the face and said, "Please let me talk to Gus alone. I promise it's important." She appeared to be softening. "Please, Georgianne. Please. It's important."

Without saying a word, she faded into the background. What luck.

Clancy and I waited patiently while she closed the parlor door and then turned to Gus, reclining on his usual sofa.

He sat at our approach. "What's up? What are you doing here at this time of night?" He patted the couch and both Clancy and I joined him.

"I really need your help. Remember how you told me that all this excitement is keeping you healthy and young?" He nodded. "Well, Gus, my friend, I've got something that'll probably make you feel like a teenager."

"I'm in. What are we going to do? Where we going?" There was no doubt why I loved this man.

"Okay, here it is. We're going to Carolyn's house. I want to see what's going on and maybe talk to her. I know why she killed her husband; now I just gotta figure out who helped her. You still willing to go?"

He grinned.

"And we're going to do it without the police."

My last sentence was lost on him, as he was halfway out of the door before I finished the question. I guess that meant "yes." We took my car.

EIGHTEEN

Clancy jumped in the back seat of the car, but managed to hang her head between Gus and me in the front. On the way to Carolyn's house, I filled in the blank spots for Gus. He already knew my suspicions about Carolyn, and he now knew the motive. I was getting nervous, and wanted a cigarette. I hadn't felt that way since the last time I'd had sex. It had been a while.

Gus didn't seem nervous, but his energy was at such a high level, I wanted to put him on a leash. I opened the window a crack to release a little of the heat. Soon, Clancy's head found the open window and behind my head I could hear her tongue flapping in the breeze.

When we arrived at Carolyn's house, I reminded Gus that all I really wanted to do was snoop around a little, and maybe talk to her. But that would depend on what we found out with our reconnaissance.

Carolyn's driveway held a car that looked vaguely familiar. I knew I'd seen it somewhere, but couldn't place it. I was relieved that it wasn't Michael's car.

As we would-be guerrillas stalked toward the house, I noticed a small figure peering furtively in the front window. This was interesting.

I turned to Gus and whispered, "I want to see who's looking in the window. I'm going to try to sneak up on her and see who it is. So just stay close by me. Close enough to help me, but far enough that you can get away if something happens to me. If she sees me, I'll just b.s. my way out of it. Keep Clancy with you." With a hand signal I motioned for Clancy to sit. I knew I sounded dramatic, but the situation didn't feel dangerous. "Don't worry, Gus. This feels real safe; just do what I asked, just in case I'm wrong. Okay?"

"Sure, but are you sure you don't want me to check this out? And you be the one who stays close by?"

I assured him that I knew what I was doing, surprising myself by my powers of persuasion. I almost convinced myself as well. Creeping forward, I felt like I was in a Grade B war movie. My adrenaline was pumping so drastically that my skin was on fire. It was almost like an energy field surrounded me. I heard Gus breathing close behind me. I trusted him. He would stick with me until the bitter end, but I sure hoped this end wouldn't be bitter.

Creeping closer to the prowler, I positioned myself directly behind her. "What are you doing?" It was difficult sounding commanding while whispering, but I think I pulled it off quite nicely.

The person whipped around—with a face that showed a state of fright that alarmed even me. "Charlie, what in the world are you doing here?" Finding scrawny Charlie Schneider peering in Carolyn's window surprised me.

"This lady in here is bad. I think she might hurt Gwen."

"Why do you think that she's going to hurt your sister?"

"Gwen's in there with her."

Oh, no. Gwen probably was here doing the same thing I was doing, trying to expose Carolyn and her accomplice. Why in the world would Gwen think she could handle this by herself? At least I had my trusty sidekicks, Gus and Clancy. And speaking of them, where were they?

No sooner had I thought the question than Gus bumped into me. I spoke quietly to him, "Do me a favor and take Charlie out to the car. Charlie, stay there and lock the door. Do not move. Will you do that?"

"I want to help Gwen."

I couldn't have Charlie trying to help. His behavior was unpredictable and I recalled the pistol brandishing of just a few nights ago. "Charlie, please go with Gus. Stay in the car and I promise I'll do what I can to keep Gwen safe. Clancy will stay with you."

Another thought came to me, "Charlie, do you have a weapon?"

He shook his head. "The cops took it at the hospital."

"Okay. Just stay in the car. I'll be right back."

223

Clancy did the predictable—tried to talk me out of being left behind, but I was able to convince her. "Please, I promise I won't have too much fun without you. Just stay with Charlie."

I assured Gus I'd wait for him to return.

Charlie and Clancy went with Gus, all three with feet dragging and heads hanging. I imagined it would take Gus a few minutes to settle Charlie down. It was hard waiting. I thought maybe I could just peek in a window while I was waiting for him to return.

I was even shorter than Charlie and couldn't see into the window. There was a wide ledge and I tried climbing up to peer inside. Perhaps I was a bit wider than Charlie was too, because I bumped against the window as I climbed into position. The "thud" was muffled, but it certainly echoed in my ears like a cannon. I convinced myself that no one heard it and proceeded to try to see something.

"Ms. Darling, perhaps you'd like to come inside to see what's happening in the house. It's much warmer and the view is better." Her voiced dripped with honeyed sarcasm. Even before I turned, I could picture Carolyn and imagined a gun in her hands.

I was wrong. She didn't have a weapon. In fact she looked weak and vulnerable. I knew better, but since I did want to go in her house, I took her up on her offer.

We walked inside. It was warm as she'd promised, but I

still shivered. Even though Charlie said Gwen was here, there was no sign of her. "So, what are you doing sneaking around my home?"

"It's no secret that I know you killed your husband. Today I found out why. You took files from your husband's office and you used those files as plots for your trashy novels." So much for my plan to be discreet.

"I wouldn't call them trashy." She smiled. She must be nuts.

"You took the files, used them as plots, your husband found out and you killed him."

"Prove it."

"I recognized patients in several of your books, *Schizoid Revenge, Bipolar Passion, Farewell My Anxious One*. I also heard Dr. Burns talking on the phone right before he was killed. He said he'd have it for you soon. My guess is you found out about him and his new girlfriend and said you wouldn't divorce him unless he allowed you continued access to the files." This was pure speculation. I was making it up as I went along, but it looked like I'd guessed right.

"You certainly think you are brilliant, don't you? But your theories are ludicrous. Why would I kill him if I needed access to his files?"

Stumped me there. "Because you did, that's why."

In walked Gus, my superhero. "You okay, Sam?"

"Yeah, I'm fine. We need to call the police. I told

Carolyn that I know everything now."

"Everything but who her accomplice is." The new voice entered the conversation with no warning. I spun around and saw—Gwen Schneider.

Gwen continued to stand there and grin. Her beautiful white teeth suddenly seemed predatory instead of just big and shiny.

My adrenaline no longer came from excitement, but rather from fear. I couldn't wait any longer. "Gus, hurry. Call George. Tell him that…"

As Gus dug for his phone, Gwen cut him off. "I wouldn't do that if I were you." The gun in her hand showed us she was serious, even though her dialogue was hackneyed.

"Gwen, what are you doing? You're innocent." My amazement was transparent. There was no way Gwen was holding a gun on my Gus.

Gwen and Carolyn looked at each other. They grinned and both grins morphed into almost maniacal laughs. Finally Gwen sauntered toward Carolyn and gave her a big kiss.

What? Had I fallen down the rabbit hole? Lewis Carroll said it right; this was getting curiouser and curiouser.

Carolyn sneered. "Close your mouth. It's most unattractive." I did.

Looking at Gus, I noticed that he didn't seem as surprised as I was. So Carolyn and Gwen were an item.

Where were my vibes? Right in the pit of my stomach. I started feeling dizzy and ill. Surprisingly enough I didn't feel scared. I'd probably pay for that later.

I'd never seen them together before, but now that I did; I noticed my body working up into a tizzy. Gee, why couldn't I throw up on them? That would certainly distract them long enough for Gus at least to make his exit.

Gwen continued to stand with one arm entwined around Carolyn while her other arm supported the gun pointing at Gus. "Move over by your old friend." She motioned for me to get close to Gus. It was hard to walk as I felt I couldn't control my legs. But I moved. Suddenly her weapon covered us both.

Gwen said, *sotto voce*, "Now all we have to do is figure out how to get rid of them."

"Whoa, Gwen, I heard that. You don't have to get rid of us. Tie us up here, and leave town. Leave the country. Leave the planet for all I care. Just leave and you won't have to do anything to hurt us."

Gwen sneered again. "This isn't the movies. You can't talk us into letting you go. This is real life and we want to stay here in Quincy." Her river rat accent reappeared. "You and Gus have got to be eliminated."

Okay, plan two. "How about letting Gus and me move out of town?"

"Shut up."

227

She was serious. All I could think about was that I needed to stall. As a crisis specialist I knew that the longer people go without using a weapon, the less likely they are to use it. I calmed enough to know it was time to chatter. "Hey you guys, I hate untidy endings, and you know I'm nosy. Before you kill us, will you just explain some things to me?"

Carolyn shook her head. "No, we are not going to explain anything to you. You're trying to stall and that's not going to work."

"Wait, honey," Gwen interrupted, "I'd love to fill the nosy little bitch in on our plans. It won't hurt anything and I'd like to let her know how wrong she's been all along. It's been such fun watching her foolish moves, trying to prove my innocence." Gwen motioned with her gun again. "Both of you sit on the love seat where I can watch you. And don't move a muscle."

It appeared to me that as long as we were sitting in Carolyn's living room we were pretty safe. Carolyn was much too fastidious to allow Gwen to make a mess here. It was also obvious to me that while Carolyn was mercenary and self-centered, Gwen was cold hearted and dangerous, the bloodthirsty leader. Of course, I'd been wrong about her before.

"What do you want to know?" Gwen looked like a cliché of a gangster in a movie from the 1930's. She curled her lip, gestured with her gun, and glared at me in a predatory manner.

"I've got lots of questions. First, which one of you did it and why?"

Before either of them could answer, I continued, "Oh God, now I see it. Gwen, when I found you on the floor in Burns' office, you hadn't just come in, had you? You were there already when Doris 'discovered' the body."

Her smile chilled me. "Go on."

"That's why you kept confessing to me. You thought I'd figure out that you'd been in the room the whole time and you were trying to convince me it was an accident. So the footprints outside the building must have been Carolyn's. Burns returned to his office after taking me to the personnel office. You two were waiting for him. Which one of you sliced him?"

Carolyn looked at her girlfriend. "If you want to talk about it, please hurry up. I want to get rid of them."

Gwen spoke to Carolyn but didn't take her eyes off us, "Don't worry. I'll hurry. I just want the satisfaction of looking at the stupid bitch's face when she realizes how we've made a fool of her."

I thought they didn't have to make a fool of me. I'd already done quite nicely on my own.

I wanted to keep Gwen talking. She'd gone over the edge and my best bet was to encourage her bragging. "So Carolyn told Burns she'd give him his freedom if he'd give her continued access to the files. He refused. So you cut him.

And after you killed him, you helped Carolyn back out the window. You probably didn't count on Doris coming into Burns' office. When she walked in, you slid to the floor behind the door and stayed quiet until the room filled up with the rest of us."

"About time you figured it all out. How we laughed at you and your amateur sleuthing. We realized pretty early you were no threat to us at all. You were just playing at crime solving. The only thing you were good at was bungling."

I let the jibe go unanswered. "I also want to know if either one of you sabotaged the gas line to my house or the brakes on my car."

"Of course not." It was Carolyn's turn to talk. "We just saw those as signs that luck was with us."

I sensed they were starting to get bored with my questions, so I decided to throw them an interesting one. "What I really want to know is how you two got together. Carolyn, I know you were Dr. Burns' sweetie while he was married to Claudia. He divorced her, married you and then started a long-term affair with Gwen. So how did you guys get so chummy?"

"I think that's a fair question." Gwen turned to Carolyn. "Do you want to answer it or shall I?"

Carolyn did not seem pleased by the whole conversation. Of course she wasn't the center of attention and she didn't like that. "You tell them if you want to. I think we need to end the conversation and get on with ending their existence. I'm bored with all the talk."

Gwen faced us again. "When Martin ended our relationship, I was mad. Really mad. I wanted to kill the little chippie he was sleeping with. But he was so discreet. I couldn't figure out who it was. Then I got mad at him instead. For dropping me and then for being so sneaky that I couldn't figure out who he was seeing. I thought Carolyn might know something. I called her and told her Martin was having an affair with someone that wasn't me. We met. We talked. The rest, as they say, is history." God, she was unattractive as a braggart.

"I have another question. Did you ever find out who Martin's new girlfriend was?"

Gwen didn't look so confident now. "No, but it doesn't matter. She doesn't have him any more."

Now it was my turn to gloat. I knew something they didn't know. Maybe I could use that as a bartering tool later.

"Okay, I have another question." Oops, I better make this interesting. Gwen and Carolyn were both starting to fidget. "Carolyn, did you send Gwen into my office to keep me busy while you were rifling through Martin's files? That was a good move and it almost worked." She nodded, she liked compliments. "The thing that made the plan fail was that Gwen kept looking at the door leading toward the kitchen. I knew something was going on so I walked through the kitchen and caught you in Martin's office."

Gwen wasn't happy by this turn of events. "Shut up, loser. Do you want to know anything else or are you ready to die?"

Okay, here goes nothing. "The other night there was quite a parade by my house. Would you explain that?"

Gwen giggled.

Carolyn's turn to talk, apparently. "It was quite a coincidence that we were both there. In fact we just discovered it today. You know Claudia Burns just returned to Quincy. I don't trust her and thought I'd check her out. As I was driving to her house I noticed she was leaving and I followed her. She went to your home, knocked, and peeked in the window. Don't know why. As she left, I looked in your windows."

Carolyn continued. "Gwen's brother Charlie has this thing about trying to protect Gwen. He was following me, because he thought I was out to hurt Gwen." She flashed a loving smile at Gwen. "Gwen was out looking for Charlie because she wanted to tell him about our relationship so he would stop worrying and would stop snooping. That's how we all ended up looking in your windows within a very short time. Rather funny when you think about it."

"Yeah, it really tickles me." God, I hate it when I resort to sarcasm.

Carolyn's recent and short bout of good humor left her.

"Gwen, we've talked long enough. Let's get out of here. We can get down to the river and kill them there. There are so many sink holes that we can load them down with bricks after they are dead and just let them sink. No cleaning up to do. And there are probably plenty of bodies down there to keep them company." Just when I thought Carolyn was the saner of the two, she went and got weird on me.

"Okay, but please," I pleaded, "please answer one more question…" They stopped walking so I continued with a question I already knew the answer to. "The thing that's driving me crazy is how did you clean up after the murder?" Looking at Gwen, I said, "There was no blood on you anywhere."

Since I sounded as if I admired their brilliance, Gwen couldn't stop from answering. "You are such a dope. Clinics are full of disposable gowns. After Martin refused to cooperate, Carolyn kept talking to him while I stepped into the closet outside his office, got some gowns, gloves, hair coverings, and booties. I looked into Martin's office, asked him to excuse us for a moment, and called Carolyn into the hallway. We went into the kitchen, covered ourselves with the disposable stuff and went into Martin's office through that door."

"Wasn't he surprised to see you both dressed like that?"

She continued, "I don't think he knew who we were right away. By the time he figured it out, it was too late."

"So you actually cut him? You're the one?"

She didn't speak but she grinned, and that gave me all the answer I needed.

I continued with my questioning. "Then you put all the disposable clothing and the scalpel in a plastic bag and helped Carolyn out of the window. She took the bag with her. That's why there were footprints leading away from but not toward the building."

"Bingo," Gwen said, "you win the door prize." She paused. "Too bad there isn't one." Again, the maniacal laughter.

It caused my spine to shiver uncontrollably.

When she stopped laughing she said, "I was the receptionist, so I was the only one who knew Carolyn had come into the clinic. She'd called him from the empty office—now it's yours—and when he got nasty on the phone we just decided to get rid of him. We figured I'd still be working there and could give new files to Carolyn. Of course, things didn't quite work out the way we'd planned."

Carolyn couldn't resist trying to stop the chatter. After all, the attention wasn't focused on her. "Will you just get rid of the bitch and the old man? You've told them everything. Sam's just stalling."

Gwen agreed to stop talking and bragging and to get the job done. "Get up. Get up. Let's go." The way she brandished that pistol, I was scared I'd die accidentally. She didn't appear to have any more expertise than Charlie did. Maybe I could get the jump on her. I thought that if there was some way I could signal Gus, or some way to let him know that he needed to deal with Carolyn, we had a chance. Carolyn was a wimp. Gwen wasn't, but we had to do something. I wasn't going to die without at least mussing up someone's hair. And if I was going to die, I wanted it to be here, so I could bleed all over Carolyn's beautiful carpet. I decided to be resolute and just go for it.

As Gus and I stood, I melodramatically clutched at my stomach and yelled, "Grab Carolyn."

Luckily Gus didn't second-guess me. He jumped up and literally threw himself at Carolyn, tackling her in a way that showed her he knew his way around a football field. At the same time I pretended to pass out on Gwen. It wasn't as picture perfect as Gus's execution, but it was dramatic and it worked. My reputation as a fainter preceded me. She dropped her gun as the nurse in her reflexively put her arms out to catch me. I immediately grabbed Gwen and put her in a basket hold—a restraint normally used only for my past psychiatric patients and younger brothers. Expertly executed and very effective.

Just as I wondered how long I could hold her, we were pleasantly interrupted. "Hold it right there. Don't move." George's voice was beautiful at that moment. I swirled around to face him and instead saw not only George, but

Michael, Pete, Rob, Georgianne, and a charging Clancy. Georgianne was replete with the ubiquitous housecoat and curlers.

I maintained the restraint hold on Gwen, but I was getting tired. Clancy revealed teeth I didn't know she had as she growled at Gwen, letting her know her bite was definitely going to be worse than her bark.

"Will someone help me here?" I yelled. Rob rushed over and relieved me of my charge.

Gus left Carolyn on the floor and went to his bride. "Darlin', I don't think I've ever seen you look so lovely." I swear to God she blushed. And she almost looked good. Hell, she did look good. Anybody who helped saved my life was beautiful.

George took charge. "Rob, Officer Radcliffe should be coming inside any minute. Read these two their rights and take them downtown. I'll be down in a little while to question them."

He looked at me. I couldn't help myself. I hugged him. Then I hugged Michael, and Pete, and Georgianne. I got on my knees and kissed my brave dog. I promised Rob a hug later, as I didn't think he'd appreciate being grabbed by his big sister as he was arresting two murderers.

On her way out the door Carolyn looked seductively at Michael in one last-ditch attempt to garner his support. Michael didn't make eye contact with her.

I stood and faced George. "Where's Charlie?" The last I knew, he was in my car with Clancy?"

"Another officer is speaking to him outside. Are you okay?"

I didn't answer; instead I asked another question. "How did you find out we were here?"

"It was Georgianne. She knew where you and Gus were going and she called me. I came right over and was rather surprised to see the rest of this gang here as well."

I looked at the beaming Georgianne. "How did you know we were here?"

"Well, you know Gus isn't well. I think it's my job as his loving wife to know his whereabouts at all times. So I listened when you were talking to him. And don't you dare call it 'eavesdropping.' I was doing it for Gus's own good, and for yours too as it turned out."

How could I be mad at the beautiful old witch? She saved us. "And what about my brothers?"

"Well, you told me your brother Rob is a police officer, so I called him, thinking that Officer Lansing could probably use a little help. And I remembered that your brother Pete is a Father, so I called him. You never know when you might need a priest. It just so happened that both young men were arriving home from work when I called and they were most happy to hear from me."

I felt Rob's stare as he and Radcliffe led the duo away.

"We're going to have a nice long talk later about your midnight activities," he said.

I bet he wanted to thank me.

Pete contributed his unwelcome thoughts. "What in the hell did you think you were doing?"

"Pete, priests shouldn't cuss."

"Stay on the subject. What did you think you were doing?"

"Well, Father Smarty-Priest, I thought I was doing exactly what I did. Gus and I solved the crime and we caught the criminals. If I hadn't pretended to faint on Gwen, she would have killed us and if Gus hadn't tackled Carolyn, why she might have…"

"If you hadn't come snooping around, you wouldn't have been in a position where you had to be theatrical to save yourself."

Male logic. Can't live with them. Period.

George hung up the telephone, where he'd been talking with the station. "Pete, will you do me a favor and give Mr. and Mrs. Granville a ride home? They look tired. I'll take Sam home in a few minutes."

Georgianne and Gus looked anything but tired. Georgianne was still glowing and Gus had the energy of a thirty-year-old. Romance was in the air tonight.

Both of them hugged me before they were escorted from the room. As he was walking out, Gus turned to me and said, "This was the best night of my life. Thanks."

The room emptied out pretty quickly. I was left with George and Michael. Michael hadn't yet spoken to me, although I could feel his eyes on me the entire time. It was time for me to hug him again. My vertigo was settling down. Maybe I was "vibed out" for the night. I now knew that Michael had nothing to do with the murder. Why did I feel dizzy around him and not around Gwen? She was one of the guilty ones.

I walked up to Michael, put my arms around him and suddenly knew. I whispered in his ear "Maybe you scare me." That's the only reason I could think of for my physical reaction to him. "Maybe you scare me, Michael."

"And maybe I should," he whispered back. His warm breath in my ear caused shivers and goosebumps, but no dizziness.

George interrupted again. "I want to give you a ride home, because I need to talk to you. O'Dear, will you follow me in Sam's car? Then I'll give you a ride back here to your car?"

Michael was much too agreeable. He said yes and took Clancy with him. George and I got into the unmarked cop car that everyone in town recognized.

The ride was only a few blocks. I sat with my head leaning back, thinking about tonight, what almost happened, and what did happen.

"Hey." He startled me a bit.

"Yeah, what?" My words were said quietly.

"First of all, I'd like to call a truce. I'm sorry about the prom. That was a long time ago and I hope you can start treating me like a human being again. I'd like to be friends."

I was feeling magnanimous. Surviving a near death experience tends to bring out the best in me. I turned to him and smiled. "Okay. I'm willing to forgive and forget."

And then he did the strangest thing. He put on the brakes, leaned over and kissed me.

And I did the strangest thing. I liked it.

This was crazy. Crazy. Michael was the guy for me, not balding old comfortable George.

"That's the way I like you, Sam. Quiet." He laughed and eased the car back into gear again.

Not only was this crazy, but Michael was behind us. I wondered if he saw anything. Oh, God, that would be awful.

We arrived at my house without us exchanging another word. I stayed in the cop car, in a semi-daze, as George got out and opened the passenger door for me. I exited slowly. Michael got out of my car, walked up to me, and handed me my keys. They each took an arm and escorted me to my front door. I was in awe of this situation. Over the past few years, I had become a Dateless Wonder. Suddenly there were two guys interested in me.

I opened my door and Clancy ran inside. I turned and

without speaking watched Michael and George walk off into the sunrise together. Okay, it was a street light, but it had the same effect. Not exactly the ending I would have planned for this adventure.

I'd probably see them both tomorrow. That would be fun. And I'd see them at the trial. That would be even more fun, because I'd get credit for solving the case. For now I needed to prepare myself for the inevitable letdown that comes after an adrenaline-laced crisis.

So I wasn't a superhero. Some might say I wasn't a hero at all. But I did solve the murder. Well, I was wrong for a while, and I was wrong about a couple of the participants, but I did solve it. That felt good. I mentally ran down the list of siblings that I needed to call in the morning and brag to.

Hard to believe that less than a week ago I was unemployed. Now, I was employed and was a hero. The only negative spin I could put on this thing was that I left the adventure the same way I entered it—with my virtue intact.

Again, not the ending I'd envisioned.

I looked at my faithful companion. "C'mon, Clancy, let's go for a walk. We've got a lot to talk about."

She smiled.

About
ANY MEAT IN THAT SOUP?
(Sam Darling Mystery #2)

When a man falls down at Samantha Darling's feet, she thinks it's pretty funny. But she stops joking when he turns up dead.

Social worker and would-be crime-solver Sam is busy trying to unravel the mystery as the death toll keeps mounting. She's thrilled to be hired by the handsome local private eye to work in the ER and investigate, but her elation quickly evaporates when she finds out that her sister Jen is being investigated for the murders.

A trio of other suspects, a poisoning scare for her best bud and canine companion Clancy, and the back-and-forth pull of Sam's attraction to the dreamy Michael and the loyal George keep her unbalanced as she tries to juggle social work, secret sleuthing, and a romantic triangle.

As usual, Sam takes her snooping to extraordinary heights. She can't seem to stop putting her nose where it doesn't belong. And this time…she may have gone too far.

ANY MEAT IN THAT SOUP?

To Rob Dufresne and Jill Dufresne Potrykus, the best kids (and adults) a mom could wish for.

ONE

He fell at my feet. Nice place for a man. Problem was, he was blue. Maybe dead.

It seemed like an eternity before a sea of color descended on him. One white coat checked for a pulse. A Mickey Mouse scrub suit listened for breath sounds. Someone in jeans and a sweater retrieved a gurney. Mickey Mouse put a finger in the man's mouth, and swept it from side to side, looking for God-knows-what.

A green scrub suit said, "On my mark. One, two, three." The sturdy group of four lifted my dinner companion and placed him on the stretcher.

My sister, Jenny—the guest of honor at this birthday party—orchestrated the procedure. As the nurse manager of the Emergency Department, she couldn't enjoy the festivities while there were chests to be pounded.

My other sister, Jill—she was the one in jeans and sweater—joined her. Even though Jill was off duty today, she was an ER resident and couldn't bear to sit and watch.

"Damn, Sam, when we tell ya to knock 'em dead, we

don't expect you to take it literally."

"Shut up, Rob." I said to my brother, the smart-ass cop. "He's not dead. I saw him breathing."

He grinned. He knew how to push my buttons. Too bad he was such a little cutie; I found it hard to stay mad at him.

After the hubbub subsided, the rest of us returned to the mundane task at hand. Eating the goodies.

A visitor might remark that we were eating in the midst of a crisis. Any one of us would reply, "Yeah. And… ?" Crises were something we were used to.

I looked around. My brothers were being their usual selves, joking with each other and happily munching on chicken wings. Other Emergency Department employees and guests relaxed in the staff lounge as they also enjoyed the food. The small dark room was made more festive with Happy Birthday signs and crepe paper throughout. Danny Jacobsen and Connie Mumford were having a heated discussion about the importance of exercise to maintain good health, as Danny ate a pulled pork sandwich and Connie started on her second. As a paramedic and nurse respectively, their experience, both in the ER and with carry-ins, kept them calm during the crisis.

"Hey, you two. For a married couple, you sure argue a lot." They both turned to look at me. "But it sounds like you were arguing the same point." I smiled as I said it.

Connie replied, "We do that all the time. We think we're

disagreeing and then notice that we're on the same side. Crazy." She looked at Danny, her bright brown eyes practically disappearing because of her huge smile.

Danny didn't say anything. Just grinned. He was a man of few words unless he was arguing with Connie.

I noticed a pale, thin guy sitting by himself in a corner. He wore a white shirt and pants, and it was hard to see where his skin ended and the fabric began. The guy would take a bite of food, and as he chewed, he kept looking from side to side and over his shoulder. He was attached to the corner and was mostly in shadow, so it wasn't easy to see him. I moved closer to Connie and asked, "Who's he?"

Connie replied, "Oh, that's Carter. He was just laid off as an EMT, but he still stops by here every day."

"I'm not one for talking about people," I fibbed, "but he looks creepy."

"I agree," she said, "but he worked here for several years. He's harmless."

At that point Jill returned, blonde ponytail pleasantly mussed, a confused look on her face.

"Who took my plate?"

"No one," I replied. "It's right where you left it. How's my date?" I took another slurp of the vegetarian vegetable soup, which was almost the only thing in that room that didn't stink of burnt flesh.

Jill's brow furrowed, then relaxed again. "First of all, he's not your date…"

I interrupted with, "Were we, or were we not, dining together?" Silence. "I think that constitutes a date."

Jill ignored me as she started munching on the Buffalo wings again. "And secondly, he'll be fine. We don't know exactly what it is yet, but it doesn't look serious. Heart looks okay, but his pulse is elevated, blood pressure is low, and he's dehydrated. Smelled like alcohol. How lucky could someone get… passing out in an emergency room." She smiled between bites. "They're admitting him to run some tests. Dougie's on duty."

Dougie was Dr. Kareem Douglas Johnson. Short, dark and handsome. And young. A resident in the ER where his mom, Loretta, worked as a technician. He was a rising star, so I had no doubt he'd take good care of…"Hey, what's the guy's name anyway?"

Jill shook her head as she munched on another bite. "Dunno. He's a homeless guy. One of our regulars. Says his name is 'Pluto,' so that's what we call him. He was hanging around outside, so I invited him to join us for Jenny's party. Gave him my plate and made another." She smiled. "Looks like he wasn't a vegetarian. He sure ate a lot of those wings before he keeled over."

I looked at Rob again. "Can't you quit licking your lips over those chicken wings? It's practically making me ill."

He made even more noise. "Just because you're a vegetarian doesn't mean that we carnivorous types can't enjoy eating flesh." He licked his lips again, but this time widened his eyes and chuckled a la Hannibal Lector.

"One of these days you'll see I'm right. It's a well know fact that people who eat meat get sick a lot more than vegetarians. And besides…"

Rob interrupted with a rather loud belch. "I don't feel so good."

I looked skyward and mouthed a silent, "Thank you, God," but my sick sibling didn't notice.

Jill quickly became a doctor again. "You want me to look you over?"

"Nope, think I'll go home. Probably got a touch of the flu. I'll be fine." I knew Rob must feel really bad, because he didn't make a wisecrack.

He exited, looking slightly green and holding his stomach.

I turned to Jill. "That sure happened fast. What do you think it is?"

"Probably just the flu. Lots of it going around. The ER's been full of people who think they're dying, but just have a stomach virus. Not much we can do for it. We just tell them to stay in bed, drink lots of fluids and to eat when they can."

"Yeah, but they don't seem to think that's enough," Jenny chimed in as she reclaimed her plate. "They're feeling so rotten that they want antibiotics at the very least. And they're disappointed when we say they need to rest and drink a lot of fluids." She took another big chomp out of a chicken wing. "Gosh, most people left before we cut the cake. You guys want some?"

"Yeah, as long as there's no meat in it." They laughed at me but I didn't react. Hell, the intense smell of chicken, pork, and beef in that small room was so overpowering it nearly grossed me out. But not enough to stop me from eating other stuff.

As Jen handed slices of cake to Jill and me, I asked again about Pluto. "So is the guy going to be okay?"

"Don't know. I was going to wait a while and then call upstairs to check. If you have a few minutes, I'll call now."

I nodded, my mouth too full of cake to talk.

By this time the room had cleared except for Jill and me. Our other brothers left soon after Rob did, but not before making fun of him for taking off sick. Jill and I sat in companionable silence. Munching.

Jen returned, minus the grin. "Nurse in ICU told me that Pluto died just a few minutes after he was admitted."

"What happened?" Jill looked up expectantly.

"Don't know for sure. They might do an autopsy to find out what happened, but the nurse I talked to said he smelled like alcohol, so maybe that had something to do with it. Dougie'll be down in a minute or so and we can ask him."

"I don't remember him smelling like booze when he was sitting by me, but the smell of this barbecued meat kind of kills my ability to smell anything else."

"'Sh'up about the meat." Jen was the sibling closest to me in age. A year younger and normally a lot nicer than I was. Yet I wasn't surprised at her "shut up." The gang got tired of my carnivore comments.

I decided to ignore her retort. "Will the cops have to come to check out Pluto's death?"

Jill and Jen both started talking at the same time, "Probably not." "Maybe."

They looked at each other and laughed. Jill continued, "It's hard to say. This death will probably fall into the gray area. Since there was no sign of physical injury and no obvious cause of death, the police might feel they need to check it out. But we have lots of deaths that fall in the gray area, and they aren't always investigated. Too bad Rob went home sick. He could've saved some other cop a trip."

Our youngest brother Rob was a rookie police officer in our hometown. He wore the "QPD" patch proudly. The Quincy Police Department was small but pretty efficient, so I expected someone to show up momentarily.

"Hi ya, Sam." The new arrival was right on cue.

I cringed. It was George Lansing, my old, un-lamented boyfriend from high school, dressed in his usual Detective Colombo-like rumpled suit.

"Hi, George."

Jen and Jill chimed in with "Hi, George."

My feelings toward George were ambivalent. He abandoned me on prom night twenty-five years ago. I've been told I hold a grudge. The jury's still out on that as far as I'm concerned.

After gracing me with his infuriating smile, he turned to Jill and said, "Jill, I was walking through the ER lobby when I heard that there was a sudden death with no known cause. Do you know anything about it?"

She nodded, "His name was Pluto, a homeless regular here in E.R. We had a little birthday party for Jen..."

"Happy birthday, Jen."

Jenny smiled and nodded her thanks.

Jill continued, "... and while he was eating, he passed out at Sam's feet."

A sound escaped from George that sounded like a snort of laughter. I glared, but he ignored me.

"What happened then?"

"We did some preliminary work on him here, but then rushed him up to ICU after we temporarily stabilized him," Jill said. "That's really all I know. It didn't look too serious from what I saw. I'm pretty confident it wasn't a heart attack from what they said... but Dougie was the doctor in charge and it was his call. I just phoned ICU a few minutes ago and they told me he died."

George took notes as Jill talked. He looked up, "I don't really know yet if we'll be investigating. We'll probably wait until after an autopsy, if they do one. But if you guys don't mind, I'll want to talk to you three individually. Just in case." He paused, then added, "And do me a favor, tell Dougie—what's his full name?"

Jill answered, "Johnson. Kareem Douglas Johnson. He's a new resident in E.R. I think you know his mom, Loretta. She's been a tech here for a long time."

"Thanks for the info. Tell him I may want to see him in a few minutes. As I said, I don't know if we'll launch an investigation until after the autopsy. Will the three of you wait for me here while I go upstairs and check things out? I'll let you know then if I want to interview you or not."

Jenny and Jill both answered in the affirmative. I did not.

"Sorry, George. I have a date tonight. With Michael. Michael O'Dear. You know, the private eye?"

"Of course, I know O'Dear. We worked together on the Burns' murder... Hell, Sam, you know that. You were there. Trying to impress me that you have a date?" His words sounded mad, but his smile said something different.

"'Course not. Just wanted you to know I can't wait all night for you."

He waited for the inevitable.

I didn't give in.

He finished for me, "You mean you won't wait for me

like you did on prom night."

I ignored the comment. "Is it okay if I go? I can talk to you tomorrow."

"Yeah, come down to the station." He turned away, then back again, continuing with his Columbo imitation. "Unless you want to meet me for breakfast?"

"Sure. Seven o'clock at The Dairy?"

He grunted and began walking toward the elevator.

"And, George?"

Another grunt as he turned to face me again.

"Don't stand me up."

I swear the final grunt had a smile in it.

TWO

"Clancy." I whistled as I walked into the carriage house. Before the whistle finished, there she was. "Hi, girl. Want to go for a quick run?"

A stupid question. Of course Clancy wanted to go for a run. She'd been inside all day and her look reminded me that I wasn't keeping up my end of our bargain. I smiled at her eagerness and her beauty. When my kids and I had brought her home from the Humane Society, we fell in love with those eyes and didn't care about what breed she was, although we found out later she was a cross between a yellow lab and a chow.

"Yeah, I know you've guarded the house all day and kept the place safe for me. I can't help it I have to work for a living."

I hooked her leash onto her collar and headed out the door. "Okay, you're right. I am later than usual. I'll tell you all about it."

As we walked and ran along our usual route in our mansion-filled neighborhood, I filled Clancy in on the events of the afternoon. She forgave me once she knew the facts.

The dogwoods were in bloom and Maine Street was ablaze with spring colors. I could even smell the delicate magnolia trees. This route never really felt like work; it could even be a meditative experience. But not today. I was in a hurry.

After a half-hour of exercise, I called it quits. "I need to get ready for Michael." As Clancy sat, she almost pulled my arm out of the socket. "Clancy, come on. I told you the other day that I had a date for dinner tonight with Michael. Don't pull this shit with me."

She stood up and it seemed as though I was watching this in slow motion. The ruff around her neck stood at attention and her blonde coat shone in the setting sun. Her regal bearing let me know that she put up with my antics because she loved me, not because she had to. She began walking slowly, ignoring my existence.

"Stop it, Clancy. You know I can't stand it when you treat me like this. I'm sorry I cussed at you. Okay?"

She smiled. I love it when she does that.

"Okay, now that you've forgiven me, I want to talk some more about today. I wonder what happened to Pluto; one minute he was fine, the next he was on the floor."

Clancy cocked her head and listened intently.

"No, I didn't do anything to him, silly. I was just talking

to him. Okay, I'm going to go over exactly what happened. I was at the clinic. My last client left at 3, and about 3:30 I went to the hospital to help surprise Jenny."

Clancy yipped.

"Yeah, she was surprised. All six of us were together but none of the out-laws or kids made it. Anyway, there was a potluck meal." Clancy looked at me with her head cocked. "No, I didn't know about it ahead of time, so I didn't bring anything. I looked around and saw chicken wings and meatballs and other gross stuff. Then I noticed some vegetable soup. I asked Loretta if there was any meat in it. She said 'no' so I helped myself to some. Pluto—that's the guy's name—came in a few minutes later. He looked around, nodded at Jill and she handed him a plateful of wings and other flesh…"

Clancy smiled again. She was almost a vegetarian herself.

"… and he sat by me. I said 'hello' but he only nodded. His mouth was full. Then suddenly he keeled over. Everyone kind of dropped their food and jumped up to help him. Well, except for me. I know my limitations. Anyway, after they wheeled him out, I didn't see him again. Hope it wasn't murder."

At that, Clancy snorted. She didn't have to remind me that the last murder that occurred in Quincy had my nose prints all over it.

We arrived home… at least almost home. We rested for

a moment in front of the big house. Ours was the carriage house behind the mansion.

"Let's be quiet when we walk by the house. I don't want Georgianne to know I'm home."

Too late. She'd already seen us. Her flowered housecoat rivaled the blossoms surrounding her house, and announced her arrival before her words.

"Yoo-hoo. Miss Darling. I mean... yoo-hoo. Sam." We'd gotten well acquainted after my boss, Dr. Burns, was murdered. Now we were on a first name basis. To my chagrin.

"Hi, Georgianne. How's Gus?" Gus was always a safe topic. He was her husband, one-half of my landlord couple and one of my best friends.

"Well, you know how sick he is..."

Yeah, I know how sick you make him.

"... but I imagine he's doing as well as can be expected."

"I've got to run, Georgianne. Nice to see you. Say 'hi' to Gus for me."

She half turned and sighed loud enough to be heard all the way to Pike County. "Well, if you don't care about your dog then..."

I had to admit she had me with that line.

"What do you mean?"

"There have been two dogs poisoned in the neighborhood, and I wanted to warn you so your darling little poochy-woochy doesn't get hurt."

At that she leaned over and pursed her dried-up lips at Clancy. And Clancy did what she always does; she betrayed me. She rolled over, exposing her stomach to Georgianne's ministrations, and Clancy's sounds of absolute ecstasy irked me even more.

"Traitor."

Georgianne didn't stop her petting, "What was that, Sam?"

"Nothing. C'mon, Clancy. Thanks for telling me about the dogs; but I don't let Clancy outside without me, so I'm not worried about her."

"Okay, just thought you'd want to know. Bye, Clancy dear. You too, Sam."

We escaped before she could change her mind and start talking again.

"God, Clancy, I think we set the world's record for ditching Georgianne. Good for us. Want a treat?"

As I opened a cabinet in my compact kitchen to get treats for both of us, I thought about what Georgianne said. Dogs poisoned. That certainly wasn't an ordinary occurrence. Especially for this ritzy neighborhood.

"Georgianne drives me crazy." I shivered. "Yeah, I know you like her. You act like her love slave. I find it sickening."

Clancy tolerated my disapproval. In fact, she thought I was overreacting. "I don't care what you say, Clancy. You don't think clearly when it comes to Georgianne."

Silence.

"Yes, I know she saved my life. Yes, I'll never forget it. You and she won't let me. Let's change the subject, okay?"

Ever since Georgianne saved me and her husband, Gus, from being killed by two murder suspects in a bizarre incident, Clancy has reminded me at every chance she gets that I'd be dead except for her friend. Yuck. Sometimes I almost wished my dog and I didn't have such a psychic connection. She was such a nag.

"Why don't you help me choose something nice to wear for my date?" We both sauntered to my climb-in closet to examine the contents.

"I have so much stuff in here. Why is it I have nothing to wear?"

Beep-beep. Beep-beep-beep.

"Shoot." My pager. I was the therapist on-call this week. The beeper's display showed the phone number of the clinic's answering service.

I punched in the number. A sweet, albeit bored, voice answered, "Quincy Community Clinic. We're here to help."

"Hi, this is Sam Darling. You paged me?"

"Hi, Sam. There's a patient in the ER who's a possible psych admission. They called less than five minutes ago."

I thanked her and tried to sound sincere. Damn. I didn't

want to postpone my date with Michael. He's the most handsome guy in town… at least of the eligible guys around my age.

I quickly poured some food in Clancy's bowl and replenished her water as I gave her my apologies. "Sorry I can't spend more time with you. Gotta go."

I rushed out of the house, barely remembering my purse and my keys. When I got into my car, I used a speed dial button on my cell phone to call Michael.

Damn. Voice mail.

"Hi, Michael. This is Sam. I'm really sorry but I'll have to take a rain check on dinner. I'm on call and just got paged for the ER. Call me later?"

Shoot. There I was, sounding like a needy female.

"Er… or I'll call you when I get home. Either way. Doesn't matter. 'Bye."

It took me only a few minutes to get to Bay General. One of the many benefits of living in a city with only 40,000 inhabitants is that you can get anywhere fast—unless you're behind a tractor.

I hadn't been gone that long from the ER and Jen's party, but the scene was quite different from when I left. The waiting room and triage room were completely full, and there were three people at the reception desk. I didn't know whom to ask about my emergency page. So I did what anyone would do if their sister was nurse manager. I pushed on the door marked Emergency Personnel Only, and walked straight into organized chaos.

I saw Jen quickly exit a room and almost run toward the adjoining one. She saw me and held up her hand in the universal sign for STOP. "Sorry, I don't have time to talk."

Quickly, before she could move out of sight, I said, "Someone paged me."

"Check with the front desk. I'll talk with you in a minute. Love you." And with that she was gone, quicker than me when there were dishes to be done.

I didn't go back to the reception desk, figuring it was still too busy, and checked with the nursing station instead. Loretta was staring at the computer. "Goshdarn thing," she said, as she not-so-gently hit the side of the monitor. The hit caused a list to appear on the monitor. I couldn't see what it said, but imagined it contained a list of patients in each room and what their symptoms were. "Goshdarn thing," she said again as the display disappeared once more.

"Sometimes you have to sacrifice a chicken," I said, shrugging my shoulders.

Loretta's round face looked up with concern, "What did you say?"

"Sometimes you have to sacrifice a chicken to get those things to work."

At that she jumped up, knocking over her chair. "You think because I'm Black and my folks were from Haiti that

I go in for all that voodoo? I'm a fine Christian woman." Even though there was a counter between us, she got so close to me I was able to tell what she had for lunch. The odor made me a little dizzy. Or maybe it was my vibes. I willed the dizziness away; there was no way I wanted any psychic B.S. distracting me right now.

"No, no, you got it wrong. I have a smart mouth. I say that line all the time about computers. Sorry if I offended you." Wow. This wasn't like Loretta at all. Even though she was a "close talker," she was a mainstay in the Bay General ER and was always known as a sweetheart. I knew she was opinionated, but so was I. Was this an overreaction, or did I just push the wrong button?

Loretta shook her head, "Nah, Sam, I'm the one who's sorry. I get frustrated with computers sometimes, and I took it out on you." She gave me a petite hand to shake in conciliation.

"No problem. Maybe you can help me. I got paged to come in and help with some behavioral health issues. Do you know…"

"Yeah," she interrupted. Everyone in the ER interrupted. They were always in a hurry. "Rooms 18 and 19 both have folks that need to be evaluated for involuntary commitments. The one in 19 is on suicide watch. We have her monitored already, so you can see Room 18 first. I'll be in and out of rooms. Let the secretary know if you need me."

She started to walk away then turned and said, "Again, I'm sorry, Sam."

"No problem." I pulled a clipboard out of my bag that contained the assessment form agreed upon by Bay General and Quincy Community Clinic. After taking a deep breath I opened the door and saw my sister Jen standing by an empty bed.

"What…"

"Shhh," she put her finger to her lips and pointed toward a closed door. "She's in the bathroom. We've just got a minute."

"Okay, what…"

"Shhh. Just listen and be quiet." Improbable, but I'd try. "There were two more deaths right after you left. Similar to Pluto. Except they came in with one symptom and then keeled over after being in the exam room alone. I'm worried and kind of afraid."

"Aw, Jen, I'm sure you didn't do anything to cause…"

She interrupted, as usual, "Of course I didn't. But three people died and they weren't in an accident together, and their hearts looked okay, and blood pressure was fine when they first came in, and…"

My turn to interrupt. "Take a breath. Tell me more."

"I can't now. And I shouldn't be telling you anything." With that she threw me a dime and I managed to catch it in my fist. "You're officially my therapist, so now you can't repeat anything I've said."

At that, the bathroom door opened slowly and a frail middle-aged woman stood in the doorway.

Jen introduced us, and with a quick good-bye, tried to exit the room. I intercepted her to give the money back. "Nope, I'm not a 'dime-a-dance woman.' I have to talk this over with someone. I'll want to check things out. I won't use your name. And you didn't tell me anything confidential, really." I crossed my fingers behind my back and pushed her out of the room.

I did what I do, first in room 18 and then again in 19. Room 18 needed more of a domestic violence shelter rather than a commitment, so I made the appropriate referrals and knew someone from the shelter would soon arrive to help her. Room 19 took more time. This teenage girl had been a "cutter" for a few years, but the cuts had become much more serious. Today her parents brought her in when she said she was going to kill herself. Since she was 18 she needed to agree to be hospitalized or she would be sent to the state hospital in Springfield. After about an hour of combination Mental Health Assessment, Lethality Assessment, and begging, she agreed to be hospitalized at Bay General on a voluntary basis, and my work was done.

A few minutes later I drove onto the driveway of my carriage house, expecting to open my door to let Clancy out. What I found instead was my friend Gus playing fetch with my dog in the near darkness.

Before I could express my surprise, Gus said, "Hi ya, Sam. I'm sorry about this. Georgie was so worried about Clancy that she forced me to check on her. Thought I might as well play with her while I was at it."

I gave him a hug. "I don't mind at all. If it was Georgianne, I'd have to act mad, just to keep up appearances." We both smiled. "But you're always welcome to take care of Clancy."

His smiled turned to a frown. "I brought my key, but didn't need it. What have I told you about locking your door?"

"This is Quincy. I don't have to lock my door."

"Sam, it wasn't that long ago when two people tried to kill you. Hell—they tried to kill both of us. Lock your door, and I mean it."

"Yes, sir. Hey, why was Georiganne worried about Clancy? I told her Clancy doesn't go outside without me."

He just raised his eyebrows and we both laughed. Georgianne was Georgianne.

"You're just the two I wanted to talk to," indicating him and Clancy.

Gus grinned. He knew it was time for another adventure.

THREE

After I told Gus what little I knew, he expressed his disappointment. I apologized, "Sorry I can't always get you involved in murder."

His gray sweater complemented his gray mood. "That's not what I mean, Sam. Not really. It's just that when I helped you solve Dr. Burns' murder I felt younger and healthier than I had in years."

I couldn't disagree.

We said our good-nights, and I slept the sleep of the almost innocent, with the windows open and the sweet smell of flowering trees enhancing my dreams.

The next morning as I was getting ready for work I knew there was something I was forgetting. I looked at Clancy for a hint. "C'mon, Clance. Tell me." And then it hit me. Breakfast with George, and I'd forgotten. Of course it wasn't as bad as him "forgetting" me on prom night, but it was bad enough. I hated to be in a position of having to apologize to him. So I rushed to the Dairy on 18th Street, right by the University, and was only a little late.

"Hi ya, Sam. I thought you weren't going to make it." George was happily munching on french toast at the counter. He kept eating as I sat and gave my order—whole grain pancakes with syrup and pecans, plus black, dark roast coffee.

I decided not to address my tardiness. "So what did you want to talk about?"

"I said I wanted to see what you knew about this Pluto character, but I thought it would be nice to have a meal with you at the city's expense."

It was hard to tell if he was kidding or not, so I chose to ignore what he said. "I really don't know much. He came in, ate chicken wings, fell over, went to the ICU, and died. That simple."

"Okay, that's pretty much what I got from the rest of the witnesses, most of them your family."

At that I smiled. Everyone but Rob and me were involved in the healthcare profession. Rob was a cop and I was a therapist-wannabe-cop. At Bay General Jen was a nurse manager, Ed was security director, Pete was a nurse/priest, and Jill was an ER resident. I've often wondered why we all got involved in service professions. Maybe it was because our parents died young. As I was musing, the pancakes appeared and I poured the luscious syrup on them. Then I tuned back in to George's ramblings.

"… and so I thought since you moved back to Quincy

maybe we could be friends again. I mean that's how we started out."

"Sorry. I was taking a mental health break. I caught the last thing you said." I took a huge bite of the steaming pancakes. "Yeah, I think we can be friends. Prom night was a long time ago and I decided at the Burns' house that I was going to forgive you."

"It's funny how looking down the barrel of a gun puts things into perspective." As a cop, George felt the same way my brother Rob did… that I should keep my nose out of police business. Of course I didn't buy what they were selling.

Breakfast was quick, and delicious, and I was soon on my way to work. Clara, our receptionist, told me my first two clients had cancelled, so I settled into my office with another cup of coffee and a pile of paperwork.

I had no sooner begun rewriting a treatment plan when my phone rang. "This is Sam Darling."

"I love your name," Michael replied. I'm glad he couldn't see my blush at the compliment.

After a mutual exchange of pleasantries Michael reminded me of our missed date last night, as if I needed reminding. He closed with, "There's something important I want to talk to you about."

As I hung up, I knew the rest of my work day was shot. How could I concentrate on helping people when Michael had something important to talk to me about? Something important. My curiosity was piqued, but there was no satisfactory answer to my questions. It was too early for him to say I love you, and too early even for me to say it. We'd been on only a few dates and one of them had taken place in my hospital room. Nevertheless, I'd fallen for him in a big way.

Even though I was thinking about Michael and what he wanted to tell me, the image of George kissing me after rescuing me from the killers kept creeping its way inside my brain. I hadn't encouraged that kiss, but I liked it. Involuntarily liked it.

I made it go away and went back to thinking about Michael. The two free hours passed much too quickly. Even though I didn't think it was possible, I was able to stop thinking about him and begin thinking about the people who trusted me to help them.

There were no more cancellations, so I was able to stay busy listening, consoling, challenging and then writing the unloved progress notes.

At the end of the workday I hurried home to Clancy. Her wagging tail stopped and the tail dropped to the floor. "I'm sorry, Clancy, I really am."

Without forgiving me, she got her leash and met me at the door. We began our walk after Clancy "watered" Georgianne's ferns. Then we headed out along our usual route, with Clancy stopping at the crosswalks until it was safe. As she did so, I again apologized. "Remember I had a dinner date with Michael last night and then got paged so I had to cancel. Well, we're just going to have dinner and that's it. I promise I'll be back as soon as I can."

She probably knew I was lying. Actually I wanted to make the dinner date last as long as possible. I didn't talk to her much more. We both enjoyed the rest of the walk through the beautiful neighborhood I lived in, courtesy of Gus and Georgianne's carriage house.

Our walk took us past extravagant mansions built by river barons in the 1800s. I noticed a few of the dogwood trees were losing their blossoms even before the date of the annual Dogwood Parade. Not a good sign, but most were still lovely and fragrant. We also passed the empty Burns' house. I shivered and so did Clancy. The location where I was nearly killed was located in my neighborhood, and there was nothing I could do about it. But I didn't have to like it.

"Thanks for helping to save me, Clancy. I love you."

She replied in her doggie growl-talk and I knew I was forgiven for leaving her yet again.

"You know, I ought to get you certified as a therapy dog. That way you could come to work with me. I know you'd be a big help."

That did it. She turned around and jumped up to give me a big sloppy kiss.

"Guess you like the idea." By this time we were almost home. "I don't know why I didn't think of this before. That way you could help people and you wouldn't have to be alone so much."

We were at the front of the mansion where Georgianne and Gus lived. And as usual our movements did not go unnoticed. This time she caught us by the front porch. "Sam, stop a moment, please."

How could I not? She said please.

"What's up, Georgianne? I'm in a hurry."

Before she could tell me, Clancy pulled away from my loose grip and went up the stairs to betray me yet again.

Georgianne petted Clancy's belly and in between "Good doggie" and "What a cute little girl you are," she finally told me what she wanted. "There were more dogs found to be poisoned. Most of them didn't die, but they got very ill. Please take care of this sweet girl."

Once again I assured her I would do so, "And I'm going out to dinner, but you won't need to send Gus to check on Clancy. She'll be fine."

I swear Georgianne "harrumphed" a bit, but her quasi-silence gave me the chance to grab Clancy's leash again, say good-bye, and rush back to my little corner of the neighborhood.

My home. The carriage house. It was absolutely perfect for Clancy and me. The main floor had a compact living room, a small dining room I used as an office, a decent kitchen, and a nice-sized master bedroom and bath. Upstairs were two more bedrooms and a bathroom. I kept the upstairs closed off now that Adam and Sarah were away at the University of Illinois. But it was easily opened when they were home on break.

As I got ready for my date, I called George and put him on speakerphone as I changed. After he answered I asked, "Have you heard about dogs being poisoned in town?"

He answered, "Not just dogs. Cats too. And squirrels, rabbits, small animals."

"What are you doing about it?" I asked as I struggled mightily to get a straight skirt over my hips.

"Sam, you sound like you're running a marathon. What in the hell are you doing?"

I stopped long enough to catch my breath, "None of your business. Answer my question."

"Same old Sam. Anyway, animals aren't normally a priority with the police. Tell Clancy I'm sorry about that."

Was he teasing me? Or did he really care about Clancy's feelings? I must have made a noise, because George repeated himself.

"As I said, animals aren't normally a priority with the police. But this has gotten to be a big deal, and we are dealing with it. That's all you need to know."

"For now. That's all I need to know for now. If you don't

get this taken care of, you'll hear from me again. 'Bye."

I hung up before he could say anything else. What in the hell was going on? Quincy was a calm, safe city, number eight on Forbes' best mid-size places to live. Had I brought violence with me when I moved home from Chicago? Animals being poisoned and people dropping dead in the ER. Were they connected or just horrible things happening at the same time?

Michael arrived just as I held my breath to pull up the zipper to the skirt. When I answered the door, instead of saying hi, he said, "Omigod, your face is red. Are you okay?"

"Yeah, I'm fine. Come in." I hastily changed the subject. "Clancy's already been walked, so we can leave right away. I"ll just get my purse."

Thirty seconds later I walked back into the living room to see Michael on the floor playing with Clancy. That's something else I liked about him. My dog thinks he's fun. I looked at Michael and appreciated what I saw. He was in jeans and a button down shirt, and the view was nice.

We left soon after, and as I got in the car I did two things at the same time—I breathed in his aftershave and I asked him where we were going. He replied, "I thought we'd go back to the Rectory. You said it's one of your favorite places, and I enjoyed the last time we ate there."

"And this time I won't get sick," I promised. But the promise was broken when I felt those same dizzy symptoms I'd felt the last time we went to dinner.

FOUR

I get these psychic vibes when I'm around evil or guilt. And apparently I get them around Michael too. I had confessed to him a while ago that I think it's because I'm scared. He'd replied that I should be. I still don't know what he meant.

So once again I'm in a romantic situation and once again I'm dizzy. Not my favorite way to show Michael I liked him.

We arrived at the Rectory, one of the popular eateries, a few blocks from St. Francis University. Another beautiful old home converted into a business. This one wasn't a former mansion, but two working class homes joined to form the restaurant. Owner Anthony Lasorda greeted us as we walked in. I got my usual hug, "Sam, it's good to see you so soon." He turned to my companion, "And I believe your name is Michael. Welcome back. Let me show you to your table."

As we walked, Michael glanced at me behind Anthony's back. I could tell he was impressed.

We ordered right away. I'd long ago memorized the

menu, and Michael remembered it from last time. My symptoms subsided, and we sat in comfortable silence as we waited for our wine to be served. Anthony himself brought it, giving us a bottle instead of the two glasses we ordered.

A few moments later we were finally alone. I loved Anthony, but he was a talker, and I was desperate to find out what Michael wanted to tell me. I did something very uncharacteristic of me. I waited for him to talk.

And waited.

The server brought our pasta, Michael's with meat in it and mine without.

Finally the compulsion was too difficult to resist. "Michael, you wanted to talk to me about something."

"Oh, yeah," he took another slug of wine and bite of pasta before he continued. "The hospital is concerned because of the recent deaths in the ER and ICU. Not the normal kind of deaths from accidents or serious illness." Bite, chew, slurp, but ever so handsomely, "No, these are people who were pretty healthy. We haven't found any connections between the patients, and that will be my first chore."

I was disappointed that what he had to tell me wasn't a profession of love. In fact it wasn't about me at all. But he looked so good as he talked, it was okay with me.

Someone came, cleared the plates, and refilled our glasses.

"Was Pluto the first patient in the series?"

"Yes, the hospital didn't think too much of it until it happened two more times. And now there are four dead. Which brings me to you…"

To me? Finally.

"I'd like you to work for me for a while. Only part-time. I know you have another job."

Before he could tell me what he wanted me to do I blurted out, "YES!" Yes, I'll work for you. Yes, I'll marry you. Yes, I'll live happily every after with you. My fantasy was interrupted when I noticed he'd begun talking again.

"So what I'd like you to do is to work part-time at the hospital, in the ER…"

"Oh, not with you then." I hoped my disappointment wasn't as evident as I'm sure it was.

"Well, you're working for me, but not with me. The hospital has agreed to hire you as a crisis intervention specialist in the ER. All the patients who've died have come through there. What do you think?"

He wants me to snoop, and I'll get paid for it. What do I think? I think I've died and gone to heaven.

FIVE

The evening ended the same way as the others I'd spent with Michael. A chaste kiss on the cheek and off he rode to save the world. Or something like that.

I took Clancy on a short walk, and spent half of it apologizing for leaving her so much and the other half telling her about the new job. She stopped and raised her eyebrows quizzically. I explained that it wouldn't take time away from her. Once I got info about getting her certified as a therapy dog there would be a good chance she could go to work at the Clinic with me, although I was pretty confident she'd be *persona non grata* in the ER.

Sleep came easily after the wine I'd consumed, and my dreams consisted of me working in the ER, solving the case, and Michael loving me. George kept interrupting every romantic interlude in the dream, and I wondered why. "Why are you here all the time?" I asked the dream George.

"You know why," was his only reply.

I awoke to an alarm and to Clancy sitting on the floor next to my bed with her leash in her mouth. "Clancy, can you wait ten minutes?" She dropped the leash and gave me exactly ten minutes.

I jumped in the shower, lathered up, and gave my short haircut a quick shampoo. I pulled on a tracksuit without benefit of underwear and took Clancy outside. "No time for a walk, Clancy. I have to get to work and talk to the boss about going part-time for a while."

Clancy was going to hear about everything going on at the hospital. As I began my explanation, I was interrupted by my least-favorite sleuth, "Hi ya, Sam."

I looked down to make sure he couldn't tell I had on no underwear. I was overly-gifted on top, and didn't want to give George a free peak. I squealed as I noticed the zipper on the old track jacket was halfway down to my navel.

"Yikes," I let go of Clancy's leash.

"Yikes? Who in the hell says that?"

"Never mind, George. What do you want?" I quickly pulled up the zipper. Too late. George was smiling that smile of his that gets under my skin. "What do you want?"

I half expected him to say, "You know." But he didn't. Instead he got rid of the smile and got to business. "I heard from O'Dear that you were going to be working for him."

"And… ?"

"And I wish you wouldn't do it." He ran his fingers through his thinning hair. "It might be dangerous. And remember the last time you did a job you weren't qualified for. You almost died."

"But I didn't." Why did I let him get to me? As an afterthought, I added, "Why would Michael feel the need to tell you I'm working for him?"

George's grin told me the zipper had gone south again. "Stop it, George."

"What do ya mean, 'stop it.' I'm not doing anything. Maybe you ought to tell the zipper to 'stop it.'"

I ignored what he said as I zipped myself up and went back to my question, "Why would Michael feel the need to tell you anything about me?"

George hesitated. "Apparently he saw me kiss you after we all rescued you."

"First of all you didn't rescue me. You got there in time to arrest the murderers. I didn't need rescuing."

"Whatever you say, Sam."

He walked a little closer until I felt I had to move or we'd be breathing each other's air.

"He saw me kiss you, and he saw you not resisting," George said, getting even closer.

"Don't you dare, George Lansing."

"You're not moving, Sam."

"Good morning, Samantha. Detective Lansing."

Georgianne, saving the day. For once I was happy to see her.

After we exchanged greetings and Georgianne had

returned inside, I told George I needed to get ready for work and I'd talk to him later. His grin let me know he'd look forward to it.

"Glad to hear you aren't wearing that to work."

"Bye, George."

"Bye, Sam."

He exited, still grinning.

SIX

I hurried to work after promising Clancy I'd check into the therapy dog certification.

My Bug was running again and I took it rather than walking. Even though work was only a few blocks away, I was in a hurry today.

Clara Schmidt, the receptionist, broke the news that Mrs. Abernathy was my first appointment. And my second.

"Sam, is that you?" Mrs. Abernathy was in my office waiting for me. As usual she greeted me enthusiastically. Mrs. Abernathy had a lot of erotic dreams and she used her therapy time to tell me all of the details.

I told her I needed to get a cup of coffee first and went into the door next to mine, the kitchen. As I poured the delicious brew into a mug I pondered again why Mrs. Abernathy would need a professional to listen to these x-rated stories. But there was no insurance company involved—Mrs. Abernathy paid cash—and so it was quite legal to charge her for the privilege of regaling me with her dreams.

Before returning to my office I gave myself a pep talk. "I know I shouldn't say this, even to myself, but Mrs. Abernathy's been passed around like the common cold. I'm not going to do what the other therapists did though. I'm going to keep her until she thinks she's done. There. I feel better now."

Mustering up my courage, I opened the door to my office. It was the first one on the left after the reception desk, so my clients didn't have to walk far to see me. Being located between the reception area and the kitchen was an ideal thing for me—I got to satisfy two of my needs, curiosity and food. I don't think people realized it, but I could hear a lot of what went on by the front door. Ditto about what went on in the kitchen, since my office used to be the butler's pantry. I had my own private door to the kitchen.

I then listened to nearly two hours of Mrs. Abernathy's erotic dreams, and did what I could to earn my keep. I commented when appropriate, tried to get her to talk about something else, then realized it was her money and her time. So I let her go on.

At the end, I said something I'd been thinking about, "Mrs. Abernathy, your dreams are quite, um, interesting. Don't you think they'd make good romance novels? Or erotica?" I had to explain what the last word meant. She might have erotic dreams, or make up erotic stories, but no one else would believe me if I were able to tell them. She was in her 70s, short, and overweight.

"No, dear, I hadn't thought of it, why?"

"Well, you have such detail in each of your dreams." Or made up stories. "I think there may be a market for them. You could use an alias if you don't want people to know who you are."

"I don't know why I'd do that. I don't mind if everyone knows that they are my books."

I didn't tell her that I thought the books would sell better if her picture wasn't on the back cover, but hell, it was up to her.

"So, I'm going to give you some homework this week. You are to write down one of your stories…"

"Dreams."

"Yes, dreams. Write one of them down and bring it to your next session. Okay?"

"Okay. Are you sure I don't need to schedule more time with you?"

"Mrs. Abernathy, I think if you start writing down your dreams, you'll find you don't need therapy. Just my opinion. I'll let you decide."

"Okay, dear."

As she left I thought how nice a cold shower would feel. She really knew her way around erotica, whether she knew what the word meant or not.

I needed a distraction, and quick. I got behind my desk

and searched the Web for "therapy dogs." A long list appeared and I investigated several of them. Either they weren't right for Clancy and me or the testing sites were too far away. Finally I found the right one—Therapy Dogs International. Clancy already met the qualifications, except for TDI's own test. And the nearest site was only a 90 minute drive from Quincy. This could work.

I quickly printed out the information, completed the forms, got Clancy's vet to fax an inoculation verification to me, and put the form in the mail to the home office. Clancy would be thrilled to know that I had thought about her as promised.

Just as I finished, Clara buzzed that my next client was here. Andrew Duesterhaus was 13 years old and, like many his age, didn't trust adults. During our first session I had been able to earn his trust through my knowledge of video games. I knew my wasted time would become valuable some day.

As Andy and I talked about his most recent behavior problems, I had a bright idea, and hoped it was ethical. As usual I didn't think things through. "Andy, have you heard about all the animals being poisoned around town?" He grunted affirmatively. "I wonder if you have any ideas about what could be happening."

He finally looked up and made eye contact. "Well, I've been thinking about it. At first I thought it was just a few animals getting into some bad meat or something. But now it's really spreading, so I don't know. Why you askin'?"

"I don't really know. I'm curious and a little worried. You know I have a dog and even though she's not outside without me, I thought what if there's some bad dog food around or something."

"Want me to check around?"

I thought long and hard before I answered. "How about this… you pass your two tests this week, and then I'll ask you to help me investigate. However, I don't want you to do anything until we speak again." I emphasized the word "anything."

I thought I might be treading a fine line in the ethics department, but having this as a reward seemed a lot more motivating than extra time on the computer. I'd worry about the consequences later.

After Andy's session I had a free hour. Dr. Burns has been my boss (for fifteen minutes, anyway) and his position hadn't been filled since his murder. So I went to the human resources office and spoke to Leonard Schnitzer, the personnel director. I told him mostly the truth—that I'd only been given a few patients so far at the clinic and asked if I could go part-time for a while. I added that I had been offered a part-time position in the ER as a crisis intervention specialist. I even suggested that perhaps I could continue working for the clinic full time and that the hospital could pay them for my time. "Just an idea."

Schnitzer seemed to like the latter part of my suggestion and said he would talk to the human resources officer at Bay General about it. I said I wanted to start the arrangement immediately since I wasn't busy at the clinic. He nodded absentmindedly since he was probably already thinking about how to make money for the clinic out of the deal.

I saw a few more clients and had ample time to complete the necessary paperwork for the day. I hoped the clinic would think about paperless charts since I was a lot faster typing than I was writing.

I arrived home to a surprise. George was sitting in his car next to my carriage house. "Hi. How long have you been here?"

He got out of the car. "Not long. I wanted to talk to you. Are you free for an early dinner?"

"I guess so." My hesitance was only because I wasn't sure what George wanted. He didn't ease my curiosity. "I just need to spend a few minutes with Clancy."

I opened the unlocked door, mentally cursing, because I knew George would say something about it. To my surprise, he didn't. Maybe he didn't lock his door either.

Clancy greeted me with kisses and turned on her back for George, so he would scratch her belly. She was easy, that's for sure.

But pretty soon she put two and two together about my

plan to have dinner with George, and froze me out. "I'm sorry, Clancy. I hate to leave you, too." I re-opened the door to take her outside. She quickly did her duty and then sat and stared at me.

Suddenly I had an idea. "George, how about we have something delivered and just eat here?"

He didn't have to think about it. Apparently he cared about Clancy too.

We debated various restaurants that delivered, but quickly decided on Quincy Pizza, Mexican, and Chinese, our town's nod to ethnic cuisines all in one restaurant. Since eating there always required a long wait, having the food delivered seemed like a good choice most of the time. After we ordered, I offered George a beer and we settled into my comfy living room furniture, he on the loveseat and me in an overstuffed chair.

Because we'd known each other since we were in school, it was only natural that we reminisced a little.

George began with, "Remember when you decided to become a vegetarian?"

"Yeah, it was in eighth grade, right after I saw someone wring a chicken's neck. That chicken kept dancing long after it was dead. It spooked me."

"Then the next day we went on a field trip. You ordered vegetable soup…"

I finished for him, "I thought vegetable soup meant

vegetarian soup. I asked the lady if there was any meat in the soup and she said…"

George continued, "… no. She said, no. When you ate it you knew there was some sort of non-vegetarian stock in the soup, and you…"

"I said to the waitress that it tasted like there was meat in the soup and she said, 'There's no meat in that soup… '"

George again, "… no meat in that soup, there's just chicken broth. And you got all red in the face and started cackling like a chicken. You even got out of the booth and did a great chicken impersonation."

We both chuckled at the memory, although I still felt embarrassment at my comedic display. It felt good to be so comfortable with my old friend. I was glad I gave up my anger and went back to liking the guy, at least most of the time.

I wanted to get back to more recent history however. "What about the deaths at the hospital? Any news on the autopsies yet?"

We were interrupted by the delivery guy, fulfilling the promise of quick delivery. George paid. I tipped. Worked out in my favor. The aroma of the pizza seemed to fill the whole room.

I set up plates, utensils, and fresh beers on the cocktail table. We began munching on the vegetarian special, and I repeated my questions. "What about the deaths at the hospital? Any news on the autopsies yet?"

He swallowed before answering. "Not yet. We might hear tomorrow on the first one. The others we had to send to Springfield to the state crime lab. We're not set up to do so many autopsies."

I smiled as sweetly as I could manage with hot cheese stuck to the roof of my mouth. "Will you let me know when you find out?"

He smiled back and only said, "Maybe." In the dim light of my living room George looked younger. I could ignore the balding head and the start of a beer gut, and see the guy I was crazy about in high school. My heart softened a little. A little.

After sinking into more talk of good and bad memories, we began to run out of conversation. Clancy came over with her leash in her mouth letting me know it had been hours since she'd been out.

George helped to quickly clean up the mess and load the dishwasher, and he stood by the door as I walked Clancy out to water the lawn. I put Clancy back in the house with a promise of a long walk in the morning.

I turned to say good-bye to George and hadn't realized how close we were. When I turned to him he put his hands on my shoulders, said, "Don't say anything," and pulled me toward him. "Since I kissed you after you were almost killed, I think about you all the time. Every time I see you I want to kiss you, but I know it's not what you want. But I'll be damned if I let this chance go by."

In shock, I didn't say anything. I stood there and melted into the arms of my high school sweetheart. The kiss was lovely, warm, and sexy as hell.

He kissed me with his soft, full lips for what seemed like forever, said "Goodnight, Sam," and turned to walk away. With my usual impulsivity I grabbed his shoulder before he was out of reach, turned him around, and kissed him again. Then, before things could get out of hand I gently pushed him toward his car.

Clancy grinned when I went into the house. "Do you like him more than Michael?" She didn't answer, but did keep grinning. I couldn't answer the question myself. I'd been out with Michael a few times and really liked him. He spoke romantically to me, but never really kissed me, except for a kiss on the cheek and the forehead, more like a relative instead of a boyfriend. And as mad as I was at George when I first saw him after returning to Quincy, I was now able to see the sweet guy I fell for in high school. Compared to Michael, George was a raging inferno—which made him a lot more attractive.

My dreams that night were similar to previous nights except when I asked George why he was there, he said, "You know why," and I did.

SEVEN

Today would be my first time working in the ER at Bay General. I planned to spend the morning at the clinic, and the afternoon and maybe evening at the hospital. Before going to work I did give Clancy the promised walk, although not as long as she expected. "I'll hear back about the therapy dog certification soon, and then we'll be together a lot." She accepted my apology and went back to bed when the walk was finished.

After an uneventful morning, I arrived at the hospital about one. Jenny told me I'd have to start with the human resources office, and that took almost an hour. Since I was already trained in the job itself, by virtue of my career choice, I only had to sign confidentiality statements, grievance procedures, and other boring papers before I was released to the ER with a huge binder full of policies and procedures.

Finally, I was allowed to start my snooping. I prayed that there would be no crises, so I could snoop to my heart's content. Jen did an orientation to the ER and gave me a mini-tour.

I knew most people who worked there, including Dr. Craig Adams. He was the only one who hadn't been to the potluck earlier in the week. Craig was a competent ER physician, but was also a crab, a dictator, and many other negative adjectives. He greeted me with a curt grunt and gave Jen some orders in a way that made me want to slap him for mistreating my sister. But when she gave me the "sister look" I figured I should keep my mouth closed.

Jen turned to me, "Okay. That's all the time I've got. I don't know what you are supposed to do when there's no mental health work to be done, but heed my words—don't interfere with how my ER runs."

Me? Interfere? Lucky she didn't know that my real job was to snoop. She'd be angry and would probably try to talk me out of it.

I felt guilty about not telling her though. It's like a giant lie. At least I really was going to do crisis work there, so that part wasn't a lie.

A Code Blue was called, taking Jenny away from watching my every move. Everyone seemed to be frantically busy, so I moseyed over to the break room. The EMTs normally hung out there when they weren't on an ambulance run. I peeked in and the room was empty. I decided to have a cup of coffee and as I filled my cup I noticed someone sitting in the corner. His pale skin was almost translucent, and his greasy hair covered his forehead.

"Aren't you Carter Callahan?" I recognized him from Jen's party.

He nodded, but didn't speak.

I stuck out my hand. "I'm Sam Darling, Jenny's sister. I think we were both in here when the guy keeled over during the carry-in."

He nodded again. And maybe, just maybe, he said, "Uh-huh." But he didn't shake my hand.

"You're kind of quiet, huh?"

"Nothin' to talk about," is what he might have said. His whisper hardly reached my ears. He didn't sound threatening; in fact, his tone conveyed no emotion at all, which set my vibes on alert.

This was boring me, but he was the only game in town, so I felt I had to talk to him. "Have you heard about the recent odd deaths in the ER?"

He nodded.

"Do you have any ideas what might have caused the deaths? Do you think they are related or just coincidental?"

"Probably murder."

His first real words and he says "probably murder." Maybe this talk would be fruitful after all.

"I'd like you to tell me why you think the patients were murdered. And please speak in full sentences. It's kind of hard pulling the words out of you."

He almost smiled. "Because we've never had this happen

before. This many people with no clear cause. It's up to five because someone died this morning."

"How were they murdered?"

"Probably poisoned."

Wow, there was more to this guy than what met the eye. I said, "The autopsy results should be back today from the first guy who died. Guess we'll find out if he was poisoned or not."

"I'd bet on it," said Carter, and he went back into silent mode.

I wondered why he was here every day. I wondered why the hospital let him just sit in the break room. Maybe the powers-that-be hadn't noticed. Jen could have a soft spot for him since he lost his job. I'd have to ask her why he got fired.

It didn't seem like I needed to say good-bye to Carter, since social skills weren't his strong suit. So I just walked out of the room with my coffee.

Loretta saw me and immediately came in way too close to tell me we weren't allowed to have coffee outside the break room, just water. I noted she'd had sausage, onion, and eggs for lunch. She was a nice lady but always gave me the shivers because of her close talking. She was a petite woman, but because of her extra-round face and her personal space violations, it felt like she was huge.

I asked what happened with the Code Blue. Her smile spread across her face as she said, "Which one? There were two. Dougie is on duty and was able to save both of them. They put them in ICU because they don't know what's wrong with them yet." She was definitely one proud mama.

"Hi ya, Sam."

I turned to look at George, standing there smiling in the ER. My face felt hot and I knew it was bright red. Thinking about last night evoked all kinds of feelings. Including embarrassment.

"Hi," I returned the greeting. I hoped he wasn't here to talk about "us."

My hopes were answered when he said, "We got the autopsy results back on Pluto. Thought you'd want to know."

In my enthusiasm, I practically jumped on the poor guy, but he didn't seem to mind. He continued to smile as I led him into a vacant exam room. "Okay, tell me."

His smile faded as my greeting wasn't exactly what he seemed to expect. So he added, "And then I have something else to talk about."

My nod seemed to suffice as agreement. "What about the autopsy?"

"Pluto was poisoned."

"Really? Poisoned?"

"Yeah. Plain old arsenic. He'd just finished eating chicken wings here, and they were the only things in his stomach, besides a little alcohol. It looked like the arsenic was on the wings."

"That doesn't make sense though. I think Jenny brought the wings, so I don't know how they'd have poison on them," I said. "And other people didn't get sick." Then I thought of Rob. "My brother Rob got an upset stomach during the potluck. I haven't talked to him since then. Has he been working?"

Since Rob was a cop on the same police force as George, George was sure to have information about him. Instead, George replied, "I dunno."

Immediately I pulled out my mobile phone and called Rob's cell number. After several rings a sleepy voice answered. "Yeah."

"Rob, this is Sam. How are you?"

"I was fine until you woke me up. I'm working nights this week."

"Sorry. I just have a few questions for you. When you left Jenny's party you were pretty sick. How long did it last and how bad did it get?"

"I threw up all night. Never had the flu so bad before. Couldn't even keep down medicine. Called in sick the next day, but have been fine since then. Why?"

"I'll tell you later. Want me to sing you a lullaby so you can go back to sleep?" The dial tone gave me his answer.

George heard my end of the conversation and I filled him in on what Rob had to say. George thought out loud, "It's probably too late to see if Rob had any poison in his system, but I'll follow up. I don't know how long arsenic stays in the system. Anyone else get sick from the food?"

I couldn't remember if any other guests got sick. But I was able to give him a list of who was there. I also wondered if there was a connection to the animal poisonings.

As George turned to leave, I asked, "What was the second thing you wanted to talk about?"

"Changed my mind. I'll save that for later. 'Bye." And just that fast, he was gone.

Lucky for me, George didn't want to talk about last night. I just wasn't ready for it. After he left I sat and thought a while. Was there a connection between Pluto dying and the other recent deaths? Was there a connection between the human deaths and the animal deaths? I bet there would be autopsies on some of the animals too, just to make sure. An involuntary shiver escaped me. I didn't know if it was from the usual coolness of the ER or because of the subject matter.

I walked out of the room and bumped into Jenny. "I need to talk to you as soon as you have a minute," was all I got to say as she whizzed past me.

Over her shoulder she said, "I have a break in a few minutes. Go to the break room and I'll meet you there."

The break room was empty when I arrived, which brought questions about Carter to the surface. He was a strange one all right. He was right about the poison, but we really didn't know if it was murder or not yet. Wonder how he knew about the poison?

Jen arrived shortly and I started with telling her about how Pluto died. "I can't believe it. Poisoned? Was it from the food at my party?" A tear formed in her eye but didn't escape to her cheek. "I'd just die if it was from my food."

I couldn't comfort her on that score. "George said our food was all that was in Pluto's stomach, and your wings in particular. The arsenic was on the wings. I'm really sorry. And remember Rob got sick too. They have no idea how it happened yet." I added, "The other unexplained deaths are being autopsied in Springfield. Hope we hear about them soon." I also told Jenny about all the animals dying, but didn't really have a lot of information on that score.

Jen seemed really shaken up, so I tried to comfort her. "Honey, I know you had nothing to do with the wings being poisoned. You are not a suspect in my book."

"It hurts so much to know someone died because of my food."

I continued to try to reassure her, "It wasn't because of your food. It was because of the arsenic on your food. Big difference."

It was unusual to see Jen as anything but calm, confident, and kind. I changed the subject for a moment to see if that would snap her out of it. "Why is Carter here all the time? I'd think if someone was fired, the hospital wouldn't want him hanging around."

She moved her head from side to side as if to clear it. "Um, the hospital doesn't know he's here. He comes in by the ambulance entrance and leaves the same way. He stays in the break room, so no one but ER staff sees him. He doesn't bother anything. Why?"

"Dunno really. I talked to him earlier and he bet me that poison was how these people died. I thought it was strange. And speaking of strange, that word describes him too. He gives me the creeps."

"Shup," Jen said, using our childhood shorthand for "shut up." Her lip quivered as she continued, "Carter's one of us. He's been with us in the trenches and he's damn good at his job."

"Why did he get fired then?"

"I hate to even tell you."

"Why?"

"Because you're such a know-it-all that you'll have it in your head that Carter poisoned people."

"Just tell me." I almost begged at this point.

"He got fired because there were some irregularities with his EMT certification. And really he's not fired; he's laid off until things get straightened out."

"Hmmm."

"Quit interrogating me." Jen had raised her voice and I was surprised at her sudden anger. "Carter's got nothing to do with this. You have your vibes—well, my gut tells me he's just weird. Not criminal. Not crazy. Just weird."

The vehemence of Jen's response let me know it was indeed time for me to "shup."

While she went back to work I decided to check work schedules against ER deaths and see if anything jumped out at me. I took old schedules and a list of the deaths I got from the secretary. In less than a week there had been six unexplained deaths, counting Pluto, though he didn't actually die in the ER but in ICU a few minutes after being admitted.

When I looked at the time of death versus who was on duty, I didn't like it one little bit. The first person who was on duty every single time was my sister Jenny. It was impossible for me to think of her as a suspect, but I knew the cops would think so—except for Rob and maybe George. There were two other people on duty for each death, Loretta and Dougie. Since Dr. Dougie Johnson was Loretta's son, Jenny put them on the schedule together whenever she could. That was three people, but I thought Carter needed to be on the list too. No one could track his exact comings and goings because of how he snuck in, but because of his weirdness and the uneasy feeling I got around him, I thought he definitely belonged on the list, maybe even at the top of it.

A slight noise disturbed my meditation. I looked up to

see Carter Callahan in his usual place in the corner. This was a sign that it was time for some in depth sleuthing.

"Hey, Carter, I want to talk and I want you to talk too. A conversation. What do you think?"

He nodded.

"Use your words."

"Uh, okay."

Now was the time for me to get to work. "I got the results of Pluto's autopsy. You were right. He was poisoned. We're not 100% sure it was murder. It could have been an accident, but I'm thinking foul play."

He sat up straight and again almost smiled. "Told you."

"Yeah, but how did you know?"

"Dunno. Just knew."

I decided to go for it. "Did you do it? Did you poison him?"

He didn't react as I thought he might. Instead he said, "What a silly question."

"It's not silly. You're the one who said the deaths were all poison and that they were murder. The only one."

"That just makes me smart, not criminal."

"You were at the party where Pluto keeled over after eating wings."

"So were you."

He had me there. "So if you aren't the murderer, who is? Any ideas?"

Carter licked his lips before answering. "The answer is clear if you know where to look."

"What does that mean? Do you have any idea who might have killed Pluto and the others?"

"I have ideas, but I'm not talking about them." With that he slumped back into the corner like the ghost he resembled.

Since it was like he wasn't there, I decided to do some thinking. I pulled out some paper and wrote down the list of folks who worked when all the patients died unexpectedly. Then I started writing why they might or might not be guilty and even how they could have pulled off the crimes.

CARTER: May or may not have been present for all the deaths. However, he was someone who had access to the ER and definitely was present for Pluto's death. Plus he was weird, just plain weird, and set my vibes going. Also he said the deaths were from poison.

JENNY: Was present for all the patient deaths, but there was no way she could have done it. She's my sister for heaven's sake.

DOUGIE: Dr. Johnson was present for all the deaths and actually worked on most of the patients. I hadn't met him yet, but hoped to soon. The problem was that everyone in the ER was always so darn busy when they worked.

LORETTA: Was at work for all the deaths, but no evidence to show she actually took care of all six people. She seemed overly proud when her son saved people.

So far, there were four suspects, counting Jenny who was definitely not the murderer. Four suspects that I knew of, but there were probably more who had access to the patients but didn't work in the ER, such as visitors, chaplains, X-ray techs, people drawing blood, etc. The list could be overwhelming. Maybe I should get that list from Human Resources and see who was working in an ancillary department when all six people died.

Suddenly I got an "aha." What if some other people were poisoned too, but they didn't die. I'd have to check on whether it was possible to ingest arsenic and just get sick but not die.

My sister, Jill, wasn't on the list because she wasn't on duty for all the deaths. As an ER resident she had an odd schedule. And she also wasn't on my suspect list because she was my sister. I wished I could do the same for Jen.

It hit me that it would have to have been a fast-acting poison if an employee administered it and the person died right away. Or would there be a way to do it surreptitiously, like put it on chicken wings, the way Pluto was poisoned.

My thoughts were interrupted by Jen poking her head into the room, "Want to go to dinner? Dougie and I are heading to the cafeteria."

Never having been one to say no to food, I jumped up and joined her. Also I'd never met the popular Dr. Johnson, and having a meal with him would let me get to know him without being viewed as an interrogator.

"Darn it!"

Jen looked concerned. "What's wrong?"

"I forgot Clancy. I didn't go home in between the Clinic and here, and she's probably standing by the door with all four of her legs crossed. Go ahead. I'll call Gus and then will catch up with you."

She nodded and exited. I had Gus on speed dial, so it wasn't long before I heard, "Hello."

Without bothering to be polite I made my quick confession. "I don't have much time to talk, but I did the unthinkable. I forgot about Clancy." I could hear Gus's gasp through the phone. "Would you please let her out? I left the door unlocked." Another gasp.

"Sam, I warned you about that. I fixed the locks so no one could break in and then you don't even use them? And yes, I'll take care of Clancy. No worries there."

He hung up before I could apologize for not using his handy-dandy locks. At least I could calm down about my sweet dog. Sweet, hell. She'd make me pay for this. And I'd do my best to make it up to her when I got home.

I hurried to the cafeteria, ran through the line, and joined Jenny and Dougie at their table. It felt funny calling Dr. Johnson by his nickname, but that was the only thing I'd ever heard him called.

You could tell he was Loretta's son. He could be described as petite too, like his mom, and had the same round face. Also he was incredibly handsome. Since he was sitting I couldn't tell his height but knew he was about 5'4", a few inches taller than his mom.

After Jen introduced us again, I began what I considered a very professional, yet undetectable, interview.

After a moment of pleasantries, I began, "Wow, you've been here for every one of the odd deaths."

He looked at me as if I'd committed a huge faux pas. "Yes, so have other people."

Jen intervened. After all, Dougie was one of her people. "He also saved a lot of other people who had similar symptoms."

Aha. New information. "Really. I didn't realize that." Note to self again: don't forget to check on how arsenic works, medical treatments that counteract it, and whether or not there were antidotes.

I continued, "So I guess you're kind of a hero."

"You betcha," said Jen.

Dougie didn't say anything, but he smiled, making him even more handsome. "I sure don't consider myself a hero, but…" He stopped abruptly, almost as if he really did consider himself a hero. Seemed odd.

Meal times were only thirty minutes when you worked in a hospital, so our discussion was short. Toward the end it hit me that I hadn't reported to Michael what I'd learned. And even worse, he hadn't checked on me.

Before I could excuse myself to call Michael, my stomach started talking to me. Me with the cast-iron stomach. And with each second it got worse. "Jen, I gotta go."

"You okay?" She was solicitous, both as a sister and a nurse.

"Nope. My stomach. Gotta go." I escaped more quickly than my middle-aged body should have been able to. Out of the corner of my eye I saw Loretta going through the line, but didn't have the time to say anything to her. I didn't want to hurl in the cafeteria. And I almost made it. Almost.

EIGHT

You'd think that hurling in front of a bunch of medical personnel would result in me getting a lot of attention. You'd think. But you'd be wrong. I was around the corner from Jen, so she didn't notice and didn't come to my aid.

I mean, what do you do when this happens and then it's finished? Do you walk away? Do you get material to clean it up? I knew I couldn't do the latter because that was the reason I was in mental health instead of health. And my innate sense of ethics wouldn't let me walk away. So I just stood there, feeling like being sick again, until someone came up and told me they called Housekeeping, and I could leave. Thank God.

I made it home in record time, raced into my house, and barely noticed that Clancy wasn't there. I heard a knock on my door but couldn't attend to it until I took care of more urgent matters.

Finally I walked into my living room and saw Gus there.

"When you didn't answer I got worried so I walked in. I heard what was going on in the other room, so thought I'd wait and make sure you were okay."

I nodded and thanked him, but didn't have the energy for much more. I collapsed on the couch and Gus threw Grandma's quilt on me. I always feel better when I'm covered by Grandma's quilt.

"Clancy?" I could barely get the word out.

"Georgianne's got her and they are practically making out on the sofa in the parlor."

I chuckled, remembering Georgianne's aversion to Clancy until she'd spent some time with her. Then it became a mutual admiration society. "I really feel horrible. Can Clancy spend the night with you guys? Normally I'd want her with me when I was sick, but I don't think I have the energy to let her outside or to even talk."

"Sure," Gus said. "Georgianne will love it." He said it without sarcasm, and I believed him.

After getting some dog food for Clancy's dinner, Gus made sure to lock the door behind him, and that was the last thing I remembered until I woke up the next morning.

I had the day off and slept in until 8 AM, late for me. A good night's sleep was restorative, and so was losing all the food in my stomach. I noted that I probably would bring my own food to the hospital in the future. However, I did remember that Jenny had told me the flu was going around. Guess I couldn't really blame hospital food after all.

Since I was off and since I felt good, I decided to do some

sleuthing on my own. I know I was only supposed to work at the hospital and funnel information to Michael, but following suspects seemed like a logical extension of my assignment.

Before leaving my house I did two things. I got Clancy and gave her an abbreviated walk—apologizing all the time—and I called Michael. "Sam Darling, private eye, reporting in."

"Not funny," Michael said. "Don't make me sorry I asked for your help. You are not a PI. You're a social worker."

Just like my brothers and George. I'm not a cop. I'm not a private investigator. Whatever. So I guess I wouldn't tell Michael about my plan to follow suspects when I could.

I told him about doing the check on who was on duty when the patients died.

"Now that's exactly the kind of thing I hoped to get from you. Good job."

He knew the way to my heart—positive reinforcement. I was ready for more. "There are four people who were always on duty," and I listed them for him. "But Jenny…"

"I know," he interrupted, "Jenny couldn't be guilty."

"Okay, as long as you know that."

"What I know, Sam, is that I can't be blinded by who is related to you, who you like or don't like. I have to go on the evidence."

I choked back a nasty retort because I still had a crush on him. Even though George and I kissed, and even though it was really nice, I still had a crush on Michael. I put aside those thoughts and said, "And the evidence will show that Jenny is innocent."

"Of course it will." Did he really believe that or was he just trying to appease me?

"Okay, that's all I know for now. I'll keep in touch."

He didn't try to keep me on the phone, which hurt my feelings, and then I mentally yelled at myself for acting like a lovesick teenager. Back to sleuthing.

All four suspects were working today, which should have set my antennas buzzing, but I didn't think that the hospital would be the best place for me to be. Instead I waited in the ER parking lot, knowing that Carter would either be coming or going in the near future. He didn't seem to stay at the hospital long, but was there several times a day, so the odds were good that I'd catch him at some point.

I sat in my blue VW bug, thinking that my car was conspicuous—too conspicuous for PI work. There was nothing I could do about it, though. My patience was rewarded about ten minutes later when Carter strolled out of the ambulance bay. Even though I knew it was him, he was so nondescript and was so "beige," that he could easily slip in and out of places without being noticed. I tried to guess which car was his, and was surprised when he sat at the bus stop. A few minutes later he boarded the bus that said Broadway on it.

You would think that it would be easy following a bus, and you would be wrong again. All the stops and starts made it impossible to be discreet. If Carter didn't know me I would have gotten on the bus myself to follow him, but that was impossible, too. So I dutifully followed the bus, and followed rather closely so no other vehicle could split us up. Since I knew the bus route I could have just gone somewhere on the route and waited, but I didn't know when Carter was going to get off.

So I followed and followed and followed, down Broadway to Fifth, south to Maine, east to Twenty-fourth, south to State, west to Eighteenth, north to Broadway, and west to the hospital. Finally, Carter got off the bus—at the same place he got on. A lot of work with little reward. Why would anyone just ride the bus for the whole route and end up where they started? I hit my steering wheel and accidentally engaged the horn. By this time I was back in the ER parking lot and Carter was near me. He reacted as most people would. He jumped. I smiled, waved, and said, "Sorry," at the same time. Carter gave me an almost imperceptible nod.

I didn't have time to berate myself as my phone rang right after the horn went off. It was Jenny, "Sam, can you come in right away?" Then she hung up.

She'd think I was Superwoman since it took me about 30 seconds to get from my car to the ER.

Jenny didn't say anything about my speed. She grabbed my arm and pulled me into an exam room. "Craig's dead. Dr. Adams is dead." She started crying and allowed me to put my arm around her for a moment before she shook off the tears and became a professional nurse again. "The cops will be here any minute."

Only a millisecond passed before I heard George's voice in the hallway. I peeked my head outside and motioned for him to come in.

His smile disappeared when he saw Jenny was in the room with me. I put aside the current drama and thought that he probably assumed we were going to make out again. Like Jen, I was able to shake off my unprofessionalism and get back to business.

"What's up?" George got right to the point.

"Dr. Adams just died," I told him.

"Was it unexpected?" He looked from me to Jen, back and forth, before Jen answered.

"Yeah. One minute he was fine and the next minute he doubled over. I checked his pulse and it was thready, his blood pressure was tanking, and his breathing was labored and all of a sudden he was gone. That fast."

"Who was with him?" George asked as he pulled out a notebook.

"Just me when he died," Jen answered. "Right before he died Loretta was with him, and Dougie spoke to him about a patient a little before that."

"Where's his body?"

"In Exam Room 10."

George stepped out of the room and told someone, "Exam Room 10. Keep everybody else out of there."

He turned back to Jenny, "You were with him. Were you with the others when they died?"

She looked confused. "Yeah, a few, but not all."

"Were you with the first guy?" He looked at his notes, "The guy you called Pluto."

She pushed the blonde hair out of her eyes and answered, "I let him join us for my birthday party, and I gave him chicken wings. I helped put him on the gurney after he collapsed. That was all the interaction I had with him. Why?"

George just shrugged his shoulders. I thought I should probably start calling him Butthead again if he thought what I thought he thought. Or something like that.

I glared at him and decided I'd get things out in the open. "Why are you asking Jen these questions? Why are you interrogating her? You know she had nothing to do with any of these deaths. Just because she made the wings, gave him the wings, and it was the wings that killed him." I thought I'd better shut up before I had her convicted and in prison.

George said, "I know she's not guilty, Sam. But I have to play this by the book. Just because she's someone I know and like doesn't mean she gets off the hook." He turned back to Jen. "I'm sorry, Jen. But we discovered that you were on duty every time someone died. Others were too, but you're the first one I'm talking to."

She nodded at him. Her face showed concern, but no fear, and that helped me relax.

George looked at me again, his sparse gray-streaked hair trying to fall into his eyes just as it did when it was fuller in high school. He'd become quite a distraction to me recently. "Sam, could you excuse us so I can talk to Jen?"

I didn't answer him, instead I looked at Jenny. "Are you okay?" She nodded. "Don't forget, if he starts treating you like a suspect, stop talking and get a lawyer."

Even though I wasn't looking at him I could feel George's glare trying to bore a hole through the back of my head. Then he said, "No need to worry about that, Jen. I'm just talking to everyone who was present for all the deaths. Then I'll talk to other people. You are no more a suspect than your sister."

I turned back to him at that remark. It reminded me of what he'd said to Dr. Burns's killer not too long ago. Virtually the same words. And he ended up arresting that person for murder not too long afterward.

I looked at Jenny again. "Just remember what I said."

She nodded.

I walked into the hallway and saw my brother Rob standing in front of Exam Room 10. He must have been the cop George had given orders to.

"Don't even start," he said.

I did my best to ignore him, but it's hard when your siblings know you so well. "Okay, I was just going to invite you over for dinner, but if you don't want to talk to me, that's fine."

I swear he chortled. I don't think I'd ever heard someone chortle before. It was like an explosive chuckle. Rob knew I didn't cook. Hell, the world knew I didn't cook. I ought to invite the world for dinner some night and show them I knew what I was doing. Nah. Probably not.

I went to my normal "go to" spot in the ER—the break room. Carter was sitting in his usual spot in the corner. I wondered if George knew that Carter was here for all the deaths too, or at least most of them. If I told him that, it would at least take the heat off of Jenny for a while. Maybe I should ask Jen if she'd ever seen Carter in the main part of the ER instead of just in the break room. My vibes weren't on high alert around him, but I thought I had some response because he was so strange.

Carter was just sitting there, almost pasted to the corner of the room. The light barely reached him. A perfect spot for eavesdropping. Maybe he knew more than he had told me so far.

"Hi." I started very gently, afraid he'd bolt if I was too aggressive.

I think he might have nodded. I do know he grunted. I took that as an encouraging sign.

"How did you know people were poisoned?"

"I told you that I just knew," he yelled. He didn't seem happy with my question. "If you know where to look, Ms. Wanna-be Sleuth, you'll find the answer. It's right under your nose."

"That sounds like you know a lot more about the deaths than you are saying."

"Duh," he said.

At least I think that's what he said. He'd slunk back into his regular persona, quiet and almost invisible. I thought it was only fair to tell him that he was a suspect.

"There are four main suspects as far as I'm concerned— Jenny, Loretta, Dougie, and… you."

Carter's laugh could have been heard across the river in West Quincy. Surprising that a seeming nonentity could make so much noise. Especially someone who normally only grunted. He didn't respond with words, just laughter. Odd. Made him seem more weird than usual, which I'd thought was an impossibility.

I went back to the ER proper and saw that Rob was still standing by Room 10, but now there was crime scene tape across the door. I avoided him, not wanting to be made fun of again. George wasn't in evidence, so I began looking for him.

No one really knew this was my day off, so I just started peeking into each room. The first one held Jenny and a doctor I didn't know, working with a patient. Jen's back was to me, so I just quietly closed the door.

In the next room I saw a flurry of activity. One of the doctors was my sister Jill. I hadn't known she was working today, but it would be good to talk to her when she was less busy. Dougie was the other doctor in there, and Loretta seemed to be assisting them. Since it appeared to be a serious situation I repeated my earlier action, closing the door without being detected.

The next few rooms were empty, silently awaiting their next patients. I continued to ignore Rob, but did notice someone had gone inside the room he was guarding. I imagined it was someone doing crime scene work, and perhaps George was there too.

I knew the whereabouts of all four of the major suspects. There was no one to follow, three of them were very busy, and the fourth was incommunicado. I wished Carter were more verbal, but then I guess he wouldn't be Carter.

Sleuthing was boring sometimes. I didn't feel grief over the loss of Dr. Adams; I'd only met him once, and he was easy to dislike. Jen had told me some tales of how she had to stand up to him several times to protect her staff from his wrath.

I stood in the nurses' station, waiting to see if George would emerge from Room 10. My patience was rewarded when he soon appeared, telling Rob to stay there until he was relieved by another officer. Rob nodded. Funny how he knew how to behave when on duty. At home he acted like one of the three stooges, easily fitting in with my other two brothers, Pete and Ed.

It was fairly easy to intercept George since he stood in the hallway for a few minutes, talking to Rob. Another person left Room 10 and walked straight to the ambulance bay exit.

George said goodbye to Rob and began walking and writing in his notebook at the same time. "Hey," I said as I got into a walking pace with him.

He stopped abruptly, turned to me, and grinned. "Hi ya," his usual greeting.

"I wonder if you have time to talk to me."

"Always. Want to talk now or do you want to meet for dinner?"

"Now if you don't mind." I noted the disappointment on his face.

We scooted into an empty exam room. I walked quickly to the window, so we wouldn't be dangerously close. I wanted to keep this professional.

George said, "I guess this isn't personal."

"Right. It's got to do with the murders. First, have you

gotten the autopsy results from Springfield on the people who died after Pluto?"

"Not yet. Today or tomorrow."

"Well, I've got an idea about a suspect. My vibes get set off when I'm around him, but it's not a horrible reaction."

"Sam, remember when Dr. Burns was murdered. Your vibes let you down."

"Stop reminding me of that. I was right on one of the murderers. I was always right about one of them."

"Yeah, but you were convinced the other murderer was innocent, because your vibes weren't present with her. So excuse me if I'm not overly excited about what you're saying."

"George Lansing, you are a pain in the butt. Here's what I know and you can do what you want with it. I'll do what I want with it too."

He rolled his eyes, which was very unattractive in a man his age. "Go ahead," he said.

"I can't prove this guy was present for all the deaths, but he's suspicious. I know he was here for some of the deaths. His name is Carter Callahan, and he was an EMT here until he got laid off because of some 'irregularities' in his certification. I haven't checked that out yet. But I did follow him and he took the bus all around town and then got off the bus here at Bay General. Right where he started. That's weird, right?" I didn't give George a chance to answer. "He's here almost all the time and hangs out in the break room. He was there a few minutes ago."

Before he could remind me, I said, "Yes, I know I'm not a cop. I'm a social worker. That's why I'm giving you this information. Happy?"

He smiled. "I'd be happier if you'd have dinner with me."

"Not tonight, but in a few days, okay?" I wanted to save a few evenings just in case Michael asked me out. Stupid. Juvenile. But oh, well…

I guessed it was time to leave when George leaned in for a kiss. I did the unforgivable move of turning my head to give him my cheek. "'Bye." I said. "See you later."

Part of me wanted to stay and avail myself of George's kisses. It had been a long, long time since I'd been in a romantic situation and George definitely seemed a lot more interested than Michael.

Since it was still early and was my day off, I went home, changed, put the leash on Clancy, and took her for a long walk in a different direction. I didn't bother talking about the investigation, and she didn't ask. We just went. Part of the way we ran, although I wasn't able to run too far. I chalked it up to having been sick yesterday.

We walked all the way to St. Francis University and back, at least a half mile each way. Clancy led the way, probably happy to finally be getting the attention she so richly deserved.

This walk was one of my favorites. To get to SFU, I had to leave the ritzy section of town and walk right by where I grew up. It was only a few blocks, but it was an extreme difference. The north side of Broadway was where I grew up, and the south side of Broadway is where I now lived. The only reason I lived in the mansion section was that I rented Gus and Georgianne's carriage house. Gus had been my friend since I was a kid, and when I moved back to Quincy he immediately offered me the carriage house. He grew up like I did, in a working class section of town. Georgianne had a lot of family money. Gus said that money got in the way sometimes, but that it was easier to deal with problems when your bills were always paid.

Clancy and I loved SFU. It was my alma mater, at least for my undergraduate degree. The old buildings towered over the campus and were magnificent reflections of the majesty of the city. Red bricks and limestone blocks. Perfect. Quincy was built on the limestone bluffs overlooking the Mississippi River, and a lot of the architecture contained limestone.

Quincy had roughly two hundred fifty full blocks of buildings on the National Historic Register. My childhood neighborhood was sandwiched in between historic blocks. Growing up, I always felt that SFU was my backyard, and I made myself at home on the tennis courts, baseball fields, and even the gym. Jen and I spent a lot of time there as kids.

For a change I just reminisced instead of working on the mysterious deaths. Until I got information on the deaths other than Pluto's, it was hard to do much brain work. But I could still follow the suspects, and check into their lives. So that's what I would do, and maybe I'd let Clancy help me.

NINE

My first thought upon waking had to do with the autopsies. My second was Clancy's therapy dog certification test. I decided to call George and ask about the former. And I'd check online for the date for Clancy's test. I'd already been notified by email that she qualified.

"Yeah." George's phone response showed that he was always on duty.

"It's me. Sam."

His tone changed. "Hi ya. How are you?"

"Good. I'm calling to find out the results of the autopsies from Springfield. Did you get them?"

"I'll check my email." His tone let me know that he was disappointed it wasn't a social call. I heard him take the phone from his ear, then he put me on speaker so he could read and talk at the same time. "Yeah, here it is. Just a second." He muttered as he read. "Okay, we have the results from two more bodies." They were bodies now, no longer patients. "Same as with Pluto. Arsenic. Maybe something else. Further tests. Will take a few more days. That's it, Sam."

"Well, at least now we know that two of them were poisoned like Pluto. That gives us three murders. We still don't know if it was accidental or intentional, though. Guess I'll have to check into it more."

"Sam…"

"Don't bother telling me what my job is or isn't. I already know." And I hung up.

I slipped on my tracksuit, with a T-shirt underneath because of the errant zipper on the jacket. "C'mon, Clancy. Let's go."

It only took a moment for us to get out the door and head for our usual morning walk through our neighborhood. Clancy led the way and I didn't have to think about the walk itself. She knew when to stop, when to go, and when to smell squirrel tracks.

"I know I haven't talked to you much about these deaths. But I'm having trouble even finding clues. If it's okay, I'll go over the suspects with you."

She turned and smiled as she walked. I knew that meant "okay."

"There are three people who were present for all the deaths, and one who may have been there for all of them." Suddenly, something hit me. "Damn. I forgot to ask George if any of the dogs had been autopsied. I wonder if they died from the same poison."

Clancy didn't like hearing that. She shrugged off a shiver

and kept going. "Sorry, Clance. Don't worry. I'll keep you safe."

We were soon at the turnaround point, and Clancy automatically did just that. I decided to forget about problems and began singing George M. Cohan songs from the first World War. That livened up both of us. Clancy seemed to march in time to the rhythm, just as thousands of soldiers had almost a century ago.

When we got home I quickly showered and dressed for work. Today I'd work at both the Clinic and the hospital. My first appointment wasn't until nine, so I took a moment to check on the therapy dog test. Luckily, I had sent everything in just in time. There was a test this weekend in Chatham, a small town near the state capitol of Springfield. I entered my credit card information to pay for the test, reminded myself to practice the necessary skills with Clancy before then, and promised Clancy I'd be home for dinner. As I left, I stopped at Michael's office on the way to the Clinic. His office was downtown in one of the old buildings that had been converted to small offices. Great for start-ups and for business's like Michael's which, only consisted of one or two people.

I found his office door open and walked in. Michael was sitting there doing two things—looking worried and looking incredibly handsome. My crush was still in full swing, even though I'd made out with George.

He didn't see me so I politely cleared my throat.

"Sam. Sorry. I'm glad to see you."

That set my pulse racing. "It's good to see you too. I came in to give you a report on the suspects."

He nodded, but looked like his mind was elsewhere.

I asked, "I have information on the autopsies. Do you?"

He shook his head so I filled him in. I also told him again about Carter, and how I'd followed him. Of course Michael reminded me that my job wasn't to follow people. As usual I ignored what he was saying. I was a grown up and knew what my job was. Then I asked him if he had any other information. He shook his head again. I wasn't getting my "evil vibes" but this sure felt funny. Normally Michael was attentive and suddenly he was almost ignoring me.

There's nothing subtle about me, so I said, "Is something wrong?"

He replied with the normal answer, "No, why?"

"You just seem preoccupied."

"Nah. There's just something I need to talk to you about."

This time I was confident he wasn't going to say he loved me, and surprisingly, I was okay with that. "Well, just do it. I'm not good at waiting." I sat down in one of the ultra-modern office chairs in front of his desk.

"I'm finding it hard to work with you on this case, because…"

Because he loved me? Because he hated me? Because...

Michael hesitated. "... because of Jenny's involvement."

My sputtering caused him to stand up and come around the desk. He sat in another chair next to me. "I know you are positive she had nothing to do with it. Since you are so biased, I wonder if you're the right person to help with the investigation."

Whew. It had nothing to do with whether he liked me or not. But, wait a minute... I jumped up and for the first time was able to tower over him. "Who in the hell do you think you are? You think my sister killed someone? Are you crazy?"

He leaned back in his chair to get away from the berserk woman in his face. "Exactly. That's exactly what I mean, Sam. Exactly."

I stopped sputtering for the moment and did something uncharacteristic. I thought before I talked. "For argument's sake, let's just say you're right. I could still do what I'm doing at the hospital. I would promise that I would quit saying I'm positive Jenny is innocent." I paused, trying hard to control my temper. "Okay, we both know that's a promise I can't keep. But I'm really enjoying working in the ER. It's exactly what I want to do. In fact, working half time at the Clinic and half time at the ER is close to my dream job." I didn't add that what actually made it my dream job was that I got to snoop.

Before Michael could speak, I added, "Do you have any evidence that Jen was involved?" I tried to act calm, and gave an Academy Award performance.

Michael went back behind his desk, seemingly convinced I was not going to do any harm.

"If you really want to know, I'll tell you." He waited, maybe to see if I was going to voice any objections. "First, as you know, Jen was there for every death."

"You're right. I do know that. Tell me something new."

"You aren't going to like this, but when Dr. Adams was murdered, I started looking at Jen more closely. They absolutely hated each other. Do you know that?"

"No. Not really. I've heard her complain about him, but nothing that got to the level of hatred." I grasped at any excuse I could think of. "But no one liked him. I've heard other staff call him a bastard."

"Relax, Sam. I don't know if I think Jenny did it. But there's a lot of evidence to show Jen has stood up to Dr. Adams many times. In fact, she was reprimanded by her supervisor recently because of how she talked to the doctor."

I hadn't heard this, and would need to talk to Jenny outside the hospital to find out her side of things.

"Besides," he continued, "the poison that killed Pluto was on the wings she brought to the party."

I shook off my anger, and had an idea. "How about if I don't investigate anything concerning Jen's involvement or lack of involvement? Would that work?"

"It would if you could only do it."

Deciding to ignore that last comment, I hurriedly went to the door before he could tell me no. With my hand on the doorknob I turned and said, "Thanks, Michael. You can trust me."

"I'm counting on it."

As I walked to the building entrance, it hit me how sad it was that neither of us flirted. It was the first time.

It was still early and I'd received a text that my 9:00 appointment was sick and had rescheduled. So I decided to stop by my house and spend a few minutes with Clancy.

Walking into the carriage house was the first time I thought that the case had entered into my world.

TEN

"Clancy, what's wrong?"

She lay on the kitchen floor, panting. Her tongue hung out as if she'd just gone for a run, but of course that wasn't the case. I repeated my stupid question, "What's wrong, girl?"

Our psychic connection wasn't working. All I could see was that she needed help. And fast.

I loaded her in my car, thankful she walked a lot and was in good shape. Still, Clancy was a hefty burden, but a burden I loved more than I could express. From the car I called the vet and was told to bring her right in. On the way I berated myself for having a vet on the outskirts of town, but I made the trip in less than 10 minutes. Luckily the trains and tractors knew better than to try to slow me down today.

Dr. Bob was waiting outside the building. He and an assistant grabbed Clancy from my arms and took her into a room. Without asking I followed them. I stroked my beautiful girl's head as they worked. Her eyes never left me, trusting that I'd make sure everything was okay. She must have also noted my tears. I couldn't stop. Clancy was my best friend.

Dr. Bob looked up and said, "Her pulse is thready and her blood pressure is really low. She feels a little cold too."

It hit me. "Check for arsenic poisoning. Please." I was desperate. "Please."

Probably because of all the recent poisonings the doctor said "yes" immediately.

"That's what I thought too," he said. "Unfortunately there's no quick way for me to test it with my equipment. I'm going to treat Clancy as if she's been poisoned. It will be best if we put her to sleep because we'll have to empty her stomach."

He must have known I'd want to stay. He added, "You can stay while she goes to sleep and then you have to leave. I promise I'll let you come back in before she wakes up. She won't even know you're out of the room."

Little did he know that Clancy understood what he was saying. What a brilliant girl! I nodded at the doctor and said, "Do whatever you need to do. She's my best friend."

"I understand." And I really believe he did.

My tears slowed a little, but didn't stop. I got close to Clancy's ear and whispered, "I love you. Everything is going to be okay." The doctor put in an IV and as I talked to Clancy her eyes closed. I kissed her and opened the door to leave. I turned to the doctor, "Please clue me in as soon as you know anything."

He nodded. I walked out and made my way to one of the uncomfortable plastic chairs in the waiting room. Time passed slowly. I counted time by noting how many people walked in and out, some with pets, some without. Some were told the doctor was involved in surgery and rescheduled. Others were seen by veterinarian assistants.

I began to pace. Then I remembered to call my office and tell them to cancel my remaining appointments for the morning. I called the ER and said I wouldn't be in for the afternoon, and left a message for Jen and Jill there. I also called George because I needed comfort. Not only did he comfort me, he walked into the waiting room before we'd even finished our conversation.

He walked in, sat down beside me, and put his arm around me. My head rested on his tweed jacket, I felt the texture of it on my cheek, and for some reason it reminded me of my Dad. And I sobbed. I didn't care that my tears and snot went on George's clothes instead of my own. He didn't seem to care either. Between my sobs and gasps for breath I told him what was wrong. And added, "She was always with me. No one else ever fed her except Gus and Georgianne. I took good care of her. I did. And someone poisoned her anyway." My sobs slowed down as George patted me and stroked my hair.

His voice was soothing as he said, "I know. Clancy is your family. Your best friend."

I looked him in the eyes and said what was bothering me the most. "It's all my fault."

"Sam, you said she was never alone outside. It's not your fault."

I inhaled in order to be able to speak. "I leave my door unlocked to my house."

"I know. But as you always say, 'It's Quincy.' It's probably not because the door was unlocked. Remember when Burns was killed, you were convinced someone broke into your house and damaged the gas furnace so you'd die?"

"Shut up, George. This is different."

My slight anger helped me pull myself together. I sat up, grabbed a tissue from the end table, and mopped up my face. I got another one to mop up George. We both grinned at my feeble attempt, which left pieces of tissue on his shirt. The grin relaxed me.

"God, I never fall apart like that. I'm sorry."

"No need. I was glad you called me," George said.

Why did I call him? I had five brothers and sisters, and numerous other relatives. Why did I call George?

He spoke again, putting his hands on either side of my face, and cupping my cheeks softly he said, "Look, let's just know Clancy is going to be okay. We just know it. We can stop worrying right now, because she is going to be fine. We just know it, Sam. We just know it." His hazel eyes looked deep into my blue ones.

That was the moment I fell in love with him again.

ELEVEN

Fell in love with him? What alternate universe was this? And when I needed a shoulder to cry on it was always my brother Pete. Always. Well, unless he was busy and then it was Jen or Jill or Ed or Rob, in any order really. Pete had some sort of "vibes" gift too. I recognized it, and although we talked about mine, we never talked about his. But it did give us a special bond.

So why did I call George? Today he behaved perfectly and said all the right things. He seemed sincere, but now I was second-guessing my choice. Omigod, I didn't say I loved him out loud, did I?

Thank God the doctor interrupted us or I would have kept ruminating about George. Clancy was the most important concern right now.

George and I stood at the same time. I couldn't speak, unusual for me. I stared at the vet and the tears started again. For the first time I noticed the smell in the waiting room—the smell of disinfectant and fear. Not a pleasant combination.

Doctor Bob didn't mince words. "I think Clancy is going to be okay. Doing a gastric lavage—I mean pumping her stomach—seemed to help a lot. Her blood pressure improved a little, although her pulse is still elevated. If it was poison, it hadn't been in her system long, or it was a small amount, or there would be more severe symptoms. I'm sending her stomach contents to the lab and she'll need to stay here tonight."

All I could think about was that she was going to be okay. I grabbed the doctor and hugged him fiercely. He was more than a foot taller than I was, but I stood on tiptoe.

I couldn't think of any questions to ask, but luckily George was more clear-headed than I was. He asked the vet, "What kind of treatment are you doing now?"

As the doctor talked we all walked in the treatment room so I could be with Clancy as she woke up. "She's quite dehydrated. And arsenic does do that. So for one thing we're keeping an IV in until both her pulse and blood pressure have normalized. There are also two drugs that are given for arsenic poisoning. I hesitate to give one of them because it can cause harm if the problem isn't poison. There are some side effects." He then explained the side effects of dimercaprol and penicillamine.

I was so sure that it was arsenic poisoning that I immediately said, "Give her the drugs." He nodded.

Clancy's big beautiful brown eyes opened, and I was

right there as the doctor promised I would be. The light in her eyes had dimmed somewhat, but was still there. I hugged and kissed her. She gently licked my face.

"Clancy, you're going to stay here tonight. I promise they'll take good care of you. I'll pick you up as soon as the doc says it's okay." I knew she understood me. She always did. Although I couldn't pick up her feelings like I usually could, I was grateful she could still pick up mine. I looked at the doctor. "I'll call later to see how she is." He nodded.

"Sam, I'll do everything I can to help Clancy. Please know that."

I took his hands. "I do. Thank you."

And with that I walked out the door. George grabbed my hand as we walked, and for once I didn't yank it away.

We walked to our cars. George asked if I wanted to go for lunch.

"Lunch? Omigosh, it feels like it's nighttime already instead of early afternoon." I clicked to unlock my car. "I don't feel like I can eat right now. I'm going to go to the hospital to work my shift."

"Are you sure that's what you should do?"

"I don't want to go home, so I might as well work. Plus, I'm more determined than ever to find out who's poisoning people and animals. I'm sure it's the same person or persons."

I got in my car, and George leaned against it with his

head in the window opening. "Okay. I know better than to try to get you to change your mind. I'll get back to work too. But you're having dinner with me tonight, and I'll accept no answer other than yes."

Normally I hate when people boss me around. But right now it was rather comforting to have someone tell me what to do. "I'm done at the hospital at six."

He smiled. "I'll be at your place at 6:15." Then he leaned in farther and kissed me. And I kissed him back. In the category of kisses, this one was sweet and loving instead of passionate and wanting. Just what I needed.

When I arrived at the ER a few minutes later I looked for Jen to apologize for being late. She was busy as usual. But she probably already knew the results of what had happened. I'd called Pete and my kids on the drive to the hospital, so I thought everyone else would be notified.

Loretta told me that two staff were sick with upset stomachs. "Probably the flu." And although the place was steadily busy, there still were no crises for me to help with. I thought that someone was going to figure out pretty soon that my position wasn't necessary. I was afraid people would then stop talking to me. So I gave myself a mental swift kick to the behind to get the job done as soon as possible.

I went into what I considered my office—the break room. Carter wasn't sitting there at the moment. I absentmindedly opened the refrigerator and worked to stifle my gag reflex. "What are science experiments doing in here?" I said to myself.

"Funny," Carter responded.

"How did you get in here? You weren't here a second ago."

"Maybe I was and maybe I wasn't."

I thought now was the time to satisfy my curiosity. "Do you go anywhere else besides the break room?"

He gave me his ghost smile, and that was answer enough.

Sleuthing didn't appeal to me as much right now, Clancy was on my mind. I called the vet and the tech said that Clancy was showing more spirit and they were confident she'd be okay and would be released in the morning.

Feeling better about Clancy, but feeling creepy about Carter, I walked out of the break room and ran into Loretta.

"Loretta, did anyone ever think to check the food in the break room?" I had to take a deep breath right away because she came in so close I'd only be able to breathe in her lunch and carbon dioxide. "The potato salad with mayo had been sitting out for hours. And there's stuff growing on some of the so-called food in the fridge."

Let me say that I was totally wrong when I thought Loretta was a close talker before. Never in my years had I ever experienced this type of "close talkery." She was so far in my face our noses were touching. I backed up against the counter of the nursing station as much as I could, but was basically trapped. With hands on her hips and her eyes flashing, Loretta yelled, "You talking about my break room food not being safe? You talking about my refrigerator being dirty? You're a fine one to talk. Jenny says there's stuff in the back of your fridge that you can't throw away because you're afraid to get close to it."

I've seen people take things personally. Me included. However I'd never experienced a sudden blow-up like this. I quickly backed out of the conversation. Guess I got on her last nerve. Maybe other people had complained, and I was just the last straw. Was it really her responsibility to keep the refrigerator clean?

I felt sick. I didn't know if my vibes were kicking in or if it was from inhaling her breath. I sat down in the nurse's station to steady myself and quickly felt better. No one else was in there, so I thought it would be a great opportunity to snoop. It wouldn't violate any laws or hospital policy since I was an employee and legally worked in the ER. I mentally rubbed my hands together, ready to dive in. There was nothing in particular I was looking for, but sometimes information just drops into your hands.

But not this time.

TWELVE

Just as I looked at the first computer screen, Jenny stepped up to the station and said three things: "What are you doing," "I'm glad Clancy is okay and we'll talk more about that later," and "There's a patient for you in Room 19."

As usual, short and to the point. I ignored her first question and I knew Pete had probably told her about Clancy. As for the third, I actually felt grateful to have real work to do to justify my existence in the ER.

"Where's the information on the patient?" I asked, quickly getting into professional mode. Luckily Jen let her first question slide, because I had no good answer.

She told me to type my username and password, which I had received on the first day from Human Resources, then showed me how to pull up the database on the computer. For some reason she added, "And although technically you have access to all the ER patient information, because we all treat all the patients, there's a rule that you don't look at anything you don't absolutely need to know. It's part of the HIPAA Law. Do you understand?"

I nodded, but that wasn't good enough for Jen.

"Do you understand?" she asked again.

"Yes. I'm a licensed clinical social worker. I know the law. I respect the law." Before she could say anything else, I added, "Yes, I know I'm nosy. But I'm ethical."

At least almost all the time.

She didn't say anything else; just ran off God knows where to do God knows what.

I turned my attention back to the computer. Jonah Landis. Wife, Kathy. I read the specifics. Jonah had become paranoid and it affected every facet of their life. So off I went to Room 19.

Jonah sat on the bed, with his wife next to him patting his shoulder.

"Is it all right if I come in?" Knowing that he was paranoid made it vital I enter the room in a non-threatening manner.

He just looked at me. Then looked at his wife. She nodded. He then looked back at me and nodded too.

"Hi, I'm Sam Darling, and I'm a social worker," I said. There was no way I'd say I was a crisis intervention specialist. That might escalate things. Social worker sounded rather innocuous.

I held out my hand. He didn't take it, but his wife did. As she did, she spoke for the first time, and she nearly blew me back on my heels.

"HELLO, I'M KATHY LANDIS AND THIS IS MY HUSBAND, JONAH."

I answered much more quietly than usual, hoping it would bring her volume down. "Nice to meet you both. What brings you here?"

Jonah looked at his wife again, and she repeated her nod. He seemed to trust her, so he finally spoke. I prepared for another onslaught of yelling. Instead, he spoke softly. "Kathy thought I should come. She thinks there's something wrong with me. But I know there's nothing wrong with me. There's something wrong with the world. Everybody knows everything about us. There are no secrets anymore." He looked around the whole room. "I think people get information about me because they keep watching me. I've reported it to the police but they don't believe me. I'm being watched."

Gosh, once he started he couldn't stop.

"They bugged my house, my phone, my car. They probably have this place bugged too, so I'm not going to tell you anything that's secret."

I nodded, and said that I needed to do a mental health assessment. He looked at his wife.

"HONEY, GO AHEAD AND DO IT. SHE'S JUST HERE TO HELP YOU."

Her volume must have done the trick, because he agreed with a nod to me.

What was it with this woman? I moved closer to her husband and away from her. My ears needed a rest. As usual I asked the patient if it was okay if his wife stayed in the room. He said it was. Then I told his wife that I wanted Jonah to answer the questions but if he didn't know the answer, or if she disagreed with the answer, she could tell me what she thought. Both of them agreed with that arrangement.

During the mental health assessment my hunch was confirmed. I gave Jonah a tentative diagnosis of schizophrenia, paranoid type. That diagnosis might stay or it might not, depending on the psychiatrist's evaluation once Jonah got on the unit.

Crap, I suddenly realized I'd forgotten to ask if he was willing to be admitted.

"Jonah, I know your fears are really bothering you. I'd like it if you would get some help so you don't have to be so scared." I knew it was imperative at this point that I didn't try to discount his fears or tell him no one was spying on him. "Being scared takes a lot of energy. You're tired, but having a hard time sleeping. If you go to the behavioral health unit, the doctor can talk to you about the possibility of medication to help you sleep."

Jonah became agitated, moving around on the bed and looking around the room frantically. I quickly added, "No one will make you take medicine if you don't want to. We only do that if someone is dangerous to themselves or someone else. You aren't dangerous. You just have a lot of fears. Okay?"

He continued looking around, but said, "Okay."

I told them I'd have to go get some more paperwork started for his admission.

Kathy said, "THANK YOU."

When I got back to the nurse's station, I asked about the proper way to get Jonah admitted. Connie Mumford pointed me to the right binder full of directions, and off I went. Contrary to when I did mental health assessments for the Clinic, I found out I was supposed to have put the MHA on the computer in the examining room. Instead I wrote it out. Crap. So I needed to transfer the info from paper to computer. Other than having to do that, I was pleased everything was computerized. I yearned for a paperless society, but the size of this binder told me that even though everything was on the computer at Bay General, it was still on paper as well.

I completed the work for Jonah's admission, including getting a doctor's signature. My sister Jill was on duty, as was Dougie. Of course I chose Jill. She skimmed over my notes, and digitally signed. She knew the psychiatrist on the unit would do a more thorough assessment, and since the patient was a voluntary admission, this was pretty much a *pro forma* admission.

I then contacted the unit to send down someone to pick up Jonah. I told Jonah and KATHY that their wait was just about over. Then I was done. And bored. Roaming around the ER only got me stern looks from people actually doing their jobs. So, with nothing else to do, I went back to the break room, my home away from home.

This time Carter really wasn't there, so I sat in a comfy looking chair and turned on the TV. It wasn't long before some paramedics came in. Danny Jacobsen sat down by me and asked if he could turn the channel. At my "yes" he switched to Jeopardy and the EMTs started yelling out answers. I soon joined in. A nice break from thinking about murder. And Clancy. At the thought of her I called the vet again and received basically the same report, with the addition that I could pick her up any time after seven tomorrow morning.

I still had about a half hour before my shift was done, so I asked Danny his thoughts on the murders. He sat forward in his chair, and said, "I think we have to find the bastard who's poisoning people and the animals too."

"Do you have any ideas about who it might be?"

"Well, I heard Jenny, Dougie, Loretta, and Carter are all suspects for one reason or another."

I used all the self control I could muster to not say anything about his suspect list. "Anything else?"

"Well, in the beginning everyone was dying, but now not so much…"

His wife, Connie Mumford walked in. After Danny kissed her, he filled her in and she added, "Yeah, no one's died since Dr. Adams. He was the seventh. Because seven people died, we now are looking for arsenic poisoning right away and treating for it. Others have lived. We haven't gotten confirmation from the lab yet that these people have been poisoned, but I bet they have. It's a much better feeling to be able to save people."

"I still want to find the SOB who's doing this," Danny chimed in again.

No more than I, Danny. No more than I.

THIRTEEN

George texted to remind me that he'd pick me up at 6:15. He also said we were going to Joe's Place, a down-home restaurant in Liberty, a small town a few miles east of Quincy.

I got home at 6:00 and was immediately struck with how empty my house was. Silence can be deafening. Knowing I was a pest I called the vet again. The answering service answered because the office was closed. As soon as I said my name, the woman gave me a message from Dr. Bob. "Clancy is doing very well. Tired, but resting comfortably." She hesitated before she read the next part, "And before you get upset about our office being closed, there is someone back by the dog runs all night. Clancy will not be alone." She stopped.

"Okay, thanks," was all I could think to say. Guess I was pretty predictable.

I hung up, and before I could think about the message, George knocked on the door.

I hadn't bothered changing my clothes or freshening up.

After all, I was having dinner with George. Comfy old George, the guy who was sweet and compassionate, and who was on my mind a lot. And although I'd come to the realization that I loved him, I also tried to make that feeling go away.

In a way I was testing him. If he still wanted to be around me the way I really am, then things might progress, whether I was ready to admit it to myself or not.

I opened the door. "Hi ya, Sam. Are you ready?" George had on jeans, so I thought that even though I hadn't cleaned up, I was still overdressed. Crap.

"Give me a minute to change. Help yourself to a beer."

I found a pair of jeans on the floor of my bedroom and quickly changed into them. That's the only concession I made to the date.

As I entered the living room, I noticed that George hadn't gotten a beer, but was just sitting there looking quite at home. He looked up. "Ready?"

I nodded and picked up my purse.

He opened the car door for me, and didn't chide me for not locking my house behind me. I suddenly burst out with, "Clancy's not there. I better lock the door."

George didn't say a word as I jumped out of the car, and ran to the door of the carriage house. It only took me a moment, but I felt more comfortable when I returned. I sank into the leather seat, feeling enveloped by the softness of the fabric.

Then it hit me. I'd have a few hours to talk to George about the murders. This was the best part of the date, uninterrupted time with the detective working on the case. "So, are you sure all these murders are connected? Were the people murdered by the same person who killed the animals? Did you…"

"Hold it, Sam. This is going to be a real date, not an excuse to get information from me."

"Couldn't it be both?" I tried to sound sweet as I touched his arm, but it sounded phony even to me.

He didn't answer.

"How about a compromise?" I almost begged.

"What kind of compromise?"

"Maybe we could talk about the murders on the way to dinner? And maybe on the way home? But not at all during dinner. That will be our date part."

"I don't like the ratio of crime to date. We'll talk about the cases on the way to dinner, and that's it."

"It's better than nothing." I smiled the smile of someone who had won the battle and planned to win the war. "Back to my questions—are you sure all these murders are connected? Were the people murdered by the same person who killed the animals?"

"You know we're not too far into the investigation yet, right? So I can give you some suppositions, but not too many facts."

"If that's what I get, that's what I get."

"Okay. We're pretty confident everything is connected. After all, arsenic powder isn't commonly found anymore."

I couldn't keep quiet. "But isn't it in rat poison?"

George took his eyes off Highway 104 for a second, "No. Not since the '60s. At least in America. There are still some developing countries who use it, but nowhere here."

"I'm surprised. I thought it was still easy to get."

"Nope. But here's the kicker. The arsenic powder found in the victims' stomachs came from rat poison. So it's either from another country, or someone has been keeping a supply of the stuff for a long, long time."

Interesting. Here I thought it would be hard to track the arsenic because it was so common. Instead it's going to be hard to track it because it's so uncommon.

George started talking again, "Did you know that arsenic is in practically everything? But in minute amounts that don't cause us any trouble."

"Yeah," I replied, "I did some research on it."

"You better hurry up with more questions. We're almost there."

Little did he know that I had a bunch. "Have you checked out the suspects? Anybody stick out as more likely to be the killer?"

"I'll tell you but you have to stay calm or I'll never talk about this again with you."

"Of course I'll stay calm." I almost laughed at him.

"I checked out Jen first…"

"Why in the hell did you check out Jenny first? She's the least likely suspect."

"Are you yelling at me, Sam? Because if you are, I'm done talking about the case." His fingers tightened on the steering wheel.

I was angry with myself for giving in to my emotions. "I'm really sorry. Please continue with why you checked out Jenny first."

George smiled as he pulled into the parking lot. "That's better. I checked out Jenny first because I agree that she's the least likely suspect and I thought it would be easy to clear her."

How could I be so mad at him all the time? He was indeed a sweet guy. "And were you able to clear her?"

"Remember to stay calm." He lifted his eyebrows, and this time he could keep looking at me since we were parked. "I wasn't able to clear her yet. Yet."

I held my temper. At least until later.

He continued, "The only thing holding us back is that she threatened Dr. Adams more than once."

I couldn't help but contribute to this, "I bet that could be said about a lot more people."

"Indeed. But none of them were present for all the deaths."

I wanted to let him know something I'd found out. "I read that it can take a half-hour for arsenic to begin working, so anyone else could have done it outside the hospital and not have been around when the symptoms showed up."

"You're absolutely right."

What? Did George just say I was absolutely right? Did he say it without being sarcastic? I needed to put this in my journal.

George took my hand. "We've been sitting in the parking lot for five minutes. Your time for asking questions is over."

I didn't say anything, but that was answer enough. George got out of the car, walked around to my side, opened my door, and took my hand as we walked into Joe's. This hand-holding thing was new, and I hadn't really experienced it since I dated George in high school. It was not unpleasant.

I hadn't been to Joe's Place since I moved back to Quincy, and it brought back a lot of memories. I couldn't help but be in a good mood, and I gave George's hand a squeeze as we walked to our table. It was a little booth, only seating two. Nestled in a corner of the large dining room. "You remembered," I said, unable to contain my smile.

"How could I forget. This was our first real date, junior year. I'd gotten my license a few months before, and was so proud to be able to drive on the highway all the way to Liberty.'"

I continued, "And we sat in this little booth. I was so nervous. I really liked you."

"Talk about nervous… I was scared to death. But once we sat in the booth and I got the courage to hold your hand, the fear went away."

"I agree," my smile widened. "Everything was pretty good that night."

"Pretty good? It was perfect."

George was a popular guy in high school. Still was. Everyone liked him. However, we'd been friends ever since kindergarten, when we were both enthusiastic about being in school and being big kids. Even though we didn't date until junior year, we spent many hours together through our school years. If the debacle on prom night hadn't happened I probably would have stayed in Quincy and married him. And I wouldn't be the person I was. My kids wouldn't be around either. I guess things turned out the way they were supposed to.

I quickly turned off those thoughts and paid attention to the menu. As usual there weren't many things for vegetarians, so I ordered the same thing I ordered back in high school. "A grilled cheese with tomatoes on it, french fries, and water. Wait, make that a chocolate shake."

George seemed surprised, "That's exactly what you ordered when we first ate here." He beamed. "So I'll do the same thing." He looked up at the waitress and said, "Double cheeseburger, french fries, chocolate shake, and we'll order dessert later."

Dessert? I was full just talking about all this food.

While we waited for our food, I called the vet again. I began with an apology but that was dismissed by the answering service, "No need to apologize. That's what we're here for. I just got a call from Dr. Bob's office. The tech said Clancy was doing so much better. They have her out of the run, and she is allowed to roam around the place. She'll definitely be ready to go home tomorrow morning." She took a breath. "Do you have any questions?"

"Nope." I was amazed at how much info she could give me without me asking anything. "Thanks and I'll be there early tomorrow."

George saw my face and must have known I was pleased with the news. He asked, "So everything is good?"

I relayed the message and he picked up my hand again.

His hand shook when he began talking, "Sam, there's been something I've been meaning to talk to you about. Since…"

The food arrived right at that moment, stopping whatever George was going to say. I wondered what it was, but quickly put it out of my mind as the joys of Joe's chocolate shake overtook all my senses.

George let go of my hand so we could pick up our sandwiches. I was surprised that I was more interested in his hand than I was in my grilled cheese and fries. I thought my life was pretty good—I had two jobs that I enjoyed, a house I loved, my family was close, my dog was healthy, and I was sitting in a booth with my high school boyfriend.

Then it happened—the door opened and in walked Michael. With a girl. And damn if the hostess didn't put them at a table close to us. What was this? The lovers' corner?

He saw us. Of course it would have been odd for him not to talk to us, so he did. "Hi, Sam. Hello, George." We returned his greeting. Then he half turned to indicate the beautiful redhead beside him. "Samantha, George, this is Jane Gordon. Jane, these are my friends Sam and George."

She extended a beautifully maintained hand with shiny red lacquer on the nails. "How do you do?" Her voice sounded like Marilyn Monroe's when Marilyn was trying to sound really smart but came off sounding really sexy.

I took her hand first and then George did. I glanced at him and noticed he was looking at Michael and not the girl. George hit a home run with that one.

I couldn't resist, "Michael, I'll need to talk to you about the case tomorrow. Will you be in the office?"

"In and out," he replied. "Text or call to see if I'm there."

All four of us exchanged more pleasantries and then they went to their table. The encounter was much less awkward than I expected. If this had happened a few days ago I would have been devastated. Funny. My crush on Michael had almost evaporated. I looked at George. Sweet, balding, old, George. The warm feeling that enveloped me was a totally different feeling than what I'd experienced with Michael. That was like a hot flash, which made me laugh when I thought about it.

"What's so funny?" George looked at me quizzically.

"Nothing. I was just thinking about how happy I am."

He took my hand again and said, "Me too." I waited but he didn't say anything about his earlier unfinished sentences. No matter. I was content.

Little did I know that my contentment wasn't destined to stay.

FOURTEEN

After a few well-executed kisses, George dropped me off at home. What was it about his kisses? He had two lips like other guys I'd kissed. But there was an extra intensity, and all the while he was gentle and caring. Though it was hard to describe why, his kisses were memorable.

I didn't sleep well. After all, I was used to having Clancy hogging the bed. It felt funny having it all to myself.

After tossing and turning most of the night, I finally slept for a while and woke up early. By the time the vet's office opened at seven I had already been in the parking lot for ten minutes. As soon as I walked in, Clancy greeted me with sloppy kisses and her version of a hug. She wasn't mad at me for leaving her there, after all. This was the first time for that.

I paid the bill with a handy credit card; no way would I have this kind of money in my checking account. The receptionist gave me a print out with instructions, which included a return in a few weeks "if necessary." Right now it didn't look like that would happen. Clancy was indeed her old self.

As we left I told her, "It's been weird talking to myself instead of talking to you." She agreed. "I have so much to talk to you about, but I have to get to work. Two important things—the therapy dog test is tomorrow in Chatham, you'll have to let me know if you're up for it. The second thing is I love George."

Clancy tried to jump on my lap. "Not while I'm driving." I pushed her back into her seat. "Does that mean you're happy?"

It did.

"Oh, one more quick thing. I'm going to have you stay with Gus and Georgianne while I'm at work. I know you're okay, but I'd worry if you were alone. Okay?"

She was always happy to spend time with my landlords, so no problem there. When I dropped her off I was grateful I had an empty stomach. First of all, Georgianne was in her usual, flower-endowed housecoat, and she made a lot of kissy noises to my friend. Gross. Clancy was my dog and no amount of kissing was going to make her belong to Georgianne.

Why couldn't I just give in and be happy that my landlords loved Clancy and Clancy loved my landlords? I didn't mind that she also adored Gus. So did I. But it would take a while for me to forgive Georgianne for the way she had initially treated me.

It occurred to me then that maybe she felt the same way

about her husband as I felt about my dog. She didn't want to share—at least not with me.

Gus shooed me out the door with the promise they'd let me know if anything changed. I parted with, "I might call too." Gus, Georgianne, and Clancy all laughed at that. Of course I'd call. I couldn't help myself.

At the office, my first client was waiting for me. It was the young computer whiz, Andy. Before I could say anything, he gave me a note from his mother that had been crumpled up in his pocket. "Andy said it was important I let you know that he did his homework every day and he did well in all his quizzes. He wouldn't tell me anything else. Please let me know if I can help further."

The kid was beaming. He was a far cry from the boy who wouldn't talk to me a few months ago. He blurted, "So now I can help you investigate about the dogs?"

I had to tread lightly here. I couldn't ask Andy to do anything that even remotely smacked of danger, plus I had to be careful of the "dual relationships" clause of my social work Code of Ethics.

For once, I thought about my words before speaking. "You can help me in one way. This may not sound important to you, Andy, but it really is. I want you to listen to what people are saying about the dog poisonings. There's not much being said about the dogs, and of course we're concentrating on the people. But I'm really worried about the dogs."

His mouth drew down into a frown, and he said, "That's all? I worked my butt off all week and this is my reward? That's nuts."

"I'm sorry, Andy. I don't think you know the importance of this. You might be the one who gets the clue that solves the case."

He brightened at that.

I continued, "Please don't do anything rash. All I'm asking you to do is keep your ears open. Don't do anything out of the ordinary. Understand?"

Andy nodded, but that wasn't enough for me.

"Say it."

"Okay, I won't do anything out of the ordinary. I'll just listen."

"And, just maybe, your listening will make you the hero of a real life adventure."

As much as he loved video games, I knew this would hook him for sure. My hope was that "just listening" would be enough motivation to get him to continue doing what he was supposed to do at school and home.

I added, "And remember you have to keep doing your homework and other responsibilities or the deal is off. This is your reward for good behavior."

Andy gleamed. It amazed me that he didn't realize he could "just listen" without having good behavior, but apparently he agreed that it was a reward. For a kid who has everything, meaningful rewards are hard to come by.

And then he said, "I do know something though." His brown eyes widened in anticipation of being able to tell me something. I nodded. He continued, "All the dogs were in one section of town."

"Where is that?"

"I dunno. I just heard some grownups talking about it."

Drat. Why hadn't I thought of that? I might have to tell Andy that it was enough information. That would surely disappoint him. Maybe I could come up with something else. And why didn't George tell me that information?

"Andy, instead of just listening, I have a better idea. Why don't you do some internet searches? A lot of investigation happens that way."

Computers were his life. "That would be cool. What do you want me to look for?"

I thought I better warn him. "Don't look up information on arsenic, because that looks suspicious if anyone would check for some reason. Okay?"

He nodded.

"However, you can look up anything and everything about the dog poisonings. Check local papers, national papers, CNN, anything. And you can let me know next session. Remember that this is a reward for good behavior, so that behavior has to continue."

He nodded again. Back to his old trick of not talking.

"Use your words, Andy."

"Yes, I understand. I won't look up arsenic, but I'll check about the dog poisonings. Can I still listen?"

I nodded.

He said, "Use your words," with a big smile on his face.

I smiled too. "Yes, you can still listen, but don't go out of your way to do so. Nothing that looks suspicious. Nothing dangerous. Understand?"

He nodded. Then, at my look he said, "I understand."

We still had some time left so we talked about his behaviors and his feelings. With many teenagers and even young adults depression is manifested as anger. Andy was one of those teenagers. And since he was only thirteen, I was committed to helping him so he didn't live a life of sadness. At least we had a good relationship, and that was a start.

As soon as he left I called Gus and had to go through Georgianne to get to him. She waxed eloquently about my dear little "poochy-woochy."

"Gus please, Georgianne. I'm in a hurry."

I heard her harrumph, but did get to Gus. "Hey, Sam, what's up?" Gus always sounded healthy when he was involved in something. Before I could even answer, Gus went on to say, "I know you're calling about Clancy. She's doing great. Georgianne and I have been fighting over her attention all morning."

My eyes misted over. "Thanks, Gus. I love you."

"You too, kiddo. And call anytime."

I finished up the morning with a few more patients, and then happily began my second job over the lunch hour. I imagined myself decked out a la Sherlock Holmes, pipe and all.

FIFTEEN

I stopped off at the hospital, even though I wasn't due to work for two more hours. I wanted to check out the one suspect I hadn't dealt with yet—Dougie. As I walked in I was greeted by an exuberant Loretta near the nurses' station.

"Two more people came in with poisoning, and Dougie saved them. Between him and Jill we are really preventing a lot of deaths."

"You are really proud of your son, aren't you?" I asked.

She gave me a funny look and got really close as was her habit. "Of course I'm proud of him. Wouldn't you be?"

She had me there, "Yes, certainly." I remembered that I really hadn't checked into Loretta's activities either. She was such a loved person, and other than her "close talking," didn't show any suspicious activities. I had to admit that her own version of Space Invaders caused my vibes to kick in, but I'd always been that way when people got too physically close without an invitation.

After telling Loretta that I was happy no one else had died, I wandered around a little bit. Jenny and some other staff were at Dr. Adams' funeral, but since the ER functioned 24/7, not everyone could go.

As I wandered, I saw Dougie come out of an examining room. He nodded at me, and kept walking. We had never really talked except for the one lunch and casual hellos, and I knew that it had to happen. So I dove in.

"Dougie." He turned around. "Are you going to lunch soon?"

"Yeah, I have some errands to run. Why?"

"I just thought we could eat together, that's all."

"Great idea. Just not today. I do have some things I need to do."

"Okay, we'll do it another day."

He hurried away. I thought that I needed to follow him. There was nothing concrete in my head, no real goal, but in the movies people always followed suspects.

I exited through the ambulance bay and jumped into my car. I didn't think Dougie knew what kind of car I drove, so I slunk down in my seat, put on my St. Francis U ball cap, and waited.

Just a scant minute after I did so, Dougie came out of the staff entrance and got in a red mini-truck. Definitely not the kind of vehicle I pegged him for. I hadn't seen many doctors drive such a modest vehicle.

He took a quick right onto Broadway and I followed as soon as traffic would let me. This was Quincy's busiest street, and I thought I'd have adequate cover. However, I didn't want to be so far back that I would lose him. I wondered if there was a class one could take to learn surveillance techniques, because I really didn't know what I was doing. I just used what I'd learned from the movies, TV, and books.

Dougie took a left on Fifth Street and then a right on Maine. When he got to Fourth Street he hung a quick right and parked on the west side of Washington Park. I was far enough back that I was able to find a spot on the Maine Street side of the park. I stayed in my car for a minute, watching as Dougie entered Holtschlag's Feed and Grain Store, one of the old, established businesses on the town square. Not many people went in there nowadays, just those looking for old-fashioned service and merchandise. Dougie came out a little later carrying a dust-covered bag on his shoulder.

As soon as he pulled away I went into the store. Mr. Holtschlag, the fourth generation to own the store, looked up expectantly. I guess two customers in a few minutes was probably a record these days.

We exchanged pleasantries. My family and his family attended St. Francis Church and had done so since the parish was founded in 1861. His store was built around the same time. I didn't feel like I could come right out and ask what Dougie had bought, but thought if I could get him away from the counter long enough I might be able to find out on my own.

So I asked for something he would have to go look for. "Do you happen to have antique pulls for ceiling fans?"

"Certainly, Miss Darling. What kind would you like?"

"I want a glass one, but I'm not sure what color or shape. Could you bring back a few?"

"Sure. I'll be right back."

"Take your time." I meant it.

As soon as Mr. Holtschlag went down a dusty aisle, I jumped behind the wooden counter. There was no computer with its itemized sales, but there was an ancient cash register, and a spindle with light-green receipts skewered on it. I grabbed the top one, desperate to see what Dougie had purchased. I squinted to attempt to read what looked like hieroglyphics. It had Dougie's name on it, Dr. Douglas Johnson. I could make out the price—$10.99 plus 88 cents tax. The item itself was harder to read. The beginning of the line said, "10 Pounds," and that was all I could see.

A throat clearing interrupted my nosing around.

"Excuse me, Miss Darling. I believe you are looking at something that doesn't concern you."

Here's where my poor lying skills would not come in handy. "Uh, Dougie is my friend, and his birthday is coming up. I thought I'd see what he bought so I would know of a possible birthday gift." Oh, God, this one was the worst lie yet. I'd have to get better at it.

"I doubt that buying rat poison would be a suitable birthday gift."

I fought to contain my elation. Rat poison. I got him. I got him.

Wait. George said that rat poison doesn't contain arsenic anymore. Unless… "Mr. Holtschlag, was that rat poison really old?" Like the rest of the store? I left the last line unsaid.

"Nope. Just got a shipment in… let me check…"

He pulled out a box from under the counter, moved his glasses from the top of his head to his eyes, and shuffled through the metal box until he found what he was looking for. "Let's see… the rat poison is new. Just came in two years ago."

New? Obviously we had different definitions for the word. However, everything is relative, and to him the poison was indeed new. Even though the rat poison was too recent to contain arsenic, I'd still tell Michael and George.

"Uh, how many have you sold?"

"Two. I remember, because…" The phone, antique like the rest of the place, interrupted him. "Excuse me." It must have been a wrong number since he hung up right away.

I continued his sentence, "You remember, because… ?"

"I forget," he replied, and I decided not to press him.

Because I felt guilty about lying, I bought one of the ceiling fan pulls. I didn't need one, but thought it might be a good gift for someone. As I stepped outside, who was waiting for me but Dougie. Since I'd never had a real conversation with him I was surprised to learn that he was a Space Invader too. Like mother, like son, I guess. My vibes went on overdrive. Even though he was quite short, he was also quite muscular and I felt a hint of threat.

"What in the hell are you doing following me?"

"I, er, I'm not following you. Were you in the store? I didn't see you when I was in there?"

"You went in as soon as I started to drive away."

Damn, my timing was a little off. And I was grateful I had a small sack in my hand that had the Holtschlag stamp on it. "I was just buying a birthday present. Wanna see it?"

"No. Just be careful, Sam. Be very careful. Sticking your nose into other people's business can cause you problems."

Sticking my nose into other people's business was what I lived for. How could that be problematic? I wondered why he was threatening me. Since my filter didn't work all the time, the words went directly from my brain to my mouth. "Why are you threatening me?"

His face lost its threat, and the veins no longer popped out on his forehead and neck, but for some reasons I still felt uncomfortable. Maybe because he remained in my face. Maybe because he was guilty of something. That's the problem with my vibes. I get them. I get physical manifestations sometimes. But I never know what they mean. I took a step back before Dougie answered. He took another step toward me. Apparently, I wasn't going to win the personal space battle.

Finally he answered, "With all the people dying, and with patients still coming in with arsenic poisoning, it's been really stressful at the hospital. I feel like the cops are watching me 24/7, and I haven't done anything wrong. Guess I'm more on edge than I thought."

What he said made sense, but I didn't think it was the whole story. "Have you been the only doctor saving the lives of the poisoned patients?"

"I don't think so. Jill's been on duty some of the time. So have a few other doctors. I'm sure I'm not the only one. Why would you ask me that?"

"Don't know. Things come to me and I say them. Sorry." My mind had drifted to "Lives of the Poisoned Patients." That would make a great short story.

Back to the present, Sam.

Dougie looked away for a moment, then back at me again. "It's okay. I guess we're all on edge. It's not a very fun place to work at the moment." He paused, looked away, then to me again, "What exactly is your job there anyway?"

I tried as best I could to explain the made-up job of crisis intervention specialist, and I think he bought it. He took a step back and I breathed deeply.

He turned away then turned back to say, "Guess I'll see you at work."

I said good-bye and he was off. This was a close call. Obviously surveillance wasn't my strong suit. I stood there for a few minutes thinking. The aftermath of my negative vibes with Dougie remained. He gave me the chills. Then it hit me that I needed to get to work. My Bug was parked in the square's diagonal parking, and it was just a short jaunt from there to Bay General. I parked in the staff parking lot closest to the ER, and I was set to work.

As I put on my ID badge I heard Loretta yell, "Dougie, hurry." I followed the commotion as Dougie and nurse Connie Mumford went toward Loretta's voice. They passed two empty rooms and went into a treatment room where Loretta was busy hooking up wires and whatnot to what looked like an elderly man. His breathing was labored and he looked a little yellow. I knew enough to recognize jaundice. From my research I remembered that jaundice was one of the symptoms of arsenic poisoning, and so was labored breathing. But of course there were many other things it could be. I knew nothing about medicine, except for what I'd read or what my kids and I had experienced. I thought maybe I could stand inside the door and watch, but if vomit happened, I'd be out of there.

Dougie went into overdrive, calling out orders which his

mom complied with, and asking Connie for equipment that sat on the side of the bed. It wasn't long before the man's breathing seemed to return to a more normal state. Dougie then asked Loretta to call ICU to send someone down to take the guy upstairs.

Exciting stuff. And Dougie was the hero again.

What's wrong with this picture? Had he had time to poison someone in the brief period since his lunch break? Or had he done it before? Did he have an accomplice? He did seem to have a big ego, and he did threaten me.

I decided I had to follow Loretta too at some point, since I hadn't done that yet. She was the last suspect on my list. I also decided I needed to be much more stealthy about my tailing someone.

In the meantime it was time to check on Clancy. I called Gus, talked to Georgianne, and found out my "sweet pooch" was wonderful and maybe they should keep her for a few days, "just in case." I quickly let her know it wasn't necessary and told her I'd be home a few hours after work, because I did plan to follow Loretta if I could.

Of course there were no crises for me to work on, so I went to the staff lounge. I wasn't surprised to find Carter in the corner, still dressed all in white, like an orderly from a few decades ago. He nodded, which I'm sure was his way of greeting me. I nodded back, and added a hello. I turned to him and asked if he had any new information about the poisonings.

He replied, "I told you everything was right under your nose. That's about all I'm telling you."

"Right under my nose," I repeated his phrase. "Right under my nose." I addressed him again, "What the hell does that mean?"

"It can be literal and/or figurative. You decide."

"I know that, Carter," I practically yelled. Actually I'd been going with the literal, and now tried to think of the figurative meaning. Under my nose… under my nose. Nothing clicked.

"There haven't been any more deaths." I sounded like I actually knew something.

"Yep, and the reason is right under your nose."

At this point I was sure Carter wasn't guilty. Although he was still weird, I was fresh out of vibes around him. Guess I got used to "weird."

I tuned him out. I only had one more hour before I was done with my part-time shift. Who could I follow? Who could I interview?

"Sam Darling to reception." The loudspeaker rudely interrupted my thoughts. I wasn't upset. Maybe there'd be an actual crisis for me to deal with. I hurried to reception where the unit secretary just turned her head toward the waiting area while she raised her eyebrows.

Immediately I thought of earlier in the year when I'd tried to deal with an out-of-control man in the ER waiting room. That's when I had met Michael. So funny that I wasn't thinking about him much, now that George… I shook my head to bring me back to the present. I saw someone sobbing as she sat in one of the plastic-coated chairs.

Immediately I went to her side and sat in an adjacent chair. "Can I help you?" I asked.

She shook her head as she continued sobbing. "No one can help. He might die."

"Who might die?"

"My grandpa. He's back there," indicating the treatment area.

So her grandpa might die. She looked to be in her sixties, close to seventy, a generous estimate. He'd probably be in his late nineties at the least. It's horrible to lose a grandparent at any age, but her sobbing made me think there might be something more.

"I'm so sorry," I said as I clicked into nice person, social worker mode. I wanted to ask what was wrong with him, but didn't know quite how to phrase it. So I just went for it. "What's the matter with your grandfather?"

"He sprained his ankle."

"He sprained his ankle," I repeated in my best counseling style. But in my head I'm saying, "He SPRAINED HIS ANKLE?"

"Yeah," snort, slobber, wail. "He was roofing his house,

and missed the last step on the ladder coming down and he sprained his ankle."

Now that I knew he probably wasn't dying, and that he was young for his age, I was able to figure out how to help. "How about if I go back and check on how he's doing?"

She nodded and I went back to the treatment area. I saw Connie Mumford and asked about the grandpa. She smiled and pointed to a room behind her. I knocked, went in, and saw someone older than Gus. But even more sprightly. He saw me and smiled a beautiful smile.

"Hi, I'm Sam, a social worker here. Your granddaughter is quite upset and thinks you're dying."

"Well, aren't you a cute young thing."

Young. Me. Well, everything is indeed relative. "So how are you doing?"

"Fine. They x-rayed my ankle, and it's just a sprain. No big deal."

"So you're not dying?" I smiled as I asked.

"We're all dying, sweetie. But not today." He continued smiling himself.

"I'll go tell your granddaughter." I excused myself and walked out. What a nice guy.

When I went back to the waiting room she was still sobbing, but was about out of liquid to expel. Must have used it all.

She looked up at me expectantly and I said to her, "Your

grandfather is fine. He did sprain his ankle but he's not dying. Would you like to go back with him?"

"Yes, please," she replied as she began to compose herself.

I led her back. As I did so I said, "Your grandfather is lucky to have someone who loves him so much."

She thanked me. As I opened the door to his room, his face lit up as he saw her, and she ran to him. Grandpa looked at me and mouthed, "Thank you." Guess the only thing involved here was love. Nice.

A successful shift. And one with a semi-crisis. Wish I could solve the poisonings as quickly as I solved this woman's problem.

As my shift wound down it hit me that I'd forgotten two things. One was to check on Clancy again. And the second was to ask George to dinner with my sibs later tonight. I wanted to surprise them with the fact that I had a date.

First things first. Gus answered this time, thank heavens. As soon as he realized it was me on the phone he said, "You don't even need to ask. Clancy is doing great. No aftereffects from the poisoning that I can see. She's sleeping on the couch with her head in Georgianne's lap."

That was a vision I couldn't unsee. "I'm so glad, Gus. You guys are so wonderful to keep her. And speaking of that... I forgot that I have a dinner with my family tonight. Could Clancy stay until 9 or 10?"

"Sure. Do you want her to just spend the night?

Georgianne would love it."

"No. I really want her home. Would 10 be too late to pick her up?"

"Nope. I'm not much of a sleeper. Stay out as late as you want."

Okay. One down and one to go. George answered on the first ring. "Yeah." His greeting didn't cheer me.

"Hi. It's Sam."

George's voice softened. "Hi ya, Sam." His usual greeting to me, but this time even warmer than usual. "What's up?"

"I know this is short notice, but if you're not busy tonight, would you like to go to dinner with my sibs and me?"

He didn't hesitate. "Sure. What time and where?"

"In about a half an hour? And I'll pick you up."

"Okay. I'll be ready."

I must admit I was happy. And I forgot all about following Loretta.

SIXTEEN

My heart beat a little faster as I pulled in front of George's house. He'd stayed in the old St. Francis University neighborhood where we grew up. I honked in front of his brick bungalow and put on some lip gloss before he came out. He did catch me primping in the rear view mirror, and I wasn't even embarrassed about it.

He slid his ample frame into the front seat of my Bug. Then he leaned over and kissed me. I kissed him back.

"Sorry I didn't ask you earlier, but I forgot all about the dinner, and I just decided it was time the family knew about 'us.'"

He put his hand on top of mine and said, "I'm glad. And I'm glad there's an 'us' for you to talk to them about. Exactly what does 'us' mean?"

I wiggled as I tried to shake off what I was thinking. I couldn't tell him that I'd decided I loved him again when he showed such compassion for Clancy. It was too early for that. Hell, it was only a few days ago I wanted Michael to love me. I was nuts. Yeah, that was the only possible explanation. I could only answer, "I don't really know. Do you?"

"Yeah, but I'm not sayin'."

He only lived a few blocks from the Rectory and we could have walked, so it was no time before we pulled into the nearly full parking lot. I didn't have the opportunity to pursue the topic, but resolved to do so when I got the chance.

We walked in to the crowded restaurant and saw my family out on the glassed in patio. Everyone knew George, especially my youngest brother Rob who was on the police force with him. Rob looked surprised. My sisters, Jen and Jill, looked smug. And Ed and Pete just looked friendly. Everyone was with their spouses expect for Rob and Pete, who were single. Pete would probably always be so, since he was a priest, but I had high expectations for Rob to be married within a few years. Everyone stood.

George hugged Jill, Jen, and Ed's wife, Angie, and shook hands with all the guys, including Jill's husband Ben and Jen's husband Manh, whom we called Manny. Looking around I was happy yet again that I'd moved back home to Quincy. I certainly missed this while living in Chicago. Yeah, it was only a four hour train ride away, but with jobs and kids, I hadn't made it home often enough. This was heaven.

We sat on an end of a huge table, and were forced into

closeness. It didn't seem that George minded since he put his hand on my knee under the table. I sure didn't mind either, but didn't know if I was ready for such intimacies. I put my hand on top of his, just to make sure it didn't stray. Brought me back to high school.

Rob finally sputtered, "You guys aren't dating, are you? Please say you aren't dating." I could only imagine him hating the fact his oldest sister was with a detective on the force.

George and I just laughed. I shrugged my shoulders in an "I can't help it" attitude. Almost simultaneously Jen and Jill said, "It's about time."

"What does that mean?" I asked.

Jen answered, "You two were perfect together in high school. I remember wondering when and if you would ever get back together."

Jill put in her two cents, "I was little but I liked George so much. I had a crush on him." She blushed a little, and glanced at her handsome Ben. "Maybe I still do," she confessed.

George said, "I remember all of you as kids. I also remember what a great family you had, and how I loved coming over there. I was so sorry when your folks died, but thought it was neat how you were all able to stay together."

"Well, you remember that I was in college by then," I said, and "DCFS let us stay together because I was old enough to act as a guardian for the younger ones, and we had other relatives who looked in on us frequently."

"Much too frequently," Ed piped in. We all laughed because he had been "the wild one" when he was young and aunts and uncles kept him in line. He had turned into a responsible adult though, partly because of his wife Angie, and partly because he was a good guy to begin with.

We spent much of the dinner reminiscing. I was surrounded by the smell of meat—the Rectory was known for its steaks and ribs—and I did my best to concentrate on my salad and French fries, a meal I considered well-rounded.

It took us at least fifteen minutes in the parking lot to say good-bye; we all hugged and spoke individually to each person. I whispered in Pete's ear, "Sorry I haven't talked to you in a while. Maybe we can do breakfast soon?"

"How about tomorrow?" he asked.

"Sorry. I'm taking Clancy to Springfield tomorrow for her therapy dog test."

That brought on questions from everyone. I promised to update them on the Darling Facebook Page, one of the many ways we chose to communicate.

Finally George and I returned to my car, parked at the far end of the lot. He walked around to my side, and opened the door for me. Before I could get in we shared another kiss that warmed me to the tips of my toes. I don't know who he'd been kissing in the many years I'd been gone, but whoever it was deserved my thanks. He knew what he was doing.

I don't remember the one minute drive to his house. When I stopped the car, George repeated his performance. Wow.

"Want to come in?" he asked.

"Yeah. No. I can't. No. Ummm, I have to pick up Clancy at Gus's house."

"Okay. The offer is out there, for whenever."

All I could do was nod. It was hard to drive home because of my weak knees. This was just crazy. A guy I loved in high school, then hated for years because he stood me up on prom night, and now I loved him again.

I was able to put George out of my mind when Clancy enthusiastically greeted me. So did Gus. His wife had gone to bed so I didn't have to deal with her calling Clancy a "dear little poochy-woochy." We stepped out on his back porch as Gus repeated that Clancy had been fine, and that it had been fun watching her.

"Any time, honey. Any time." Then he said, "I thought I was going to help you out with this case like I did the last one... ?" He made it a question instead of a statement and his disappointment was evident.

"I'm sorry. I'm working two jobs, and I'm taking Clancy to Chatham to get certified tomorrow, and I'm kind of dating George."

"Whoa. I need to be brought up to speed on a lot of stuff. Could you use a companion on the trip?" Clancy looked up at him. "Besides Clancy, I mean." Clancy smiled at her friend.

"Well, it would be nice. Even though Clancy is a great listener, she's not the best conversationalist." I looked down at her, "Don't pout. You know it's true."

I looked at Gus again. "I'm leaving at 6 in the morning."

"Well, I better get to sleep then." He walked back in his house with a lively step.

Clancy and I hit the sack practically the minute we got into the carriage house. Before I drifted off, I apologized to her, "Sorry I haven't told you everything that's going on. I'll fill you in tomorrow. Love you…"

It seemed like only a moment later that I heard the noise of the alarm clock. It was abrupt and unwelcoming.

SEVENTEEN

Gus was waiting by my car at 6 AM with two coffees in his hand. I had planned to stop for a caffeine fix along the way, but was grateful I didn't have to. Clancy didn't like being relegated to the backseat, but since it was Gus, she didn't complain too much.

During the almost two hour drive Gus asked a lot of questions. I answered them, making sure to include Clancy in the conversation. Gus seemed appeased after he found out what little I knew.

He finally said, "Maybe I could do some checking around about the dog poisonings. Or follow some of your suspects."

I nixed that immediately, taking my eyes off the road for a moment. "Gus, you were a huge help in the Burns murder case, but your wife would kill me if I got you involved in another one."

"Sam, please. You know how I love helping you."

I couldn't say no to him. He was the one who'd always been there for me, and not just for giving me the carriage house when I moved back to Quincy. "Okay. I'll let you check on the dogs. Maybe you could get George to tell you some of the names of the dog owners. Then we can interview them together. We might be able to find some commonalities."

"Thanks, Sam. You won't be sorry."

I certainly hoped not.

Then I filled him in on the George situation. "I'm glad you're happy for me."

"Happy doesn't begin to cover it. I'm thrilled. You'll finally have a social life." Gus squirmed in his seat like a little girl at a One Direction concert.

"I already had a social life," I sputtered. "It just so happens that it revolved around my dog, my family, and you."

We arrived just in time for Clancy's test. There were about twenty dogs there with their owners. We'd been told that we couldn't bring in any treats or food; the dogs had to follow the commands because they wanted to, not because they were going to be rewarded with treats.

Clancy had to redo the skills she'd already demonstrated to earn the Canine Good Citizenship Test. She'd been through all the levels of obedience class at the Quincy Kennel Club, and I know she remembered how to do them.

She didn't always obey me, and I didn't expect her to. I treated her as a friend and not a subservient species.

However, there were times she had to do what I said. If I yelled STOP she knew it was an emergency and always did what I asked then. Normally I didn't have to give her too many commands, because she just knew how to behave. I'd warned her ahead of time, however, that today she had to pretend she was "just a dog," and that she needed to do what I asked. I could tell she knew how important this was, so I had no worries.

She did great on the earlier skills she already knew; then came the new stuff. I had her sit on my left side with a loose leash. Four people approached her, each with a different apparatus—a wheelchair, a walker, a cane, and crutches. She continued to sit but looked expectantly at each person. When the wheelchair came so close that the person could touch Clancy, she graciously offered her head to be petted. The same thing happened with the other people. Whew! Passed that one with flying colors.

The next part of the test consisted of four or five people approaching Clancy quickly and invading her space. It reminded me of Loretta and her son Dr. Dougie. Clancy was startled but continued to sit, looking at me to see what I wanted her to do. "Good dog, Clancy. Keep sitting. Good girl." She looked up at the individuals who were so close she could lick all of them if she chose. Luckily, she didn't choose that option.

Other people and dogs were going through the same

exercises and with varying degrees of success. I felt bad for the ones who had to leave. I believe that dogs love to have a job to do. And being a therapy dog seemed like a great job to have. Of course that's just my opinion. I'd have to ask Clancy later about it.

She breezed through a few more tests, then it was time for the final one. She had to walk over a hot dog without trying to eat it. A few dogs passed, and a few failed that task. Two dogs were able to grab the hot dog without their owners even knowing it.

I had to stop the "just a dog" charade for a moment. I got down by Clancy and asked, "Have you ever picked up food on our walks without me knowing it?" She looked away, which was like a big guilty sign wrapped around her.

"Aha," I yelled, disturbing everyone in the facility. "Sorry," I said quickly, not wanting to ruin Clancy's chances of getting certified. Some folks continued to look at me, but most went back to the business at hand.

At last it was our turn for the hot dog exercise. I got down to Clancy's level and said, "Don't you dare!" She knew exactly what I meant. Since I'm a vegetarian there isn't meat in my house, except for what is in Clancy's dog food, so having a hot dog sitting right in front of her would certainly be tempting. "Don't you dare," I repeated. She looked at me with her "you're only human" countenance.

As we sailed over the hot dog as quickly as my short legs

could manage, I prayed silently for Clancy to be able to resist the temptation. As we crossed the finish line I looked back to see a hot dog, right where it was supposed to be. I heard Gus cheer from the bleachers.

"Clancy, you are awesome!"

Her look said, "Of course I am."

"I'm going to buy you a hamburger on the way home."

Then she broke protocol and jumped up on me. I didn't care, but she wasn't supposed to do this. A woman approached me with a clipboard, and unfastened a paper to give me. She said, "She jumped up on you after the exercise was completed, so it's not a problem." She smiled then and said, "Congratulations to you and Clancy. You both did a nice job, and Clancy will be receiving her certificate in a week or so."

I couldn't help it. I hugged the woman.

Gus had a hug for both me and Clancy. My grin was so big my cheeks hurt. Before we even got outside I told Gus, "Two things. First we're going to buy Clancy a hamburger somewhere. Second, I figured out how she got poisoned."

"How?" He got closer as we walked.

"Did you see those two dogs who got the hot dog and their owner didn't even know?"

"Yeah."

"That had to be what happened to Clancy. I never let her eat stuff when we're outside or on our walk. She had to have done it quickly, without me looking. Plus she looked guilty when I asked her."

Gus was one of my friends and family who didn't roll his eyes when I talked about Clancy knowing things. He asked, "What are you going to do about it?"

"I guess I'll tell Michael and George." Omigod. Michael was my boss in the investigation and I forgot to go see him yesterday. Crap. I promised myself I'd call him when we got on the road and see if he had time to meet when I got back to Quincy. I'd call George from the car too.

But first things first. We got in the car and drove to the first fast food place with a drive through. A bored voice said, "Help you?"

I ordered a double burger with no bun and no condiments and heard the voice say something about "one of those crazy no-carb diets." I ignored it because I was in such a good mood. I also ordered a sweet tea for me and a cup of coffee for Gus.

After I paid for and received the purchases, I handed the bag to Gus, who promptly unwrapped the treasures and leaned around and gave them to Clancy. She did not eat like someone with manners. I could hear the "gulp" and the satisfied belch. I know she would have verbalized a "thank you" if she could have. This was indeed an unusual treat for her.

The rest of the trip was uneventful. Gus and I sang

World War I and II era songs, which is what we did when we first met when I was in grade school. He was one of my oldest friends.

When we arrived home, Gus hugged both Clancy and me and turned to go into his house. Before he'd taken two steps he turned around and said, "You forgot to call Michael and George."

I slapped my head, then thanked Gus for his reminder. I thought about a thing I'd seen on Facebook. "Two things that bother me about aging are losing my short-term memory and losing my short-term memory." My memory may be suffering, but Gus was in his eighties and as sharp as ever.

Clancy relieved herself on Georgianne's plants. For some reason I couldn't rejoice in that as much as I used to.

Clancy led the way into our home. I immediately sat down on the couch and called Michael. It was Saturday, but I was sure he wouldn't mind being bothered.

The first thing out of his mouth after the hellos was, "Looks like you and Lansing have become quite the item."

I didn't know what to say so I didn't say anything.

It was only a short silence, and he broke it. "Interesting."

Even though I didn't know what "interesting" meant, I thought he might be a little upset that I was with George. "You didn't act like you wanted anything else from me. I mean, you said things, but you didn't act on them."

His chuckle made me smile. "Your directness is one of the things I like about you."

I didn't know what else to say about the situation, and it seemed that Michael wasn't as upset as I thought, or wished, he'd be. I guessed there would be no duels fought over me, but if truth be told, it was okay. I had George and I loved him.

I decided to continue. "Who was the woman with you at Joe's Place?"

"Just a business associate."

I thought he was a one-man operation. Maybe he had others like me who worked as needed for him. And when I say "like me," I meant only in the sense that we were both women. The resemblance ended there.

Putting aside those errant thoughts, I said, "I wanted to tell you something I came up with." I then went through the tale of the hot dog at the therapy dog test.

Michael said, "Sounds plausible. Maybe meat was poisoned, and somehow made its way to both dogs and humans. Let's hold onto that and think about it for a while."

I disconnected, then wondered what went wrong. Michael always said really nice things to me, and was flirtatious, but never made a move.

I'd think about that later. I immediately called George, to give him basically the same information. The phone call ended differently however. He thanked me, and then started talking about personal matters.

He made me feel like a teenager, all mushy and gooey-eyed, when I wanted to concentrate on murder. After we ended the conversation, I sat and thought about two things—George and the murder. My thoughts were convoluted, but both subjects made me smile. George, for obvious reasons, and the murder because I figured out something important.

Now to find out who poisoned the meat, and how it got to both dogs and humans.

EIGHTEEN

I woke up the next morning, and decided to skip Sunday church. I felt guilty but had a good reason. I was going to snoop.

I put on a pair of jeans and a T-shirt, filled a vacuum mug with coffee, put Clancy on a leash, and set off. There was no coherent plan. That's not what I was good at. I was good at impulsive and sometimes stupid behavior… but it got the job done. Kind of.

Shaking off any doubts, I talked to Clancy out loud, making my plan as we went. "I think Loretta goes to the Full Gospel Praise the Spirit Church of Divine Love." I could feel Clancy's doubt. "I'm not making this up."

I thought I'd go to her church. And then do what? Well, I hadn't gotten that far yet. I'd go to her church and wait. That's what I'd do. I told Clancy as much. No response from her. That must mean I was on the right track.

Right track or not, that's what I was going to do. And since Clancy was riding shotgun, that's what she was going to do too.

I had no problem finding the church because I'd volunteered there earlier in the month, debriefing some kids and families after a traumatic event in the community. Even though I poked fun at the name of the church, the members were the warmest and most welcoming people at any church I'd been to, including my own.

So I parked. And waited. And waited. And waited. I'd forgotten that this church had long services. We Catholics knew which priest took how long saying the Mass. And if we were in a hurry we went to the half-hour version, and if we really felt like worshipping we went to the full hour Mass. Nothing like this.

I scooted around in my seat, wishing I'd brought water for Clancy and me, but then I'd have to find a bathroom. As it was, I was just bored, but not uncomfortable. "Sorry, Clancy. I'd forgotten how boring stakeouts were supposed to be. The only other one we did was much more exciting, wasn't it? A half hour from start to finish, and we caught the murderers at the end." I smiled at the memory, conveniently skipping over the part where I almost got killed.

My reverie was interrupted by a pounding on my car window. It was Loretta, and she was steaming. I imagined her blood boiling. I put the window down and she stuck her head in. Because I still had my seatbelt on I couldn't move very far away. As usual I could count how many cavities she'd had repaired. What was up with this woman?

My vibes were in high gear as I started sweating, and the dizziness almost made me swoon. I tuned in to what she was saying rather than what I was experiencing and caught her in mid-sentence, "… and just who do you think you are? Just because your sister is the boss in the ER doesn't give you the right to follow innocent people like me. Get the hell away from here."

She pulled her head out and gave my car a push forward. It appeared she actually thought she could make my car move. In her current mood, I had no doubt she could do it.

"Now, now, Sister Johnson, what seems to be the matter?" Dr. Simmons' soft voice had a calming influence on both of us. This demeanor belied his preaching ability. He was able to "raise the roof" when he was on the pulpit. Outside the pulpit he was the calmest man in town.

Loretta hesitated, then said, "I was just asking her politely to leave. She's blocking the fire hydrant."

I wanted to scream, "Liar, liar, pants on fire," but caught myself in time. I was sure Dr. Simmons had already heard what Loretta had really said, but was just being diplomatic.

Loretta had the sense to at least look sheepish. She looked at the ground and said, "Sorry, Pastor. I get worked up sometimes."

"Yes, sister. Use that energy for the Lord instead of for whatever you were doing."

"Yes, Pastor, I will."

Dr. Simmons turned to me, "Hello again, Sam. What brings you to church this morning? You're a little late for the service."

What could I say? I couldn't lie to Dr. Simmons. So I told the truth. "I'm following Loretta."

Her "So there!" look pissed me off. Now she knew what I was up to, and there was nothing I could do about it.

When I told Dr. Simmons that Loretta was a subject in a murder investigation he started laughing. I wanted to tell him what I suspected, but couldn't, with her standing right there.

I pulled away, with Dr. Simmons still laughing and Loretta still fuming. I was really good at this investigating stuff.

What they didn't know, however, was that I waited a few blocks away, in an alley, hoping that Loretta would drive my way.

And a few minutes later my hopes were answered when her little green sedan passed by. I waited a moment before pulling behind her. Again, I wished I had a special, nondescript car for surveillance. My beloved blue Bug stuck out like a butterfly at a caterpillar convention.

I decided to just stay close to her, since she'd probably already suspected I'd be following her. She even waved at me a few times as we drove through the city. When she arrived home at a neat little frame house, I parked behind her. She opened her trunk and I craned my neck to see what was inside. I even undid my seatbelt to give me a better stretch.

Inside the trunk was a bag full of something or other. It kind of looked like the bag I saw Dougie carry from Holtschlag's Feed and Grain Store. I'd need to get a closer look so I'd know for sure.

So, before I had a chance to think things through, I jumped out of my car and said, "Hey, Loretta."

She'd known I was there already, but probably hadn't suspected that I'd get out of my car. She glanced down at the contents of her trunk and quickly closed it.

Damn. I still wasn't 100% sure it was rat poison, but it did have the same colors as the bag Dougie had carried— red and yellow.

She didn't say anything, but walked to the house. This was the first time she hadn't gotten in my face to talk to me, and I rather enjoyed it.

As I got back in my car I started talking to Clancy. "It looked like the same bag. But what does that matter? There's no arsenic in rat poison anymore. Is this significant? Or was Dougie just buying rat poison for his mother's rat problem?" My head hurt from the possibilities and improbabilities. Clancy calmed me with her presence as she was normally able to do. Soon my adrenaline had slowed and I was breathing normally. "Thanks, Clancy." She smiled. Clancy would make an excellent therapy dog.

"That reminds me. I'm going to put in a formal request tomorrow for you to work as a therapy dog at the clinic. Sure hope they say yes."

I could tell she hoped so too.

I called George as I pulled into the courtyard at home. I left a message inviting him to come over, that I had some news for him.

Then I decided a nap was in order. Clancy and I slept until my phone rang. George said he was on his way over, and I couldn't tell him I had a nap face. So I said okay.

I jumped up, ran my fingers through my hair and licked my lips. This would have to do.

The doorbell rang shortly thereafter, and I was glad I hadn't been home long enough to mess up the place too much.

Opening the door, I grinned stupidly. Then I really did feel stupid when it was Carter Callahan from the hospital.

"Er... hi," was all I could come up with.

He gave his usual nod and began to step through the doorway.

"Um, Carter, I'm kind of busy. What do you want?"

"I'm here to tell you who killed the people."

NINETEEN

I quickly changed my attitude. "Why are you standing outside? Come on in." As I started to close the door I saw George's car pull in next to mine. Carter must have taken the bus again.

I left the door open for George and ushered Carter into the living room. George came in and I gave him a peck on the cheek.

He looked me up and down until I blushed. Finally he said, "You don't have any pants on."

Crap. I'd taken off my jeans to take the nap and forgot to put them back on. I quickly excused myself, ran to my bedroom and fixed the situation.

When I got back to the living room I saw Carter and George each drinking a beer.

George looked up, "That's better." He smiled that smile. "Carter was waiting until you got back. He said he knows who killed those patients."

Carter nodded, as he usually does. I sat down, noticing that George had gotten a beer for me. A mid-afternoon

Sunday beer. Seemed like a good idea to me.

I didn't want to spook Carter, so I held back a little, which meant I gave him about a minute to tell us what he wanted to say before I asked.

"So, uh Carter…" He didn't take the hint, so I had to ask, "What did you want to talk about again?"

"I thought I'd tell you who the killer is. I kept telling you it was right under your nose, but you didn't seem to get it."

I couldn't let it go. "Well, I figured out how the dogs might have gotten poisoned. It was right under their noses." I waited, but he didn't say anything, so I continued. "This is what I called you about yesterday, "I looked at George when I said it. "I know how the dogs were poisoned, especially Clancy. She must have picked up some meat when I wasn't looking. I noticed it at the therapy dog test. Some dogs were able to grab a piece of meat off the floor when they were walking with their owners, and the owners didn't even notice it. That had to have happened with Clancy, and maybe the other dogs."

Neither guy reacted.

"C'mon, you guys. That has to be what happened."

George looked pained as he said, "You already told me that last night. I didn't want to burst your bubble, but that's kind of obvious, Sam."

"Not to me," I blustered. "I know Clancy doesn't eat anything that I or someone else she knows doesn't give her.

So this was a huge deal when I came up with it."

I saw the look on George's face. "Don't you dare give me that condescending look!"

And then to Carter, "Tell me what you want to tell me or get out."

He stood up and started for the door.

"Wait!" I grabbed him by the back of his shirt and pushed him back onto the couch. "Tell me!" This was the first time I wasn't worried about scaring him off.

Carter had absolutely no emotion on his face. Just like always. He shrugged his shoulders and said, "It's Loretta."

"I knew it. That's what I think too."

George remained calm. "How do you know it's Loretta? Carter first." He was in his police detective mode.

Carter answered, "You know how sometimes I sit in the corner and no one knows I'm there?"

George and I nodded in unison.

"Well, I was doing that when Loretta and Dougie came in. Loretta said something about she was sorry it happened, but Dougie better not say anything. And Dougie said he didn't know if he could keep quiet any longer, that he felt guilty. Then they noticed I was there and both left real fast."

"Great. I just knew it was her. Because she's so short and stands so close to me, she is literally right under my nose. Nice clue, Carter. Why didn't you tell me before?"

"You're getting paid to figure this all out. I thought I'd

give you a clue to help, but I wasn't going to do your job for you. It's taken so long that I thought I'd tell you."

I couldn't believe it. "How do you know I'm getting paid to snoop?"

He gave a little smile and said, "I sit. I listen."

George's turn. "Sounds to me like it could be either one. Or both. Sam, what made you think that Loretta is the murderer?"

"Okay, this may not be enough for you, but I saw Dougie buy a sack of rat poison at Holtschlag's. Then I saw the same bag in Loretta's trunk. At least I think it was the same bag. Looked like it anyway."

"That's circumstantial, but it does give me something to follow up. Again, it points to both of them, not just Loretta." He paused a moment, then continued, "You do remember that there's no arsenic in rat poison, don't you?"

I could do nothing but say, "Yes."

"Still it's something for me to check out. Is that why you asked me to come over?"

"Part of the reason…"

"What's the other part?" His voice got a little huskier.

I moved my head toward Carter. Once again, he was sitting somewhere unnoticed.

Carter said, "The buses don't run at this hour. Guess I'll have to walk home."

Unhappily, and with great disappointment, I said,

"George, maybe you can take him home."

George didn't look happy either. "Yeah. Okay."

He let Carter out the door first, then partially shut it. George grabbed me and gave me a smooch of which songs are written. I had never experienced one like it, and only hoped I had a future full of them. They just kept getting better and better.

"See ya later," he said.

I couldn't talk.

TWENTY

I cleaned up the house a little. Then I noticed Clancy staring at me. She'd never seen me in this state over a man. I ignored her stare and told her it was time for bed.

Normally I'd find it hard to sleep because pieces of the murder puzzle would be floating around in my head and I would be problem solving. Tonight was different. George occupied my mind. Just George. How could I have let all this time go by without forgiving him for a teenage wrongdoing? I wasted so much time.

Perhaps this was the way it was supposed to be. Meeting again in our mid-40s, at a time when we were more sensible, more settled. At least George was. I was feeling like a teenager with a giant crush on the coolest guy in school.

How did my fickle emotions move so quickly between Michael and George? Maybe after I saw George at the hospital, I didn't want to think of him, so fell for the first handsome hunk I saw. Actually I didn't care why it happened, I just knew that I was with the right guy now.

When I finally slept, my dreams weren't of George.

Instead I saw Loretta and Dougie passing that bag of rat poison back and forth between them like it was a hot potato. When I awoke I quickly wrote down all the details of the dream, because I normally forget them almost immediately.

At this point I was convinced Carter was innocent. Dougie and Loretta were the two suspects left that I actually suspected, although I was pretty sure Loretta was the villain. My vibes went crazy around her, and only less so around her son. Some months ago when my boss was murdered, my vibes pointed me toward the murderer, but they also pointed me in the wrong direction more than once.

I had to remind myself that I felt the strange, "vibe-ish" sensations around Carter too. And just because I kind of liked him and his weirdness doesn't mean he wasn't guilty.

Lying there ruminating over all the possibilities wasn't getting me to work on time. "Clancy, I'm sorry. No walk this morning." I quickly pulled on some sweats and let her out to the courtyard. "Don't pout. I'll walk you tonight. Just do what you have to do, and hurry."

She didn't hurry. That was her way of telling me off. I waited as she watered Georgianne's plants and returned to the carriage house. "Forgive me," I pleaded as I dropped the sweats and jumped into the shower. Yelling over the shower noise, I said, "I have to go to work. Today's the day I ask about you working as a therapy dog at the clinic."

Finally, I'd found the lever to get Clancy to relent on the guilt trip.

A scant half-hour later I ran into the office. Clara Schmitt, the receptionist, greeted me cheerily, "Hi, Sam. Your eight o'clock cancelled."

I didn't take out my frustration on her, but I was getting pretty tired of my early appointments always canceling. However, the upside was that I'd have time to talk to HR about Clancy. Since my boss was killed, that position still hadn't been filled. We therapists were all kind of supervising ourselves for the time being.

I walked to the other side of the building to Human Resources, to the office of Leonard Schnitzer. He was decked out as usual in his bowtie and checkered sport coat. I had taken the time to write up a program proposal and I handed it to him. He glanced at it and said, "No."

I was prepared for that. I gave Schnitzer a second paper, citing various references concerning the efficacy of canine therapy. He remained unconvinced. "No."

No problem. The third paper contained one sentence, "I'll go to the board."

I didn't want to have to go there, but knew this one would work. Schnitzer had an inordinate fear of the Board of Directors discovering his incompetencies. Since he had been in charge after Dr. Burns was killed, he lived in constant fear of being found out.

He stuttered, so I knew I had him. "Perhaps I was too hasty, Ms. Darling. Let me look at your proposal again, and I'll get back to you tomorrow."

"That will be satisfactory, Leonard." When with him, I used the same formal, stilted English he did, but I refused to call him Mister. Another childish thing. I had a hard time using a respectful title for someone I didn't respect.

I spent the rest of that first hour going over my dream again. Loretta and Dougie throwing that rat poison back and forth, back and forth. Could they be in it together?

I guessed they could be, but my money—if I had any—was on Loretta. She's the one who had ended up with the rat poison that didn't contain arsenic anyway. Why was I so focused on the rat poison? I was sure it would still poison people, and dogs, but there was no arsenic. But it seemed like too much of a coincidence.

I wondered if there was another readily available source for arsenic. Guess I needed to do more research.

Mrs. Schmidt announced that my 9:00 had arrived. I checked my schedule and smiled when I saw that it was Mrs. Abernathy. She sometimes got on my nerves with her vivid recitations of her sexual dreams, but she was never boring.

I ushered Mrs. Abernathy into my office and began by asking if I could call her by her given name, Hazel. She agreed, and asked if she could call me Samantha. I laughed at that. It was very seldom I heard my full name. I suggested she call me Sam. She said she couldn't do that. So Samantha it was.

We began the session with a review of the homework I'd given her. Last week I had suggested she think about writing down a dream and see what she thought about publishing it.

Hazel sat her rotund body in the comfortable love seat in my office. She looked like she belonged there, all cozy and content, just missing a roaring fire, a teapot and a cat. She sighed heavily, and her flowered dress heaved as her ample bosom rose upward a little from its usual place around her waist.

"Well, Samantha, I have been thinking about your suggestion. I'd like to try it. I believe my dreams are important enough for the world to know about them. So how will I go about it?"

She had me there. I promised her I'd do some research for her since she didn't have a computer. "Why don't you continue writing down your dreams, and if they seem related, maybe you can string them together to make a longer story?"

Hazel seemed confused but nodded.

I asked if she had any more questions about the book, and she shook her head no. Then I tried the impossible… to get her to talk about her issues. I knew it wouldn't work, but I was almost desperate to get her to be a real client, to talk about things that are making her unhappy. Instead she was happy, pleasant to talk to, and disinterested in talking about problems. "It brings me down, Samantha." That's what she said, and I had to honor it, although I was surprised at the way she phrased it.

Certainly I used counseling skills to help her dig a little, but if she wasn't interested, she wasn't interested. I sighed and asked if she wanted to talk about anything else.

She did. She wanted to know if she'd have to pay a percentage of her income to me because I came up with the idea. I assured her I didn't want anything. Hazel smiled, and that was the end of the session.

It certainly didn't take up a full hour. I had 15 minutes before my 10:00 showed up. I quickly finished the progress note, which was difficult to write, then took a chance and visited Schnitzer's office.

He saw me coming and ducked into a nearby men's room. He didn't know me very well if he thought that was a significant deterrent. I followed him and caught him hiding in a stall.

A noise from another stall convinced me we weren't alone. I took Schnitzer's hand, and not unkindly led him from the bathroom into the hall.

"May we talk in your office?" I asked in the nicest tone I could muster.

I pretended he had a choice. When in his office I

dropped his hand and asked, "I don't mean to disturb you, but I wondered if you'd had a chance to decide a little early."

He was sweating, even though the room was cool. Did I intimidate him? If so, he wasn't the first person.

"Yes, as it so happens, I have decided that a therapy dog is just what we need, and I'm glad I thought of it."

I coughed to cover my indignation, then realized that I didn't care who got the credit, I just wanted Clancy to be able to work with me. Schnitzer and I worked out details quickly and he said he would draw up a contract for me to sign.

No problems there. I'd just cross out what I didn't like.

The important thing was that Clancy would be a daily fixture here at the clinic. I couldn't wait to tell her.

TWENTY-ONE

My 10:00 and 11:00 appointments came and went with minimal drama and some actual therapy.

Before going to my afternoon job at the hospital, I ran home during my break to tell Clancy the good news. When I pulled into my courtyard there was another car parked there—Loretta's. What in the world was she doing at my house?

As I got out of my car, Loretta walked up to me, too close as usual. My vibes went into overdrive and I stepped back without thinking. She must have been used to that, and took a step forward for every step I took backward, just like her son had done.

I said a quick hello and added, "I have to let Clancy out." I walked to my door and opened it without a key. My first thought was, "Damn. Now she knows I don't lock up my house." It was quickly followed by a note to self, to begin locking that door.

Clancy came right to the door and stepped over the threshold. She looked at Loretta and I thought she might sense something amiss and start growling or something, normally completely out of character for her. Instead, she took a few more steps forward and nuzzled Loretta's side. An initial look of distaste crossed Loretta's face, but it was quickly replaced by rapture. Reminded me of how Georgianne had been with Clancy at first—disgust changing into adoration.

If Clancy loved her, then how could she be the murderer? I just didn't get it.

Clancy reluctantly tore herself away from Loretta's scrubs and went to water the ferns. Finally Loretta looked like she was ready to talk.

Instead of telling me why she was there, she started asking questions about Clancy—what kind of dog, how old, where did I get her, would she have puppies, could she get one, and so on.

I answered a few questions and then asked, "What are you doing here, Loretta? And how did you know where I lived?"

"It's called a phone book, Sam."

Smart ass.

"And I came over on my break to talk to you about the rat poison in my trunk."

Aha. She was ready to confess. I was uncharacteristically quiet.

"You see, my mother has a problem with mice. She lives

in an old house and can't afford an exterminator. We ran out of the first bag we'd bought, so Dougie bought the rat poison, then gave it to me. And that's it. Nothing suspicious at all." She smiled. But she looked like the cat that swallowed the canary.

I found it suspicious anyway. But now I knew where the first bag of poison went. Holtschlag had been ready to tell me, but had changed his mind. Why would Loretta make a trip to my house just to tell me about her mom's problem with mice? Must be nervous. Maybe guilty. I decided to go with what she was saying.

"Makes sense to me. But why couldn't you wait until you saw me at work to tell me?"

"Oh, you know how busy we get in the ER. No time to chat. Besides, Dougie thought…"

"Dougie? What did he think?" Damn, why did I interrupt her in the middle of telling me what he thought?

"Oh, nothing," was all she said about him. Damn again. "Guess I'll get back. I only get a half-hour for my lunch break."

"Bye," was all I could come up with.

As I put Clancy back in the house, she gave me a look that let me know she caught my stupidity.

"I know it was stupid, Clance. But I can't help getting excited about stuff and then I interrupt people."

It was only a few minutes later that I entered the ER. My

carriage house was right in the center of town and I was close to everything.

Jenny saw me right away and her first words surprised me, "You and George?" She hugged me. "I'm so happy for you." I was grinning pretty big by then. Until she said, "We all thought you'd be alone forever."

"Why?" I practically whined.

"Nothing bad. It's just because you're independent, and well, a little bossy. And kind of stubborn. And…"

I cut her off before she could continue the litany of my many faults. "Okay, that's enough. I'm glad you're happy for me though."

She looked relieved that I wasn't mad. How could I be mad? The family loved George and so did I.

It was seldom Jenny stopped her work long enough to talk to me. Being the nurse manager kept her busy. I took advantage of the infrequent lull to ask a few questions. First, though, I wanted to let her know that no one thought she was guilty.

"Of course they don't. So what are your questions?"

I was surprised she wasn't at all anxious that she was on the suspect list, but started with my questions, "Is Loretta here?"

"I think she just came back from lunch. Why?"

I didn't answer, but asked another one instead, "Is Dougie working too?"

"Nope, he's not coming in until later."

My final question, "Do you really need me today?"

"Sam, we've never really needed you."

I put aside my hurt feelings to say, "Would it be okay if I took off for a few hours?"

"Sure, just make sure it's noted on your time sheet."

Thanking her, I backed away and turned around and ran into none other than Loretta. Was she eavesdropping? Or just being her usual space-invader self?

"Hello again." I decided to be friendly.

"Hi," she said letting me note that she'd recently eaten onions. "Why are you taking off?"

"It's personal," I lied, knowing I was going to snoop on her son.

"Okay, see you later," she said, but her eyes told me it was anything but okay.

I scooted out from under her stare and quickly exited the hospital. I felt a presence near me as I walked. None other than Carter Callahan following me. I whipped around and faced him. "What are you doing?"

He answered softly and without emotion, "I'm following you so you don't get killed."

That was certainly to the point. "I'm not going to get killed." I couldn't just stop there. "Why do you think I'm going to be killed?"

"Because you're following the murderer," he said.

"Wait. I thought you said it was Loretta who did it."

"I changed my mind. It's Dougie."

This confused the heck out of me. I kept going back and forth between the two, just like the rat poison in my dream—back and forth, back and forth.

"What made you change your mind?" I asked.

Carter looked at me as if I were stupid. "Doesn't matter. I just know."

"Get in the car," was all I could say at that moment.

He climbed in the passenger seat of my Bug and connected his seatbelt. He was so slight that I feared he would slide right out of the seatbelt if we got in a wreck. After he was settled, he said, "Let's go."

Overall, this was probably more talking than I'd ever gotten out of Carter Callahan. Was this how he was when he was excited?

"What are we doing?" he asked quietly, as we were driving out of the hospital parking lot.

"Well, I thought I'd follow Dougie a little."

Carter wrinkled his nose. "Do you know where he is?"

I hesitated. "Not exactly. I thought I'd just drive around until… okay, I didn't think this through very well. But the town is small and—"

And just that quickly I realized that we were behind Dougie's truck. I gave Carter a look that surely demonstrated my superiority over him. He slouched a little in his seat.

"Don't worry," I said, "I won't rub it in. Much."

Once again, I didn't know what I was doing when it came to tailing a suspect, and I knew I really wasn't supposed to be doing this anyway. But my curiosity, which others might call nosiness, is genetic, and there is no cure.

Since my car stood out and I didn't know what I was doing, I decided to once again just get right behind him. Sure, I didn't know what good that would do, but I didn't have another plan.

Carter reminded me over and over again that I was too close to Dougie. I turned to tell him to "Shup" and BAM! I hit the back of Dougie's truck.

We both pulled over to the side of the road. It was Broadway, the busiest street in town. I got out of my car to see if there was damage, and there wasn't. At least I couldn't see any. His truck was old, and my car was dirty. I could see where they came in contact, because that part of my car was clean.

Dougie got out of his truck a moment later. He stormed over to me and began screaming. He positioned himself toe to toe with me, looked me in the eye, and was practically frothing at the mouth. I couldn't understand him. I was too busy wishing that I wasn't backed up against the front of my car. There was no way to escape his space invasion rant.

I understood his anger. But I didn't understand his rage.

Finally, I managed to scoot out sideways from his attack.

I walked around him to get a little room. As I did, I saw the back of his truck and the damn rat poison was there.

Back and forth. Back and forth. What did it mean?

I'd soon find out.

TWENTY-TWO

"Do you want me to call the police?" I asked Dougie when he stopped screaming to take a breath.

Aha! That did it. He calmed down slightly and said, "No, I'll take care of my truck. You take care of your car." He started to walk to the driver's side door, then turned and pointed a finger at me. "You just better mind your own business. Understand?"

I understood all right. He was protecting his mother. Or maybe himself. I was confused as hell.

Carter had other ideas. "See I told you he was guilty." Carter didn't even know about the rat poison in the back of his truck.

I had an idea. "Want to check out Holtschlag's with me?"

He nodded. Getting back into character.

I drove the short distance downtown, parked on the square at Washington Park, and Carter and I crossed the street to the store.

Mr. Holtschlag was behind the counter as usual. He

looked up, "May I help… ? Oh, it's you."

"Yes, it's me and this is my friend, Carter." They did a mutual nod thing. "I wonder if you have any more of the rat poison that you sold Dr. Johnson the other day."

He nodded again, and began walking down an aisle. Carter and I followed him. I loved the smell of this place. Old wood. Plus lots of miscellaneous smells you'd find in a Feed and Grain Store. We walked down the aisle, stepping over boxes, dodging mini-columns of whatnot, until we finally arrived at the destination—the storeroom in back.

"Here's what I have," the proprietor said, indicating stacks of bags.

I thanked him and then hit myself in the head. The stacks were taller than I, and there were several brands. I turned to Carter, "The bag is yellow and red."

Carter, like the savant that he is, said, "There they are" right away. He pointed to one of the stacks behind the first row. It towered over us by several feet. I looked at the retreating figure of Mr. Holtschlag and knew he wouldn't want to help me.

There was no way we could pull out a bag from the middle of the stack, and I couldn't reach the second row anyway. I turned to Carter, "Look for a ladder or something to climb on."

After a rudimentary search, we found the ladder in a corner of the storeroom, looking as old as the place itself. It wasn't a stepladder, it was the kind that had to be leaned up against a wall, but it would do.

Carter apparently had a fear of heights, because he insisted I be the one to climb the ladder. We placed it so it leaned against the first tower of bags. Grateful I'd remembered to wear pants instead of a skirt, I climbed slowly, praying this old ladder would support this old body.

It did. I grabbed the topmost bag from the appropriate row, and was going to hand it down to Carter. As I held it I teetered back and forth, back and forth. There's something about these bags of rat poison that made back and forth happen. As I teetered backward, self preservation took hold and I dropped the bag as I held on to the ladder with a grip that would rival super-glue.

Unfortunately the bag didn't fare as well as I did. When it landed, several feet from Carter, it exploded in a burst of powder that filled the air around us. I cussed and I heard Mr. Holtschlag screaming as he ran back toward the storeroom. "Get out of there. Get out of there. That bag has arsenic in it."

I did something I didn't think was possible. I jumped off the ladder and beat Carter to the front of the store.

"What?" I said to Holtschlag. "Rat poison doesn't contain arsenic any more."

He mopped the beads of perspiration off his forehead with a handkerchief that looked as old as the store and the ladder. "Not in the states. But there are still some countries that use it. I've got to sit down."

Carter and I helped the old guy to a stool behind the counter.

I couldn't help myself, "Why in the hell would you buy rat poison with arsenic in it?"

"I don't think I ought to tell you."

I gave him my big sister glare. It can stop a mortal at twenty paces. He couldn't help but relent.

"A… a… customer ordered it," he stuttered.

"Who," I demanded.

Again he said, "I don't think I ought to tell you."

I moved so that I was even closer to him than Loretta or Dougie would have been. "Tell me." I waited a beat. "Or I'll call the cops right now." I held up my cell phone for good effect.

He looked like he was going to relent. I didn't let him know that I was going to tell the cops anyway, just not that second.

Holtschlag's shoulders relaxed. His arm muscles followed suit. He slumped on the stool, and a tear rolled down his well-lined cheek.

"You scare me," he said.

"Good, because I mean what I say."

He gulped, righted himself by holding on to the counter, and said, "Dr. Johnson had it special ordered from Haiti."

"Dougie ordered that whole stack?"

Shaking his head, Holtschlag said, "It was so cheap I thought I'd order more and make a little money."

"Isn't it illegal to have arsenic in rat poison in the states?"

"Probably. I don't know. I didn't check." He looked defeated, his eyes downcast, tears now flowing freely. "Don't let them take my store from me." He grabbed my arms. "Please."

He looked pathetic. "I'll do what I can. But you do know that people died because of that rat poison."

Panic replaced the tears. "No. I didn't. I didn't… I didn't know… I swear."

I had a hard time believing him, because it was all over the news, but it didn't matter what I thought. He was going to have to face the consequences of his actions. I was confident it wouldn't be accessory to murder, or anything that huge, but there would certainly be consequences.

Carter stayed with him while I stepped outside to make the phone call. Normally I'd call my brother Rob first with a scoop like this. He was still considered new on the force and I like to help him as much as I can.

But I'd been working on this with George. Besides, he was my guy, and I needed to notify him. I had him on speed dial already, and waited patiently for him to answer. It wasn't to be. So after listening to a much-too-long message, I told him what I knew about Holtschlag's and the rat poison, and said that Carter and I were going to confront Dougie. Once again, not thinking things through. I did have the good sense to invite George to join us, but of course I didn't know exactly where we'd be.

I saw through the window that Mr. Holtschlag seemed to be breathing normally, and I motioned to Carter to come outside. "Let's go," I said when he got there, echoing his earlier words.

As we buckled ourselves into my car, I suddenly remembered I needed to tell Michael too, since he was the one who hired me. Before we took off, I called him with the same result as George. I left a similar message.

I entertained a momentary fantasy that they were somewhere together fighting over me, but that wasn't really what I wanted anymore, and the vision soon vanished. I loved George, and Michael was just a friend. A very handsome friend, but that was it.

"Are you ready for an adventure?" I asked Carter.

He actually smiled.

Then it hit me. Gus had wanted an adventure. I couldn't do this without him. He was with me the last time I confronted a murderer, and even though it was a fiasco, it did have a happy ending.

"We're going to pick up someone."

Carter didn't respond, so that meant he was back to normal.

The sun was getting close to the Mississippi River, and I realized that it would soon be dusk. I wasn't frightened because Quincy was a safe town, and besides, I'd have Carter and Gus with me. None of us carried guns. I didn't like 'em. And I hoped Dougie had the same feeling.

I didn't bother calling Gus because we were so close to the house. I parked in front and bounded up the stairs to the front porch, or veranda as Georgianne called it. I knocked and rang the bell at the same time. My adrenaline was pumping at full steam and it was hard standing still.

Georgianne answered the door and I didn't give her a chance to remind me that Gus was ill. I barged right past her and saw Gus sitting in a recliner in the parlor. His recliner was Georgianne's one concession to normality in the mansion.

"Want to have an adventure?"

Gus bounded out of the recliner and we both almost flew off the porch heading to my car. He did turn to yell back to Georgianne, "I love you."

Gus wouldn't fit very well in the backseat, but the back seemed to have been made for Carter. Carter was silent, and I was able to fill Gus in on what we were going to do.

He beamed. "Do you think we'll need everybody's help like we did last time, or can we do this one alone?"

I didn't like the implication. "Of course we can do this alone. No one knows where we're going, except I left messages for George and Michael. They'll probably call me and I can tell them we need them or we don't need them. We'll see how it goes."

Unfortunately, my impulsivity was leading us right into danger. And I was too stupid to notice.

TWENTY-THREE

Without a plan we'd be doomed to wander around aimlessly. I pulled over to the curb on Tenth Street, near the hospital. And I turned to my accomplices.

"Anybody got a plan?"

Blankness from Carter and a shoulder shrug from Gus. I'd have to be the one to decide.

"Okay. Dougie is supposed to be working this evening. Let's make sure he's here." I dialed the hospital and keyed in the ER extension. The receptionist answered my question by saying that Dougie called in sick.

"He's sick, or at least he said he is," I told them. "So I guess we ought to try his house first. Make sense?"

Two enthusiastic nods told me I was on the right track. I wished George or Michael would call me back. They'd tell me what to do, and they'd let me know if I was making a mistake. They would probably be more than happy to tell me. My stomach was communicating something to me, but I didn't know what it meant. I just knew we were getting close to the murderer, at least if I believed Carter.

My hunch still told me Loretta was the villain, but Dougie had threatened me twice and he had been the one with the rat poison the last time I checked. Or was it Loretta? Back and forth, back and forth. Damn it! I was getting my dreams mixed up with reality.

It was a short drive to Dougie's house, just like anywhere else in Quincy. His truck was in the driveway. I parked on the street in front of a neighbor's house, and told Gus and Carter to stay in the car.

"That's what you always say," Gus said.

"And last time you didn't listen. Please do it this time. Please."

He nodded, but didn't say anything.

I coughed as I got out of the car, followed swiftly by Carter coughing too. I leaned back in the car and fished a cough drop out of the glove box. "Carter, if you need one, there's a few more left in there."

Then I started walking, but as usual didn't have a plan. I didn't know if I should just go up to his door and knock—the straightforward approach—or if I should try to look in a few windows, and check in the backyard.

The last time I tried looking in someone's window I ended up with a gun brandished in my face. So I decided to go up to the door.

The door was ajar; I took that as an invitation to snoop. I pushed it a few inches more. Just enough for me to get my head through and look without actually going in the house. If caught I'd say that I was getting ready to ring the doorbell. That was as much of a plan as I could muster.

I did just what I had hastily planned—pushed the door with my toe, and kept my hand near the doorbell, just in case. I angled my head around to get a look at as much of the interior as possible, but no luck. Just a house with furniture, "stuff," and the end of a red and yellow bag sticking out from behind the couch. Bingo!

My phone picked a particularly bad time to whistle, telling me I had a text. I quickly turned off the sound, hoping no one inside had heard the noise. No one inside had. But a voice from behind me said, "Paying a social call?"

Just knowing it was Dougie, I turned and prepared to lie. Michael's face surprised me. I whispered, "What are you doing here?"

"I got your message and figured you'd be tailing one of the suspects. I found out Loretta was working, so I tried here. And I see suspect number three is in your car. Friends with Callahan?"

I didn't have time to answer him. Dougie came to the door. He said, "Hmmm. Were you guys going to ring the doorbell or were you going to talk all day on my step?"

I gave him my best phony smile and asked if I could come in.

"That's not convenient right now. What is it you want?"

I tried again. "I'd rather sit down if it's okay."

"It's not okay. Unless you have a search warrant. Oh, I forgot, neither of you are police, so I'm going to have to ask you to leave before I call them and tell them you're trespassing."

I hate a smart ass, unless it's me. "I see the rat poison behind your couch." He quickly turned to look. I continued, "Michael, will you please call George and let him know we've caught Dougie with the murder weapon."

"No need," another voice chimed in. George walked up the sidewalk, followed by Gus and Carter.

I immediately told Gus and Carter to get back in the car. I swear Carter coughed out, "You're not the boss of me."

Then my stomach spoke to me again. And not kindly. I began coughing and it sounded like Carter and I were playing a duet. I managed to tell George two things: One, that a rat poison bag had exploded at Holtschlag's and Carter and I inhaled it; and two, that I loved him.

That was when everything faded to black.

TWENTY-FOUR

I awoke hearing beeps and feeling pinpricks in my arm. I tried to talk but something in my throat would only let me issue guttural sounds.

My sister, Jill, was leaning over me looking into my eyes shining the brightest light I'd ever seen. She must have seen the panic I felt and used her best "doctor voice" to try and calm me.

I pointed to the tube and she nodded and said, "We'll take it out soon. You vomited a lot and we needed that to stop, so the tube is just going to your stomach. Don't worry, it's not a ventilator."

That did help me relax a little. I shot my eyebrows up questioningly, and she said, "George brought you in." She nodded to the other side of my bed where my hero stood. "And you can talk just fine. You'll just have to get used to the NG tube."

Tears threatened to fall. George was already holding my hand, and leaned over and kissed my cheek. I squeezed his hand, but still needed to know more. "What's happening?" I whispered.

George took over then. "Carter and you both had a reaction to the rat poison. You most likely had a slight case of arsenic poisoning."

I squeaked, "Slight?" I wanted to yell, "SLIGHT?"

"Yes, slight. You're going to be fine. At least that's what Jill says. Carter's going to be okay too."

Jill excused herself to go check on Carter for me. I still was confused, and George must have known it. My stomach, my head, and my throat hurt. I didn't like talking with this tube down my throat. It felt like it was as big as a tunnel.

He continued, "We have Dr. Johnson in custody, but he contends he's innocent. He won't talk more and is lawyered up. We took the bag of rat stuff from his house and it's being analyzed now. Looks like it does contain arsenic though; it says so on the bag."

George leaned over and kissed my cheek again. "I can't believe I'm talking and you haven't interrupted me once."

I managed to grunt and kicked him in the side with my foot. He laughed at me. "Is it okay if I leave you alone for a minute? I have a call to make."

I nodded.

As he walked toward the door, he turned and said, "I love you too."

The most romantic words George had ever said to me, and he's leaving, while I'm lying in a hospital bed with a tube down my throat and needles in my arm. Something was horribly wrong with this picture.

I wasn't surprised Dougie hadn't confessed. Why would he? But it looked like Carter was right and I owed Loretta an apology. She probably wouldn't accept it because her shining star, baby boy was in jail and accused of several murders and attempted murders. For some reason, it just didn't feel right to me. Although my vibes were present around him, they weren't the "omigod, I'm in the presence of a murderer" type of vibes. More like "get out of my face" vibes.

Couldn't do anything about it anyway. I was stuck in my own brand of jail, and I wanted the damn tube out. Immediately. I rang the call bell, and the smiling nurse immediately retreated when she saw my face. A moment later Jill returned.

"Sam, wait just a few more minutes. We want to see if any more juice is coming out of your stomach. If it's about done, then I'll take the tube out. Promise."

I held up five fingers and croaked, "Five."

"Yeah, five minutes ought to do it."

I pointed toward the door and arched my eyebrows.

"Carter is about in the same position you are. Because he's so much younger, he…"

She stopped before I kicked her too.

"Anyway, he's going to be fine."

Her pager went off and she said, "I'll be back in a few minutes to take out your tube."

I held up four fingers. All she did was laugh as she left.

I must have dozed off. The next thing I knew I couldn't breathe. My eyes popped open to see Loretta even closer than usual. Her cinnamon-scented breath would have gagged me if I'd been able to gag. As it was I had a stupid tube down my throat, two petite hands trying to kill me, and my arms incapacitated with needles in them.

She let go for a split second as both my legs scissored up and kicked her in the head. It must have pissed her off because she slugged me. I thought that at least she wasn't choking me. Where was Jill? Where was George?

I began panicking again as she choked me after slugging me one more time. I was able to kick her again, but was losing what little strength I had.

Throughout the struggle she was talking through clenched teeth. I could make out something about her baby and what I was doing to him. I would have loved to have answered, but I was being choked to death with a stupid tube in me.

Just as I thought I was going to die, a big, beautiful, blonde, furry creature came flying through the air. Clancy knocked what little air I had left out of me. But even better she landed on Loretta and put her teeth around Loretta's arm and pulled. Loretta didn't scream but she let go of me immediately. Clancy continued pulling her until Loretta was off the bed; then Clancy knocked her to the floor. My brave canine stood over Loretta with her teeth bared, just daring Loretta to move.

At that point I noticed that Gus had entered the room.

"Are you okay, honey?" he asked, leaning over me and looking as mad as I'd ever seen him when he turned around to glare at Loretta.

I nodded while I was sobbing, making as much noise as I could with the damn, damn, damn tube down my throat. When would this end?

George ran into the room, followed quickly by Jill. Once he saw that I seemed to be alive and breathing, George took out his handcuffs and read Loretta her rights. He asked a security guard, who also appeared, to watch Loretta in the corner for a minute.

He held my hand while Jill deflated the balloon inside my stomach so the tube would come out easily. I had to cough more, and didn't know if it was from the tube coming out or if it was from inhaling the arsenic, but I didn't care. I was rid of the tube and I was alive.

Now that Loretta was safely away from me, Clancy jumped on my bed and nuzzled against me. "Oh my sweet girl," were the first words I said as I hugged her the best I could considering I was still tied up to IV poles.

"What happened?" George asked, still holding my hand

and gazing at me as though he wanted to wrap his arms around me despite the crowd.

Loretta was in the corner and screeched to anyone who would listen, "You had my boy arrested. He's the only good thing in my life, and it's all your fault he's in jail and his career is ruined."

"His career isn't ruined if he's innocent," George said. "Is there anything you want to say?"

"No. Yes. I don't know." She looked at George, then at me, and then back at George.

"I can have Dougie out of jail this afternoon if he's not the one who's been killing people," George said to her.

Loretta started sobbing. "I didn't mean for anyone to die."

It was hard to hear what else she said because she was sobbing from her very soul. After a few minutes, she began talking again. "You don't understand what it's like. He's the first one in our family to go to college, and he ended up being a doctor. But no one here recognized his brilliance. Everyone was always bragging about Jill." She glared at me as if that was my fault. "I had to do something to show people what a wonderful doctor Douglas is."

George prompted her with, "So you…"

"So I thought it wouldn't hurt anyone very much if I put just a little rat poison on some food. I was very careful and I practiced on dogs first."

Clancy growled and no one blamed her.

"Once I got good enough at poisoning dogs that they stopped dying, but just got sick, I decided to begin on people."

Outraged as I was, I was able to squeak out a few words, "But there were some dogs poisoned after people started dying."

"Yes, there was some leftover meat I'd had for the dogs. I just threw it in a trash bin on Maine Street. They must have gotten it there."

And some of it dropped on the sidewalk and my dog almost died from eating it, I thought. I choked up and couldn't get any words out. All I could do was hug my sweet heroine, Clancy.

George asked another question, "How did you know to order rat poison from Haiti?"

She didn't answer, but her worried expression told us there was an interesting answer there somewhere.

I hated to change the subject but had to ask Gus, "How did you get permission to bring Clancy up to see me?"

"Permission?" was all he said. He winked, and I swear Clancy smiled.

TWENTY-FIVE

Jill said she would release me in a few hours. In the meantime no one made a move to remove Clancy from my bed.

My brother Rob arrived with another officer to take Loretta to the station. After a quick hug, and an "I love you," he left. But I knew I'd hear a lecture later, about the fact that I wasn't a cop. Boy, oh boy, I'd heard that often enough. And it probably wasn't the last time.

Michael walked in. I'd forgotten all about him. I didn't have to ask where he'd been, because he started talking right away.

"I'm sorry I haven't been here sooner, but I kept in touch and knew you were okay. I went to Loretta's house with the police and we saw some white powder in her garage. Figured it's the rat poison, and we'll find out from Dr. Johnson why he had it."

He walked over and gave me a quick hug. George and Clancy allowed it.

Gus had gone to be with Carter because he didn't have

anyone with him, and there was no one to call. I had a feeling Gus would be just the poison antidote Carter needed.

Michael left pretty quickly. I thought about how fast things, and my affections, had changed. Just a short time ago I had yearned for Michael to return my interest, but now I knew that had been a passing fancy.

George took Clancy and me home a few hours later. I still had on the gown from the ER, so he put me to bed, and I conked out immediately after getting a sweet, loving kiss. My last thought before falling asleep was that I wanted more.

I woke up to someone whistling. When I opened my eyes I could see the sunshine beaming onto the carpet, letting me know I really needed to vacuum. George bounded in with coffee and toast.

He said, "This is all the food I could find."

"It's perfect," I replied as I tried to sit up.

"And don't worry. Clancy has already been out."

A movement on the other side of the bed caught my attention. Clancy snuggled up next to me as she always did when I was in bed.

"Have you been here all night?" I asked George.

"Yeah."

"Where did you sleep?"

"Well, I was kind of worried about you, so I just slept by

you so I'd be there if you needed anything."

"Thank you," was all I could say. Then I thought of something else, "Where did Clancy sleep?"

"Well, we both wanted to be by you so she slept on one side of you and I slept on the other. A little crowded, but you were well-guarded."

After grinning, I began devouring the toast, and took a sip of the coffee, swallowing gingerly because of my throat. "Have you heard anything yet?"

He knew what I meant.

"Yeah, I've been on the phone with the station. Dougie is innocent of everything except not reporting his mom. He bought the rat poison innocently enough. Loretta told him that his grandma had some rats and wanted the type of product she remembered from her childhood in Haiti. He wasn't aware it contained arsenic, but even if he had known, it's unlikely he would have suspected his mom was up to no good."

"So that explains why he bought it. Why did he have it at his house?"

"Well, this is where he committed a crime. After he noticed he was always on duty when the poisoned patients came to the ER, he started to suspect that his own mother might be behind the poisonings. She kept calling for him whenever a new patient came in; that gave her away, and he wanted to stop her. So he took the bag back from her and stashed it at his house. He wanted to see if the poisonings would stop if he had the bag."

"Did they?"

"There were a few more. Loretta had some of the powder at her home. But no one else died. She'd figured out the dosage by then."

I had one more question. "I understand how the dogs were poisoned. How did she do it to people?"

He frowned as he said, "Well, the first victim, Pluto, was poisoned at the party. This was Loretta's first attempt, so she scattered some of the poison on a few wings, and she used too little. Other people got somewhat ill, but that was it. Not enough to make their nausea look like more than the flu—or to have them admitted to the hospital so that Dr. Dougie would have to save them. But because Pluto's immune system was compromised from living on the street for many years, and because of his alcoholism, he was more susceptible. He was doomed."

"So she used more the next time, to make even healthy people ill… and she used too much?"

George nodded, sadly. "And finally," he said, "she found just the right dosage."

"But how was she able to poison the people in the hospital, like Dr. Adams?"

"Funny thing about that," he said. "Some people were poisoned right there in the ER. When they asked for a soda or coffee, she would put a little rat poison in it. She could gauge the dose pretty well by then, even accounting for body mass. She's a nurse, after all."

My curiosity wasn't satisfied yet. "What about the other people?"

"Well, she went to a lot of church and community functions. Sprinkle, sprinkle, and there you have it."

He leaned over and kissed me.

"Because you've been through a lot I'm not going to give you a long lecture. But you are a social worker..."

"Not a cop. I know, I know, I know. But I can't help myself." I kissed him back. "And if I hadn't snooped at Holtschlag's, you would have never known about the rat poison."

He was mercifully quiet, staying true to his word of not lecturing me too much. I finished the toast and slurped up the last of the coffee. I looked at Clancy, then I looked at George. I was pretty content at that moment. Pretty content.

"George, please take Clancy to the living room and turn on Animal Planet. That will occupy her for a while. I'm going to jump in the shower and I'll see you in a minute."

He looked at me with mischief in his eyes. One of the many reasons I loved him. Without a word to me, he called Clancy and they disappeared into the living room. It was only a moment before I heard the TV telling Clancy all about wildlife in Idaho.

As I climbed out of bed I felt a little dizzy, so I moved slowly. Besides the dizziness, I had a sore throat, but other than that I felt pretty good. I steadied myself against the bedstead and stood for a moment.

I felt some strong arms hold on to me, making me feel safe. And loved.

George whispered, "It looks like you might need some help taking that shower. I could call one of your sisters, of course. Or..."

I smiled, and repeated, "Or..." as I took his hand and pulled him toward me.

About
CAN YOU PICTURE THIS?
(Sam Darling Mystery #3)

If Sam had known when she knocked over the guy's bicycle that it would put her knee-deep in murder again, she might have thought twice.

Richie Klingman, the only representative of the "paparazzi" in Quincy, chases Sam down with his camera in an attempt to grab a quick shot of the local celebrity sleuth. But when the flashbulb goes off in her face, she goes off on him—or on his bike—and down it falls, Richie and all.

Turns out that one of the photos Richie took caught the precise moment of a murder on film. The next thing Sam knows, Richie himself has been stabbed and is in the hospital with a serious chest wound.

Sam is stumped. There are no suspects. Instead there are round-the-clock police protecting Sam and her kids, who are home from college for the summer. And there is round-the-clock involvement with her old high school beau George, whom Sam has finally forgiven for standing her up on prom night.

When at last a suspect emerges, Sam is confronted with her own mortality yet again. In this third book of the Sam Darling mystery series, you'll be wondering whodunit right up until the picture is fully exposed and the murderer comes to light.

CAN YOU PICTURE THIS?

To Kayla and Hunter. My angels.

ONE

Richie howled as I shoved his bike away from me in surprise. Not my fault he fell over.

His flash went off again as he dropped to the ground. Richie, all lean and no fat, must have felt the fall much more than I would have. But again, not my fault.

"You can't just push people over like that, Sam," he yelled.

I wanted to retort with, "Yes, I can," but I didn't. Instead I leaned over to help him up. He rejected my arm as I offered it, so I moved to pick up his bicycle.

He reacted by grabbing the handlebars and taking it back. I guess I wasn't surprised. Richie's bicycle was his livelihood. While he righted the bike and looked it over for damage, I found his hat lying in the gravel on the side of the street.

Instantly he jerked the hat out of my hand too. I'd never seen Richie this mad before. Normally he was a pretty easy-going dude; this was a new side to him. He cleaned the hat against his threadbare jeans and brushed the gravel off his T-shirt and pants.

Trying to be the bigger person—literally and figuratively—I said, "I'm really sorry, Richie. Your flash going off right in my face surprised me, and I pushed your bike away without thinking. I hope there's no damage." I patted the camera that he'd managed to keep clutched in his hand as he fell.

With more dignity than I'd ever seen him muster, he shook the rest of the dust off his body and replaced the porkpie hat on his head. Then, with a look of horror, he let out another yowl, which pretty much undid the attempt at dignity.

"Where are they? Did you take 'em? Where are they?" He took off his hat again, looked it over, and checked his clothing, but the panicked look remained.

"Where are what?" It seemed we'd gotten his belongings and his vehicle. What else could it be?

His look bored through me. "You took them. I know you did." Richie took a step toward me as he said it, and I saw his fist balled at his side.

"I didn't take anything, Richie, and you're beginning to piss me off. Even more than you already did with that damn camera flash." I was tempted to smash that camera against Richie's bird-chest, but I composed myself. "Now tell me what you're missing and I'll help you find it."

"Two things. First the badge that goes in my hat."

I knew that badge well. Everyone in town did. Richie was

never seen without that piece of paper in his hatband that said, "PRESS." He didn't actually work for Quincy's single newspaper, but he freelanced as a photographer and sold pictures to the paper whenever he could. He, his bicycle, camera, and hat were well known around the city.

"Okay," I said. "That's one. Tell me the second thing."

"Pictures. I lost pictures."

Richie was a rare breed. He still used a Polaroid instant camera. However, I knew he had a hard time finding film for it since his camera model had been discontinued, so WalMart special ordered the film for him. Or *the* WalMart, as he calls it.

"I'll help you look for your pictures. They've got to be around here somewhere."

"Yeah, you should. It's all your fault they're missing."

"Richie, you took a close-up picture. The flash went off in my face. I couldn't see. I lashed out. That's what happened. If you want to take a close-up picture of someone you need to warn them." I'd had it. He was bugging me and so was the heat. The humidity in Quincy could be intense in the summer. I was tired of both of them.

"I don't have to warn anybody. I'm a paparazzi." He practically whined.

In a fully superior voice I corrected him, "You're a paparazzo. Paparazzi is the plural. You're the only photographer in town who ambushes people."

As we talked we looked for the missing photos. It was only a moment before Richie yelled, "Aha! Found them," and held up a handful of pictures.

Minutes later I found the precious badge, which seemed to be made out of cardboard. It was folded in half. When I unfolded it, I noticed that it didn't just say "PRESS." It said, "PRESS HERE."

I handed it to Richie with a big grin on my face. A laugh escaped despite my best intentions, and I could see from his look that he was offended by it. He stepped back as if he'd been hit.

"You're mean."

Well, I'd been told that before, but it didn't mean it was true. "Sorry, Richie. I just thought it was funny." I handed him the cardboard before he could grab that too.

As an afterthought, I said, "Why did you feel the need to take a close-up picture of me? You've never done that before."

"Well, you just helped solve another murder, and—"

"Helped solve a murder? I *solved* it. And I solved the murder before that, too. Sure I had a little help, but I did it."

"If you'd quit talking for a minute, I'm about to give you a compliment," he said.

I shut up.

"You helped solve another murder and you're developing

quite a reputation in Quincy."

I must admit my head was swelling as he spoke. "Quite a reputation," I repeated, smiling.

Richie looked like someone who had something more to say.

"Spit it out, Richie."

"Well, part of the reputation is that there hadn't been any murders in Quincy for years… until you returned. Now we've had two situations in less than six months. People are saying that—"

"That what?" In my mind, I was wringing his scrawny neck.

"That maybe it's you. Maybe you brought some bad juju with you from Chicago and now it's making problems in our little town."

"That's BS. You need to tell everyone who talks about me that I solved the murders, but I didn't cause them."

When I said those words, I had no idea that I was about to find myself knee-deep in murder once again.

TWO

I sent Richie on his way, but I was not in a good mood.

How could people think the murders had anything to do with me? That was crazy. I solved two murders. Well, actually eight murders. The first one was my boss, and the next seven were people poisoned at the hospital. Again... I didn't cause them... I solved them.

Luckily I had enough self-esteem that Richie's statement couldn't bring me down. In fact it was kind of cool that I had enough celebrity for Richie to seek me out. Normally he just rode around town shooting pictures of random people and events, hoping to get a money shot. Maybe someday, if he stopped gossiping about me, I might prove to him how it would be cheaper to buy a digital camera and just develop the good shots, instead of buying so much special-ordered Polaroid film.

I continued my walk down the beautiful, tree-lined streets near the carriage house where I lived. Normally I'd have my dog, Clancy, with me, but my neighbors and landlords, Georgianne and Gus, had asked if they could take her to the dog park today. Of course, Clancy would rather go there than on our routine walk. So I was alone, taking in the summer flowers, trees, and mansions along the way. My kids, Adam and Sarah, were home from the U of I for the summer, but both were sleeping in today—Adam after a late date and Sarah after working all night in the hospital kitchen.

My pleasant reverie was interrupted by a loud voice calling my name.

"Sam. Sam. Sam!" Each "Sam" was followed by a deep gulp of air, almost like someone were drowning.

Reluctantly, I turned, and saw Richie flying toward me on his bike. He was riding on the sidewalk and would have bowled me over if I hadn't stepped aside. His brakes screeched and he almost went butt over handlebars as he stopped.

"Sam," he repeated, and it sounded like he couldn't catch his breath. "Asthma," he whispered and the sound came from the deepest part of his lungs. He pulled an inhaler out of his pocket and breathed in a big squirt of the medication.

I waited until he could breathe before I spoke, but didn't try to contain my emotion. "What? Do you have more gossip to report about me?" Of course, sarcasm dripped off my words.

He only said one more word. "Look." Richie thrust one of his Polaroid pictures at me.

It took a moment for my middle-aged eyes to adjust focus. I looked at the picture, and grabbed Richie's arm as dizziness overtook me.

My stupid, pain-in-the-butt psychic vibes were attacking me again. And that only happens big time when there's a murder. Just like the last two times I'd gotten myself in deep with a murder investigation, I felt my vibes pulling me in. I let go of Richie's arm and looked at the picture again as my dizziness diminished.

The picture showed a guy sitting against a building. What was shocking was that he was in the process of being stabbed by someone in a bright blue hoodie. You could only see the hood—the face was hidden.

It occurred to me that only in Quincy would a murderer wear a bright blue hoodie. Whatever happened to criminals wearing black and trying to be innocuous?

"Richie, when did you take this picture?"

"I dunno." Richie was shaking, so I took his arm again and set him down gently on a bank on Maine Street. He looked incongruous in the midst of such glory. Yet, in another way, he fit right in since he was such a fixture in town. "I really don't know. I've been out today since about 5 AM. I wanted to see if I could catch some early birds going into taverns." He looked at me. "You know. Gossip sells on the internet. I don't just provide pictures to the Quincy paper," I nodded, encouraging him to continue.

"Sometimes I sell them to Michael. And most of the time I don't look at the pictures until later. I take them while I'm riding, so I can't look at them right away. I was in some places more than once today. So it was sometime after 5 and before now." He looked at his watch. "Between 5 and 10:30."

The light in the picture was dim, but it wasn't dark enough for it to be before dawn. And he said sometimes he sold pictures to Michael O'Dear. Michael was the only private investigator in town, and my previous love interest. Even though he hadn't reciprocated my feelings, I had been momentarily sure I was in love with him.

Then I got back on track and finally thought of the right thing to do. "Richie, we need to go to the police right away. I know Detective Lansing will want to know about this." I felt warm as I mentioned his name. George Lansing had been my boyfriend in high school, and we recently reconnected. *Really* reconnected. I blushed as I thought about him, but it was a happy blush, not an embarrassed one.

I shook my head to get me back in the present. "We need to go to my house and get my car. You can leave your bike there, and I'll bring you back to it after we're done at the police station."

Richie nodded his assent.

Luckily we were only a few blocks from my home. We

walked to the back of my landlords' mansion, regal with its red brick and white stone, and reached the red brick carriage house behind it. I told Richie to park his bike and to stay by my car. As usual, my house wasn't locked and I opened the door and reached around the corner for my car keys, hanging on a hook near the door.

It felt funny not to be greeted by my Clancy, and it also felt funny having to be quiet so I didn't wake my kids. They were seldom home any more, but Clancy usually was.

I unlocked my VW Bug, almost the same color as the hoodie on the "stabber," just not quite as bright. From the driver's seat I unlocked the other door for Richie. For the first time it hit me that I didn't lock my house, but I locked my car. No explaining it.

We rode in silence to the police station, except for Richie's occasional, "Watch out," "There's a car," and "You're going too fast." Because of the situation I chose to ignore the backseat driving coming from the front seat.

We got lucky and I found a parking spot right in front of the station. The police station was on Fifth Street and connected to it, between Fifth and Sixth on Vermont, was the County Courthouse. We went in through the Fifth Street door and stopped at the reception desk. The reception area was utilitarian, with not much in the way of decoration. I asked if Officer Lansing was in.

The receptionist replied from behind a sliding glass

window that he was in a meeting but should be done shortly. I left a message with my name attached, and Richie and I found a seat to wait for him.

As we sat, I looked at the floor while I was thinking. Soon I noticed two shined black shoes in front of me. My eyes slowly moved upward, and I saw the blue uniform belonging to my baby brother, Rob.

"What are you doing here?" Rob said it in a voice that showed he knew I was up to no good.

"Just here to see George," I said. I wanted to call Rob "Mr. Smarty-Pants Baby Cop," because… well, just because. But I didn't because I didn't want to embarrass him at work.

"It's never that simple with you," he said. "You say you're just here to see George, but I bet it's about something you shouldn't be involved in."

"It's not my fault," I sputtered.

"Yeah, right. It never is," was how he answered. Another policeman I recognized as Jimmy Mansfield called to Rob to hurry up.

As they exited the station, Rob turned and said, "You used to come down and tell me things. Now that you and George are together, you come down and give him all your information. Maybe you'll think of telling me stuff again sometime? Love you." And with that he was gone.

Rob made me mad, but he had a valid point. When I

was working on solving my boss's murder, I told him everything. At that point, I was still mad at George for standing me up on prom night 25 years ago. That reminded me—our 25th reunion was coming up soon; I needed to remember to talk to George about that. I'd been on the planning committee and was really looking forward to the celebration.

As my thoughts flitted from topic to topic I had to remind myself to stay in the present. *Stay in the present, Sam,* I repeated in my thoughts. *This is some serious stuff you and Richie are dealing with.*

I'd almost forgotten about Richie, sitting at my side quietly, and holding onto his camera and pictures for dear life. I'd kept the one in question. I wanted to make sure we didn't lose it on the way.

"Damn." I checked my pockets and looked on the floor around me. "Richie, did I give the picture back to you?"

He shook his head. "You had it. Insisted you would take better care of it than I would." His sneer told me what he thought of that.

"Damn," I said again, as I saw George walk to the lobby. He wore khakis, a white shirt and a brown blazer with a tie I'd given him. He had a loving, expectant look on his face that quickly turned to puzzled when he saw me with Richie.

"Hi ya, Sam," George approached me and gave me a peck on the cheek. "Hey, Richie. What's up?" He looked back at me as he asked it.

"Well," I said, scared to be confessing my screw up. "Well, Richie accidentally took a picture of a stabbing. We don't know if the victim is dead or not, but it looked pretty serious. It happened between 5 and 10 AM. The light makes it look like it was around 6 to 8, wouldn't you agree, Richie?"

He nodded. Richie had a smile on his face that showed his excitement.

George looked thoughtful and said, "We've not had any reports of a stabbing, at least not that that I'm aware of. Why don't you two come in back with me?"

He took my arm solicitously and we went into the police station proper. A hive of cops and support personnel kept the place buzzing. George ushered us to his corner of the world, and we sat—him on one side of the desk and Richie and I on the other.

I still hadn't confessed.

"Where's the photo?" George asked with great interest.

"You see, I… I mean Richie…" At Richie's growl I went back to, "Well, I… I…"

"Sam, spit it out," George said, all business now.

"I think I lost it."

"Lost it?" His face showed his disbelief. He wasn't too upset. He hadn't noticed yet that it was a Polaroid camera. "Well, it's still on the camera, right?"

I looked at the camera. Richie looked at the camera. George looked at the camera.

"What in the hell are you doing using this kind of camera, Richie? Haven't you ever heard of digital? And, Sam, why in the hell would you be so careless as to lose the only picture of the so-called crime?"

"So-called crime? You don't believe us? Just because it's going to be easier on you to pretend it didn't happen, that doesn't mean it didn't happen. Richie and I both saw the picture. We have it in our brains. You might want to have someone interview us separately about what we saw."

"Don't tell me how to do my job!"

Now his voice was raised and his face was red. Because he was losing his hair, I could see the redness all over his head. I didn't think I'd ever seen George this angry since we had started dating. He was usually sweet and very understanding of my sometimes ditzy ways.

More quietly George added, "We do have to take a statement though. It's policy.

Ignoring his last comment, I stood. "C'mon, Richie," I said, trying to sound dignified. "Let's go solve this one ourselves."

THREE

The thing that really made me mad was that George didn't try to stop us. The only thing in his favor was that when I looked back at him, he wasn't laughing. When Richie and I got outside the police station, my phone whistled, signifying an incoming text.

I stopped to read it. Richie stopped a few steps ahead. "It's from George," I whispered to myself, happy that he was going to apologize.

Instead, the text said, "I love you. See you tonight."

See you tonight? After he practically called me a liar. Yeah, right. Then another whistle. "You're right. There I said it. Please come back in so we can get a description of the picture you saw."

What a guy. Not afraid to say he was wrong. It would be hard for me to do, but he didn't have all the "quirks" I had. Maybe eventually some of his more positive characteristics would rub off on me.

I said to Richie, "George wants us to come back in and describe what we saw." There was a look of satisfaction on my face that I wasn't proud of. So I promised myself I wouldn't gloat when I saw George.

As Richie and I walked back into the station, I literally ran into George rushing out.

Over his shoulder he said, "Sorry. Just got a call. Have to go. Officer Darling will talk to you."

I couldn't be mad at George, even though it would have been fun to be able to feel superior for a moment. And even though Rob was a "lowly" newbie, it was cool of George to have my brother be the one to interview us.

The receptionist buzzed us through and Rob met us on the other side of the door.

Right away, I said, "You just left. What happened?"

"Oh, Jimmy just wanted to talk to me about something. I came in by the back way." He motioned for Richie to take a seat in the hall and he ushered me into an interrogation room. It was a stereotypical interview room. Not much different than the ones on TV—metal table and cinderblock walls. Ugly and cold.

"I thought I'd interview you first, because you're older and more likely to forget what you saw."

I was ready to punch his cute face, but then I noticed the grin. My baby brother was teasing me. And he sure knew how to get to me. "Okay, okay," I said. "Let's get this over with while I still remember."

"Why don't you just tell me what happened," Rob said

as he turned on a digital recorder. "Is it okay if I tape this?"

I nodded, and then realizing that it was an audio recording, said, "Yes," too. Then I began.

"This morning I ran into Richie. He startled me by taking a flash photo of my face while I was walking, so I shoved his bike away. Naturally, he fell over, and he was upset at me. Then I…"

"Sam, I don't need all the 'before' details. Tell me about the picture."

I didn't like it, but complied. "Well, if you don't want the whole scenario… for context… Richie showed me a photo of a man collapsed against a building. Another man, in a bright blue hoodie, was stabbing him in cold blood, right at the time the picture was taken. It looked like a rather large knife being pushed inside the guy. I'd say it was near his heart, but not quite that high. Definitely on the left side though." I paused a moment. "Oh, I forgot. Richie told me it was taken between 5 and 10 AM, or maybe 10:30 AM. I can't remember."

"Good, Sam. Good. Now close your eyes and see if there are any other details you can remember." My little brother was good at this.

I did as he asked, and visualized what the instant photo looked like. "The light in the photo showed it couldn't have been taken as early as 5. It was too light for that hour. So I guess I'd say 6 to 8. Sorry I can't be more exact about that."

I scrunched up my face as I tried to see more.

"Relax a little more," Rob suggested. "Don't try to force it. Do you remember where the sunlight was coming from?"

I felt my shoulders and my face relax. "From the left maybe. And the building, the building had limestone blocks on the bottom. It was white above the foundation." But many of Quincy's buildings had limestone blocks in them. The city was built on limestone bluffs overlooking the Mississippi River, so that didn't narrow things down too much.

"Good. Good. Was there anything else in the picture? Grass, streets, lights, vehicles?"

Deliberately relaxing my shoulders again, I went back to the picture in my mind. "I saw a green bush, a little grass, and some blacktop maybe. Not a sidewalk. Something looked familiar, but I'm not sure what."

"Okay, Sam. Open your eyes."

As I did, I looked at my baby brother in a new light. Not only was he a rookie cop, he was also someone who would make detective in the future. I was sure of it.

He then said, "You did a great job. When you sit out in the hall, relax and think about the picture. If you come up with anything else, let me know when I'm finished talking with Richie."

I nodded, and got up to leave, but not before I said, "You did a great job, too."

Richie and I exchanged places and I could imagine what he was saying to Rob. The one thing I hadn't remembered to ask Richie was where he had ridden that morning. I'd have to ask later.

But the next time I saw him he was in no position to talk.

FOUR

While I sat, waiting for Rob to finish talking to Richie, I realized it had been a long time between bathroom breaks. My phone rang as I looked down the long, green-tiled hallway and saw the universal sign for bathroom sticking out from the wall. I answered my phone, thinking that I still had a few minutes before Richie would be done.

The phone call was a computer reminder that I had a reunion committee meeting on Wednesday night. I quickly made sure the appointment was in the calendar of my smart phone as I walked briskly to the women's bathroom. There were only two stalls inside and both were occupied, so I leaned against another green tiled wall and waited. Waited with my legs crossed. As I uncrossed and sat I felt the universal relief that only comes from this situation.

I hadn't planned to be away that long, but as I washed my hands I thought that I wasn't gone long enough for Richie to be done with the interview. When I tried to exit the ladies' room, there were two women trying to get in. They wouldn't budge, so I had to back up and step aside to let them enter. I did take an extra moment to give them dirty looks, but of course, it didn't change anything.

I looked back down the hall and saw that the row of metal chairs was empty, so I felt relief that Richie wasn't done yet. But when I got to the chairs, I also noticed that the door to the interrogation room was open and the light was off.

Hurrying out to the lobby, I didn't see Richie or Rob there either. I asked the receptionist to page Rob. In a few minutes he appeared looking a little confused.

"Where's Richie?" we both said together.

Rob started talking right away. "When we were finished we thought you must have gone to the car, since you weren't in the hallway. So Richie went out to your car."

"I was in the bathroom," I said. "He's probably waiting out there for me."

But he wasn't.

I retraced our route, reversing it and driving from the police station to my home, impatient with every traffic light, but no Richie. I didn't know if he had a cell phone or not, but at any rate I didn't know how to contact him. And when I got home his bike was still parked next to the carriage house. I left again, thinking he might have walked a different way. Again, no luck.

By then I was worried, but not yet frantic. I called Rob on his cell and told his voice mail of my concerns. I called

George, and left a little more detail since he hadn't been in on the interviews. I even called Michael to see if he had Richie's cell phone number, but there was no answer. I called the Quincy Whig, but the newspaper employee told me they were not allowed to give out private numbers.

I returned home and decided to stop thinking about Richie, knowing he would turn up sooner or later. As I entered the house, I heard the TV and the sounds of laughter. The picture I saw in the living room was one that made my heart smile. My grown-up kids, Adam and Sarah, were sitting on the couch watching TV and laughing. For a brief moment it brought me back to their childhood days when they'd watch cartoons together on a Saturday morning. Sure it was Saturday morning now, but near lunchtime instead of early morning. But when I got inside far enough to see what they were watching, I saw the TV was turned to the Cartoon Channel.

"Some things never change," I said as I wiggled between the two of them on the couch.

Adam lowered the sound with the remote and put his arm around me. Sarah did the same on the other side of me.

"We made a Mommy Sandwich," Sarah said. Same thing she used to say when she was small when both kids hugged me at the same time.

This was a slice of heaven. "You guys hungry? It's lunchtime."

"Nope," Sarah answered. "We just finished breakfast a little bit ago."

"Okay. Remember we're going out to dinner with George tonight."

Adam said, "Yep, we remember and were just talking about it. We want to meet the guy you've hated all our lives and then suddenly love."

"Wha… wha… what?" I sputtered. "How did you know about that?"

Sarah and Adam both smiled as Sarah answered for them. "You have a lot of brothers and sisters. Most of them are very happy to share the latest news with their sweet niece and nephew."

Adam joined in, "By the way, when is Clancy coming home? We saw your note that she was at the dog park, but shouldn't she be home by now?"

"Yeah. I see Gus's car outside. I'll run over there and see."

I wiggled out the opposite of how I wiggled in, and realized that when the kids were here I missed them more than when they were gone. It didn't make sense, but when they were away at school I knew they were fine and they were happy. But when they were home I looked ahead to when they had to leave and it made me sad. Dumb.

I went over to Gus and Georgianne's place, knocked on the back door and let myself in. Gus walked into the kitchen, put his finger to his lips, and beckoned me to follow him quietly. So I did. We walked through the kitchen, breakfast room, and dining room, and reached the room that Georgianne called a parlor, I saw her sound asleep and snoring on the old-fashioned velvet couch. And my big beautiful dog was lying on top of her asleep as well. Clancy did manage to open one eye as we approached, but was too tired to keep it open.

A few months ago I would have thought this was an abomination. At that time Georgianne was not a friend of mine, to put it nicely. I had always loved Gus, and tolerated Georgianne because of that. Now I grudgingly admitted I loved them both—Gus more than Georgianne, however.

"She really had a workout at the dog park," Gus said.

"Which one? Clancy or Georgianne," I teased. Then I added, "I really miss Clancy," I whispered. "Bring her home as soon as they wake up. Okay?"

Gus nodded, and I walked out the way I walked in—quietly. I held the screen door as I exited. Life without Clancy was not a good life for me. She helped me every day by being my confidante and a loving friend. She also worked with me at the Clinic as a therapy dog. This just started a few months ago, after we solved the poisoning murders. Our psychic connection gave me a dog who not only listened well, but communicated her thoughts to me some of the time.

As I walked down the porch steps toward my little corner

of this heaven, I saw that Richie's bike was gone. He must've grabbed it and left before I could see him.

A voice boomed, "Hello."

I turned to see a tall elderly woman that I didn't recognize. From first glance I could tell she was a character. She had flaming red hair with earrings to the ground and boobs to the sky. I wondered how she did that at her age.

"Hello, I'm Sam Darling. I live here," indicating the carriage house.

"I'm Julieanne Harmon, Georgianne's younger—much younger—sister."

We shook hands as we introduced ourselves. Then I said, "Georgianne is asleep. I just went in and talked to Gus."

"Thanks. I'll go in quietly. Hope to see you again." With that, she hugged me so hard my stomach touched my spine. Then she and her booming, dramatic voice began walking up the stairs to see her sister and Gus.

When I went inside my home I asked if anyone had knocked while I was gone. At their simultaneous "no" answer, I had a quick thought that they should have been twins instead of two years apart.

As I made myself a quick peanut butter sandwich, I reflected on how lucky I was to have such great kids. At 21, Adam had just finished his junior year at the U of I and was searching for his place in the world. Sarah, now 19, was going to be a sophomore there in the fall. She worked at the hospital at night, helping a registered dietitian plan appropriate menus for patients with differing needs. I stood in the kitchen, eating, and looked into the living room at my loves. Adam with his dark hair and dark eyes. Sarah with her golden hair and blue eyes. My ex-husband and I had always said we each had a reproduction of ourselves. I silently hoped that Adam didn't turn out like his father, however.

I told them I was going to take a nap, but that I wanted them to wake me if anyone came by.

"God, Mom, are you that desperate for company?" Adam came by the sarcastic gene honestly.

There was no way I wanted to get into the Richie thing with them, so I just let his jibe flow off of me. When I got to my room, I did what I usually do there. I took off my jeans, and pulled the covers over my head. My bed was lonely without Clancy. She'd been my sleeping buddy for several years.

Now George had changed things a bit.

FIVE

I woke to Sarah crawling into bed with me and giving me a hug. Felt like old times. Whenever I'd overslept when she was a kid, she would wake me this way. "Hi, sweetie," I said. "I love having you home."

"Love being here," she said. "It's time for you to get up. I'll wait and take a nap after our dinner and before I go to work."

"Okay, sweetie. I'll get a quick shower." I jumped out of bed as quickly as I could. Seeing George always gave me energy. It was then I noticed Clancy was back. She'd been sleeping with me and I hadn't even known it. I guessed that Gus must have brought her home while I was sleeping.

Sarah stayed in my bed and turned on the TV, watching the news. Clancy curled up next to her and Sarah petted her absentmindedly. My shower took just a few minutes. I'd already showered earlier that morning and washed my hair then. I wrapped myself in my terry-cloth robe and walked back into my bedroom. I laughed as I realized Sarah and I had traded places. She and Clancy were both sound asleep.

I crawled into bed with them and woke Sarah up. She smiled as she realized the tables had turned.

"We've got to get going, honey," I reminded her. "What are you going to wear?"

"A skirt, I thought," she answered. "Okay with you?" She smiled as she said it.

"Perfect, and make sure your brother at least puts on clean jeans."

About a half hour later George walked in the front door, kissed me, and stayed quiet as I introduced him to my kids.

Sarah shook his hand with a smile. Adam said, "Good to meet you. I've heard a lot about you."

George looked at me as he said, "Your mom talked about me?"

"A little. Mostly it was from our aunts and uncles. Seems like everyone likes you."

"But we'll make up our own minds," Sarah piped in teasingly.

"She's not kidding. We'll make up our own minds," Adam said.

"Well, I've sure heard a lot about you two. Your mom is proud of both of you, and was really looking forward to you coming home for part of the summer." He turned to me again. "I'm sorry, Sam, but we have to make it an early night. I have to work tomorrow on this case we picked up."

"But tomorrow's Sunday." I hate it when I sound like a

petulant child, but it happens.

A few unattractive whines from me later, and after bidding good-bye to Clancy, we were in the car heading to the restaurant. "I thought we'd go somewhere different tonight," George said as he drove. "I have reservations for us at the Boat Dock."

"Good thinking," said Adam. "I've only been there once. Great food." The Boat Dock was a restaurant built out over Quincy Bay, an offshoot of the Mississippi. They had a reputation for wonderful fish dishes, with fresh fish bought each day from folks who'd caught them in the river. Of course, that didn't impress me as a vegetarian, but what did impress me was the fact that they had the largest salad bar in town.

I smiled as George reached over and took my hand. I leaned back into the seat, thinking that I must be the luckiest girl alive. Then I went and ruined it by asking, "What's the case you caught?"

And George ruined it even more by saying, "Not tonight, Sam. Please. Let's just have a lovely evening with no talk of crime, murder, and me warning you to stay out of those things."

I pulled my hand away. I could imagine my adult children making faces in the back seat. This must seem like an instant replay of the relationship I had with their father, right at the moment before a fight started. For their sakes I decided to surprise them by letting it drop. I'd deal with George later about it.

I was the one who was surprised when George said, "I'll tell you one thing. One thing. It was the guy you and Richie described—the guy who was stabbed. Don't ask any more questions. That is all I'm going to say." When I opened my mouth to speak, he repeated, "That's all I'm going to say." It sounded final so I relented.

He was a great guy, but had a thing about me "meddling" in police work. I knew he was just trying to protect me, but it made me mad sometimes. And of course it didn't stop me from meddling.

So I held my tongue. Almost impossible for me to do in situations like this. I counted it as a personal victory.

We rode in silence to the Boat Dock. Since it had started raining a little, George dropped us off at the entrance and went to park the car. The summertime humidity hit us full force. Although the temperature had mellowed a bit, we could always count on the humidity to drain our energy.

"You're mad, Mom. Admit it," Adam said as we waited just inside the door of the restaurant.

"Mad? Me? At what? Of course I'm not mad." I thought I did some of my best acting.

"We know you're mad. We've known you for a long time," Sarah chimed in. "When you deny something to us, you always start with a question or two, like you need time to think before you answer."

I just looked at them. They knew me pretty well. So I decided to shake off whatever petty anger I felt toward George, and enjoy this evening. Tonight was the first time my kids had met George, and I wanted them to like him as much as I did.

Right on cue, George entered the restaurant, took off his jacket and shook off the water. He smiled at me and I melted, forgetting for a while that I'd ever been upset with him. He went to the hostess and said he had a reservation for four.

We were led to a table overlooking the water. There were lights strung outside over some boat docks that made the place look magical. And even more lights were strung on wire over our table, but nowhere else inside. The outside ones looked like twinkling stars reflected in the bay. Those inside were like little faerie lights surrounding our table.

"What's this?" I asked, after taking a moment to enjoy the view.

I swear George beamed as he said, "Happy birthday, Sam. I know it's not until July 4th, but I wanted to surprise you and I wanted your family here with you."

I turned and kissed him. This time not the quick peck you do in public. I really kissed him, at least until I heard Adam and Sarah making noises.

"Sorry, you guys," I said to them, and to George I said,

"Thank you so much. This is a wonderful surprise."

He continued beaming as he actually pulled out my chair for me. The ambiance of the place lent itself to romance, even though my children were here. I had to work on holding the menu with my left hand because my right one was busy holding George's hand.

Content. Happy. And soon to be eating a fabulous meal. What could go wrong?

SIX

What could go wrong, indeed?

I'm a born optimist, but everything was just a little too perfect. I was with the man I loved, and the kids I adored were with me too. I'd been surprised with an early birthday present, and I was going to eat a scrumptious meal. The lights weren't candles, but right or wrong I felt they were flattering. My smile was genuine and so big that even my teeth hurt.

Then it happened.

George's phone dinged, signifying a text message. He smiled as he said, "I'm not going to check it. I'm off tonight. I worked hard to get a sub for tonight. That's why I'm working Sunday."

Against my better judgment I said, "You probably should check it. It might be any kind of emergency."

He shrugged his shoulders, smiled, and said, "Okay, if you think I should. I want Adam and Sarah to be witnesses that I'm only doing this because you suggested I check it." Both Sarah and Adam smiled too as he said it.

As George looked at the text his brow furrowed. It seemed he took a very long time before his head came back up and he looked at me.

"Oh, no," was what I said.

"Oh, yes," was what he said.

He took in all three of us as he continued, "I'm really sorry, you guys. I have to go in. It's urgent or I wouldn't do it." Then just to me, "This was an important night for me. I'm so sorry, Sam." He leaned over and kissed me.

I just nodded. Then, not wanting him to think I was angry with him, I said, "I love you."

George looked surprised. Probably because I said it in front of Adam and Sarah. "I love you too." He kissed me again and started to walk away. Then, in what I've come to love as his Columbo imitation, he turned back and said, "I'll take care of paying for your meal on the way out. Please enjoy it. And, Sam, if I get done early enough I'll call you tonight. Otherwise, I'll talk to you tomorrow." With that he was gone.

My sigh was big enough to fill the whole restaurant.

"You love him?" Sarah asked.

"You said you love him," said Adam at the same time.

"Yep." They hadn't heard me say this to a man since the divorce from their dad a few years back. I tore myself away from looking at the door George used to make his exit, and looked at them instead.

"Yeah, I do. And it surprised the hell out of me too."

The well-dressed server came and took our order on an electronic tablet. Impressive. After the initial disappointment of George being gone, I relaxed and enjoyed the rest of the meal with my kids, at a restaurant we hadn't been to before as a family.

When we were finished I realized that George had driven us in his car. The hostess came up to us when she noticed we were finished and asked if there was anything else we needed. I said, "Maybe you could call us a cab." She nodded.

A few minutes later she said, "Your ride is here."

We exited the restaurant and saw the town's one and only limo service with a car waiting for us. It wasn't a stretch limo, but a limo nonetheless. Flabbergasted, I turned back to tell the hostess there'd been a mistake. She couldn't stop her smile. "Officer Lansing took care of this as he left."

I shook my head to clear it. George thought of everything.

"C'mon kids. Let's see how the other half lives."

The limo driver, dressed in a black suit, with black tie and white shirt, and complete with the requisite hat, opened the door for us. I sank into the leather seat and missed George.

Not for long, though. The ride home was full of giggles. Maybe the drinks Adam and I had might have caused a few of the laughs, but I was as relaxed as I'd been in a long time.

The limo driver wouldn't accept a tip, and said it had already been taken care of.

We walked into the unlocked carriage house and were greeted by Clancy, who was definitely ready to go out. Adam said, "Take it easy, Mom. I'll take her out. C'mon, girl." Clancy bounded toward him and off they went.

Sarah took the opportunity of being alone with me to say, "You seem really happy with George."

I gave her hug, and then said, "I am, honey. And I'm continually amazed that I hated the man for almost 25 years. I was stupid. Just stupid. Well, stupid and stubborn. He's a great guy, and I'm lucky that he cares for me."

"But you did seem to be upset with him on the way to restaurant."

"I was," I said, "but decided to let it go. The thing is, he always tries to get me to butt out of investigations that I have every right to be involved in."

"Mom, you're a social worker—"

"Not a cop! I know, I know. I've sure heard that a gazillion times. But I can't help being curious. And while you were away at school I solved several murders."

"Yeah, but you ended up in the hospital last time, and someone tried to kill you while you were there. I worry about you. A lot."

I just hugged her again and let it drop. How could I explain to her the compulsion I felt to help out? My vibes led me in the right direction, at least most of the time, and I had to help.

Adam brought in a panting Clancy. "We ran around in circles for a little bit." He hugged her, then she sidled over to Sarah for the same thing. For her next move, Clancy went to my bedroom door and stood, waiting for me to join her.

I hugged and kissed my kids, then did just that, following Clancy's lead. Sarah hadn't gotten a decent nap before going to work, but she said she'd drink a little caffeine and be okay.

Ah, the young.

That was the last coherent thought I had before waking up the next morning. It was a Sunday, so I planned to go to Mass and hoped the kids would go with me. As a lifelong Catholic, I had been feeling conflicted about how sleeping with George fit in with my faith. I hoped that getting back to weekly Mass would help me.

My cell phone rang as I was getting out of bed.

After my hello, I heard, "Sam, I need to talk to you. Right away."

"Okay. Come on over."

George sounded serious. Too serious.

I jumped up and put on a pair of jeans and a lightweight sweater. Sarah was still at work, and Adam had fallen asleep on the couch instead of going up to his room. I roused him, said I was expecting company, and asked if he'd go upstairs.

He mumbled something that sounded affirmative, and slowly walked to the stairs.

I quickly took Clancy outside for a potty break, and as I was going back in the house, George pulled up. I waited for him to get out of the car, and ran to him with a kiss and hug.

"Thank you so, so much for my birthday present," I said, accentuating each "so" with a kiss.

He responded, but seemed distracted. "I'm glad you liked it, Sam. Can we go inside to talk?"

The immature part of me thought, *Omigod, is he breaking up with me?* I knew better than that, but there are times when I revert back to an unsure teenager.

Instead, I said, "What's wrong?"

He guided me toward the door, and waited until we were inside before speaking. "Let's sit down," indicating the couch.

"What's wrong?" I repeated.

His face told me he wanted to soften the blow, but he just said it.

"Richie was stabbed last night."

SEVEN

I couldn't speak.

George held me as we sat on the couch. He handed me his handkerchief because my tears were flowing and I couldn't seem to stop them. Finally, I hiccuped and it broke the tension.

"I'll wash this," I said as I showed George his wet handkerchief.

He nodded.

"'I'll wash this.' What a stupid thing to say." I pulled away enough to turn toward him. "Is Richie okay? He isn't—"

"He's alive. They texted me when we were at the restaurant to tell me that an injured man was found in the bushes on the side of the John Wood mansion. It was Richie. Sitting in the same place the other guy was found. Richie was bloody and unconscious—but breathing."

I felt more tears on my cheeks. I gestured for George to go on as I used his handkerchief to catch them.

"We knew right away that the crime might be related to

the stabbing you and Richie saw in the photo."

"Was it? Was it related?"

George shook his head and said, "Probably. It would be too much of a coincidence to have two guys stabbed in the same location several hours apart. Richie is at least alive, lucky for him."

"Omigod, I can't believe it." I fell back against the back of the couch. "I feel like a close friend was attacked, and I hardly knew him. Do you think he was stabbed because he took the picture?"

George answered, "Well, the killer could have seen Richie ride by on his bicycle, and maybe he saw him take the picture. We don't know anything yet, except…"

"Except what?"

"Except Richie was wearing a bright blue hoodie when we found him, with a white T-shirt. Of course there was blood all over him."

"He wasn't wearing either of those things when we saw him yesterday. Can I see the hoodie? I can tell you if it was the same color the killer was wearing."

He nodded. "I had to leave it at the station, of course, but I was hoping you could come down and take a look at it."

"Yes. I want to. Can we go now?"

"Sure, hon." He pushed my tear-wet hair behind my ears. "Are you sure you feel like it right now?"

I said, "Yes. I want to go now. The sooner I see it, the more likely I am to remember the exact color." Then I thought of something else, "Can we visit Richie? Is he at Bay General?"

"That's where he is, but the last time I checked he was still in the ER. I'll check again in a little while."

I left a note for Sarah, let Clancy go upstairs with Adam, and walked out of the house with George's arm around my shoulder. I felt so bad for poor Richie. The only thing he was guilty of was annoying me by taking my picture, and he had the unfortunate bad luck to take a picture of a murder in progress. And for that he got himself stabbed.

We rode to the station in silence. George parked near the police vehicles in the staff parking lot. I sat there stunned until George opened my door for me. Even though he was in his job arena he still put his arm around me to walk me through the employee entrance into the station.

He checked out the hoodie from the evidence locker and as soon as I saw it I knew. "It's the one," I said.

"Wait. Wait just a minute," George said as he walked me to an interview room.

As soon as we got inside and he'd closed the door, I said, "That's it. It's the one." I took it and held it to my cheek, thinking of Richie. "It's crazy that the killer wore a blue hoodie in the first stabbing and the victim wore a blue hoodie in the second stabbing."

I looked up at George and said, "I forgot to ask you about the details of the attack. You said he was stabbed?"

George nodded. "Stabbed above the stomach, near the heart on the left side, same place as where you said the other guy was being stabbed in the picture. And there's more. There are more than one person's prints on it. Richie's were on top. He said the murderer took his hands and made him push in the knife, maybe to make it look like suicide. Then he tried to pull it out, but couldn't quite do it."

"I don't get it. Why compound the first murder with an attempted murder? We couldn't see what the murderer looked like in the picture. And why didn't Richie die? What was different about this attack?"

"First, he—or she for that matter—couldn't have known whether his face showed in the picture or not. He probably felt it was safer to get rid of the photographer. But Richie didn't have the picture on him. Which means that the guy is probably still looking for it. Second, I don't know why Richie is still alive. I'm just grateful he is because we can interview him about the attack. He is being guarded by police, so he's protected."

"What are you going to do?"

He sat on the table right in front of me, and said, "You're not going to like this, Sam, but we have to keep you in protective custody."

I stood up and walked away. "No, you can't do that. I

have a life. I have kids. I have a job."

He followed me and took my arm, gently but firmly. "Sam, I love you. But even if you were a total stranger I'd put you in protective custody. We don't know; the guy might have seen Richie with you later. We just don't know."

"What does it mean—protective custody? Do I have to stay here? Can I stay at home with you watching me?"

He sat me down again, and I saw both love and worry on his face. "I'll probably hate myself for saying this, but I think we can have police at your house, watching you. But this means you can't leave; you have to stay there. Can you promise me this?"

I nodded, but then thought this deserved words. "Yes, I can promise."

And at the time I meant it.

EIGHT

I rode home with George in his car, and he said that my brother Rob would be on duty with him to begin with, as part of the protective team, and that someone else would take over at night. I nodded dumbly, unsure of what to say or even how to behave.

We arrived at my house in a few minutes. When I saw it the first thing that came to me was, "My kids. What about Adam? Sarah? Clancy?" I didn't think my children would mind my putting Clancy in the same category as them.

He walked around his car and met me in front of it, "Adam and Sarah will have to stay elsewhere. But I think it would be okay for Clancy to stay."

I smiled. "I definitely want the kids to be safe, and they can go somewhere else. But Clancy has saved my butt more than once; I feel better when she's with me."

George smiled too, "Guess she's not just a therapy dog for your patients."

I nudged him as we walked through the unlocked door. Clancy greeted us enthusiastically, and I told her to listen while George and I explained the situation to my kids and to my brother, who had already arrived. Clancy pulled back from me, almost like she knew I was going to say things she didn't like.

I phoned Father Brother, the nickname for my priest brother, Pete. He had a few extra rooms in his place, and I asked if Adam and Sarah could stay there for a few days.

"What's wrong?" he asked, concerned evident in his voice.

"Don't get excited, but a pal of mine was attacked and we don't know if his attacker saw me with him or not."

He raised his voice, "You say don't get excited and then tell me this!"

"Calm down. You're a priest."

"I'm also your brother, dammit."

"Pete, stop it. Priests don't cuss."

"Don't try to change the subject. Tell me what's up," he demanded.

"I did. I was talking with someone, gave him a ride somewhere, later he ended up in the ER. We're not sure if the murderer thinks I know something or not, so basically I'm in protective custody in my own house."

"Why can't they keep you at the police station or put you in another house?" he asked.

Growing weary of the questions, I sighed and handed my phone to George. I saw him change from boyfriend to cop before my eyes. As I walked upstairs to get the kids, I heard him say that Rob would be there too. Of course! I should have told one brother that another brother would be helping. That would have sold Pete on the deal.

Sarah and Adam were not pleased at waking up—especially Sarah, because she'd just gone to bed after working all night. She didn't exactly complain, but repeatedly rubbed her eyes while saying she just fell asleep. Adam had no problem complaining, as usual. I told them both that George would explain everything when they came downstairs, and that they needed to hurry.

George said that he'd convinced Pete to quit nagging me and he told Pete that he loved me and…

"You told him you loved me?" Suddenly I wished we were really alone.

"Of course. I've told you. You've told me…"

I interrupted, "I was first."

"Yeah, but I knew it first. I just didn't want to scare you off. Anyway, since we both know it and have verbalized it, and your kids know, there's no reason everyone else can't know. Right?"

"Right." My smile felt good in the middle of this mess. I patted George's shoulder when I walked by him. As I did, the scent of a familiar aftershave brought me back to high school. I remembered the same thing from the way he smelled so long ago, but I couldn't identify it. I'd have to ask him later.

My feelings were close to the surface and I almost cried when the kids stumbled down the stairs. They looked so young, with tousled hair, both in T-shirts and gym shorts. I quickly made coffee, and while it brewed, I pulled out their favorite cereals and milk. Just as I had when they were children, Adam loved Count Chocula. And Sarah had favored Wheaties ever since she had seen her first athlete pictured on the box.

I stayed in the cozy kitchen, not wanting to face my children. I knew I was abdicating the responsibility of explaining things, making George do it. Not very mature, but I also knew how they were going to react, and I figured I'd put the pieces back together when Adam exploded and Sarah started crying.

Nothing. Coffee brewed. I poured four cups, fixed each one the way each person liked it, took them into the living room, and waited. They sat huddled together in the same room, but talking quietly.

"For heaven's sake, you guys. Any reactions?" I couldn't help myself.

George said, "I told them in the beginning to stay calm for you. And they have. You've raised two great people."

Sarah stood and I noticed she had tears in her eyes, but they hadn't fallen. Wordlessly she came to me and hugged me, guiding my head to her shoulder the way I used to do hers.

"Dammit, now you've got me crying," I said.

Adam said, "I'm upset about this. Who wouldn't be? You could be in danger. But George convinced me that getting angry would only make things worse."

I went to him and hugged him too, and started to feel a little better. Turning to George I said, "Can they drive themselves? Or should someone take them to Pete's?"

He replied, "I've got a ride arranged. You two better finish your coffee and get packed."

Sarah asked, "How many days should we plan for?"

"Hard to say. Why don't you pack for two or three and if we need to readjust, we will."

"What about work? I work five nights a week," she continued, worry evidenced in her voice.

"We'll call in for you for the next few days."

"When we get to Uncle Pete's, do we have to stay inside?" she continued. "Can we go for walks? What about the grocery store?"

"You are so much like your mother." George ran his hand through his thinning hair. "You sure have a lot of questions."

"But they're legitimate questions, George," I said, standing by my girl with my arm on her shoulder.

"Indeed they are. I just felt bombarded for a moment."

"Welcome to my world," said Adam, laughing. It was good to hear laughter.

George answered Sarah's questions, "For the time being you need to stay inside. Pete can get anything you need. He said he'll stay there with you instead of going to work."

The two young ones took their coffee mugs with them upstairs. I could hear them moving about, and it reminded me of when they were young and we lived in Chicago. I felt grateful that I had them in my life, even though time was rushing by and they'd soon be gone. That thought was even more depressing than thinking about a murderer perhaps trying to kill me.

I shook off both those thoughts. For some reason I always had to physically do a head and shoulder shake to make disagreeable thoughts or emotions go away. It was weird, but…

George came over and interrupted my reverie with, "I'm thinking it might just be a better idea to move you somewhere else. Not a lot of people know about us; maybe you and Clancy can stay at my place for a few days. We can still have another officer or two there at all times. What do you think?"

My immediate impulse to say "no," quickly changed to an "okay." It might be fun to stay at George's. Spending so much time together would certainly force us to get to know each other more quickly. We'd see how compatible we were without having to "date" for a long time. This was actually a great idea. At my age, I couldn't afford to spend years dating someone and then deciding it wouldn't go anywhere. This would be more like "fast forward" dating.

"Okay," I finally said aloud. "Okay."

"You're not going to argue with me about this?" George asked, his eyebrows raised in surprise.

"Nope. When you're right, you're right."

He hugged me so hard it knocked my breath out of me. I didn't complain. I knew he was excited to win an argument with me, even though the argument was non-existent. In fact he was kind of cute in his excitement.

Clancy and I went to my room so I could pack. "George," I yelled, "will you please put some of Clancy's dry food in a gallon plastic bag? They're in the third drawer, and her food is on the floor in the cupboard."

"Sure," he yelled back. For a moment I could tell that Clancy had a hard time deciding who she wanted to stay with. I was packing and she wanted to make sure I didn't leave without her, but George was messing with her food. She chose food over love, and trotted out to the kitchen.

I smiled as I packed a few things in a gym bag. A sudden realization hit, and I shrieked as I dumped out the contents on my bed, and started over. I'd only packed white "granny panties" and plain cotton bras. Not only that, my summer pajamas were threadbare and a few of my favorites had holes in the elbows and knees. I didn't even own sexy nightgowns or pajamas. What was I going to do? I started looking through my bureau as I thought. I didn't know if I was going to sleep with George in his bedroom. I assumed I would. We'd been intimate for a few months, but because of our work schedules we'd only been able to "get together" once a week or so, and it was usually spontaneous.

In the bottom of my bra drawer I found two that were a little sexier than my plain cotton ones. I packed them plus one of my better white cotton bras. No lace, strictly utilitarian. I'd save that one for the day I was going home.

Then in my underwear drawer I found some granny panties that were at least flowered, with colors that hadn't faded. I replaced my white ones with those. Instead of my "holey" pajamas, I put a few sleeveless T's and two pairs of short gym shorts that hadn't seen the light of day in years. I definitely needed to do some lingerie shopping in the near future.

I met my kids back in the living room. They both had backpacks which I'm sure included their iPads. That reminded me I needed to pack my laptop. We could easily stay in touch via phone or computer. I hugged them both, almost desperately, and said, "I love you so much. Take care of yourselves, and do whatever the cops and Uncle Pete tell you to do. I'll talk to you every day, and I'm sure we'll all be home soon."

Clancy circled around them, looking anxious, until I told her they were just going to their Uncle Pete's. She was able to relax then and give them both doggy good-bye kisses.

It was only a few moments later that George and I were ready to leave. I made sure the coffee pot was turned off, and that there was nothing else I needed to take care of. This time I did lock the door, and heard George say, "About time." But I could hear the grin in his voice.

"I have to tell Gus what's going on."

He nodded, and I bounded up Gus and Georgianne's back stairs. Gus opened the door before I knocked. After we greeted each other, I explained to Gus what was going on.

"Do you need me to do anything?" He seemed excited. "Want us to keep Clancy? I can help you know."

He'd been involved in every murder I had solved so far (or helped to solve, as George would say).

"Thanks, but Clancy is going with me," I said, hating to leave him out of this. "You could keep an eye on my place. If you notice anything odd, call the police. Do not—and I repeat—do not do anything else. Don't go out back. Just watch my place from your house. It might even be good for you to park on the street instead of back here. That way you won't have to come out here at all. Got it?"

"Yeah, I got it."

"Good," I said.

George's laughter could not be contained.

I gave him my patented "look" but it didn't do any good. He kept laughing.

"What's so funny?"

"You told Gus the same things I tell you. Hope it works better with him."

I couldn't argue with him. It was true. My curiosity and my stubbornness apparently knew no bounds.

But I smiled. Even though a murderer might be after me, I was getting a chance to "play house" with George. Nothing wrong with that.

NINE

We left my blue Bug next to the carriage house, loaded up George's nondescript police car, and took off. Clancy didn't like being in the back seat, but there was only room for George and me in front. "Sorry, Clancy. You'll be back in a place of honor as soon as we get to George's." She seemed to understand.

I had only been to the outside of George's house since I'd moved back to Quincy. We always seemed to be at mine. As a kid I was at his home frequently; in grade school George and I were friends and played baseball together a lot in the summer. At night we played Kick the Can and other games that took a lot of energy. When we played in his yard, his mom gave us drinks, and the same thing happened with my mom when we played in our yard. I expected the house to be a typical bachelor pad with maybe a few remnants of his childhood, since he still lived in the house he grew up in. HIs parents were gone, like mine, and he was fortunate enough to have inherited a lovely bungalow, two blocks from St. Francis and a few houses away from where I grew up.

I loved this neighborhood. Even though it was nothing like the mansion-filled place I lived now, it was only four blocks away. The neighborhood contained mostly brick bungalows, and all the yards were neatly mowed, with mature trees and riotous colors of summer flowers everywhere you looked. As we drove by his house in order to get to the alley, we also had to drive by the house I grew up in. Nostalgia swept over me, and I missed my parents deeply.

We pulled into George's garage through the alley and he hurried me through the yard into his house via the back door. Clancy followed close behind.

The first thing I noticed was how comfy the eat-in kitchen looked. He'd updated the appliances from when we were kids, and the bright yellow patterned wallpaper had been replaced with a light yellow wash on the walls, white curtains on the window, and hardwood floors. An antique-looking wooden table completed the kitchen picture. This was a kitchen I could fall in love with.

"This surprises me," I said.

"Why? Too frou-frou?

"Not at all," I answered. "It's actually perfect." Clancy had already moved on to another room. So I dropped my purse on the floor, stepped toward George, touched his arm with my right hand and put my left behind his head, pulling him toward me. I kissed him the way he always kissed me, warmly, passionately, and lovingly. When I was finished I noted the happy, albeit surprised, look on his face.

"Guess you do like it. Hope you like the other rooms just as much."

We left my stuff on the kitchen floor and he led me to the dining room, which was a big room that was basically empty except for an old hutch that held what looked to be childhood treasures and things left by his parents. The room had maroon walls, hardwood floors, the hutch, and that was basically it.

"This one has possibilities," I said, and George smiled again.

"Yeah, I don't do much entertaining. So I just never got around to buying any new furniture for this room." He held my hand. "Maybe you can help me with it."

Next we walked into the living room. It looked comfy, and the décor was lighter than what I'd seen in the dining room. There was a brick fireplace, and hugging the walls were a love seat, couch, and a recliner. On the walls were pictures of George and his parents at various stages of George's life. As an only child, he probably hadn't known what to expect when he walked into our house the first time in elementary school.

On a wall near the fireplace was a picture of us as kids—all of us in the neighborhood. There must have been 20 kids in the picture, and George and I were standing next to each other. He looked tough in his white T-shirt and blue jeans. I basically wore the same outfit, signifying my status as a tomboy and someone who could be trusted when chosen for a team. What I hadn't really noticed when I saw this picture at my own house was that my face was turned toward him. Maybe I was falling in love with George even then. I touched the picture lovingly, and was reminded of so much cherished history I shared with this man.

I looked around again. This room was clean and neat, but for some reason you could tell a man lived here.

"Finally," I said as I noticed a pair of sneakers by the front door.

"Finally, what?" asked George.

"Finally, I found something out of place."

"Well, I'm kind of neat, but not overly so, believe me. I have housekeepers who come in every two weeks, and I have to put things away so they can dust and sweep. I am not a neat freak."

"Good. 'Cause I'm not either."

"I know," he said with a grin on his face.

We continued the tour. His bedroom was on the main floor, and the bathroom sat between it and a second smaller bedroom he'd turned into an office. He told me that on the second floor there was a loft bedroom that ran the length of the house, and he'd added another bathroom up there.

"And my next project is to redo the basement for yet

another guest room and bath."

"Wow. There's a lot of depth to you. I had no idea."

His face got serious. "We might as well deal with this now. Sleeping arrangements."

My heart rate increased.

"I'd like you to stay with me in my bedroom, but I don't want to push you. Staying together for a few days or more is a little different than the times we've slept together. What do you think?"

"There's nowhere else I'd rather be," was all I said.

He stepped toward me, then took a deep breath and turned toward the kitchen. "It's about dinnertime. Let's put your stuff in the bedroom, and I'll make dinner."

"All this and you cook too. How did I get so lucky?"

George made a pasta and vegetable dish, with vegetables from his garden and some fresh mozzarella.

"I can't believe you fix up houses, cook, and garden… plus you're a damn good cop and a wonderful boyfriend." I paused to look at him and smiled. "You might want to take notes, George. I'm not always going to be this nice."

He laughed as he made iced tea, and I worked on a salad. It wasn't long before he dished up the pasta to accompany the salad. We sat in the kitchen while we ate, and chatted about everything except sleeping together and murder.

"Remind me to call the office in the morning and tell them I'll be out a few days." I looked up at him as I spoke.

He nodded, mouth full of food.

Then suddenly I yelled, "Omigod, where's Clancy?"

We both jumped up to search and we found her stretched out on George's bed. Staking her claim.

"Hope you have Animal Planet, so we can distract her while we… get busy." I whispered because I really didn't want Clancy hearing this.

"I can't believe you said 'get busy' instead of have sex, make love, or one of a thousand different ways to say it." He hugged me, laughing. "And yes, I have cable, so we can keep Clancy busy while we get busy."

"Stop making fun of me."

"That's the way your entire family communicates. I was just practicing," he said. As he walked out of his room he answered his buzzing cell phone. "Lansing. Yeah. I don't know. Maybe sit in the street in a car. I'll keep the floodlights on in back so no one can sneak up on us. Okay."

Before I could ask about the call, he said, "Your brother. Said he's the only one who can watch the house tonight. Mansfield is assigned elsewhere. So I told him to stay in front. But now I'm second-guessing myself about the decision to relocate. We probably should have stayed at your house where's there's only one entrance. I don't know."

"It's okay." I hugged him. "The murderer probably doesn't even know about me. And if he does, he doesn't know where I am. I feel safe with you."

He hugged me back, but his mind seemed elsewhere.

I tried to distract him by walking seductively toward the kitchen.

George said, "Something wrong, hon? You look like you're hurt."

I ignored the unintended jibe and said, "Nope. I'm fine. Let's clean up the kitchen," and muttered under my breath about men who can't tell the difference between sexy and hurt.

We worked together, putting food away and doing dishes. I soon forgot my pique and relaxed, thinking about how great it was to be staying with the man I loved.

After the kitchen was cleaned, he said, "I'm going to take a shower. See you in a few minutes." He gave me a quick kiss and went to his bedroom.

I sat at the kitchen table for a minute and Clancy came up to me. She nuzzled against my leg, and I petted her absentmindedly.

"I know I've been ignoring you, girl. I'm sorry. I'm just not used to having a boyfriend, and then there's this whole stupid murder thing. I feel like crap. Richie got stabbed and I don't know what's going to happen or how long before we can go home."

She talked back in doggie talk. Her soft growl was comforting, but then she added another element to her message. She had to go out. I knew I had a few more minutes before George was done, so I put the leash on her and went out to the back yard.

The floodlights hadn't been turned on yet, so I leaned back through the door and turned them on. As I did, I heard a rustling sound. Clancy growled then barked. A moment later I saw a blue hoodie running from the bushes near the back porch out to the alley. The first thing I thought of was that George was going to be pissed.

And I was right.

TEN

"What in the hell were you thinking?"

"Obviously I thought I'd get away with it, and I wouldn't have to explain myself."

He stood there with a towel around his waist and I was distracted. Even though George had a "middle aged spread," he didn't look bad. Not bad at all. I found it difficult to concentrate on my transgression.

"I'm sorry, George. I really am. The truth is that I didn't think. I forgot I was in trouble and just felt like I was at my boyfriend's house because I want to be here, not because I have to be here."

"You could have been killed, Sam. I'd never forgive myself if you were hurt on my watch." He grabbed me and held me close for a moment, then quickly backed up. "I better go get dressed," he said with a red face.

I laughed. "It's okay to just put on pajamas if you want. It's getting late."

"We're still going to talk about this," George said, and pointed to a chair. "Now sit and do not move. Or I'll take you with me."

I raised my eyebrows and showed him an evil grin.

He was back in two minutes wearing a T-shirt and gym shorts—the same thing I'd brought for myself. That made me feel warm.

He paced the dining room as he called Rob to tell him of the guy in the yard.

"I don't know if he is involved in what happened to Richie or not, but we better be alert." Rob must have said he'd go around to the back as well as the front of the house. "Sounds good, Rob. Glad to hear it. And if you are walking around the house it'll keep you awake." Then a soft chuckle.

"That was really stupid." He was all business as he sat on the love seat in the living room and pointed toward the other end for me to join him.

"I know. I didn't think. I'm really sorry."

"You can't do it again," he said as he grabbed my hands, and held them as if by holding them he could keep me there and keep me safe.

"I won't," I promised. "I'll let you take Clancy outside, or at the very least we'll do it together. Okay?"

"Okay to the first. I'll do it. And if you noticed, all the blinds are drawn. I want you to stay away from the windows. Oh, and Rob said there would be two guys overnight after all, so I'll be able to sleep."

"I promised you I'll be careful and I will." I added and

moved closer. "Shouldn't you turn on Animal Planet in the living room now?"

For different reasons, he and Clancy both smiled. And that night I enjoyed some very personal protective custody indeed.

The next morning, I woke up with a smile still on my face. I turned to hug George, and found that Clancy had maneuvered her way in between us. So I hugged her instead. I laughed as I did so, which woke up George. He leaned on his elbow and looked at me over Clancy.

"This is cozy," he said.

"Yes, it is. Maybe you should get a king-sized bed."

He laughed and said, "I don't think it would fit in this room. The bedrooms were built small in bungalows. Guess you were supposed to spend your time in the living room and not the bedroom."

He stood up and said, "I'll give you the shower first. I'll take Clancy out."

"Thanks." As I gathered my things and went into the bathroom, I thought that even in the midst of this mess, I was happy. Very happy.

Before I jumped in the shower I called my office and said I'd be out for a few days. Clara Schmidt, the receptionist, said she'd call my clients and reschedule them. With that finished, I was able to get ready for another day that I got to spend with my sweeties. I counted Clancy.

CAN YOU PICTURE THIS?

George brought Clancy back in, and while he was showering I was able to spend time with my sweet dog. I fed her and gave her fresh water, and we had time for "girl talk" while I made breakfast. She isn't much of a conversationalist, but we understood each other just fine. She stayed right by my side, standing guard as I chopped up onions and green peppers. The pungent odor kept me alert. The thought of George kept me happy.

When George entered into the kitchen he came up behind me and hugged me. I leaned against him and inhaled his clean, manly scent.

"What's that aftershave you use? It reminds me of high school."

"You recognized that? I bought it just for you." I could hear the smile in his voice. "It's Hai Karate. Same thing I used to put on back when we first dated. Not easy to get now, but it was worth the effort since you noticed."

"I appreciate it." I turned long enough to give him a quick kiss, then got back to my task. "I hope you like hash browns."

"I do."

"I make them with lots of stuff—onion, peppers, tomatoes, and cheese. I learned that when I volunteered in Mississippi after Hurricane Katrina. Every mile or so they had a Waffle House which made the best hash browns I'd ever tasted. You had some veggies left over from dinner." I moved around the kitchen opening cabinets until I found plates and glasses. "I scrambled up a few eggs too. One of my many vices is that I love salt and pepper. I went light on the salt, but put in a lot of black pepper. Hope it's okay. I'm not much of a cook."

"It smells great," he said. "It's nice having someone cook for me."

"Will you pour the coffee? And butter the toast? Everything is just about ready."

I had to admit that breakfast was wonderful. It felt like a little family. George, Clancy, and me. I felt comfortable. And loved.

Then damn reality had to insert itself.

George answered his cell while he was still eating. He became serious immediately. "Yeah, I'll be right there. Don't move the body."

I gasped. "Another body? Another murder?"

"Yeah," he said, wiping his hands and mouth with his napkin after taking one last bite. "You're coming with me. I can't leave you alone."

I didn't argue. And didn't even ask if I could take Clancy. Of course, I'd take her, no question about it.

We left everything on the table and went dressed as we were. I had on jeans with a short sleeve cotton sweater and he had on jeans and a St. Francis High School T-shirt.

"Where did they find him… it… the body?"

"The exact same spot. In the alley, against the John Wood Mansion. Same as the first man who was murdered, and same as where Richie was found."

He parked illegally on 12th Street, and I told Clancy to stay in the car. I knew I wouldn't be allowed to stay in the car without George, plus I didn't want to. I was anxious to find out what had happened.

When we reached the spot, I saw that a screen had been placed to shield the body. I took a deep breath before moving around it.

The sight made me gag. Every reason I didn't go into the medical field surfaced. A man in a bright blue hoodie, also wearing a previously white T-shirt, jeans, and brown boots. Something horrible that looked like it might have come from his brain was splattered on his left side, and a handgun lay on the ground near his right side. The smell of gunpowder along with the coppery smell of blood sickened me.

It looked like a suicide. I hoped I was right and I hoped the guy was the murderer. If so, I wouldn't have any more worries about him hurting me too.

I stood off to the side while George talked to the uniformed cop by the body. I noticed another cop standing near me. It was Jimmy Mansfield, this time in uniform too, and he said he was assigned to me for the day. I gave him a half smile, thanked him, then quickly turned back to watch what George was doing.

A few minutes later, George nodded, and the other guy placed a covering over the dead man.

"Well?" I asked, when George walked back to me.

"We're not sure of anything yet, except that it looks like a suicide," he answered.

"It's hard to say, but he looks about the same size as the guy in the picture. Damn, I wish I knew where that picture was."

"Probably totally gone. No use worrying about it," George said. "Let's go back to my house."

"Okay. Don't you have work to do on this case?"

"Yeah, but I can do it at home. Cell phone, computer, Skype. That's how I'll stay in touch, because it's more important that I keep you safe. Once we have the body identified and have some evidence he's the murderer, then you'll be free."

"That'll be nice, but I do kind of like this protective custody thing."

He grinned as he opened the car door. He nodded at a cop in a car behind us as we took off. That was the first time I noticed we were being followed. I saw that it was Jimmy, the cop who told me he was assigned to me. Guess Rob was busy or maybe off today after working all night.

As soon as my thoughts went to Rob, my phone rang and it was him. I said, "Hi," and told George we could go ahead and drive home, that the phone call was from Rob.

"I just heard," Rob said. "Was it the murderer?"

"Don't know for sure. He was about the same size, but in the picture I just saw him mostly from the back. I saw some of his side, but nothing of his face. It was just awful seeing the body."

"I know. It never gets easy."

"Will you please tell the others? Especially Pete and my kids? I don't really want to talk about it any more."

"Sure thing, sis. Love you. And be careful."

"Love you too."

We pulled up to a red light, and George turned to me. "I love that about you."

"What?" I smiled.

"That you guys always say, 'I love you' when you leave each other or before you hang up the phone."

"Mom and Dad always did that. And it gave me a little comfort knowing that the last thing they heard from me was 'I love you.' And it was the last thing I heard from them too."

I rode the rest of the way in silence to George's house, feeling content. He parked in the garage again and we walked into his kitchen a few moments later. Clancy sat and looked up expectantly.

"Hungry, girl?" I couldn't help but smile when I looked at her.

George got her food and a bowl while I filled another bowl with water. It was still early so I made the bed while George worked on the computer. I heard his voice at times when I sat to read on my iPad. I must have dozed off on the couch because the next thing I knew I felt Clancy giving me doggy kisses.

"Clancy, stop," I said, my eyes still closed. "I'm awake." I moved to push her away and discovered it wasn't Clancy after all, but George.

I pulled him to me, and we got a little amorous until he stood up and said, "Forgot. I'm on duty. Damn."

I smiled, and stretched, then sat up again. I got up and followed George into the second bedroom that he'd converted to an office. "Any news yet?"

He knew what I meant.

"Not really. The first and last dudes didn't have an ID on them, so we're running the last one's prints. We already ran the first one's and he's not on the database. We're also checking their bites, and we'll run those too, against dental records. I don't know anything right now."

"Do I get to… er… have to stay here tonight?" Oops. I didn't want to sound like I was ready to move in. I just really enjoyed being here with George.

He answered right away without looking up. "I think tonight, yeah. We don't know if the last guy was the murderer or not. We don't know who it was in my backyard last night. We don't know much of anything except we have two bodies, someone in the hospital, and not much information."

The day passed in a leisurely way for me, but not so much for George. He stayed on the phone and/or the computer all day, stopping only for a light lunch I'd put together with leftovers from yesterday. Around 5:30 I heard him sigh and say to someone on the other end of his phone call, "I'm done for today. Call me if you have any, and I mean any, news."

I stood behind him by then, and I leaned down and hugged him from behind. The chair got in the way, but I needed him to feel how much I cared about him.

"I love you. I hope you know how much." As I stood up he swiveled his office chair around to face me and pulled me to his lap.

"No one will hurt you, Sam. I'll take care of you."

"And sometimes, George, I'll take care of you."

ELEVEN

The evening was more pleasant than the one before, and not only because there was no extra person in the back yard. It was quiet. I read while George sat on the couch by me, watching something on the tube. A while after that, George read while I watched TV. Later, we found a show we both liked—a re-run of *Bones*—and sat together, whispering so Clancy didn't hear everything we said. After that show we sat in the silence and I enjoyed it.

I hadn't experienced this kind of peace before. No thoughts of will he drink too much, is he cheating on me, does he love me… no thoughts like the ones that had cluttered my mind in previous relationships.

Maybe he's "the *one*," I thought, and then laughed aloud at myself. I had thought my ex-husband Joe was *the one* too. And I'd quickly found out how wrong I was. Joe was a man who was a good father, sometimes a great father, but he was a lousy husband. Going hot and cold, loving then not, being attentive and then ignoring me; it was a roller coaster of a marriage that didn't suit me. I never knew whether Joe would come home right after work or at two in the morning. He wasn't abusive to me, at least not physically. Verbal and emotional abuse was another story.

My children knew nothing of this. And never would, at least not from me. I'd told Pete when I was in the midst of the divorce; he was the one who advised me to get an annulment "just in case." So I did; it was on the grounds of fraud, since Joe wasn't staying true to the promise of fidelity. It took a while, but finally was approved.

I didn't tell anyone else the reason for my divorce, not even my sisters or Gus. I don't know if I was embarrassed or just didn't want to bore them with my problems. There were some suspicions, of that I was sure. But no certainty on their part.

But George was different. I would bet my very life on that. He was a smart ass, which I did love. However, he wasn't cruel with his comments. He almost seemed to be a member of the family with his ready sarcastic wit. And he wasn't afraid to be loving, even in front of others. His kindness and compassion left me feeling so much in love that I could hardly stand it. Surely he had his faults, but they were more than bearable.

We'd made a big chef salad for dinner, with some ham on George's portion, and George broke out some wine, since technically he wasn't on duty. He limited both of us to one glass, just in case we had to react quickly at any time.

I didn't object since I wasn't much of a runner even sober. Drunken staggering would make me even slower if a bad guy were chasing me.

The rest of the evening was as pleasant as before dinner. And the night was… well, the night was pretty darn fantastic.

I awoke with both a smile and a dog butt on my face. George had already gotten up, and I heard him whistling in the shower. Clancy had to go out, but I wasn't going to make the same mistake again. I called to George, saying, "Can you hurry and take Clancy outside?"

"Yep," he yelled back. And it was just a moment before he came back into the bedroom and landed on the bed to give me a hug.

He jumped up and said, "C'mon, Clancy, let's go outside."

She reacted predictably, leaping off the bed and running around George until they finally walked out of the bedroom. I stretched luxuriously, content with my life. Well, except for the part where I couldn't work and couldn't go home. Couldn't see my kids either. I guessed I wasn't as content as I'd thought.

"I betcha I'll get to go home today," I said aloud. Then, not troubled by anything for the moment, I got up and showered, and even sang while I did so. Today was going to be a glorious day.

Or so I thought.

TWELVE

It wasn't long before breakfast was finished and cleaned up. "Y'know, I don't think I've ever cleaned off a table so much. Lots of times things sit there until I get around to it."

"I noticed," George said.

With the mood I was in, I couldn't even get sarcastic with him, much less mad.

"I need to know how Richie is. It's stupid, but I feel partially responsible."

"I'm glad you realize that it's stupid. You did nothing to hurt him. And I'll check on Richie in a little while."

"Do you think I can go home today?" I asked him, changing the subject.

"We'll see. I'm going to check with the station."

He called and spoke to his captain, who told him they had no reason to think the suicide was the murderer, but no reason to think he wasn't. In other words they didn't know much of anything yet. George asked when the autopsy would be conducted and was told it would probably be today.

When he hung up, George added, "At least that might tell us whether he was a suicide or a homicide."

I had no idea that they thought it might not be suicide. I felt a shiver that was part fear and part excitement. "Wow. That would make a big difference in everything, wouldn't it? What makes you think it might not be suicide? And can I still go home today?" I stopped when George held up his hand.

"You and your daughter with the questions…. Anyway, the answers are yes, it looked too perfect, and I don't know." Then he said, "Do you really want to leave here?"

It was my turn to say, "I don't know." I added, "I don't want to leave you, that's for sure, but I'd love to be in my cozy little carriage house with my kids there… and you, of course." I hugged him to let him know that I wasn't trying to escape him, or his lovely home.

I could see he was having an internal dialogue, trying to decide if it was safe for me to go to work and to stay at my own place. Finally he said, "I don't want you to leave, but that's just selfish. I've enjoyed having you and Clancy here the last few nights. But somehow it just feels like you'd be safe going home. And to work too."

I kissed him. Kissed him seriously and thoroughly.

"Before I go, maybe we can get Clancy to watch the Animal Planet one more time," he said, his eyes flashing. I looked at George and grinned back.

After all, who knew when we'd be able to have some private time again? We'd both be busy with work, plus I'd have the kids, and I'd neglected the rest of my family since I had fallen in love with George.

Clancy hadn't watched so much TV since I'd gotten her. Now here she was, eight years old, and I was getting her addicted to the boob tube. But it was worth it.

Later we had another cup of coffee while watching a show with Clancy on the migratory patterns of the Canada goose. She seemed enthralled. I leaned over Clancy so I could talk to George.

"I keep wondering how Richie is doing. Can you check, please?"

"Sure. I forgot to call, but I'll do it now. Since he was a crime victim I can get some information from the hospital." He called and spoke to the nurse manager of the floor Richie'd been moved to. He spoke for a few minutes, and his eyebrows shot up in disbelief, before thanking her and putting his phone down.

"He's doing really well," he said before I could even question him about it. "And the thing that flabbergasted me was the reason he didn't die."

"What. Tell me." I couldn't contain myself.

"He was stabbed the same way as the first guy, but he has a rare condition called," he looked down to consult his notes, "dextrocardia. It means his heart is on the right instead of the left side of his chest. So even though the knife went in the same place, it didn't hit his heart. He'll be fine. He's going to be discharged in the next few days."

"Wow. I've heard of that, but don't think I've ever met anyone who had it. And I sure didn't know what it was called." I had to think about it for a while. What amazing luck Richie had. "We need to visit him."

George agreed. "We can go this evening or tomorrow. I have lots of work to catch up on."

Later that morning, after checking with the station again, George said I could probably stay at my house safely. As he drove me home, my mind was cluttered with useless facts, and my vibes had deserted me... at least for the moment. Even Clancy wasn't able to help me. Our connection was lessened when there was an abundance of people around.

I realized it was too late for me to go to work because the agency would have already called my clients to cancel for today. But I did phone in a message for the receptionist, Clara Schmidt, to let her know I'd be there tomorrow.

George said he'd pick me up later so we could go to visit Richie at the hospital, then dropped me and Clancy off at my house. I sighed as I walked through the door to my domain. This was my very first home ever where I'd had a bedroom to myself, not to mention the luxury of a bathroom attached. When I was young, I had shared with my sisters, and of course I shared with Joe while I was married.

There was something so right about having a place of my own. I wondered if I ever could share a place with someone again. My kids didn't count. They were part of me, plus they were seldom home anyway. Adam would graduate after one more year and he'd most likely move out as soon as he could. Sarah had a few more years at school and I hoped she would consider this place her home until she finished.

I dropped my bag on the floor and plopped my body onto the couch. And there I sat with my feet on the coffee table until my kids walked in. Without any prompting one sat on either side of me. I took both their hands and held them close for a short time. We didn't even talk. Just sat in silence until Clancy let me know she needed to go out.

"I'll take her," Adam said.

"No need, hon," I said, getting up, "I want to take her for a little walk."

"I'll go with you," said Adam and Sarah at the same time.

I smiled at how sweet they were both being.

"Nope. I need to be by myself a little and enjoy my freedom."

Clancy got excited at the sight of her leash, because it meant she was going for a real walk and not just a pee in the courtyard. As we exited my house, the mansion's back door opened and out walked Georgianne in her loud, flowered housecoat.

"Yoo-hoo, Sam!" Even though I was standing a few feet

away from her back porch she still yelled as if I couldn't see or hear her.

"Good morning," I said, happy with the world for the moment, and that world included even Georgianne's housecoat.

"Are you home for good?" she asked. "Gus has been worried about you."

"Welcome home, Sam. I missed you and Clancy." Gus stuck his head out of the door and yelled his greeting.

Seeing the two of them, Clancy pulled on her leash until I let go, and she ran up the stairs to greet her friends. After she gave them each doggie kisses, she rolled onto her back so they could apply some well-placed belly rubs.

Georgianne looked up, "I wanted to ask you, Sam, if you would like to play cards tonight. My regular group is playing, but it's a special night because my sister is here and she adores card games. Please say you're free."

Normally I'm quick enough with the excuses, but not this time.

"Sure, what time?" All was right in my world. I could afford to spend time with Georgianne. Plus, I'd get to see Gus.

"Come over at seven. Would your children like to play?"

Thankfully, for them, I was able to say that I thought they were both busy. They loved Gus and Georgianne, but I thought the card game with old folks might be asking too much of them.

I was finally able to extract Clancy from their ministrations and took off. Today we went on our normal walk through the lovely neighborhood we lived in. It seemed it had been a long time since I was able to talk to Clancy like I'd always done.

"So, girl, what did you think about staying with George?"

I had to grin at her smile.

"Me too, Clancy. Me too."

I marveled at the blooming flowers and the squirrels and bunnies scampering on the park-like lawns. Even though these sights were almost daily occurrences during my summer walks, I still felt immensely lucky.

Out of the blue the hair stood up on my neck. Something was wrong somewhere. My stomach was tied up in knots and I felt dizzy enough that I had to sit down on a bank. It was daylight, so I shouldn't have felt threatened, but I did. Clancy's low growl told me she was getting the same vibes I was.

I looked back and forth, back and forth, but nothing was there. Just the cars on Maine Street, a busy thoroughfare as usual. The sidewalks were empty, which was kind of strange, but not too much out of the ordinary on a work day in a residential neighborhood. I willed myself to relax my shoulders, which were up around my neck.

Breathe deeply, Sam. Just breathe deeply.

That calmed me enough that I was able to stand up. I brushed the grass and dirt off my butt and told Clancy everything was going to be all right. My vibes were still telling me something was wrong, but I couldn't see anything.

Starting to walk again, I felt Clancy pull behind me and she began barking frantically. I couldn't hold her, and as I turned around to see what she was going after, I saw a blue hoodie on a figure escaping over a high wooden fence in a side yard. Clancy stood at the fence barking, but she couldn't jump over it. I was okay with that. If something ever happened to her, they'd have to bury me along with her.

"Clancy, get over here right now!" I seldom used that commanding tone of voice with her, because she usually knew how to behave. And it seemed that once more she might have saved my life, or at least saved me from something unpleasant. She looked at me, barked one more time for good measure in the direction the blue hoodie had taken, then came back to me. I knelt and hugged her, telling her over and over how much I loved her. She'd been with me since she was a pup that my kids picked out at the Quincy Humane Society. I couldn't imagine my life without her.

A few months ago, Clancy had been poisoned, along with many other dogs, some of whom died. I'd been frantic, and George had comforted me. It was the moment when I first knew that I loved him. I wasn't able to explain it.

Clancy accepted my love and my thanks. Once I was able to walk again, I turned around to go home—this time we didn't walk all the way to my job at the Quincy Community Clinic, like we typically did.

"Omigod, girl. I wish I knew what just happened." My mind was full of confusion. "I have to trust our instincts and figure that the guy was up to no good. Right? Even though he didn't do anything to us. I mean, you barked, and I felt my vibes. It had to be a dangerous situation. Plus, he ran away." Clancy was looking at me with her most alert expression.

"What a weasel." As usual, while we walked, I kept up a running commentary with Clancy. "Should I tell George? I mean the guy did have on a blue hoodie."

Clancy thought I should tell him. But she was more of a worrywart than I was.

"I don't know, Clance. I don't want to have to be under protective custody again. It was glorious being with George, but I hate being confined." I thought for about a half block. "Nope. Not going to tell him. Not just yet anyway. And if you give me away, you will be in big trouble, young lady."

At that time, an out-of-breath cop in a blue uniform ran up to me. I recognized Jimmy Mansfield, who had been assigned to me earlier.

"I saw what happened," he said, in between gulping breaths. "I was sitting at the light and got out of my car and chased the guy a few blocks. He had a big head start, and I couldn't catch him. Sorry."

He took another deep breath, then seemed to breathe more normally rather quickly.

"Are you okay?"

"Yeah, thanks," I answered, feeling tired just looking at him.

Clancy gave a low growl again. I couldn't feel whether it was left over from the crisis or whether she was growling at Jimmy. Sometimes our psychic connection seems to flow only one way.

Then it hit me.

"Oh shit. You're going to tell George, aren't you?"

THIRTEEN

"Well, of course I am," he answered in a Dudley Do-Right manner. "That's the right thing to do."

I nodded, as if I agreed, and he didn't ask what the "oh, shit" was about. So I played along and was pleased that at least George wouldn't have an excuse to get mad at me.

I thanked him again for trying to help us, and walked the short distance to my home. I knew it wouldn't be long before George called me or came over. I expected a lecture from him, so I didn't tell the kids because I didn't need a lecture from them too.

I heard them upstairs, so I slunk to my bedroom and quietly closed the door. Of course I had my cell phone with me, so I could answer George's call and get what was coming to me. I took off my jeans and pulled the covers over my head. What had happened finally hit me, and the tears started.

Clancy tried to wiggle under the covers to comfort me, but had to do it from on top of the bedspread. I uncovered my head, tears flowing down my face, and let her give me a kiss. She only gave me one, because I'd taught her not to lick my face—unless it was an extreme emergency. Guess she thought this qualified. And I agreed.

We cuddled until my phone buzzed.

"Hello," I said, knowing who it was.

"Sam, are you okay?" George asked.

"Perfectly fine," I lied.

"I'm outside the house, and I'm coming in."

"No problem. It's probably unlocked."

It was only a second later he came into my bedroom, yelling.

"Unlocked? Why in the hell would you leave your door unlocked after what just happened?" He jumped on the bed, on the opposite side of Clancy, and hugged me.

I couldn't help it. I cried again. His yelling was because he was scared for me and he loved me. I knew he wasn't horribly mad, just upset at how stupid I am sometimes.

After I calmed again, I apologized.

"Sorry about the door. You know it's one of my many bad habits. And you don't have to worry about what happened today. Clancy saved me, then Jimmy chased the guy. I don't know what would have happened, but I felt safe. Clancy is amazing." I turned to her. "Aren't you, girl? You are freakin' amazing."

She finally smiled and that relaxed me because it meant there was no danger around right now. I told George I wanted to take a nap and then I was going to play cards at Gus and Georgianne's. He could come along and keep Gus company if he wanted.

"Well, I'm certainly not going to leave you alone, even walking the few steps to their house." He gave me a kiss on the forehead. "Take your nap, and then you are moving back to my house again after your card game."

"No," I begged, "please can we stay here? You can get some things while the kids are here with me. But no need to tell them what happened."

"Too late," Adam said, standing in my doorway.

"George called me before he called you, Mom," Sarah added. Then, turning to George, she said, "We'll watch her while you go home and get some things."

Reluctantly George agreed, warning me one last time, "Stay put. Don't even leave your bedroom."

I didn't have to agree. My kids did it for me. Sarah lay down by me when George got up, and Clancy stayed on her own side. Adam said he'd be in the living room, with the door to my bedroom open. I felt very safe and very loved.

During my short nap, I dreamed in color of blue hoodies everywhere. Ballet dancers wore them, people riding unicycles wore them, police, firemen, priests, everyone. Everyone had on a blue hoodie. They didn't scare me. Blue hoodies weren't threatening. But that all changed when I looked down and saw that I wore one too. My scream echoed in my head, but no one heard me.

It wasn't long before George returned, waking me as he walked into my room. I felt my pulse start to slow and hoped that my fearful heavy breathing didn't cause him concern.

"What time do you play cards?" George put a duffel bag on the floor, and looked pleased that all was well.

I looked at the clock and yelped, "Now." Then sweeping aside my covers I said, "Move on out everyone, I need to get dressed."

"Sorry. I said you weren't to be left alone. Sarah, will you stay with your mom while she gets dressed?"

Sarah nodded without speaking.

I loved that George was sensitive enough to not flaunt the fact that he'd seen me undressed before. Sarah sat on my bed and talked to me while I put on a clean, and non-wrinkled, shirt. I used the same jeans I'd discarded to the floor prior to my nap.

I heard George and Adam raise their voices in the living room, but didn't think much of it. Maybe there was a baseball game on or something.

While Sarah and I were still alone, she took advantage of the momentary privacy.

"I'm going to work tonight. No one is going to stop me."

And I knew that was true. Short of hogtying her, George wasn't going to keep her from work any longer.

I didn't say anything, but knew George was in for a battle.

She repeated her statement to him.

"Now, Sarah," George said. And that was all he got to say before she launched into a tirade worthy of her mother.

"Well, we need to have someone go to work with you. A cop," He said when she was finished. She rolled her eyes, but George wasn't intimidated. He continued, "Maybe your brother… I'll need to check. In the meantime," he looked at all of us one by one, "… don't go anywhere."

He went into the kitchen and made a call, keeping his voice low so we couldn't hear what he was saying. Sarah, Adam, Clancy, and I didn't say anything. I guess we all wanted to hear what he said. At least I did. It looked like he ended the call and made another one. By the way his head was moving, he got the result he wanted, then he made one more call. Another positive response. By now I was confused, wondering why he had to make three calls. He soon un-confused me.

"Okay, here's the deal. I'm staying with you, Sam, for obvious reasons." He smiled at his little joke, which was welcome at this point, but his demeanor changed immediately.

"While you were getting ready," George looked at me then glared at Adam, "Adam informed me that he was going out with friends. I said, 'It's Tuesday. Why would you go out on a Tuesday night?' He looked at me like I was nuts and reminded me he was young and they go out any night they want to."

I joined in on the glaring at Adam.

Adam wasn't scared. He knew my glare was worse than my bite.

"So here's what's going to happen," George went on. "Officer Jimmy Mansfield is going to work with you, Sarah. He's not going to wear his uniform so he won't embarrass you too much."

Sarah nodded and didn't say a word.

"And as for you, Adam, your uncle Rob is going out with you and your buddies." He stopped Adam before he could say anything. "Rob is pretty close to your age, so it won't look weird that he's with you."

"I wasn't going to complain," Adam said, sounding defensive, "Uncle Rob is closer in age to me than he is to my mom. And he's kind of cool… for a cop." Then he actually smiled.

I sighed with relief. I felt that both of my kids would be safe tonight. I was confident Rob would take good care of Adam, and his friends. Plus, he wouldn't drink, and would be alert. And Jimmy Mansfield had already saved me once. He'd take good care of my baby girl.

Sarah said she was going to take a nap until it was time for work, and George let her know Jimmy would pick her up about 20 minutes before she had to be at the hospital.

Rob called Adam's phone and I could hear Adam agreeing to whatever Rob said, ending the conversation with, "Okay. See you then."

After my kids and I exchanged "I love yous," I knew I could relax and enjoy my card game.

George and I took Clancy and a six-pack of beer with us and walked through the courtyard to Gus and Georgianne's house. The back door was open and I heard laughter coming from the dining room.

George and I walked in to see Georgianne, her sister Julianne, Gus, and two other older women I didn't know. I introduced George, and we were introduced to Lily and Mae, old friends of Georgianne's.

"We like to have four or five for our card games, and unfortunately one of our members is in the hospital and another wasn't feeling well," Georgianne said. "I thought you might enjoy a game with us."

Yeah, right. You're all at least 40 years older than I am. I'm sure this will be a laugh riot.

But when Georgianne said, "We recently started calling ourselves the Game of Crones," I figured it would be fun after all.

Gus told George, "I got a great cop movie from the forties. It's got George Raft and Edward G. Robinson. Thought maybe you hadn't seen it yet." He led George into the living room. As he walked by me, George kissed the top of my head, and I noticed wistful looks on the other women's faces.

Georgianne surprised the hell out of me. She was actually fun. Still a little snooty, but more relaxed than I'd ever seen her. This group had been playing cards every Tuesday night for more than 40 years, meaning they started about my age.

The game was a rummy variation, and over time, they'd developed their own rules. It was fun but with some bittersweet moments. Mae asked several times each hand what the wild card was. It changed each hand and it was hard for her to retain the memory.

As a therapist, I noticed signs of early dementia; whether it was Alzheimer's or not was up to a doctor to diagnose. But dementia definitely. I thought that it wouldn't be long and they'd be losing another member.

The other three were sharp as tacks, and I had to work hard to keep up with them, their cards, and their banter. Georgianne had a side table full of edible goodies and of course I spent some quality time there.

Julianne was certainly funny, loud, and theatric, making me wish I'd known her when she was younger. Suddenly she stood up, threw out her arms and yelled, "I LOVE MEN!" I didn't know where that came from, but it was endearing rather than uncomfortable.

"That reminds me of my third, or was it my fourth,

husband," she said at one point, and went on to tell a bizarre story involving outdoor sex and fire ants. Normally I'd be grossed out thinking of an eighty-something-year-old woman having sex, but I'd already begun liking this group, and hoped I could continue playing whenever they needed a fifth.

Clancy moved from George and Gus to the card table throughout the evening. I couldn't help but think that I'd been neglecting my precious dog and vowed to remedy that situation as soon as I could.

The group had a lot more energy than I, and we played until nearly 11. I yawned as we played but no one seemed to notice. They were enjoying themselves too much. I knew I had to get up really early for work—that is, I would if George let me go. I hadn't had the Clinic cancel my patients for the rest of the week, and was anxious to work instead of sitting around being scared.

After our good-byes, George and I walked hand in hand across the courtyard, with Clancy close by on my free side. George had made me lock the door, but evidently the kids hadn't locked it when they left, so it was unlocked yet again.

George was not pleased.

"Damn it. What is it with your family and locking doors?"

I couldn't help but smile. George was indeed a fierce protector. I touched his arm, he turned around, and I kissed him.

"I'm sorry. I guess we're incorrigible," I whispered as I stood on tiptoe to kiss him again.

As usual the kiss was exquisite and my body tingled from head to toe. As we finished we heard a smattering of applause from Georgianne's back porch where she and her sister were standing. I laughed and curtseyed. George stood there with a grin on his face. I waved goodnight to them and we went inside my cozy haven.

George quickly searched through the whole place, which only took a minute. At that point I was glad of the carriage house's coziness.

Sarah was at work, I assumed with Jimmy at her side, and Adam still wasn't home. Of course, he and Rob probably hadn't gone out until ten or so. I imagined George and I would have a few hours of privacy left.

I told Clancy I was sorry and that I loved her as I turned on Animal Planet. She lay on the couch, watching the mating dance of the mongoose. George had already gone into my bedroom and when I got there I heard him singing in the shower. "I guess this is my new normal," I said to myself as I dropped my clothes and joined him.

FOURTEEN

I'd set my alarm for 6 and let out a cuss word when it went off. Normally I'm a morning person, but I'd had a late night. I jumped up and took a quick shower, dressing in the bathroom so I wouldn't wake George. He looked so young lying there, without worry lines crossing his face. I felt bad that I caused much of his worries. Clancy lay next to him. That was her usual routine. She stayed in bed until I was ready to go to work, then she went outside to take care of business. After that, since she's been working with me as a therapy dog, she just jumps into the car and goes to the office with me, or we walk to work together.

I knew I couldn't leave without letting George know. That would cause him undue stress. So I leaned over and kissed him. He awoke smiling, but frowned when he saw I was dressed. "Where do you think you're going?"

"George, I have to go to work. I've already called in for two days. I need to get back there. I haven't been employed long enough to have vacation or sick time."

"You're not going. Period."

"Uh, yeah. You're going to have to learn that doesn't work with me."

"Damn it, Sam."

I felt sorry for him so I gave a little. "You can come to work with me, but you can't stay in the room when I have a client. What they tell me is confidential."

"I can wait right outside the door."

He knew where my office was. When my boss was murdered some months back, George had interviewed me. That was when I was still calling him Butthead instead of George.

"Well then you better hurry up and get ready. I want to stop and get bagels for my co-workers before I go to work."

He did hurry. I took Clancy outside while George was finishing up. When George came out, I already had my car going, with Clancy in the back seat.

"Hmm, guess we're taking your car today, huh?"

"Get in and I'll explain." He did, and then I did. "I love the fact you are so protective, even when I'm not in trouble. It's been many years since I've had someone take care of me and make me feel safe. Maybe it's actually the first time it's happened since I've been an adult." I looked over before I started backing out into the alley. George looked pensive, but not unhappy. "But sometimes I have to assert my independence. I've been on my own a while. Even when I was married I felt like I was on my own. I get… I don't know… I get itchy when I feel confined."

That's when he got mad.

"You feel confined because I like to take care of you? You feel confined because I love you?"

I pulled the car over immediately and put it in park. "George, that's not what I meant at all. Omigod, I adore being loved by you. I feel safe. I feel happy. You are a tremendous man and I'm thrilled we're together. I feel like the luckiest woman in the world." That, at least, got rid of his frown, and what I'd said was true.

"But," he said, "you feel confined or trapped or what?"

"Definitely not trapped, George. Definitely not trapped. Perhaps 'confined' was the wrong word. I just need to be in control of my own life at times. And this horrible murderer has impacted my life in ways I don't like. The only good thing is that I get to spend so much time with you. I love that."

I guessed I must have explained myself better that time, because George put his arm around me as I drove, easy enough to do in my small Bug.

"Damn, woman, you drive me crazy," he said softly. Then he added, "I love you."

I parked illegally at the Bread Company. It's great to have a cop with you. He wouldn't stay in the car though, insisting he wasn't going to leave me alone. We walked in, and I must have strutted a bit. People looked at us, and several smiled and said hello. This was my breakfast hangout when I ate alone and the regulars had never seen me with a man. The Dairy was the Darling family breakfast place but the Bread Company was where I went to read or check Facebook over my coffee and bagel.

Ron greeted me and asked if I wanted my usual mug of coffee and whole grain bagel. I said, "Nope, can't stay today. I want a baker's dozen of assorted bagels." He grinned and kept glancing at George. I finally introduced them, but ended up just saying, "This is my friend, George."

I mentally berated myself before the sentence was even completed. George was much more than my friend, but I didn't know how he felt being called a boyfriend when he was technically on duty. Hell, I didn't know how I even felt about it. Boyfriend was such an odd word to call a 43-year-old man.

"Friend, huh?" As we walked out, I could tell he was teasing me.

I told him of my dilemma.

He said that it was no big deal. I was happy to be able to relax on that score.

We arrived at work a few minutes before I was due to be there, and Clancy jumped out of the Bug, eager to get to work. No leash needed here. She loved her job.

As we walked through the front door I introduced George to Clara Schmidt, the Clinic's receptionist. He explained to her what was going on and that he'd be there all day. She said she'd inform our personnel director, and in fact acted as if this were an everyday occurrence—a cop in the waiting room.

The personnel director was acting as an operations director. Ever since my boss was murdered, the Clinic had been a little disorganized.

I reminded George that there was another entrance to my office in addition to the one near the reception area. Since my office had been the butler's pantry when the clinic was a private residence, I also had a door to the kitchen. That one I used frequently, utilizing my seemingly bottomless coffee cup and trying to fulfill my endless search for snacks. I left Clancy in my office, walked George into the kitchen, and began to set up the bagels and cream cheese.

"Why did you bring bagels?" George asked as he got coffee for both of us.

"I dunno. We're usually pretty busy here, and every now and then someone brings in treats. It's kind of a way to bond with each other, even though we seldom talk."

"Nice," he said.

"When I don't have a patient you can stay in here with me," I told him as we returned to my office. "You'll be much more comfortable in the love seat or the big chair." Plus, it would be nice for me to have him there.

As had been the case recently, my eight o'clock had cancelled. So I told George he was welcome to use my space as his office until 9.

Meanwhile I went back to the kitchen and got bagels and cream cheese for both of us. When I returned to my office I saw that George was sitting in the overstuffed chair near the small fireplace, and was getting out his phone. Clancy curled up around his feet. I liked the look of that.

"I'm going to call the station," he said. "Want to see if the autopsy results are in yet."

I was good at tuning out other people's voices, being the oldest of six. That was the only way I could ever do homework or read a book. I'd just use other people's voices as background noise while I worked or read. But this was different. Today I wanted to hear what George said.

"Yeah," he said to me when he disconnected from the call. "It was a suicide. Forensics found the powder burns on his hand, and the autopsy investigation revealed that the weapon had to have been placed on the victim's temple. They are about ninety-five percent sure it was a suicide."

"That's all? Ninety-five percent?"

"Well, without a suicide note, or other evidence, it's virtually impossible to be one hundred percent sure. I mean someone could have put the guy's hand on the gun, pulled the trigger, and we might never know. Maybe we'll find more evidence when we figure out who he was." He paused and then added, "There's more, Sam."

I felt a sudden worry and then nodded for him to continue.

"He was full of cancer. The coroner said that the guy would've died in a matter of days."

"That's interesting," I said. "And a not uncommon reason for suicide." I booted up my computer while continuing the conversation, "What are the chances you'll find out his identity?"

"Pretty good actually. Most people aren't completely off-grid. They leave traces of their existence throughout their lives. Especially if they've ever been arrested or been to the dentist. We'll find out who this guy is. And hopefully we'll find out if he's the killer… and then why he did what he did."

The hour passed quickly, George on the phone or his laptop and me finishing up some paperwork, the bane of my existence.

It wasn't long until Clara announced via my phone intercom, "Your nine o'clock is here, Sam."

I thanked her and asked George if he would exit by the kitchen door, so he didn't see my client, just in case they knew each other. He complied, but kissed me before he left.

"Don't do anything stupid," were the words he left me with.

I opened the door to the waiting room and welcomed

Hazel Abernathy, a seventy-something-year-old woman with an incredibly vivid erotic dream life. And that's all she wanted to talk about. Because she paid cash, I had no requirements to meet from the Department of Mental Health, Medicaid, Medicare, or any insurance company. Even though, as a psychotherapist, I felt obligated to try to help anyone who walked through my door, Hazel insisted she had no problems other than wanting to talk about her dreams. So I let her.

A few months ago I had made the gentle suggestion that she might want to write them down and try to make a book out of them, and Hazel responded with enthusiasm. I wasn't sure these were all dreams, and thought some of them might be fantasy musings of an active, but bored, mind. She insisted they were dreams, so that's what I called them.

Romantic novels weren't my interest; I much preferred mysteries, suspense, thrillers, and sci-fi. However, I had done some research to be able to help her with what she wanted to do. I'd given Hazel an "outline" of an erotic romance and suggested she think about putting her dreams into that format. My sister-in-law loved what she called "housewife porn," and I had gotten some ideas from her. Of course I didn't tell her why I was interested.

Today Hazel was beaming as she greeted me.

"Samantha, I've found a publisher! It was much easier than I thought it would be." I'd never seen her so happy.

"Big Butt Publishing wants my first manuscript, and they gave me a contract for it and the others. Thanks to you, I'm going to be a published author."

I'd never really heard of Big Butt Publishing, but the name itself gave me pause. "Hazel, that's great. But your dreams are erotica and not porn. That publishing company sounds like it publishes pornography."

"What? Do you think that's what they're looking for? My dreams are not porn." Her mouth drew down and she looked like she was going to cry. "They are beautiful, sensuous expressions of love and romance. I was a bit surprised at the name of the company, but thought I was just being a prude."

"A prude is never what I'd call you, Hazel." Worried, I continued with, "Have you signed the contract yet?"

"No. I have it with me and am going to see my lawyer after our appointment."

"Great. Please make sure he checks on the company too, and not just the contract."

"If you insist I do that, then I shall." She then went on to talk about her recent dreams, and I listened with my usual amazement at her imagination… or subconscious.

When her time was up, I looked in the kitchen to find George. I pulled him into my office, with the doors closed, and kissed him with a fiery intensity that surprised him.

I disengaged reluctantly. "Sorry, George. I just heard

some things that made me think of you." Clancy just lay on her pillow, watching, and I thought she was probably judging us.

"No need to apologize," George said. "I could take more of that." He moved closer to me but I put up my hand in the universal sign for "stop."

I said, "I'd love to, but I only have one minute before my next appointment. And since there's nowhere to take a cold shower here I think it's wisest if I keep a little distance between us."

"Okay, if you have to."

The rest of the day was pretty uneventful except for my lunch hour, where I apologetically told Clancy she needed to stay in my office and George and I went out to lunch, a first for us on a weekday.

"I love this," I said to George over a huge grilled cheese sandwich, "but I do feel guilty about Clancy."

"I have an idea," he said, and ordered a hamburger plain, with no bun.

When we got back to the clinic, George gave Clancy the hamburger as an "I'm sorry" gift, and when she'd finished inhaling it, he took her outside for a short walk while I prepared for my next patient.

At 5, I quickly finished up my progress notes, and we headed out. Clancy hadn't had much work to do today as a therapy dog. Hazel petted her when Clancy greeted her upon her arrival, but then was so caught up in her dreams that Clancy got to sleep through the session. I had met with two children during the afternoon, so Clancy did get a workout then. She showed her sensitivity when one of the children began sobbing during the session. Clancy climbed up on the love seat the girl was sitting on, and gently laid her head on the girl's lap.

That was one of Clancy's major strengths—empathy. She had an innate sense of when people needed her. On her first day at work, without warning, she had jumped up on a man's lap—a hard thing to do when a dog is her size. But she did it, and the man began crying as he hugged and petted Clancy. She knew he was sad before I did. She was an amazing addition to my practice. I was glad she worked with me, and not only because I loved being with her. It also made leaving her at other times less difficult for me.

Like tonight.

FIFTEEN

As we walked out of the back door of the clinic to my car, George asked, "What shall we do for dinner tonight?"

"Well, I have a final meeting with the committee before our reunion this weekend. I guess you get to be on the committee too since you won't let me go alone." I laughed at this, because George hated meetings. Said he had enough of them on his job.

"What time is the meeting?"

"It's at 6:30 and we'll have dinner there."

"Where's there?"

"We've been meeting at Little Sprout's." Little Sprout was another mainstay of Quincy. Located on North 12th, it was a place my parents used to take us on the rare occasions we could afford to eat out as a family. Dad had been friends with the original owner, and I think Little Sprout (the owner's nickname) might have given Dad a discount because of the six kids.

I turned to George. "How about the two of us visiting

Richie before the meeting? We can drop off Clancy and then go right away." Turning back to Clancy I said, "I know you won't mind, girl. You are always tired after working all day." I smiled as I said it, because she was funny. She came home after work and collapsed, just like I had always done pre-George.

Since George agreed with my suggestion, we dropped off Clancy at my locked house, and only 10 minutes later we were at the hospital. We went into the room Richie was supposed to have been in, but it was empty.

"Omigod, George, he died."

"Don't go jumping to conclusions," he said. "I'll check."

I followed him as he went to the nurse's station, flashed his badge, and was told that Richie had taken off AMA.

"Against medical advice? Why would he do that?" I asked George.

He shrugged his shoulders at me and continued with the nurse, "Was there something that happened to cause him to leave so suddenly?"

"I don't know," she replied, clearly preoccupied with what she was doing. "Sorry."

"Where are the police that were guarding him? Why wasn't I notified?" George was clearly frustrated.

She mimicked George's shoulder shrug, and went back to work.

"I don't get it," I said to George. "One minute he's in

the bed and the next minute he's gone. Do you think he's safe?"

"My gut feeling is that the suicide was the murderer. So, yes, I think Richie is safe in that respect. But medically, I don't know."

I was worried about Richie, but there was something else niggling at my brain. There was something peculiar going on. Something I couldn't articulate yet. My vibes had been causing my stomach to rebel ever since I had touched Richie's empty bed, and the vibes continued to intensify. That must mean the murderer had been here. And maybe he'd been here when Richie was still there. Maybe he took Richie with him. Or maybe, like us, he came in too late. I was just sure he'd been there. My vibes didn't lie. Well, they were wrong sometimes, but not this time. I was sure of it.

George called the station. When he finished the short conversation he turned to me.

"There was only one cop on duty at the time—Jimmy Mansfield. He reported that Richie signed himself out, and refused police protection, so Jimmy returned to the station."

"I don't get it," I said.

"Yeah, me either."

"Should you leave me and go check on him?" I was trying to be generous, but I really didn't want George to leave me.

"Nah. Captain's going to ask someone else to check on Richie. I'm okay."

Since I couldn't think of anything else I wanted to say, I was uncharacteristically quiet during the drive to Little Sprout's. As usual, the parking lot was full, but we were able to jump in a spot vacated by an early eater. The committee had a small room reserved for our dinner meeting, and George was greeted enthusiastically. I wanted to say, "Hey, I'm here too," but I was afraid it would come off as bitchy instead of just sarcastic.

We seemed to have been the last to arrive, and George went around the table, alternating shaking hands and hugging people. He had been popular in high school and was even more so now. I was popular by association. Since I dated him back in school I had been invited to all the parties and activities. Even now, people always acted as if they liked me. But my self-image didn't always buy it.

The chair of the reunion committee was Cal, officially Calvin Joseph Wade, George's best friend in elementary and high school. Another guy from the neighborhood. He was involved in George not picking me up on prom night. Although I had totally forgiven George a few months ago, I still hadn't gotten there with Cal.

If grudge-holding were an Olympic event, I'd be the record holder. One of my many faults.

Next to Cal was Marilyn Driscoll. She was legally blind but could see shapes and some facial features. Plus of course she would have recognized our voices, and she exclaimed her delight at George's presence. Her husband Frank sat next to her. He had gone to Gem City High School, the public high school in town. Despite the fierce rivalry between GCHS and St. Francis High School, the classes mingled a lot for social activities. Frank came to the meetings because he drove his wife, but he was also a contributor of ideas. The one thing that bothered me just a tiny little bit was that he always wore his GCHS letterman's jacket, now 25 years old. I didn't know his motive, and should have asked. The blue and white jacket had a brighter shade of blue than the blue and gold of our SFHS colors.

"That's it," I shrieked, pointing at Frank. He had just sat down again after shaking hands with George, but jumped up as if someone had shot him.

"What's it?" he yelled back at me.

"The color. The color on your jacket. It's the same color as the murderer."

Now it was Frank's turn to yell. "What in the hell are you talking about?"

I turned to George, who had been greeting Gloria Rosenthal and William "Stretch" Smith on the other side of the table. "George," I yelled.

"I heard you," he said. "People all over town heard you, honey." His rebuke was softened by the endearment, yet I still felt a sting.

He excused us and pulled me out of the room. "You've

got to learn how to control your impulses. You do have great investigative instincts with an ability to put differing ideas together, but you have a hard time waiting when it comes to information."

He had his hands on my shoulders and looked me in the eyes. I felt like I'd been reprimanded by a teacher in grade school. Hell, in high school and college too. Even though I felt hurt, I knew he was right. So I said it.

"Even though my feelings are hurt, I know you're right. Can we talk more about my faults later?" I asked the question sincerely.

"Sure. Right now I want to ask you a few questions about the case, and then we're going inside for the meeting. Okay?" He continued to make intense eye contact.

I nodded.

"Okay," he said as he let go of my shoulders and seemed to relax. "I think you made a really good point about the colors being the same. However, if you remember, neither hoodie had any insignia on it."

"Yeah, but it was the same color. That color blue is an exact color, not just close. I wonder if it means anything. Maybe it had something to do with the rivalry between schools. It's a stretch, but not beyond possibility." I looked up at him.

I could see he thought it was a stretch too, but he didn't deny it was a possibility.

"Here's my next question," he said very slowly. "Do you think at our age you can learn to not blurt things out inappropriately?"

I almost yelled at him, but stopped myself. "I don't think you realize how many times I have held my tongue. Ever since I saw you again when I moved back to town. Plus, as a therapist, I'm great at not always saying what I'm thinking. But sometimes I just can't seem to help myself when I'm not at work." Before he could say anything, I added, "I promise I'll look at this flaw and see if I can change. I'll do my best."

George didn't say anything, but put his arms around me and hugged me, making things feel right again. I worried as we started to go back to the room that our friends would think I'd been reprimanded. But George did just what I would want a boyfriend to do. He walked in holding my hand and smiling at me. Then he won my heart all over again.

"Sorry for the interruption. Sam is so helpful in solving crimes and sometimes her ideas just flow out of her. So let's get back to the task at hand."

I sighed and smiled at the man I loved.

He finished saying hello to everyone by speaking to Vic Carruthers and Cynthia Wayne Carruthers, a couple who married on graduation day, so they had recently celebrated their 25th anniversary.

I chose a seat by Cindy. I didn't have many close friends because of having my sibs as my best friends growing up, and of course always having George. There were also several cousins my age whom I hung around with. However, Cindy was an exception. She'd been my best friend of all our schoolmates. She'd had other friends, of course. I think I was the only one who had friends by association. But Cindy liked me for me, and I had never forgotten that.

We hadn't seen each other often over the intervening years, but we did swap Christmas cards. It was only after I moved back to Quincy and we ended up on the reunion committee together a few months ago that we had reconnected.

She was the only one in the group who knew how serious my relationship with George had become. The others knew we were dating; how could I not tell everyone? But I'd held back enough that they didn't know I was hopelessly in love.

Cal opened the meeting and each of us reported on our assignments. We went around the table until all the details had been covered.

"Sounds like everything is all set," Cal said. "Let's make sure we arrive early on Friday at the Boat Club, and on Saturday at the Boat Dock. Anything else?"

There was nothing else, so the meeting ended. George and I were invited to stay for a beer with some of the gang, but we both declined, knowing that there was a possibility that my life still might be in danger.

How casually I let that thought come and go, as if it were an everyday occurrence. "My life might still be in danger" was thought of as easily as "I should let Clancy out." Yet I felt protected. How fortunate for me that I was dating a police detective.

George opened my car door and didn't make a crack about me driving. Smart man.

It was hard for me to drive because I kept thinking about the blue in Frank Driscoll's jacket.

"That color has to mean something, George. It just has to."

"I think it's an interesting addition to the info we've gathered, but it doesn't have to mean anything. We're constantly getting information that looks important on the surface, but we have to sift through it all and see what's really important versus what is irrelevant. It takes a lot of time and effort to do that. A lot of detective work."

"I know. I know. But sometimes my vibes let me cut through the bull and get right to the answer."

"Yes," George said, "I'm sure that's true. But I can't just go on your vibes. I can't arrest people on your vibes. I can't chase people on your vibes. The only thing I can do is figure out an excuse to interview people you think are guilty. And I do that without complaining."

"Too much. Without complaining too much," I had to add.

Ignoring my comment George said, "So what are your vibes telling you now?"

"Well, there's something about that color blue. I don't know if it has to do with the high school or not. I just know that the color on the hooded sweatshirts is really important."

"I'm sorry, Sam, but that's pretty obvious. The killer wore it, put it on Richie when he was stabbed, and had it on himself when he committed suicide."

"At least we hope the killer committed suicide." The first time I'd ever hoped someone had killed themselves. It didn't sit right with me as a therapist, but it was an honest feeling.

It was time. I had to tell him.

"When we were at the hospital, my vibes went into overdrive when I touched Richie's bed. The killer had to have been there with him at some point. I mean, obviously before he committed suicide, I guess." I waited for his snort of derision, but there was none. He was quiet and looked thoughtful.

"And, George, I haven't told you this before, but when Richie handed me that first picture my vibes really started bothering me. There was something about that picture… I really wish I could see it again."

"Maybe you will."

I wish he hadn't said that.

SIXTEEN

The next day was both the Fourth of July and my birthday, a combination I had endured all my life. We needed to get some sleep. George had promised me that we'd be staying up late tomorrow night. I didn't know what he had planned, but smiled as I dropped George at his house with the promise that I'd still be careful.

"Yes, I'll lock the door. Yes, I'll check in the backseat of my car. Yes, I'll call you if I have to leave, and you can go with me."

"Wait a minute," he said. "Let me follow you home and make sure you get inside. I'll feel better."

I didn't argue. And waited while he went into his garage. After the weird episode on my walk, I would do everything I could do to keep safe. I was really glad to be out of protective custody. I didn't really know why George wasn't arguing that point, but I didn't want to ask, afraid he'd change his mind.

It was just a moment before his headlights blinked behind my car, letting me know I could go.

We talked on the phone while we drove. Both of us had hands free set-ups so we were within the law. It felt funny because we'd been together for the last several nights, but we both knew that we needed to get back to normal as soon as we could. Plus, with my kids at home, I didn't want George and me to be practically living together.

In a few minutes we were there. He and I got out of the car at the same time. We kissed good night.

"Make sure you don't let anyone else in the house. Don't go out without telling me. Understand?"

"Yes, sir. I'll be good."

He didn't leave until he saw me unlock my door and step inside.

When I walked into my home there was Jimmy Mansfield sitting on my couch, petting Clancy. My first reaction was panic.

"Where are they? Are they okay? Why are you here?" My questions peppered the poor guy so much that he put his arms up in self-defense.

"Sam. Sam. Sam," was all he said until I shut up. Then he quickly said, "They're okay. I'm not here as a cop."

"Then what are you doing here?"

"Well,…"

He was rescued by my daughter Sarah, who walked into the room at that point.

"Mom, leave him alone." She turned to Jimmy and said,

"I'm so sorry. My mother can be rather overzealous when it comes to my brother and me."

Turning back to me she said, "Mom, Jimmy and I are going out tonight. I don't have to work."

"Oh… oh." I was grateful Sarah was okay, but felt stupid at my impulsive behavior. So I added, "Have fun."

"Where's Adam?" I asked.

"I think he's upstairs taking a nap," she responded with a shrug. "He talked about going out with his friends again tonight. Including Uncle Rob."

So both my kids are hanging out with the guys who were their bodyguards last night. Interesting.

I excused myself and took Clancy outside, thinking about one of my many faults. George was probably right. I was turning 43 tomorrow, and it was definitely time to grow up in a few areas. In elementary school I had always gotten in trouble for talking. I was thrown off the cheerleading squad in 8th grade at St. Francis Elementary School for "talking in line repeatedly." And I was given an F in Conduct that same year for my comment to Sister Margaret when I said, "Pipe down, Maggie." So when people talk about my impulsivity, they aren't telling me something I don't already know. And I'm much too old for it to be charming.

I knew I needed to think things out much more carefully than I had been. And that included my life with George.

"C'mon, Clancy, let's go to bed," I said as she finished her business. We walked back into the house and I noticed that Sarah and Jimmy were sitting rather close on the couch. Deciding to mind my own business for once in my life, I said goodnight to them and took Clancy with me into my room.

"Maybe I need to get some therapy myself," I whispered to my best friend as I crawled into bed.

She didn't say anything, because she was already snoring.

I snuggled up to Clancy until her snoring started bothering me, and I turned to my other side. It did feel good though to have her in the bed. It helped me not miss George so much.

"Maybe I do need to talk to someone," I whispered again before I fell asleep.

I sat up abruptly as I awoke to noises that scared the hell out of me—banging, horns blowing, yelling. At the foot of my bed stood Adam, Sarah, and George, each making obnoxious noises of some kind. Adam held two saucepan lids, Sarah had a whistle, and George blew on a birthday horn.

I blinked and smiled and groaned when I realized what was going on. I was definitely glad I had a T-shirt on. Sarah led in the singing with her usual exuberance, and even dour Adam was grinning.

I also noticed that Clancy was with them. Normally she

wouldn't enjoy the noise, but she was smiling. My surprise was keeping me quiet.

Finally George said, "Happy birthday, honey. Welcome to my age." He leaned over and gave me a kiss on the cheek. He was quickly followed by Adam and then Sarah. Sarah excused herself and left my bedroom.

Soon we heard her voice saying, "It's ready. Come in."

I expected some coffee and toast, which is what the kids had always made for my breakfast in bed ever since they were little. After asking Adam and George to leave so I could put on some sweats, I looked around for some clean ones. Failing that, I put on some dirty sweats, anchored a bra in place, and kept on my oversized T-shirt.

Stumbling out of my bedroom I noticed it was dark in the kitchen. Too tired to care, I kept walking. Of course I noticed something was up. But when I got to my living room and still didn't see anyone, I got suspicious. I looked around, which didn't take long, and then went upstairs to look at Sarah and Adam's bedrooms. Even Clancy was gone.

Finally I opened the door and walked outside. What I saw startled me and once again I couldn't talk. There stood George, Sarah, Adam, and all of my sibs and most of their spouses. Everyone was raising a glass of something or other. I couldn't tell if it was orange juice or champagne.

"You guys," was all I said when I could finally talk. My eyes were filled with happy tears, but all at once I remembered what I looked like, and shrieked. "Yikes!"

"I told you, Sam," said George, "no one says 'Yikes' anymore."

"She does," said Adam. I smiled at him sticking up for his old mom. At the same time I tried to cover myself with my hands, even though I was already covered by raggedy clothes.

Since they were all relatives, except for George, I relaxed and just let it go. George had seen me at my worst and at my best, and still said he loved me.

"So what's this? Whose idea was it? Don't you all have to be at work? Why is it so dark? Where's breakfast?"

George looked into Adam's dark eyes for sympathy, "Was she always like this, with the questions one after another."

"I'm afraid so." Then Adam addressed me, "Mom, we wanted to have a birthday party for you. It's the Fourth of July and no one has to work. Thought you'd remember that. Anyway, we couldn't get everyone together easily, so this was our compromise. We knew you didn't have to work today, so George took a day off too—"

"And then," Sarah continued, "we decided to have a breakfast party. Everyone was able to clear an hour or so early in the morning before the holiday got into full swing, so that's what we did."

"Thank you," I said as I hugged all three of them and

made my way down the line of all the rest of my family. Jenny first, the only sib shorter than I was. Her dark blonde hair was natural, unlike mine. Her husband Manh was on duty at the hospital and couldn't be there, she said, but sent his well wishes.

Ed and Angie were next. I wondered if we always stood in birth order without thinking, or if this was something they had planned. He was tall and slender, an anomaly, but did have the tow-colored hair and blue eyes that were the norm. Pete was another anomaly. One because he was even taller than Ed and two because he was a priest. Not much celibacy going around our family. Everyone had kids except Pete and Rob, who wasn't married yet. Jill had her usual blonde pony tail. She and her husband Ben stood holding hands, which made me smile. Rob was the only one with a hint of red in his hair.

I must have been in shock because I hadn't noticed my nieces and nephews moving about—Rosie and Annie, Jack and Marty, Alice, Susan, John, Robert, and Skeeter.

I was attacked with hugs and cries of "Happy Birthday, Aunt Sam!" Smiling was the only thing I could do, except hug back.

Robert had on a blue GCHS sweatshirt. I remarked on it. He reminded me that he went there instead of St. Francis High because of a special program they had for students who were bright but had a learning disability. I told him I'd want to talk to him a little later, because he was the only one in the family who went there.

In the meantime, George took my arm and escorted me toward Gus and Georgianne's. I dutifully went up the back stairs with him, followed closely by Clancy, but George wouldn't answer any of my questions about why we were there.

As he opened the screen door I smelled some lovely food. Both Georgianne and Gus had on aprons and we followed them as they carried food from the kitchen, past the breakfast room/butler's pantry, and into the formal dining room. Of course. My house couldn't hold everyone so George and the kids had to be resourceful and make other arrangements.

I stopped Gus before he went back into the kitchen.

"Gus, this is so sweet. Thank you."

"I would have been mad to have been left out. You getting me involved in your shenanigans has made a new man of me. So it's I who should thank you."

I hugged him and then approached Georgianne.

"Thanks, Georgianne. I appreciate this so much."

"Nonsense, Samantha. I'm pleased we could be in on the surprise." Then she hugged me, which upped the quality of surprise exponentially.

There weren't enough chairs for everyone, but Gus spread tablecloths on the floor and the next generation ate there, even the ones in college. Clancy sat with them, saliva dripping from her mouth. But she didn't dare to take anything without permission.

Then Georgianne put some scrambled eggs in a small bowl, put it on the floor, and in a voice others used for talking to infants, said, "Here, you sweet little poochy-woochy."

And Clancy did what Clancy always does, she showed Georgianne how much she loved her by rolling over on her back so her belly could be rubbed. Even before eating the eggs. These two had developed a very close relationship since Clancy and I had moved into the carriage house. In the beginning I hated it because of my intense dislike of Georgianne. Then I began to tolerate it. Now I loved it. My feelings about their relationship echoed the way my feelings about Georgianne had changed.

Even before I cleaned my plate, I sat back and surveyed the room. I thought that I must be the luckiest gal alive. The man I loved was sitting next to me. My two kids were there. All my sibs and most of the in-laws. And tons of nieces and nephews.

As I thought about them, my eye was caught again by Robert's blue Gem City High School sweatshirt. I also saw his plate was about empty, and quickly finished my breakfast.

"Robert, can we talk for a minute?" I asked, as I pulled

his chair back from the table.

"Yeah, but I was gonna get more of…", he tried to talk but I cut him off.

"You can get more in a minute. This is important."

"Yeah, but…"

"Okay, okay," I said, but grudgingly. "Hurry up, hon. I *really* want to talk to you."

The strange look he gave me didn't cause me any trouble. I was used to it. My nieces and nephews loved me, but I was an oddity among a group of people who were not a traditional family anyway. Jenny and I had raised the smaller sibs after our parents died, so I was kind of a grandma figure to some of the younger nieces and nephews. Robert was one of the older kids, so he saw me as an aunt, and not a grandma.

Everyone knew that patience was not a virtue I possessed. So I grumbled, shuffled my feet, came off like I had restless leg syndrome, and in general was insufferable. My vibes were making me uncomfortable. I just knew that the unusual blue color was a major clue in the mystery.

"Sam, what's the matter?" asked George. "This is a party. Why are you so antsy?"

"I have an idea about the murder. I *have* to talk to Robert, but he keeps wanting to eat."

"Come here," he said as he stood. He put an arm around me and smiled, so it was hard for me to be mad, but I knew he was going to yell at me. In a nice way of course. After all, he was George.

"Stop it," was all he said, as we stood alone in the kitchen.

After that, it was easy for me to be mad.

"What in the world are you talking about?" I almost yelled.

"Shh. There's no need to upset the others." His head moved almost imperceptibly in the direction of the dining room.

"George, you're shushing me. You're actually shushing me!" George had always been so kind and understanding, and seemed to even like my idiosyncrasies. I guess he'd had his fill.

"You're going to break up with me, aren't you?" I continued with a whiny voice even I didn't recognize.

"Of course not. Why do you think that every time we have a disagreement I'm going to break up with you?"

"It's a long story, but my ex-husband threw it up to me every time we got in an argument. He always threatened to leave. Maybe I'm not over that yet."

George took my hands as he said, "I'm not him."

"I know," I said as I started to lean into him.

"Don't try to change the subject, and don't try to hug me out of talking to you about your behavior."

I was silent.

George continued, "You sat there like a little kid. At least you didn't make faces, but it was obvious you were impatient. We all put a lot of effort into making your birthday special, and I'd appreciate it if you acted your age."

"You're right." And then at George's request, I repeated it. "You're right," I said again.

Inside I felt turmoil. I recognized he was 100% right. Normally my sibs would tease me out of my moods. But it seems they were letting George deal with me assertively, instead of the passive-aggressive family way using sarcasm. I made another silent promise to myself to improve. And said to myself yet again, *Maybe I should talk to someone about this.* It was almost a "physician heal thyself" moment.

I tuned back into George just as he was ending his message with, "… I love you, Sam."

What a great thing to hear after berating myself, and being corrected by George.

"I love you, too."

By the time we walked back into the dining room, Robert was finished eating, and was exhibiting my previous behaviors as he waited. I felt relieved that I wasn't the only one who couldn't wait.

I walked up to him and asked appropriately and maturely, "Are you done, hon?"

He said yes, so I asked him to walk into the kitchen with me.

I started with asking him how school was going for him.

He said that since he started on his ADHD medicine, he was having an easier time of it.

After my aunt duties were satisfied, I told him about the murders and how the murderer had worn the same color of hoodie, but without the GCHS logo.

"Do you have any notions of how they could be connected?" I asked him.

"Well, there's a huge rivalry between GC and St. Francis. I know my family at St. Francis feel that way, but at Gem City there's even more. It's like animosity. Hatred. I don't know why, except a lot of times St. Francis beats GC in sports and St. Francis is a lot smaller." He paused for a deep breath. "Have you checked to see if the victims were from the same school?"

"No, I haven't. And that's an excellent idea. Thanks." I hugged Robert as I thanked him. And like a typical teenage male he half-heartedly hugged me back.

I couldn't wait to tell George this idea, but as soon as I returned to the table and sat, Gus went into the kitchen and returned with a cake. There were so many candles that there was a danger of the smoke alarm going off.

After they sang happy birthday to me, and before I blew out the candles, I said, "I'm so grateful for all of you in my life." I couldn't say any more because of the lump in my throat. I made a wish and blew out the candles.

When I was able to talk again I said, "Six months ago, you guys surprised me in the ER, congratulating me on my new job after my return to Quincy. Today you did it again. I loved it! But I promise that I won't fall prey to this one more time. I'll be on the lookout from now on."

People smiled and chatted, some of them loudly. As I looked around the table, and around the blanket on the floor, I knew I was absolutely blessed. What a crew! And they loved me.

As soon as the cake was eaten, some people had to go to work. A lot of us didn't have traditional jobs with regular holidays off. Others stayed, along with the kids, and gave me presents. Tears again on my part.

Each gift was thoughtfully purchased or made and showed how well people knew me. Gus and Georgianne gave me gourmet coffees from around the world. Generous and appreciated. Jenny and Manh had bought an SFU hoodie, in brown and white, along with a baseball cap in the same colors. Pete and Rob joined forces to give me gifts for Clancy—a pink blanket with paw prints on it, and a new leash and collar in bright pink. I sure wouldn't miss her in the snow with those on. Ed and Angie went in with Jill and Ben to get me gift certificates to the Dairy and the Rectory.

The kids made me drawings, which warmed my heart. Some of them were quite sophisticated in their technique.

Soon, the gathering broke up. I thanked everyone, and

George, my kids, and I went back to my house. As we placed my gifts on the dining room table, I was struck by the brown hoodie I'd been given. What was it about the blue hoodie in the murders? I couldn't let it go.

"George, Robert gave me an idea. Why don't we check to see if all the victims went to the same school? That might give us more info about why the person used the blue hoodie."

"Yeah, good idea," he said, but seemed to have his mind elsewhere.

"What are you thinking about?"

"Us. Well, us and what a great family you have."

"Thanks." I went to give him a hug.

"I love you, Sam."

"I love you, too." But I was beginning to get worried because of the tone of his voice.

By then Adam and Sarah knew they needed to vanish. So they did, and they took Clancy upstairs with them.

George took a step back and took my hands before he spoke.

"I don't know if I can do this anymore."

SEVENTEEN

For a moment I was too stunned to say anything.

"Get out," were the first words out of my mouth.

"But you don't even know what I—"

"Please leave."

He waited a beat, and the look on his face showed both anger and hurt. As George opened the door to leave, he said, "You really need to work on that."

I ran to my bedroom, threw myself on the bed and began crying. He was going to break up with me. Despite what he had said earlier. I was sure of it.

Or was he? For a moment I feared I had done something terrible. Caused him to walk out when he just wanted to talk to me.

The tears came hotter and faster.

What in the hell is wrong with me that I would sabotage the best relationship I ever had? Now I would never know if I had ended it with my own stupid temper.

I heard a noise and turned over. George hadn't left after all. He'd returned and just stood in the doorway. It was now or never for me. I rolled off the bed, and stood at a respectful distance from George.

"You probably shouldn't forgive me. But I'm begging you to. I am so very sorry. I was stupid, impulsive, and immature. I don't know why. But I promise I'll get help…" Then I finished the thought, "… whether or not you stay with me."

"Sam, what I said a few minutes ago is still true." He held up his hand in the universal stop motion.

He'd done that before, when I'd just returned to Quincy and was involved in a murder investigation. At that time, it enraged me. Now, it was what I deserved. So I didn't interrupt him.

He seemed to relax and put his hand down.

"What I said before still holds true. I love you. I love you a lot." He ran his hand through his thinning hair. "But you drive me crazy."

He walked over, sat on the bed, and patted for me to sit as well.

"I do want you to get help. Your impulsiveness has gotten worse since we've been together." He covered my hand with his. "I hope it has nothing to do with me, but I suspect it might."

I wanted to talk but waited for a few seconds to make sure he was done.

"I don't know why I'm doing this. I know that it could

be sabotaging our relationship, and trust me, it's the last thing I want to do. You are the best guy I've ever known, and certainly the best guy I've ever dated."

He gave a rueful smile.

I continued, "And whether or not you stay with me, I promise I will see someone for therapy to figure this out."

"Stop it. Stop it now." He stood, and there was uncharacteristic anger in his voice, and his face was beet red as he said, "Every damn time there's a problem you think I'm going to leave you. Stop it. I AM NOT JOE! I'm not going to leave you. When I say I love you, I mean I love you. You. With every fault, with every good thing, with every laugh, with every tear, with every impulsive and stupid move. I love you."

By then I was bawling. I didn't deserve him. Even when he was saying that he'd never leave me, he was not a weakling. He was a man. A real man who knew what it took to make a relationship work.

"Why haven't you ever been married?" I said, changing the subject, and wiping the tears and snot off my face with a handkerchief George handed me. "I mean, I think you are the best catch there is. Why haven't you ever gotten married?"

"Guess I was waiting for you."

The answer thrilled me, but there had to be more than that.

"Have you ever been engaged?"

"Kind of. Not really. Well maybe. Yes."

Surprised, I said, "It doesn't sound definite."

"It was on my part, I thought. Not on hers. She wore my ring, but wasn't committed to the relationship. I don't really want to talk about it."

"Okay. Was it someone I knew? Was she pretty? How long ago was this? Do you still think about her?" I was breathless from my questioning.

Finally, George smiled. Then he laughed. "There's my Sam."

"We're going out," Sarah yelled from the other room.

"Clancy's going with us," was Adam's contribution. "So we'll all be… you know… out."

"For a while," Sarah said. I heard the leash being clipped to Clancy's collar and the door slam as they left together. I looked at the man I loved.

George grinned at me and then kissed me. And then we made up in the best way we knew how.

It wasn't even noon and it was already my favorite birthday ever.

Later, I stared at the ceiling and thought about how I had been acting. *I'll talk to Marian Dougherty in the morning.* Marian was also a therapist at the Quincy Community Clinic. I'd met her on my first day as she helped clear out the office where my boss had been murdered. *Yeah. She'll be good. I'll talk to her tomorrow.*

Then my mind went back to the argument with George. It came back to me that before I'd told him to leave, he'd said that he didn't know if he "could do this anymore."

He was dozing but I tapped him on the shoulder. More than once. Finally he opened his eyes, saw my face near his, and smiled. Then he must have noticed my quizzical look.

"What's the matter?" he asked.

"I'm not trying to start an argument, but I think we left something unfinished." I took my time so I didn't say anything stupid. "You said, 'I can't do this anymore,' while looking at me. What did you mean?" I was careful that my tone wasn't accusatory.

He hesitated, then said, "I don't think I'm ready to talk about it now. But just know it had nothing to do with breaking up with you." He took my chin in his hand, and gently kissed me.

"Okay. I trust you." I kissed him back. "And I want you to know I'm talking to a therapist tomorrow at work, and I'll set something up. Would you be willing to come in for a session sometime later?"

"Sure, but why?"

"Well, it's often helpful for a couple to meet with an objective third party to work out some kinks. It may not be necessary, but just in case it is, I'm glad you said yes."

I sat up, and started toward the shower. I'd been

surprised with my party this morning, and hadn't even brushed my teeth.

I turned around, and said, "It's tough when a therapist needs a therapist. But it happens all the time. We're human. However, it will be hard for me to allow someone else to help me through this, since I know all the techniques she's likely to use. And I'm a little stubborn." At that I was rewarded with a grin from George. "But I'm going to do it. You are worth it." I paused and smiled. "We are worth it."

When I'd finished my shower, I found George in the living room watching ESPN. I figured it was time to get back to the murders, so I did.

"Honey," I said, "I'm going to get on the computer for a while. Okay?"

"Sure. It's your birthday," he said, with his face still directed toward the TV. "But later, I have plans for us."

I went over and hugged him, then set up my laptop on the small dining room table that sometimes doubled as my desk. I could see George from there, and my heart leaped as I noted how perfectly he fit here. Right on my couch. Watching TV. And every now and then he would turn and smile at me.

If my life were a musical, as I'd often wished it were, this would be the moment to break out into song.

Finally pulling myself back to reality, I decided that I'd had enough distractions for the day. Back to the mystery at hand.

I pulled up Google and did a search on Richie Klingman. He'd gone to GCHS, as I'd anticipated. It hit me that I still didn't know the names of the two dead guys.

"Hey, George, did you ever get the names of the guys who were murdered?"

"Yeah. I don't have the info handy. Check out the online newspaper." Our local paper had gone with a digital edition as well as their paper one. So I did a search and came up with the names.

"Did they identify them with imprints of their teeth?"

"Yep," he said, finally turning away from the tube for a moment. "Everything is accessible nowadays." He turned back right away, lest he miss some statistic. I loved sports and yelled at games with the best of them. But all the stats bored me.

I turned my attention from the bigger screen to the little screen before me. I plugged in the first of the three names I got from the paper, John Delacourt. He was from Quincy and went to St. Francis High School. Creighton Jameson was next. He and his family moved here when he was in high school, and he also went to SFHS. So two out of three went to St. Francis. Richie was the only one of the three from GC. They all graduated the same year, so they probably knew each other. That didn't give me any information that helped with the blue hoodie notion. But I could check it out with Richie whether he knew the other two or not.

I decided to delve some more. The obituary for Delacourt stated he played football, basketball, and baseball for SFHS.

"An all-around jock," I said aloud. I looked over at George to make sure that my talking hadn't disturbed him.

Some of the same information surfaced when I looked at Jameson's obit. He had played basketball and baseball for SFHS. It also said donations in his memory could be made to the local arm of the American Cancer Society. Jameson was the guy we assumed was the murderer, and according to the Coroner's report, his cancer was so far advanced that he would have lived for only a few days longer if he hadn't taken his own life.

I thought that Richie himself had played soccer, or wrestled or something, for GC, but I wasn't sure. I could check with him on that too.

The stuff I learned online was interesting, but it didn't get me any closer to figuring out the mystery of the blue hoodie. Or the reason Creighton Jameson killed Delacourt, tried to kill Richie, and then killed himself. A suicide didn't surprise me, if Jameson was that ill, but I couldn't see him killing the other two. At least I couldn't come up with the reason. A little more snooping might help.

Whoever killed Delacourt, and I assumed it was Jameson, had pushed the knife in below the heart and then angled it upward so that it ended up in the heart. But when he'd stabbed Richie, he missed the heart because of the dextrocardia. Why did he make Richie hold on to the knife itself? He hadn't done that with Jameson. Maybe he'd wanted people to think Richie had killed the first guy and then committed suicide.

Lots of questions… and no real answers. My vibes were dormant again. They usually came to life only when I was around a criminal, or sometimes around a victim or a clue. Nothing today. Nada.

I had an idea.

"I'd like to take a walk."

"What?" George asked, still engrossed in a show about the Cardinals, and how they were doing in the pennant race.

"I'd like to take a walk."

"Okay, I'll go with you." I knew he just said that because it was my birthday. He normally didn't take walks with me.

"I'll go by myself. It's kind of relaxing to walk without Clancy every now and then. I'll be back in a little while. Just walking in the neighborhood."

He nodded. I grabbed my cell phone and went to the door.

"I think I'll stop by work for a minute and see if Marian happens to be there." We often went in on our off time to catch up on paperwork. There was always a lot to do.

George wisely didn't say anything but, "Have a nice walk." Surprisingly, he didn't act like I needed a guard.

As soon as I got past Gus and Georgianne's house I dialed 411 and got the number of Creighton Jameson's wife. The operator connected me "at no extra charge," and I waited impatiently for someone to answer as I walked slowly down Maine Street.

"Hello," a soft voice finally said.

After finding out this was indeed Mrs. Jameson, Enid Jameson, I introduced myself and asked if I could stop by.

"I guess so," she said, "but why do you want to talk to me. Do I know you?"

"No, ma'am. But I'm working as a consultant with the police, and I'd like to talk to you. It will just be a few minutes, I promise." I crossed my fingers as I fibbed. It would all be worth it if I figured out the solution to these murders.

She acquiesced and I told her I'd be there in about an hour or so if that was convenient. It was.

I kept walking until I hit the Quincy Community Clinic, located between 14th and 16th on Maine. I used my key. The lobby was empty, but I heard soft noises that let me know there were some people in the big house.

I walked to the other side of the converted house to see if Marian was busy. Her door was open and she was at her desk doing paperwork, her height hidden behind her desk. She looked up as I began to speak. After we exchanged hellos, I got to the reason for my visit.

"Marian, I wonder if you'd be kind enough to be my therapist?"

"Of course," she said as she stood to come nearer. "I have time now if it's an emergency." She towered over me, but I didn't feel intimidated by her. Her kind face made her height irrelevant.

"It's not an emergency, but it is kind of urgent. Something is causing a lot of trouble in my life, and I'd like to talk about it."

Marian ushered me in and closed the door.

"Since we don't have clients today, now would be perfect."

I sighed and a tear escaped. Once I started I couldn't stop. I spent the next 45 minutes giving her details on all my faults, primarily my impulsivity, and when I left her office I had a huge smile on my face.

How could she do that? How could she figure it out in less than an hour?

Of course I diagnosed people myself within 53 minutes, the traditional therapy hour. I wondered how many people walked out of my office as happy as I walked out of Marian's.

I left a note for myself to ask Clara to schedule another appointment with Marian for the following week. I wanted Marian to be able to "get credit" for seeing me, plus my insurance would pay for it. If I told my clients that there was no shame in seeing a therapist, then I needed to live that myself.

"I am happy. My life is good," I said aloud as I exited the Clinic.

I remained amazed that such a short period of time could make this significant a difference in my attitude. But it did. And I couldn't wait to tell George. And all my brothers and sisters who had teased me for years.

I walked down to 14th and Maine and turned right. Enid lived in a large home converted into apartments on 14th and Hampshire, so it was a short jaunt.

I knocked on the appropriate door, and it was answered by a teenage boy. He had a sad or sullen face, I couldn't tell which, but after I introduced myself and asked for his mother, he stepped aside so I could enter.

"Mom, she's here." A quick yell brought Mrs. Jameson to the foyer. She was dressed informally in jeans and what might have been one of her husband's dress shirts.

"Please come in," was all she said, as she led me to the living room.

She indicated that I should sit, and asked, "Why are you here?"

Saying no to an offer of tea or coffee, I said, "I consult with the police on certain cases," a little white lie. "And I have a few questions to ask about your husband's death." I didn't say suicide on purpose. First of all, it's a word fraught with emotion and judgment. Secondly, I wasn't totally convinced he had committed suicide. It wasn't anything that anyone told me. It was just a feeling.

After saying a few things to make her a little more comfortable, I was ready to approach the subject.

"Enid," she'd told me to call her that, "I want to ask how Creighton died."

At her almost imperceptible nod, I continued, "Do you believe Creighton killed himself?"

Damn, the waterworks started. Normally, my straightforward approach worked well. This time, not so much.

"I'm sorry, Enid. I didn't mean to make you cry."

"No, no, it's okay," she said. "It's just that you're the first person to ask that since the police. Everyone just assumes it was suicide, and…"

"And… what?" I asked, tired of waiting.

"And… I don't think he killed himself."

EIGHTEEN

She looked around as if she didn't want anyone to hear her.

"What do you mean?" I asked.

"Just what I said. I don't think he committed suicide." At that she looked around again, and her voice dipped even lower. "I think Creighton was killed."

"Did he have any enemies that you knew of?"

"Not what you would call enemies," she shook her head as she answered. "I don't know if everyone loved him or not, but I'm pretty sure no one hated him enough to do this. No. It can't be someone we knew. Except…"

"Except what?"

She hesitated before continuing. And sent her son to the kitchen for a glass of water.

"Except he only had a few days, maybe a week, to live."

"I'm aware of that. The coroner's report said as much. Do you think he might have killed himself to spare you a drawn out suffering and death?"

"No. I'm sure of this. He was a fine Christian man. He

would never, under any circumstances, kill himself. We'd even talked about it. He told me he would never do it."

I thanked her for her time, expressed my condolences, and walked back toward my house. What if her words were true? What if Creighton Jameson hadn't killed himself?

That meant the killer was still out there. That meant the guy who ran from Clancy and me was probably the killer, and not a prankster.

George was going to kill me when he found out what I was up to. I knew it. At least he would if the killer didn't do it first.

Suddenly frightened for the first time, I ran a few blocks. By the time I opened my door and stepped inside I was out of breath and hot.

"Omigod, Sam. What's wrong?" George had jumped up at my entrance. He walked to the door and picked me up, no mean feat. He lay me on the couch and put his hand on my forehead. "You have a fever."

"No, I don't," I said as I tried to sit up. He pushed me back down and I tried again to sit up. This went on like a bad Three Stooges movie. Finally, I pushed him away and succeeded in sitting. "I'm fine, I promise. I just ran a few blocks, that's all."

He sat on the edge of the couch, but didn't take his eyes off me.

"Why did you run? Exercise?"

"Yeah." Another white lie. "Exercise."

"Well, I don't believe you." His handsome face said the same things as his words. "Now tell me the truth."

He knew me. And wasn't afraid to challenge me.

"The truth is that I don't think Creighton Jameson killed himself, and neither does his wife."

"What do you mean?"

So I told him. I left nothing out, except the fact that I was now a little bit afraid. Well, maybe a lot afraid. But I didn't want to be under house arrest or protective custody or whatever. How could I solve this murder for George if I couldn't continue my investigation? So I didn't mention the fact that I was probably still in danger.

But that wasn't all of it. There was something else, nagging me. Something else besides the blue hoodie. My vibes were vibrating, trying to tell me something. I just couldn't bring it to the surface.

At that point my kids walked back in and Clancy bounded over to me. I hadn't seen as much of her as usual since the kids had been home, and since George and I became a thing. I hugged her and didn't let go, putting my head against hers. She could tell something was wrong, and didn't leave my side.

"Oops, looks like we came home at the wrong time. George, next time put a necktie on the doorknob so we know to stay away," Adam said, raising his eyebrows at my still-pink face and the fact that I was breathing a bit harder than normal.

"Adam," Sarah said as she fake punched him.

George was speechless. I just laughed.

"You guys have the wrong idea. I just ran a few blocks and it's taking me a while to recover." In the recent past my running had fallen by the wayside, in favor of slow, leisurely walks. "Sit, you two, and talk to me."

"Can't, Mom," Adam answered. "Gotta run." And he did that, literally. He ran up the stairs, and ran back down with a different shirt on. A quick kiss for me and off he went.

Sarah sat on the love seat, looking over at George and me on the couch. I was still holding on to Clancy, but did allow her a little breathing room.

"How was your date with Jimmy last night?" I asked.

Sarah smiled shyly.

"Did I know about this?" George asked. "Why didn't I know about this?"

"You went home last night, and that's when I found out about the date. I didn't think to mention it this morning. Sorry." I gave George's hand a squeeze to show there was no harm meant. "So... ," I said, turning my attention back to Sarah.

"So... ," she repeated, with a hint of red on her cheeks, "we went for a late meal at the Rectory. I saw some folks from school and we joined them."

"Did Jimmy go to St. Francis?"

"No, he went to GCHS, but we know some of the same people."

Then it hit me. I couldn't express any emotion over it in front of Sarah. But I thought of something I hadn't known before. Something that had been bugging me. *Jimmy.* I knew I had to talk to George privately, but I did want to finish the conversation with Sarah first.

"So you had a good time?"

"Yes, Mom. I had a good time. Anything else?" When I shook my head no, she continued, "Then I'd like to take a nap. I need to work tonight, and I got up awfully early this morning for your surprise."

I nodded, and she came over and kissed me, saying, "Happy birthday. I love you."

"I love you, too, sweetie." But I wanted to say, now hurry along. I couldn't wait to talk to George.

As soon as Sarah was safely out of earshot I turned to George.

"I think Jimmy might be involved."

"What do you mean, involved? You think he's dating someone else while he's going out with Sarah? I don't think he's that kind of guy. But if he is, he'll be very sorry."

"I love that you're protective, but it's not that. In fact it's worse."

"Worse?"

"Yeah. He might be the killer."

NINETEEN

"Sam, you must be overheated. This is crazy. Jimmy Mansfield is no more a killer than I am."

"Don't be so sure," I said.

"Okay, reasons," he demanded. "Give me reasons. Give me facts, not just feelings."

"Remember that he was the one who came up to me right after the guy in the blue hoodie tried to attack me? Clancy chased the guy up to a fence, but then couldn't go over it. Just a few minutes later, Jimmy came round the corner. He said he tried to get the guy, but couldn't. I remember that he didn't look hot or sweaty. He looked very put together for someone who had just tried to chase a bad guy. He was gasping for breath, but that could have been phony."

George just looked at me.

"And Sarah said he went to GCHS. I don't know if that's important, but it seems to me that it should be." I wanted some affirmation from George. "With the sweatshirt color and all."

"You're letting your imagination get carried away, Sam. Don't get me wrong. I love your imaginative, creative side. But you can't go accusing good cops of murder. You just can't."

"George, right now you have zero suspects. Zero. There's no one to investigate. There's no one to question. Zero."

"Yeah, but that'll change." He sounded a little defensive, and I couldn't blame him.

The last murders I had helped solve had involved logical suspects from the start. Too many. But it at least it gave the cops someone to question, and me someone to spy on. This time wasn't as much fun. I was just as scared, but didn't know who I was scared of. I needed a suspect. And fast.

Then came the blow I was dreading.

"Sam, I'm going to have to put you under protective custody again."

"Okay."

"Whoa." George looked at me with his eyebrows raised. "What's wrong? That's not like you to agree so easily."

"I hate protective custody. Hate it. But I love having to be with you. That's all. Nothing wrong."

We made a quick sandwich for my birthday lunch, and George said not to eat too much. It was obvious to me that he was excited about his surprise. In the afternoon, while he watched TV and worked in the living room, I sat in the dining room and caught up on Facebook.

"Hey," I said, "why don't we call Richie and see what's up with him?"

"Good idea. I'll call the station and get his number."

A few minutes later George had the number and in no time at all I overheard him say, "Hello."

I heard George ask Richie how things were going. Then a long pause as Richie spoke.

"Invite him over," I said, interrupting as usual.

George did just that. When he finished the call he said, "He'll be right over."

"I wonder how he'll get here. Will he be well enough to ride his bike?"

"Guess we'll see," George said, un-muting the sound of the ball game again.

I went back to my computer, until we heard a knock on the door.

George got the door, and in walked Richie, looking no worse for the wear.

He sat in the living room and I joined the two guys.

"How are you?" I asked as I gently hugged him. "Are you okay? Did you see who did this to you? Have the police asked you to describe him? Did he look like the same guy in the picture?"

"I'm okay. Wow! You're worse than the police are. I'm pretty sore. But I'm able to ride my bike, and take pictures, and that's what's important to me. I feel awful lucky. And yeah, the police interviewed me when I was in the hospital. I don't really remember the guys face. And I don't know how I got the hoodie on me. I don't remember much."

"Well, you're lucky that you have that dextrocardia thing." I wanted to be sympathetic, but thought Richie should know what was going on. "I hate to have to tell you this, but we discovered that the last guy might not have committed suicide, and that it might have been another murder."

He looked shocked, and sat back in the overstuffed chair. The purple on the chair made him look even more pale than the blood loss had already done. I was used to Richie having a suntan because of all the bike riding he did. This look was different.

George took over. "You need to be in protective custody. By now the killer knows you aren't dead. He or she might try again. We have to keep you safe."

Richie shook his head and raised his arms to protest what George was saying.

"No. I won't go into protective custody," Richie said. "I don't want anyone guarding me or watching me. It was bad enough when I was in the hospital, and I had fun trying to fool them. But I couldn't live like that. I'll keep myself safe, never you mind."

I couldn't help but go back to the photo.

"I'm so sorry I lost the picture, Richie. It might have

helped us figure out who the murderer is."

George was smart enough not to correct me on the "us."

"I know you didn't do it on purpose, Sam. It's okay."

"I really think you should be in protective custody," George said again. "The murderer is bound to know you aren't dead. He might try again, and I'd like to make sure you are safe."

"I appreciate it," Richie replied. "I really do. But I can't accept it. I can't allow it. Just can't."

"Well, we'll be looking out for you from a distance whether you like it or not, Richie. We have to do the best we can to prevent you from being injured again, or worse."

George's words sounded ominous, and they would have been enough to have convinced me. But Richie would not change his mind.

"Whatever you have to do, Detective," Richie said.

I thought his reply was weird. Why did he get so formal all of a sudden? Strange.

"I gotta go," Richie said and that was that. He was out the door and gone before I could get off the couch.

"He's one strange dude," I muttered. Then turned back to what I thought was important.

"Honey," I said, "I really think you need to check on Jimmy. Remember the first night I was at your house?"

George looked distracted as he mumbled, "Yeah."

"Well, he couldn't guard the back like he was supposed

to because he was busy somewhere else. He knew Rob would be in the front and the back wouldn't be guarded. Maybe it was him in the blue hoodie in the backyard. He got scared off, so no damage was done. But maybe that was him."

"Maybe it was a lot of people, Sam."

"Yeah, but please check him out."

"I will, but not in a big way. Because I don't suspect him. He's a good cop. But I'll make a few calls to see where he was assigned that night. Will that be enough?"

"Yeah, and please find out if he was always where he was assigned."

"Okay. Now I need to run home and get some clothes so I can stay over tonight and guard you." A brief smile flitted across his face. "You need to come with me."

Seeing the face I made, he amended it to, "Okay then. Why don't you stay here and get ready for tonight? Don't forget that we're going out for your birthday, murder investigation or not. Dress up a little and I'll be back in an hour." He faced me squarely. "Don't let anyone in. Do you understand me?"

Clancy stood beside him, seeming to echo his sentiments.

"I'll be fine," I insisted. "Sarah is upstairs sleeping, Adam is out, so I'll let him in, but no one else. Well, except Gus and Georgianne. It's their house after all. And if one of my brothers or sisters comes by I'll have to let them in."

"You know what I mean," he said, raising his voice. So I knew he was serious.

"Okay. I'll be good. And I'll just go and get changed for tonight. First I might just sit for a minute. Everything seems to be moving so fast."

"Sit for a few minutes then get dressed. I want to surprise you again."

I kissed him, then closed the door after him.

Tonight was indeed going to be a surprise.

TWENTY

Collapsing on the couch seemed like a good thing to do. So I did it.

I lay there, trying to relax. I knew George was going to check on Jimmy but I wondered if I should too. It was an awful idea. What if the young man Sarah went out with was indeed the killer?

The thought bothered me so much that I stood up and paced a bit. Jimmy was a viable suspect, but I wondered why I didn't have any bad vibes around him. When I met him, I simply saw a nice young man. I didn't want to believe he was guilty, but I needed someone to grill.

I plopped down on the love seat, trying to think of something else besides Jimmy and my concern about Sarah being involved with him. My thoughts went back to the conversation I'd had with Marian.

She'd begun by asking what brought me there. A standard question we therapists employ to start the conversation. So I told her about my impulsivity and gave her several examples of how it had been problematic.

Marian said she had an idea and started going down a list of symptoms that we use with kids and adolescents. At my replies, she nodded. I quickly figured out where she was going and when I did I sat there in disbelief.

"Me? ADHD?"

"It appears that way, Sam. I noticed it the first day you came to work, the day our boss was killed."

"But I'm not hyper. Not very often anyway."

"I see that. But I also see that you hit every symptom for the impulsivity section and most in the inattentive section."

"Yeah. I'm not hyper, but I am so easily distracted, and then there's the damn impulsiveness." I sat up straight. "Thank you so much, Marian. Even though I've diagnosed kids with this disorder for many years, I've not applied the same criteria to myself." I slowly shook my head. "I shouldn't be surprised, but I am. Me. ADHD. That explains so much. I always want to be thoughtful before I react. I really do. But it's like I can't help it." My sigh filled the room.

"So what do you want to do?" Marian asked.

"Well, with any other adult in this situation, I'd suggest they see a psychiatrist for medication. I don't know about me though... I just don't know. Maybe I can ask my family doctor about some medication."

"Think about it," she said. "That would be my recommendation to you, by the way. Get some meds. Only because this trait has made your life difficult and you've already tried to change on your own. It's up to you, of course."

Remembering her recommendation now, I realized that I should really tell George about my meeting with Marian as soon as he returned. What I had learned was important, and I wanted to share it with George… talk it out, and get his perspective. He could help me decide what to do.

A knock on the door grabbed my attention. I looked through the glass and saw it was Richie. Impulsively I opened the door. Even as I did, I thought, *Should I really do this? Sure. It's only Richie.*

He walked in quickly and closed the door behind him. He had a stupid grin on his face, his GC T-shirt on, and something in his hand. He didn't greet me, just stood there with his hand out toward me. I finally realized I was supposed to take what was in his hand.

"Ah, the picture. Where did you find it? Did you have it the whole time?" I glanced at it, then stared at it, then stared at Richie, then back at the picture.

"There's something about the build of the murderer," I said. "Something familiar. Do you recognize him?"

Looking back at Richie again, I finally focused on him, and nearly fell to my knees.

"And what in the hell are you doing with a gun in your hand?"

TWENTY-ONE

He laughed at my confusion.

Clancy went for him immediately. As she did, he kicked at her blindly, and hit her hard in her ribs. I heard a "whoof" as the breath was knocked out of her, and she fell down near the door.

My beloved Clancy. She was lying on the floor, still, but at least I could tell that she was breathing.

"Sam, I'm sorry. Your dog is okay, as far as dogs go. I'm sure she'll be all right. And I really like you as a person. Maybe you're a little pushy, a little bossy, but—"

"Okay, okay. Get to the compliment."

Oddly, I realized that it was the same thing I'd said to Richie at the beginning of this misadventure. It was hard to speak to him in a normal tone of voice when his gun was pointed at me. That and the fact that I wanted to throttle him for kicking my dog.

But I knew it was critical—more than critical, it was a matter of life or death—that I remained calm and used my therapeutic skills to my utmost ability. Or it would be the last therapy I ever did.

Richie smirked. I hate smirks.

"You seem to forget, Sam. I'm the one with the gun. I'm the one to decide if and when I'll give a compliment. There you are, showing how pushy and bossy you are."

"And nosy. Don't forget nosy." I turned my attention to Clancy, who was alert, but remained on the floor. I could hear her low growl and knew she was planning another assault on Richie.

"Clancy, don't. Just stay there. I promise I'll be okay. Just stay there. Stay." She looked at me with absolute trust in her eyes. She put her head down, but her ears were on high alert. I knew that if Richie tried to hurt me she would attack.

"Put the dog in the closet," he ordered, pointing toward the small coat closet near the door.

"Clancy, please. Go in there. I'll be fine. Just go."

And with one last growl and bark at Richie, she went into the closet.

"Now, let's talk," I said to him.

"Shut up," Richie yelled suddenly, as he closed the closet door. "Shut up. You sound just like my mother. I hated her. Don't make me kill you, Sam."

"Sorry, Richie." I kept my voice calm and modulated. The more he talked, the more likely I was to live to see George again. And everyone else. My children, my family. I turned off the chatter in my brain before I became too emotional to focus on the crisis before me.

"I won't make you kill me, Richie. I promise. You're the boss. But can I ask a question, please?"

He frowned but it looked like he nodded a little. So I took a chance.

"Why did you do it, Richie? What would make a nice guy like you kill people? I don't get it."

"That's because you're kind of nice. You don't see the bad stuff in people unless we throw it in your face. You didn't even make me search my pockets looking for the lost picture. It was inside my shirt pocket all the time."

"Guess I wasn't as smart as you." *Keep complimenting him,* I told myself.

"You're darn tootin'. I'm a lot smarter than people give me credit for. And I'm a damn good athlete."

"You are?" which I quickly changed to, "You are." But back to the subject at hand. I kept my voice even, although I could feel every nerve at attention.

"Why did you do it, Richie?" I asked again.

"The first guy was kind of random. I knew he'd gone to St. Francis High, so I automatically hated him. By the way, I hate you too."

As he said it I shrugged my shoulders as if to say that it was a natural feeling. "But why kill him?"

"Didn't you hear me? He went to SF. I hate the school and hate the people who went there."

"I'm sorry. I don't understand."

"I was a good athlete. But every time we played against SF I wasn't allowed to play. They always beat us, and coach said I wasn't good enough to play. I *was* good enough." His voice was rising. This wasn't a good sign. I had to diffuse the tension. He went on, getting louder. "Mom said I wasn't good enough too. Wrong. Wrong. I was a great athlete. I hate SF graduates. Hate 'em."

I nodded, and spoke again, my voice calm. "Okay, what about Creighton Jameson?"

"Beyond the obvious that he went to St. Francis, he was going to die anyway, so what's the big loss? I made him the decoy. So no one would know it was me. They'd figure he felt bad about it and decided to kill himself. Then the cops— including your boyfriend—would close the case." I could hear the satisfaction in Richie's voice. "I mean don't act like the world is going to miss Jameson. He was toast anyway."

Omigod, he's a psychopath! And I knew I really had to keep him talking, plus I had to keep complimenting him.

"And everyone would believe he was the murderer."

"Of course," he nodded as he spoke.

"Tell me more." I had to keep the conversation—such as it was—going.

"What do you want me to tell? There's one model of the old-style Polaroid camera that has an automatic timer on it. You can set up a shot and then be in it." He smiled as he said this. "Not many people know that. So for the first guy, it was easy for me to set up the camera on my bike, throw on my blue hoodie, and presto—one vagrant gone."

He walked around the living room, but kept the gun pretty much facing my way. "I knew I wouldn't be a suspect because of the type of camera I used. Then when I made the brilliant move of stabbing myself in the chest—well, that sealed the deal on me being innocent. You stupid, stupid people. Of course, my heart is in the wrong place. Literally."

He let out with a maniacal laugh. The kind the villain always did in the old movies. I halfway expected him to pull out a black cape and twirl on a pencil-thin mustache. At that moment a Jimmy Buffett tune surfaced in my brain. *I wish I had a pencil-thin mustache, the Boston Blackie kind.* I cursed my ADHD and forced myself to focus.

"You made some brilliant moves, Richie. I wish you'd done it in a legal way, so people could really appreciate you as a free man. They won't give so much admiration to a criminal."

"*Criminal?* You ignorant female." His voice got lower and more serious. "Shut up and do what I say."

"Just tell me what to do and I'll do it." I could feel my heart beating.

"I want you to write a note. Get some paper." I did. "You need a pen too. Don't drag this out anymore than you already have."

"I don't have a pen," I said, as meekly as I could. "I mean I can't find a pen. I know I have one. Do you want me to keep looking?"

Richie took a pen out of his PRESS hat and threw it at me. "Here's a damn pen. Now sit down at the table and write what I tell you."

"Okay," I said, still compliant, and knowing he wanted me to write a suicide note.

"Please don't forget to take your pen with you after you kill me. I don't want anyone to be able to use it as a clue to trace it back to you." I didn't want to sound too bossy and set him off, but wanted to drag things out.

"See," he said. "That's what I mean. Sometimes you're a really nice lady."

I was immensely grateful that he didn't catch on to my procrastination.

"Hey, Richie, I just thought of something. Would you like something to drink? I have iced tea or I could make some coffee."

Damn, that was one too many distractions.

"Are you trying to drag this out so you get rescued?" He wagged the gun around like he was doing a flag routine.

"No. Yes. Yes, I guess I am. I don't want to die. I have two kids, a dog, and a boyfriend. Plus a job I love. Why would I want to hurry up my death?"

"That makes sense," Richie said, "but it's not enough

reason for me not to kill you. You're the only one, the only damn one, to almost figure it out."

"I told you I was nosy. I can't help it. I wish there was a twelve-step group for curiosity. I'd join. Hell, I'd be the poster child for the group. My mom was the same way. Guess I got it from her."

"Shut up, Sam." Richie was getting antsy. "I can't stand here all day with a gun pointed at you. Sooner or later someone is going to show up."

"That's my fondest hope," I whispered.

"Well, the door's locked and I'm sure not going to open it."

"But, Richie, that door is the only way out. Since this was a carriage house, the windows are small. If someone comes to the door you won't be able to get out without being seen." I needed to come up with a plan, and fast.

I could feel my brain going into overdrive. Maybe some of that crazy activity would be useful for once. *Think.*

"Wait, let me show you where there's another escape route, just in case someone barges in on us." It sounded crazy to me, that I would actually try to help him escape when I knew he was trying to kill me, but he might be just crazy enough to believe it. I prayed.

"Okay. But hurry." God bless Richie. He bit on that one.

"I will," I said. "Just follow me."

He did and I could imagine the gun pointed right at the

back of my head, although the reality was that it probably was moving all over the place.

At this point I had no idea what I was going to do, I just knew I had to keep stalling. As we were walking to my bedroom I heard the front door rattle, and then George's muffled voice yell, "Hey, Sam. You locked your door. Amazing. Open up, hon, I have something to tell you."

Richie put his finger to his lips, warning me not to make any noise. But I could tell he was getting nervous about how he was going to escape.

I didn't want to make noise anyway. Sarah was upstairs and I didn't want her to barge into this situation. But knowing her, she'd have on headphones with music playing.

"Hurry, I told him. George has a key," I lied, "and he'll be in any second."

"You hurry," he countermanded. And I did. I ushered him to my bedroom and then to the adjoining bathroom.

This was my moment. I was thinking as fast as I could. What was my story?

"If you stand on the edge of the bathtub and put your hand on the window ledge, you'll feel a lock." He was climbing up. He believed me. *What to say?*

"Push the lock and part of the wall will fall away, letting you virtually walk out of here." That was nuts. A fantasy. *Keep talking.*

"I know that sounds wild, but it's…it's because this place

is a carriage house. It's the old part of the wall that used to be there when carriages actually came in and out. A great big opening."

I didn't know where this was coming from. Some part of my mind that was intent on survival. Richie was up there and feeling for the lock.

"It's on the opposite side of the house as the front door, so George will never know," I said.

"Gee, thanks," Richie said, gullible as ever, and then he stretched his arm above the tub and reached up to the high windowsill. As he did, he had to balance himself against the wall. For an instant I saw the gun pointed at the ceiling instead of at me. I took that moment to move faster than I thought possible, stepping out and slamming the bathroom door.

I heard him yell at me to stop, and then I heard the explosion of gunfire, echoing in the tiled bathroom. I heard the bullet hit the door. It didn't go through it, but I felt lucky that I was off to the side, already heading toward the front door. I only had a moment's head start, so I grabbed some dining room chairs as I passed them and pushed them down behind me. I knew they wouldn't stop bullets, but they might trip up Richie.

Hearing more gunshots, and breathing heavily, I finally reached the front door and grabbed the doorknob. Just as I touched it two things happened. The door opened, and I got shot.

TWENTY-TWO

I didn't lose consciousness, but my butt hurt like hell. I wanted some attention, but didn't want to let on that I was shot in my butt. I was actually feeling pretty relieved to be alive.

So I lay there, on my stomach, and stayed quiet—for once—while the man I loved took care of the man that shot me.

"Richie," George said, his own gun in his hand and pointed at the murderer, "don't do anything you'll be sorry for. You're in deep enough trouble already, and I don't want you to make it worse for yourself."

From the floor, I could see that Richie was shaking, and unarmed. I was trembling myself. After all, I was the one who'd been shot in the butt.

George started to tell Richie what to do, but Richie interrupted.

"I'm sorry, George." He started to sob. "I'm sorry, Sam. I don't know what happened. It just snowballed. Not my fault."

"Shut up," I said, brave now that I could see Richie didn't have a gun. "George, he kicked Clancy. Help her. Then help me."

"First things first, Sam." George turned his attention back to Richie, whose gun I now saw sitting on the floor. "Kick it over to me." Richie did. "Now turn around and put your hands behind your back." Richie complied and George cuffed him. He had another set of cuffs and he righted one of the chairs and attached Richie to it.

George called in for backup immediately. He also called for an ambulance. Then he read Richie his rights before Richie could say anything else.

George's proximity made me feel better, but damn, my butt hurt. That was secondary to my dog in the closet however.

As George opened the closet door, Clancy came out slowly. I could tell her ribs hurt, but she let me know she was okay by coming over and licking my... butt?

"Clancy," I quickly said, "I'm okay. Someone will take care of the wound. Come here." And she gingerly walked toward my face and nuzzled me. I found it immensely comforting.

Police arrived first. Two of them came in and carted Richie off. As he left I noticed tears running down his face. He tried to turn to me, but couldn't because the officers were leading him quickly toward the door. I did catch his words, however.

"I'm sorry, Sam. I'm really sorry. Especially about the dog."

His remorse didn't touch me as a victim. As a social worker, I hoped he would get some help in prison and maybe be put in the forensic mental health ward. But that wasn't up to me.

When the ambulance arrived I insisted that Clancy get taken as well. George warned them not to argue with me, and they didn't. Clancy and I shared the gurney. It was a tight squeeze but the only difference from every bedtime was that my dear sweet girl was hurting and my butt cheek was bleeding.

"Drop her off at Dr. Bob's first." I turned my head to George, desperate for him to agree with me.

He sighed heavily, knowing this was a battle he wouldn't win.

"Yeah, do what she says."

I smiled, in spite of my pain, in spite of my worry. George called Dr. Bob's office to let them know what had happened to Clancy. The ambulance driver and George gently carried in my girl, and when George returned to the ambulance he said he'd be checking on Clancy. I knew that he loved Clancy almost as much as I did, so I was able to relax a little. In fact, if my butt hadn't hurt so much I would have fallen asleep.

George interrupted my relaxed state.

"What in the hell were you doing?"

I knew what he meant.

"Well, once I figured out what Richie had done, I thought I could trap him into confessing. I didn't let him in knowing he was the murderer. Even I wouldn't do that."

At George's expression, I rethought that. "Okay. Maybe I would have. But I didn't."

George was scowling at me, and caressing my cheek at the same time. It was an interesting combination.

"To tell the truth, I let him in without thinking. I didn't figure out he did it until after I let him in, and he showed me the picture. Or maybe it was after I saw the gun." I could hear George breathing hard, and I knew he wanted to yell at me. "Anyway, don't say anything. I know it's a problem. And I felt safe because I knew you'd be right back. And you were."

"That's not going to get you out of the doghouse." Even though his words were harsh, his tone was warm and he put his hand on my back. If I hadn't been lying on my stomach I would have kissed him.

"I know. I should know better by now. In my head it's always a smooth operation. I solve the crime and nobody gets hurt." I suddenly thought of something as the ambulance stopped at the entrance to the ER. As they wheeled me in, I yelled at George, "Call Dr. Bob and find out how Clancy is doing."

I was immensely grateful that my sister Jill was on duty and available to be my physician. As soon as she saw me she said, "What have you done now?"

"Is that how you treat all your patients?"

"Nope. Just you. What happened?" she asked as a nurse took my vital signs.

I told her all the details, while trying to make myself sound good and Richie sound evil.

"I'll lay off for now, just until we're done treating you," Jill said. "Then I'll turn into your sister instead of your doctor."

She gave some orders to the nurse. I heard "bullet," I heard "sutures," I heard "injection," and I signed a paper agreeing to treatment.

Someone started an IV, and before long I was out.

I awoke in the same room in the ER, with George holding my hand and me lying on my side. At least it was a different position. I felt some pain in my butt, but felt kind of groggy too, which was okay by me.

George explained the procedure to me and that everything had gone well. I grinned at him, in my dopey haze, and saw my knight in shining armor. My George.

"I love you," I said. "Did you see my butt?"

"I love you, too," he responded, "and don't worry about your butt. And even though you are out of the woods medically, you are still in trouble with me."

I nodded, then changed the subject.

"How's Clancy?"

"She's fine," he said. "Doc said she's going to be sore for a while, but no ribs are broken and he doesn't think there'll be any permanent damage. Gus is going to pick her up later. She'll probably be home before we will."

"Good. When can I leave here?"

"Jill said you have to be completely awake and alert. She'll be back in to check on you soon." He patted my shoulder, almost absentmindedly, as we talked.

Now that things were getting clearer I remembered something.

"When Richie and I were in the carriage house, and you couldn't get in the front door, you yelled that you had something to tell me. What is it?"

"Not now, Sam," George said. At my insistence he gave in and told me.

"I've been promoted to Chief of Detectives."

"I'm so proud of you," I gushed. And not knowing when to leave well enough alone, I added, "I probably helped you get that promotion, because I've solved so many murders since I've been back."

George gave me a look that silenced me immediately. But not for long.

"And I have something to tell you." I had even more to say than usual. The medication made it all seem very pleasant. "I have ADHD, and that's why I'm so impulsive and stupid. Well, ADHD doesn't make you stupid, I just do stupid things. But I can't help it sometimes. And sometimes I can." I thought a moment. "I'm talking and I can't shut up."

I started crying, not from his look which was now kind and loving, but from the whole experience. I was groggy, in pain, worried about my dog, and even worried about Richie. I noticed a look of compassion on George's face. He put down the railing on his side of the bed, moved me over, and slid in next to me. He put my head on his shoulder, and sweetly and softly sang to me.

Who knew George could sing?

I felt like I was in heaven. If heaven included sore butts.

If only Clancy were on the other side of me, I thought that I could fall asleep between my two loves forever.

And who knows… maybe I will.

More to come!

A sample from the next book in the series follows, as well as a bonus short story.

Buy the fourth Sam Darling mystery,
"Will You Marry Me?" right now.

Or read on for the first chapter…

About
"Will You Marry Me?"

There's a Chicken Convention in town as Sam Darling takes her curiosity on the road and tries to solve another murder—and this time the feathers are flying!

Savvy sleuth Sam and her canine sidekick Clancy are at it again in the fourth book in Jerilyn Dufresne's bestselling cozy mystery series. Sam and her sweetheart George are headed off for a well-earned vacation. That is, until Clancy digs up a mysterious human bone. With help from the Bobs—Bob Bob, Jim Bob, Joe Bob, Mike Bob, Billy Bob, and Mary Bob—Sam jumps in as always to help figure out who done it.

How far will Sam go to solve the case? Far enough to squeeze into a fluffy chicken suit and infiltrate the world of those who love to cluck. Once again, intrepid Sam goes from the frying pan into the fire… but will she get burned?

ONE

My excitement about our trip could not be dampened. George and I were going away and we were taking Clancy with us. What could be better?

Gus and Georgianne, my landlords, were at my carriage house pretending to listen to my instructions on how to care for the place in my absence.

"Calm down, Sam," Gus said. "You act like we've never been in this place before. We watched it when you were in the hospital after getting shot in the bottom, when you were poisoned, when you had to stay at George's because your life was threatened, when…"

"Okay, okay," I said, "I'm convinced." I didn't want to hear a litany of the times I'd been hospitalized or otherwise unable to be in my cozy nest. Or rather their cozy nest. They owned it, plus the mansion that sat in front of it.

I looked down at my dog, Clancy, sitting faithfully at my side. Her thoughts intruded on the talking. She was amused by Gus's speech.

"Clancy, that's not nice. Are you sure you want to go with us?"

Her thoughts were kinder after that, and her soft growl meant she gave in.

"George is going to pick up Clancy and me in a few minutes. I know I've forgotten something. I just know it," I said as I continued to look around.

Recently I'd begun taking medicine for ADHD and my system was still getting used to my brain slowing down a bit. It was a welcome respite from my normally unwelcome impulsiveness and inattention, but at times there was a brain fog I didn't like.

"If you forgot something just give me a call. Hell, you're never without that fancy phone of yours." Gus was allowed to tease me. He was almost an adopted grandpa and my best friend. Well, besides Clancy.

"Samantha, we are honored you want us to watch your place. I'd be pleased to check every room while you're away. On a daily basis." Georgianne was my friend too, but I didn't quite trust this offer.

"That's okay, and not necessary. I'm sure it will be fine. There are no plants to water—I've killed them. I'm taking my dog with me. Everything inside is in working order. I stopped my mail. So all you have to do is keep an eye on the outside."

I prayed that Georgianne could keep her paws off my house. Even though I inherited my nosy gene from my mom, I preferred to call myself curious. I saved the nosy moniker for Georgianne.

But I loved her. Couldn't help it. She was my best friend's wife.

I was still looking around when George walked in. We kissed, and my day was made. Nothing could bring me down when I had George and Clancy at my side. I felt like I could conquer the world, and was ready to leave Quincy so I could do it.

A quick kiss and hug for Gus and Georgianne, and a conscious locking of my door, and we were off.

"I love you," was all I could think to say to them as we waved goodbye. The air was crisp but tolerable and the sight and smell of leaves falling off the trees announced the middle of autumn without the need for a calendar. I left my window open so I could smell the season.

There was also a whiff of George's Hai Karate aftershave, which always took me back to high school. He was my friend from kindergarten on, but was my boyfriend in high school. That relationship ended abruptly when he stood me up for prom. Twenty-five years later, I've not only forgiven him, I've fallen in love with him again.

He started chatting about something. He was the Chief of Detectives at Quincy Police Department, and was probably talking about a case, but I drifted off, thinking about how the last several months had made me love him even more than before.

Finally, I tuned back in.

"So it's really important that you and Clancy come with me to the Grand Canyon. It's the first place I want to travel to as a couple, er… um… a triple." George was adorable, always making sure to include Clancy in everything. She was the only reason we were driving rather than flying.

"You know," I whispered, "we could have left Clancy with Gus. She would have been fine, and we could have flown, giving us more time there."

Clancy, relegated to the back seat of the rented SUV, perked up her ears and started "talking." Her low growl sounded kind, but then she put in the inflections that would let anyone know she was unhappy with that remark. Not only do Clancy and I have a psychic connection, sort of, she also "talks" quite eloquently once you learn to understand her language.

"I know," George said to her. "Don't worry. I wanted you with us on this trip."

"Sounds like you two are in collusion." I couldn't help but smile. I loved them both so much, and to see their connection intensified my feeling of joy.

It felt great to be on vacation. Even though I'd started work as a therapist at the Quincy Community Clinic less than a year ago, and didn't really have vacation time saved up, I still felt the need for relaxation. A few months ago, I was in the ER with a bullet in my butt. Prior to that I'd been hospitalized because I'd been poisoned. I still couldn't believe people in Quincy had actually tried to kill me. Shaking off any fear, I was determined to enjoy this trip.

George crossed the Mississippi into Missouri and drove south on US-61. We planned to drive to St. Louis and take I-44 southwest. He had it all planned out, but I wasn't too interested. I listened to the music, looked at George, and absentmindedly reached back to pet Clancy.

What a wonderful life I had. And to think—the excitement we were going to experience on the trip was planned, not accidental. Rare for me, recently.

I noticed George yawning.

"Honey, didn't you sleep last night?"

"Not much. Between planning for the trip and finishing up paperwork on some cases, I didn't get too much shuteye."

"Let me drive for a while, and you can rest." I wanted to pull my weight on this trip so George didn't have to do everything. After all, I had been the single parent who took my kids camping, backpacking, spelunking, and climbing, and I drove all over the USA. I was a pretty capable person, and there was no reason to change just because I was in a relationship.

"Okay," he said, without argument. "I'll make it to St. Louis, and once we're on I-44, it'll be yours."

I smiled, feeling like I'd won a non-existent argument.

Just as he had promised, George pulled over after we hit

44. We changed places, and Clancy didn't move a muscle. I hooked up my iPhone to George's radio and listened to my own songs as I drove. George was asleep before I even had the Bluetooth set up.

I sang and grinned. Belted out song after song after song. Poor George was so exhausted that my bellowing didn't even wake him.

Time passed quickly, and before I knew it we were nearing Springfield, MO. On an impulse, I turned south on US-65 toward Branson. I wanted to see the famous city where people flocked from all over the world to see the shows.

The journey was easy and definitely not exciting. I drove around the town, rather than through it, deciding at the last minute that there was nothing there of interest to me.

Clancy's whine let me know she needed a bathroom break, and the needle on the gas gauge informed me the car needed filling. I took a random exit and drove on a narrow road until I reached a town. The sign said "Crackertown, 'We're the Ritz of the Ozarks.' Population: Varies."

The whole sign made me giggle.

As I slowed to thirty miles an hour, George woke up, stretched, leaned over to kiss me, and asked where we were.

To say he exploded might be an understatement. And since George was usually such an easygoing guy with me, my eyebrows shot up and my mouth opened, but nothing came out.

Finally I was able to talk.

"I'm sorry. I didn't think you'd mind." I was used to saying "I'm sorry" to George because I messed up a lot. But things had gotten better since I started taking ADHD medication.

"Oh my, I just remembered what I forgot."

"What?" George asked in the middle of his anger.

"You're going to be mad," I promised him.

"Tell me now while I'm already mad."

"I forgot my meds for my impulsiveness. I am so, so sorry." My impulsivity and inattention have caused a lot of trouble for us, and make me unlikeable. Well, except to my family, including my dog and my George. But still, I knew I was hard to put up with.

George's handsome face was red, as was the top of his head where hair used to be.

"Honey," I said. "Please try to relax. I don't want you to have a stroke on our vacation." Even Clancy looked concerned.

"We can call Gus and have him send your meds."

I nodded, then yelled, "NO! I don't remember where they are, and I refuse to let Georgianne have an excuse to look through my house. I couldn't bear it." I touched his shoulder. "Please. Let's just see how I am. If it's not too bad, I can wait until I get home for the meds. If I'm so annoying you want to throttle me, I'll have Gus look for the bottle and overnight it. Or I can call my pharmacist to send the prescription to a place nearby. Okay?"

George was the sweetest guy in the universe. "Okay. But no more unplanned detours. We have to make it to the Grand Canyon."

Smiling, I pulled over to the first gas station I could find.

"Will you please pump the gas?" I asked. "I'll take Clancy for a little walk."

George didn't say anything, so I assumed assent.

"C'mon, Clance, wanna go potty?" Clancy quickly jumped out of the open back door and immediately sat so I could hook on her leash. I saw some grass between the gas station and a small restaurant, so I headed there.

Clancy began pulling me, which was unusual, but I realized it had been a long time since she had gotten a potty break. She peed immediately when we got to the grass, but continued pulling. I let her take the lead because I was now intrigued about what could be attracting her.

I thought it was probably some meat. Since I'm a vegetarian she doesn't get meat scraps at home, so when she's around any kind of meat, she goes bonkers. I knew I'd need to be careful she didn't get into any spoiled food, but I still let her have the lead.

Clancy stayed on the grass, moving to the part between the station and the blacktop road, and began digging. And digging. She surprised me with how intent and focused she was.

Finally she stopped digging, but kept her nose down in the hole she'd dug. It was obvious she had something, and she began pulling with great force. I found myself rooting for her to succeed. She hunkered down and used all her Lab/Chow strength to give one final jerk. She pulled so hard that when she succeeded she fell onto her butt, then rolled over. But she held on to her prize. A very long bone.

She didn't chew on it, which surprised me. She placed it at my feet as if it were a prize or a gift. Then it hit me.

"George, come here. Hurry."

He rushed over, probably because he thought I was in some sort of trouble. But this time was different.

"What does this look like?"

"Damn it. It's a human bone." He petted Clancy as he said it. "Good job, girl." But his face didn't say the same thing.

His face said, "There goes our vacation."

The fourth Sam Darling mystery, "Will You Marry Me?" is available now.

And don't forget—there's a bonus short story, **Sam's Prom Night Fiasco**, *starting on the next page!*

Read on for how to contact the author and join her mailing list so that you'll get the news first about each book before it's released.

Sam Darling mystery series bonus story!

Sam's Prom Night Fiasco

Samantha

" S top obsessing, Sam. He'll ask you." My best friend, Cynthia Wayne, pulled her ponytail down yet again as she continued to give me her best dating advice.

I made a pouty face in the bathroom mirror and then tried to apply the pink glossy lipstick that Madonna recommended. "Easy for you to say, Cindy. You and Vic have hands practically welded together and you already have your wedding planned. You know you have a prom date." I pouted again. "Unlike me."

Cindy, finally satisfied with her side-swept ponytail, a la her idol Cindy Lauper, changed the subject. "Got a cigarette?"

"Of course. But I'm not going to get caught smoking in school again. Sister Evangelista will have me expelled and I won't get to graduate. And won't my folks just be thrilled about that." I looked over my shoulder to make sure no one was listening. "I'll let you have one after school. It's the best I can do."

Although I wasn't averse to rule breaking, I had to

graduate. I was the oldest of six kids and was expected to go to college. I looked at my best friend, "My folks would have a cow if I got expelled. Crap, the last time I got called to the principal's office I walked in and my parents were there. My parents! Can you imagine the humiliation? The horror? I have to sit down just thinking about it." I moved and sat in an empty stall.

"You are such a drama queen," Cindy said. She was about the only person who I'd let get away with that. "Get out of there. It's gross."

I walked back to the mirror, and checked my lipstick again. I'd already chewed it off. Why couldn't I just stay still? I reapplied my lipstick and said, "Anyway, back to the important topic. I'll just die if George doesn't ask me to prom. It's only two weeks away. We're going steady; I don't know what's wrong with the goof. Does he just assume we're going? Does he like someone else?" I turned to Cindy. "I'll just die." I could feel the tears starting behind my heavily mascaraed eyes.

I looked in the mirror again. "Maybe he doesn't like me since I started using makeup," I said. "I don't know why I let you talk me into it."

"You can't be a tomboy forever," Cindy said. "You've got to grow up sometime. And now's the time. Now quit whining and let's get to Math Analysis before Miss Pulliam shuts the door. C'mon." She grabbed me by the arm and pulled me—books and all.

I gave my makeup one last swipe, making sure I didn't enter the classroom with raccoon eyes. It was bad enough getting teased and called "ditzy" because I couldn't stay focused on one thing. It would be even worse to be called "raccoon."

"That reminds me," I said, screeching to a halt outside the door to our math class. "I need to apologize to Gloria for calling her a 'raccoon.' It wasn't nice."

"Where did that come from? Oh, never mind," said my long-suffering friend. She was probably used to how my mind worked, or didn't work.

We walked through the door just as Miss Pulliam moved to shut it.

"Glad you could join us, girls," she said. But she said it with such a melodious voice and a smile on her face that it was almost impossible for me to get mad at her.

Cindy and I sat beside each other in Math Analysis. I loved being in an advanced placement class. I thought it was cool being smart, although most of the other kids didn't agree. I leaned over to Cindy and whispered, "We have to finish the conversation about you-know-who."

"Samantha," the teacher said, "why don't you tell us the answer to number one on your homework."

"I would, Miss Pulliam, if I had it. I mean if I had it with me. Oh, heck, I didn't do it. I had to work last night at the

Dairy, and was really tired when I got home. So I just went to bed."

"You had plenty of time to complete the assignment, Sam. You had three days."

"I know, Miss Pulliam. I'm really, genuinely, truly, absolutely sorry, and promise it won't happen again."

"Drama queen," whispered Cindy.

"See me after class," Miss Pulliam said to me.

"Yes, Miss Pulliam." Dutifully chastised in front of the class, I opened my book to the appropriate page. Luckily I didn't care what the other students in this class thought of me. They were all nerds, which Cindy and I would never be. Not in a million years. Smart, maybe. Nerd, never.

The class passed quickly. I loved Math Analysis. It came easy to me but still didn't put me to sleep. What I dreaded was talking to the teacher afterward. I hated being in trouble, even though it was a fairly common occurrence.

The bell rang and I sadly watched everyone else walk to the door. I sat until the last possible moment. As I slowly walked to the teacher's desk, like a doomed prisoner toward the guillotine, I glanced to the right and saw George waiting for me at the door. He looked confused. George looked confused a lot when it came to me. I often wondered what he saw in me. He was Mr. Jock and Mr. Popular, and I was… me.

"Ahem." Miss Pulliam cleared her throat and I realized I

was standing in front of her desk but gazing at George. I shrugged my shoulders at my boyfriend and turned my attention to my teacher.

"Angelique, I am so sorry."

"What did you call me, Samantha?"

"Crap. I am so sorry, Miss Pulliam."

"Please don't use vulgar words."

"Yes, Miss Pulliam. I mean, no, Miss Pulliam. I won't."

She smiled and indicated a chair next to her desk. "Please sit."

And then began the usual lecture. One I'd heard my entire life—you're so smart, you're so talented, you don't work, you procrastinate, you don't pay attention, you're impulsive, you have a smart mouth.

The difference this time was that I really listened. Miss Pulliam was one of my favorite teachers. I could imagine that she had a life outside the walls of St. Francis High School. She was pretty, and she wore lipstick and high heels. Totally unlike the nuns. Some of them were okay, but I couldn't picture them outside of school. It was almost as if after school they went into a hyperbaric chamber until the next day.

After what seemed like an eternity, I was finally released. By that time, George was sitting on the floor against the far wall.

"'Bout time," he said, standing up. He looked so

handsome in his letterman's jacket, polo shirt, and khakis. School policy dictated no jeans, and no T-shirts, which explained the collared shirt and khakis. "What happened? You in trouble again?" He smiled as he said it, and he took my hand.

I found it hard to get mad at him. I loved this guy. We'd been friends our whole lives, living a few doors away from each other. Suddenly, in high school, our relationship changed to boyfriend and girlfriend. I didn't know how it happened. One day we were playing baseball, the next day we were kissing.

I didn't complain.

George

"Go ahead and ask her," Cal said, as George parked at the Dairy.

"Quit talking about it." George locked his car and walked with his friend to the front door of their after-school hangout.

"Well, it's obvious it's on your mind. You talk about it yourself all the time." Cal was a little shorter than George and had to walk quickly to keep up.

"At least shut up about it now. I don't want Sam to know."

"I don't get you," Cal said, moving toward an empty table in the corner of the ice cream shop. "You hang out with Sam every chance you get, you talk to her on the phone every night, you hardly ever have time for me any more. But you haven't asked her to prom yet? That's just stupid. Hell, I have a date and I'm not even dating anybody."

George pulled out a menu from behind the napkin holder, although it was an unnecessary effort. He knew what he wanted. He'd grown up a few blocks away and had been in here several times a week whole life.

"Shut up!" This time George raised his voice, then immediately quieted and smiled as he looked up at his girlfriend.

Sam greeted them, holding on to an order pad. "Hi. What can I getcha?" She gave a small smile to Cal, and saved her huge grin for George. "Do you want the usual?" she asked George, almost sweetly. At his nod she turned to Cal, "What about you?"

Cal quickly scanned the menu and ordered the same thing George had—a cheeseburger, fries, and a chocolate shake. Pretty standard fare for many high school students after school.

"Okay," Sam said, "I'll get the order in right away." She looked at George again, "I get off work in about an hour. Want to pick me up?"

George nodded, with the same smile Sam showed.

"Oh, for cryin' out loud," Cal said when Sam had gone. "You two lovebirds are so sickening sweet. Why in the hell don't you ask her to prom? I don't get it."

"Keep your voice down. And I mean it." Cal obeyed George's icy glare, and George continued. "The truth is that I don't think she'd say yes."

"Of course she'd say yes. She's a girl, she's a senior; of course she'd want to go to prom. You're a dork."

"Cal, you forget. This is Sam. She can hit a baseball

further than a lot of guys on the team. She completed an unassisted double play. She's not into girly things like dressing up for prom."

"You are dense, my friend. Dense." Cal shook his head at George's reasoning.

George didn't reply. He just waited for his food and milkshake to arrive. However, the furrow on his forehead showed that he was concentrating on something.

Samantha

"So, what's up?" I asked George. We were parked in front of my house in his '65 Chevy. No one else I knew had a car more than 20 years old, but this was George's pride and joy. We'd been sitting in silence for a few minutes. Usually by now we'd be kissing, and he'd be trying to go to second base, even though he knew better. But instead we were just sitting.

He didn't answer my question, so I went to my dark, insecure place—"You're going to break up with me, aren't you?"

"Of course not. But I get pretty tired of you always thinking I'm going to break up with you. No. I'm trying to figure out a way to ask you something."

"Okay," I said. I was a little nervous. What if he was going to ask me to go all the way? Of course, I'd say no, but he was a guy and I loved him and I thought he'd ask. In fact, I'd probably be disappointed if he didn't at some point.

George looked around, adjusted the rear view mirror, and looked everywhere but at me.

"You're scaring me, George. What's wrong?"

"Nothing's wrong, Sam." He finally looked at me, took both my hands, and glanced to the heavens before asking, "Will you go to prom with me?"

"Yes," I said. "Yes," I said again. I threw my arms around his neck and kissed him. Hugging him, I whispered, "I thought you'd never ask."

"Really," he said. He wiped some perspiration from this forehead with one hand, but kept a firm grip on me with his other one.

"I already have a dress," I admitted. "So I've been waiting for you to ask." I gave him another kiss, then said, "What took you so long?"

"I didn't know if you'd want to go, so I've been holding off. And now it's just less than two weeks away, so it seems wrong somehow to ask you this late. But you're the only person I'd want to go with."

"I should think so," I said with a grin.

I turned and faced the front, but couldn't stop grinning.

"I'm going to prom," I whispered. "I'm going to prom."

George

"I don't know what color tux I should get. Is this the right color? I don't know. She said her dress is blue. Does that matter?" George turned and was admonished by the guy measuring him.

"Please, sir. Stand still." Bob Tucker, of Tuxes by Tucker moved his hands effortlessly over the fabric. "I've been doing this for 40 years, but even I can't work magic when you keep moving." He took a pin out of his mouth and deftly placed it on a cuff. "This is a black tux. I've already worked on it for 20 minutes. So you are going to wear a black tux. It goes with everything. When you're an old man you'll look back at your prom pictures and know you looked good. Others, in their baby blue or maroon tuxes, will laugh at themselves later. Don't worry. Your girlfriend will love it."

"Okay. If you say so." George looked unsure but obeyed.

A few minutes later he walked out of the shop with his usual blue jeans back on. It was warm and he had left his jacket at home. He hopped in his car, rolled down all the windows, and thought about tomorrow night.

The prom was like a rite of passage. He'd pick Sam up at six, go to dinner at the Rectory, then at eight go to the dance. Afterward was when the real fun began though. Cal was having an all-night party at his parents' farm. George had no hope that he and Sam would have sex. She'd been very clear about that and he knew it wasn't a battle he was willing to die in. But it would be fun to drink beer and stay out all night, and know he wouldn't get yelled at about it.

It's going to be the best night ever.

Samantha

"Jenny, get out of the bathroom. I need to put on my makeup. Hurry." My sister Jen was a junior but had a date with a senior, Max McCall. He wasn't someone I particularly liked, but Jen said it didn't matter; she just wanted to go to prom.

So here she was hogging the bathroom when it should be me having extra mirror time.

Jenny threw open the door, rolled her eyes, and moved back to the mirror.

"Thank you," I said, and tried to keep the sarcasm out of my voice. I moved in front of her to get a good view of my blue eye shadow with white highlights but she pushed me away with a hip.

Jen was shorter than I but just as tough. No one noticed her toughness though because she was so darn sweet. I was the only one she was mean to, and I knew the strength under the sugar.

"You should be a nun," I said, trying to wiggle back to the mirror.

"What a stupid thing to say. Why?" she responded. "Why should I be a nun?"

"Because you're sweet on the outside and iron underneath." I laughed at my metaphor, and loved that I knew what a metaphor was. Then I really laughed, "Like an iron penguin."

"That's just dumb," Jen said. "Now, move your butt. Move it," she commanded.

"Even though you are made of metal," I laughed, "I'm still not scared of you."

She laughed too, and the rest of our primping time went surprisingly well.

Once we finished with our hair and makeup and had given each other a high-five, we started to walk back to the bedroom we shared. In the hall, our baby brother, three-year-old Rob, looked at us with his mouth open. "Pwetty," he said. We both leaned down to kiss him.

"Pretty," I heard again, and saw five-year-old Jill, who ran up and hugged me and then she hugged Jen. Jenny and I giggled and I knew this was going to be a great night. I looked pretty and George was going to fall more in love with me than he already was.

George

"George, it's for you," his mom yelled up the stairs. George gave up on fixing his tie and went downstairs, taking the phone from his mother before he even landed on the bottom step.

"Yo," he said, and his smile quickly went away. "No," he said next.

On the other end of the transmission, about three miles away, Cal explained a predicament. "I can't help it. I'm stuck in the mud on the way to town. My dad's gone and can't help me. It's not too bad, and it's dry around where it's stuck. It's just a little car. We can push it out. No problem. Then we can pick up our dates and go to the Rectory."

"Shut up for a minute and I'll answer you." George ran his hand through his thick hair, still wet where it curled around his ears. "Let me think." He moved from one foot to another, running possibilities through his mind. Finally, after a huge sigh, he said, "Yeah. I'll be there in a minute."

"Thanks, buddy. You won't regret it." George could hear

the relief in his friend's voice.

Cal gave directions to where he car was stuck, then said, "I'll walk back to the car and will see you there."

George quickly finished getting ready, and decided to worry about the tie later. "'Bye, Mom, Dad. I'm going out to Cal's to help him get his car going." He decided not to tell them about the mud, because he was sure they'd try to talk him out of it.

As he started his car and backed out of the driveway, he thought he probably should have called Sam, in case he was late. *Nah, I'll be done in plenty of time,* he thought. *Besides, Sam'll understand.*

This was the most wrong he'd ever been.

Samantha

With every passing moment Sam's foot tapped quicker and louder. The loud tick-tock of the clock on the mantle underscored the fact that George was late. Very late.

Her mom sat down on the couch and put her arm around Sam. "I'm sure there's a good explanation. George is a good boy, sweetheart. He'd never stand you up on purpose. Especially not on prom night. Are you sure about not calling his house? Maybe something is wrong."

"Mom, no." I practically begged her as I threw myself against her. "No."

"Honey, why not?" she asked as she stroked my hair.

"If something was wrong someone would have called us. Everyone knows tonight is prom. So if there was a problem, someone would have called. Think about it." I let out with a wail, and the echoes of Cindy calling me Drama Queen haunted me. "Plus girls don't call boys. Ever."

It felt good to have my mom to lean on, and I knew I'd lean on her my whole life.

My mom gently said, "You've called him before,

Samantha. And I think it's time to call him again." She kissed my forehead and told me she loved me, just as she'd done my whole life. "I've got to get the dinner dishes finished. Are you sure you don't want something before it's all put away?"

I slowly shook my head. I wondered where my brothers and sister were. I knew Jen was at the prom, and that thought brought on a fresh onslaught of tears. But Ed, Pete, Rob, and Jill were nowhere in sight. Dad wasn't around either. I thought he probably had taken the others out somewhere so they didn't witness my humiliation. Or maybe because Dad knew they'd get on my nerves and suffer my wrath.

"What's going to happen to me?" I said aloud. "My life is ruined."

And there was nothing drama-queeny about that.

George

"Now," said George. "Press slowly on the accelerator while I push the car. Slowly."

The wheels started turning but then the car suddenly jerked and the tires dug deeper into the mud, covering George and his gorgeous black tux. George screamed, "STOP!" However, Cal didn't hear him.

"STOP!" yelled George again, this time even louder. The noise of the whirling tires and the smell of burning rubber soon ended but not until George was not only covered in mud, he was sitting in it.

Cal turned off the motor and opened the door. He jumped over the mud onto grass.

The situation was so dire that even Cal didn't say anything for a moment.

"Aw, man. I. Am. So. Sorry." He spoke slowly as to accentuate the depth of his feeling.

George still hadn't moved or said a word.

"Are you okay?" Cal asked.

"Am I okay? How the hell do you think I am?" George

finally said. "Give me a hand."

Cal recoiled from George's muddy hand. "Wait," he said, and opened the back door of his car. "I had this for the make out party." He pulled out a blanket, wrapped it around his arm, and gingerly held out his hand to grab George's.

"Why are you being so stinkin' careful?" George asked. His tux made a sickening thwump as it pulled free of the black mud. George rolled onto the grass and collapsed.

"Well," said Cal, taking a few steps backward, "I'm still clean and thought I would go to the prom."

"Why, you nasty weasel. I wouldn't be in this mess if it weren't for you." George tried to get up but was weighed down by the mud.

"I know. But unless you have another tux stashed somewhere, you can't go to prom, but I can."

"You could give me your tux," George suggested.

"You know that wouldn't work. You're taller than I am and my shoulders are wider. My tux would never fit you."

"You're a self-serving snake, you know that?"

"Maybe. But there's no sense both of us missing the prom." Cal reached for the blanket. "Here. Wrap yourself in this and you can sit in the passenger seat of your car. I'll drive."

"Why would I let you drive my car?" George asked as he covered his muddy body with the blanket.

"Because you would get mud everywhere. Just wrap up every part of yourself and sit. You'll be fine and I'll give you ride home."

"You'll give ME a ride home?"

"Well, you don't expect me to pick up Mary Sue on my bicycle, do you? I kind of thought you'd let me use your car."

"I have no words, Cal. I have no words." George shook his head, but as he did so he wrapped up snuggly and wiggled onto the passenger seat.

George continued, thinking aloud, "I don't know what to do. Sam'll never believe this happened. She's not very trusting anyway, kind of thinks most guys are only good for baseball. She won't believe me. I know she won't."

"I could tell her," Cal suggested.

"She wouldn't believe you. She hates you."

"Yeah, but…"

"But nothing. She'd think you were just lying for me."

"Yeah, but… if she is so sweet on you, why wouldn't she trust you?"

"I don't know. Because she's Sam, I guess. And this is so damn embarrassing. I was so stupid to come out here."

"…and help your best friend? That makes me feel like crap."

"At least you don't look like crap." At that, George finally smiled.

George's smile faded quickly. "I don't know what to do. What am I gonna do?" He looked to his best friend for advice.

"Maybe I could drop you off at her house and she could see how muddy you are. She'd believe you then."

"Yeah, but she'd be pissed that I put you ahead of her. I don't know what to do."

Cal thought for a moment before speaking, unusual for him. "Since you don't want to call her, maybe you could have your mom call her. Or maybe have your mom call her mom."

"That's like a mountain of stupidity." George wiped away a tear that threatened to escape, then realized he'd wiped mud on his face. "Just take me home."

"Can I use your car?"

"Yeah. Somebody ought to."

"Thanks, buddy. What should I tell everyone at the dance who asks where you are?"

George hesitated, then said, "Just tell them you don't know. I'll figure it out."

Samantha

The phone rang. "Mom, will you get that please?" I had no intention of talking to George, if that's who it was.

"It's for you, dear," her mom said holding out the phone toward me.

"Is it him?"

Mom nodded.

"Tell him I'm not accepting phone calls from anyone named George Lansing."

Mom put the phone back to her ear. "I'm sorry, George, she's not going to talk to you." A moment of silence, then she said, "Of course, I'll tell her."

I looked at her, wanting to know what he said, but also felt my heart harden as I waited.

"He said he has a good reason for what happened last night. He's sorry and he really wants to talk to you."

I allowed her to put an arm around me, "Mom, I just don't think there's any good reason for him not to call last night if he couldn't make it. I'm so embarrassed. And hurt. I thought he was a guy I could trust. I really loved him."

"I know, dear." Mom rocked me a little. "But these things have a way of working out."

"Not this time, Mom. Not this time."

Dear Diary,

 Men suck.

 I'll never speak to George again as long as I live. He ruined my life. He's a despicable, low-life, slime-eating scoundrel.

 He broke my heart.

 No one will ever do that again.

 Sincerely,

 Samantha

Little did I know…

The fourth Sam Darling mystery, "Will You Marry Me?" is available now.

Read on for how to contact the author and join her mailing list so that you'll get the news first about each book before it's released.

ACKNOWLEDGMENTS

The idea for Triple Trouble came from my publisher, Patrice Fitzgerald of eFitzgerald Publishing. I thank her for her foresight in putting the first three books together. We've been a good team.

Each book has its own set of acknowledgments in the individual books. However, I want to make sure I reiterate a lot of them, because the books would not have been completed without the following people:

The aforementioned Patrice Fitzgerald; encouragement from fellow writers (you know who you are); writing and critique groups that I've been fortunate to be a member of; my beta readers, Jan Smith, Nikki Shields, Donna Welsh, and Beth Lane; Toni Taylor from Tiger Imagery for her lovely photographs and Keri Knutsen for turning them into perfect cover art; Jason Anderson of Polgarus Studio for his excellent formatting; Kristen Theissen, Kathy Vogel, Joe Osier, Richie Klauser, Panera Bread Company

(Ron Frillman), my Game of Crones, and Gloria Rosenthal.

And to my much-appreciated readers! Please let me hear what you think by posting a brief review. Indie writers depend upon reviews because we don't have the big budgets of large publishing companies. And if you enjoyed these books and the other Sam Darling mysteries, please tell your friends.

As usual, the people depicted in this book are the result of my imagination only, and bear no resemblance to actual people. The exception is, when the Darling sibs are being sarcastic, that accurately describes my five brothers.

Bestselling author Jerilyn Bozarth Dufresne is the oldest in a family of nine children, which is where she got the inspiration for the Darling Family—although her sibs fight a lot more and have cornered the market on sarcasm. She returned to her hometown of Quincy, Illinois after having lived a nomadic life in her middle years.

Jerilyn currently works as an outpatient therapist at a local mental health clinic and teaches at Quincy University. She and her dog Gus live with, and are tolerated by, two cats.

To hear first about new books by Jerilyn, sign up at http://eepurl.com/z30jv . Your email will never be made public and you can opt out at any time.

Manufactured by Amazon.ca
Bolton, ON